GOD
OF
RUIN

RINA KENT

To the psychos,
May we enjoy them in fiction but never encounter them in real life

AUTHOR NOTE

Hello reader friend,

If you haven't read my books before, you might not know this, but I write darker stories that can be upsetting and disturbing. My books and main characters aren't for the faint of heart.

This book contains primal kink, somnophilia and mentions of childhood trauma. I trust you know your triggers before you proceed.

God of Ruin is a complete STANDALONE.

For more things Rina Kent, visit www.rinakent.com

LEGACY OF GODS TREE

ROYAL ELITE UNIVERSITY

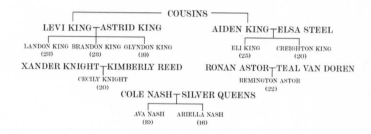

COUSINS

LEVI KING ⊤ ASTRID KING

LANDON KING BRANDON KING GLYNDON KING
(23)   (23)   (19)

AIDEN KING ⊤ ELSA STEEL

ELI KING   CREIGHTON KING
(25)   (20)

XANDER KNIGHT ⊤ KIMBERLY REED

CECILY KNIGHT
(20)

RONAN ASTOR ⊤ TEAL VAN DOREN

REMINGTON ASTOR
(22)

COLE NASH ⊤ SILVER QUEENS

AVA NASH   ARIELLA NASH
(19)   (16)

THE KING'S U'S COLLEGE

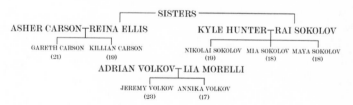

SISTERS

ASHER CARSON ⊤ REINA ELLIS

GARETH CARSON KILLIAN CARSON
(21)   (19)

KYLE HUNTER ⊤ RAI SOKOLOV

NIKOLAI SOKOLOV MIA SOKOLOV MAYA SOKOLOV
(19)   (18)   (18)

ADRIAN VOLKOV ⊤ LIA MORELLI

JEREMY VOLKOV ANNIKA VOLKOV
(23)   (17)

I'm out for revenge.

After careful planning, I gave the man who messed with my family a taste of his own medicine.

I thought it'd end there.

It didn't.

Landon King is a genius artist, a posh rich boy, and my worst nightmare.

He's decided that I'm the new addition to his chess game.

Too bad for him, I'm no pawn.

If he hits, I hit back, twice as hard and with the same hostility.

He says he'll ruin me.

Little does he know that ruination goes both ways.

PLAYLIST

Blood on Your Hands – Veda & Adam Arcadia
Angel of Small Death & The Codeine Scene – Hozier
RUNRUNRUN – Dutch Melrose
Roman Empire – MISSIO
The Worst in Me – Bad Omens
Skins – The Haunting
Don't Say I Didn't Warn You – VOILA & Craig Owens
Supernatural – Barns Courtney
Rude Boy – Rihanna
Happiness is a Butterfly – Lana Del Rey
Artistry – Jacob Lee
Bad Decisions – Bad Omens
Last Cigarette – MOTHICA & AU/Ra
Anarchist – YUNGBLUD
Colors – Halsey

You can find the complete playlist on Spotify.

GOD
OF
RUIN

ONE

Mia

TONIGHT, A CERTAIN EYESORE PRESENCE WILL GET A TASTE of his own medicine.

I stride through the darkness of the night with a chip on my shoulder and rage boiling in the very marrow of my soul.

My fingers splay on the strap of the mask covering my face. Breath condenses against the plastic and sweat coats my upper lip.

The place where my plans will take place materializes in front of me—huge, imposing, and dreadfully heartless.

Not empty, though.

These types of hedonistic meccas are often brimming with wannabes who like to think they're worth more than their parents' bank accounts.

But, oh well, none of my plans would have meaning in the absence of a crowd.

The dazzling lights of what can only be called a mansion slash through the night with the brightness of a falling star.

There's nothing modest about what I'm looking at. It's a huge three-story architectural wonder whose front brims with wide, tall windows.

That's where all the lights shine through, particularly on the first floor. LED strips cover the trees in the vast garden surrounding the property. I can't help feeling bad for the poor trees that are being suffocated for some random celebration.

The mansion's exterior boasts a welcoming Victorian-like vibe that promises great fun, but I'm not fooled.

Inside that mansion lurks skin-crawling danger wrapped in a dazzling appearance.

And tonight? I'm going straight for that danger's throat and bringing him to his damn knees.

"Slow down, Mia!" a feminine voice calls, crowded with frustration.

I throw a glance back to find my twin sister, Maya, holding her carnival mask with golden ornaments in hand as she pants.

My eyes grow wide behind my own mask and I pull her to the side before we cross the property's gate.

She struggles under my firm grip, her whines resembling those of a petulant child.

"Ugh, you're hurting me." She releases herself from my merciless hold after a long struggle. It's no secret that I'm the twin who loves strength training. Maya is more interested in massages and sculpting her model body.

We're under a tall tree with bent branches that offers some form of camouflage from any onlookers.

Maya hikes a hand up her hip over the skintight glittery black dress that leaves nothing to the imagination. My sister has always been proud of her slim hourglass figure and C-cup breasts, and she's never shied away from showing them off.

We're identical twins, so we have the same petite facial structure, almond-shaped light-blue eyes, and full lips, though hers are slightly bigger than mine. Our hair is shiny platinum blonde, but she keeps hers long—currently swishing to her lower back—while mine falls just below my shoulders.

Usually, I'd have a ton of ribbons in mine, but since I'm trying to stay under the radar, I have it in a ponytail tied with only one blue ribbon.

I'm also wearing my least attention-grabbing outfit—a simple strapless leather dress that reaches the tops of my knees.

My boots for the night are the tamest I have and the only ones that aren't chunky or covered with chains.

Maya, however, chose to wear heels, as usual, not seeming to care about whether or not that would hinder our mission.

I point at the mask in her hand and gesticulate to her face, then sign, "You're supposed to be wearing that! They have cameras around, and you might have just offered them a front-row seat to our identities."

She rolls her eyes dramatically, proving her position as the ultimate drama queen I know. "Relax. The camera range only starts once we're close to the gate. And I was going to put it on, if you'd been patient for, like, two seconds."

"Don't mess with me." I snatch the mask and smash it to her face, then strap it around her head so that it's secured.

She whines and groans. "You're running my hair, idiot. Let go. I'll do it myself."

I only release her once I'm satisfied with the mask's placement. She glares at me through the eyeholes as she proceeds to fix her hair.

"Don't give me that," I sign. "You know how much effort it took for me to get a goddamn invitation to this pretentious event. The last thing I need is for something to go wrong."

"Yeah, yeah." She throws her hand in the air with obvious exasperation. "I've heard the story about your sacrifices a thousand times, to the point that I can recite them back."

"In that case, stick to the plan and stop giving me headaches."

"Yes, ma'am." She does a mock salute and I make a face behind my mask.

Since she can only see my eyes, Maya can't get the full picture, but she still smirks anyway like an annoying idiot.

My twin sister has always been my best friend, but she often drives me up the wall with her shenanigans.

After I make sure neither of our faces is showing, we start walking toward the mansion again.

Or more accurately—the Elites' compound.

When I first came to Brighton Island, I had to learn a few rules. The most important one is that there are two rival colleges on this island. The one I belong to is American and called The King's U. It's funded by powerful people whose pockets are filled with new money. The kind whose source or motives are hard to pinpoint.

My parents are included in the group of powerful people. We're Russian mafia royalty and they happen to be leaders in the New York Bratva.

The other college is Royal Elite University—or REU. British, loaded with old money and pretentious aristocracy.

Our college has two clubs: the Heathens, with which our loyalty lies since my brother and cousins are members; and the Serpents, who are second on my shit list.

First on that list, however, is the Elites. The secret club and the holy grail of REU.

While the Heathens are full of mafia heirs and American royalty, the Elites are...dangerously different.

They appear elegant and suave, but there's a nefarious undertone lurking beneath the surface.

Maya and I are infiltrating their mansion and party. It's impossible to get an invitation to these close-circle gatherings unless you're part of the club or their family and friends.

Lucky for me, I managed to snag two invitations that were meant for someone who's part of the family.

When Maya and I arrive at the entrance, a large man stops us. Masks are mandatory tonight, and he's wearing a black carnival one with golden ornaments.

From my research, I gathered that mask nights are important nights. They're not only a members' meeting, but they're also when they celebrate wins and announce plans for the future.

It's the main reason why I waited such a long time to execute my plan. There needed to be this level of significance for the mission to be satisfying.

I reach into my bag and show him the black invitation card with

'Elites VIP' written in gold. After Maya does the same, he takes and scans them with a special gadget.

Geez. No wonder it's impossible to get into these things. They even scan invitations to make sure there are no forgeries.

Once the light goes green, he nods more to himself than to us and motions behind him at his colleague, who's in a similar mask.

"You'll leave all your personal belongings here. No phones or cameras are allowed inside." His gruff voice with a barely understandable British accent fills the air. "If we find out you snuck any communication devices inside, you'll be thrown out."

Maya releases an exasperated sound as we ditch our bags. "You better protect it with your life. Actually, since this is a special edition Hermes and is, therefore, worth more than your life, lose it and I'll use your skin as my new bag. Capisce?"

The man shows no reaction to her dramatics, and I grab her arm and then basically push her inside a dimly lit hallway.

"You just made him take note of us," I sign discreetly. "What happened to our plans about blending in, idiot?"

"Excuse you. My bag is worth more than this mission."

"Are you telling me a bag is worth more than getting revenge for our brother?"

"Well, since he can get that himself—which he should've by now, but I'm not sure why he hasn't—I think…yes?"

"Maya!"

"What? I had to pull strings to get that bag."

"Then maybe you shouldn't have brought it on a night like this?"

"It's my lucky bag. Of course I'm bringing it to your suicidal mission."

"I have everything planned. It's not suicidal."

"It will be when Niko finds out."

I wince at the thought of our older brother, Nikolai, catching a whiff of this. Pissed off is going to be the milder reaction.

Maya's eyes twinkle behind the mask with a mischievous grin. "He'll skin us alive."

I lift my chin. "Don't care. I'll deal with him once I'm done with our revenge."

Our conversation comes to a slow halt as we exit the hallway and find ourselves in a main hall.

Huge chandeliers hang from the high ceilings, illuminating a glittery interior, marble flooring, and ornate pillars.

All the attendees wear masks similar to ours and are dressed up in fitted tuxedos and elegant party gowns. I definitely look the least sophisticated of the bunch, while Maya blends right in.

"I told you so," she whispers in my ear in reference to her earlier suggestion that I wear a showier dress.

I elbow her side, but she only laughs in mock reaction.

If she weren't my sister, I would've kicked her in the face a long time ago.

We each grab a drink from a passing waiter, but I don't take a sip. One, I'd have to lift my mask, and I'd rather not reveal anything about my identity. Two, I'm such a lightweight that even a beer can get me tipsy. So I only pretend to drink while keeping my attention on the people mingling about.

Some of them are dancing to unknown classical music like they're a bunch of middle-aged couples. Others are talking and laughing at what I'm sure are boring topics.

The subject of my revenge, who should be somewhere in the middle of the charade, isn't here.

"Do you see him?" Maya signs, as is our habit whenever we don't want someone to eavesdrop on us.

I shake my head.

My foot taps on the floor in a manic rhythm. This is bad.

That asshole is the star of the show, so unless he shows his ugly self, our plan is practically null and void.

All of a sudden, the lights dim. My eyes adjust to the darkness, but I can only see shadows and silhouettes of other attendees.

My spine jerks upright and my manic tapping comes to a halt, mainly because the panic is too great to be contained by mere tapping.

Sweat trickles down my spine and the rotten stench of mold invades my nostrils.

I'm not going back there...I'm not...

"Hey." Maya's soft voice fills my ears as she wraps an arm around my shoulders. "It's going to be okay. You're not alone, Mia."

I stare into her eyes, which are identical and yet somehow different from mine. As the seconds tick by, my breathing slows back to normal.

She's right. I'm not alone, and I'm definitely not back in that humid, dark place from ten years ago.

I flash her a tentative smile because I'm so thankful for having her, but at the same time, I'm so ashamed of my weakness.

My inability to get my shit together even after all this time.

Every year, I say this is the year I get over it, but so far, I haven't had any luck.

"I'm okay," I sign, then force myself to focus on the scene.

Sure enough, a few newcomers dressed in gowns and tuxedos walk in as if they not only own the place, but also expect everyone in it to worship at their feet. They're wearing luxurious masks and are holding their noses in the air as if it's their mission to judge the world.

Our target is in their midst.

No doubt about it.

In fact, he's probably the one in the middle who has one hand in his pocket and the other hanging nonchalantly at his side.

My blood boils and it takes every ounce of my control not to jump for his throat and claw his eyes out.

Stay patient, Mia. Everything is sweeter in its own time.

Maya and I exchange a look, our twin hunch activating at the same time, and we nod at each other.

We slip between the party people who are too mesmerized, by whom I assume are the club leaders, to notice us.

For the first time in forever, I'm thankful for the darkness. Maya and I go unnoticed all the way to the designated hallway.

While it's true that getting invited to an Elites party is a highly selective process, gaining access to the mansion they use as a compound isn't as hard.

Especially since I'm friends with someone who lives here.

Not sure he'll still consider me a friend after I'm done with his asshole of a brother, but, hey, he knew I would never forgive him for kidnapping Niko and, in retrospect, causing his injury.

Someone needs to teach that bastard a lesson, and what am I if not a Good Samaritan?

Since I had access to the mansion yesterday, I managed to stack our weapon of destruction within the party's main event.

All we have to do is go up and hit the button for all hell to break loose.

But before we can do that, we have to make sure what I planted is still in place.

To do that, Maya will check the power supply and I need to reach the trigger button.

There's no need for any communication outlet because we're the type of twins who feel each other no matter what.

If everything is all right, I'll get a hunch before I push the button.

We slide our palms against each other and tap the back of our hands together in our special shake, then part ways.

I reach the second floor, and since everyone is busy with the pretentious assholes, I don't encounter any of the invitees. But there are definitely guards and cameras, which is why I'm pretending to go to the bathroom.

Once I'm there, however, I hop on the sink and remove the vent cover, jump into the airway, and close it behind me. I'm slim enough to fit. Once I'm inside the tight space, I breathe deeper and start crawling.

You're going to be all right, Mia.

This is not that place from ten years ago.

You're just serving justice for Niko.

I'm so close to relapsing into my illogical panic, but I don't. It takes me about five minutes to get to the other end. By the time I reach my destination, I've inhaled more dust than a vacuum and I'm sweating like a pig.

I slowly open the vent cover and once I listen in to make sure there's no one in this bathroom, I maneuver my way out until I land on the sink, then jump to the floor.

Phase one. Done.

Maya should've gotten to the other side by now. She doesn't need to do any jumping or crawling. Nor can I ever convince her to 'lower' her 'sublime' status.

She probably just needs to flirt with a guard if she encounters one.

I tap my mask to make sure it's in place, then check my reflection in the mirror, smooth my hair, and dust my dress. Once I'm satisfied with my look, I exit the men's bathroom. Anyone could walk in and ask what I'm doing here, but oh well, even if I'm caught, I'll pretend that I got here by mistake.

All I have to do is reach the control panel at the corner and activate the timer.

The moment I'm out the door, the hair on the back of my neck stands on end.

However, before I can turn around and inspect the source of the intrusion, I'm pushed back inside the bathroom with a blinding force.

I'm too disoriented to focus, let alone try to stop the inhuman, raw power I'm handled with.

My back hits the wall and I groan, then lift my hand, ready to flip whoever it is a thousand fingers while kicking them.

All my plans come to a halt when my gaze clashes with dark-blue eyes.

Familiar eyes.

The eyes of my enemy and the target of my revenge.

Landon fucking King.

TWO

Mia

THIS ISN'T PART OF THE PLAN.

In fact, it's so far away from the plan that I can hear meticulously laid-out scenarios crash like broken china.

I'm standing in front of none other than *the* Landon King. A charming god, a genius sculptor, and, most importantly, an insufferable bastard.

His hand squeezes my upper arm, pressing it against the wall with a power that renders me immobile.

My lips clamp together even as condensation covers the interior of the mask. Sweat trickles in the valley between my breasts and glues the dress to my back.

Any attempts to control my breathing end in epic failure. The air coming through my mask's nostril openings wraps a noose around my neck—suffocating, nefarious, and as dangerous as the eyes staring down at me.

They're all that's visible beneath his white Venetian carnival mask that's decorated with elegant golden lines. On other people, it would look tame, welcoming even, but on this man, it's nothing short of a horror scene.

One distinctive feature gives him away. The eyes.

They're a dark, shiny blue, like an ocean that's twinkling under the silver moonlight. Deep, mysterious, and…deadly.

I've heard so much about Landon, but this is the first time I've believed he's a lethal danger whose path I shouldn't cross. Unless I'm in the mood to be drowned in his ocean so fast that no one will find a trace of me.

Too bad for him, I'm the type who likes swimming in open water.

I let my hand fall to my side, abandoning the flipping-off idea, but I lift my chin. I've been so looking forward to kicking this asshole in the face that I'm barely holding on.

Yes, his appearance has ruffled my plan, but it's far from ruined. I just need to abandon his eyesore company and go on about my business.

"Care to explain what your insignificant presence is doing here?" His suave British accent echoes in the empty space like a lullaby.

This is what I've hated about the bastard ever since I met him that one time when he was vandalizing my cousin's car. He has a natural way of sounding haughtily elegant while delivering cold-blooded threats.

I'm ninety percent sure he's emotionally checked out and has no link whatsoever with the human side of himself. And while I don't give two fucks about his relationship with his feelings, it makes it tricky to deal with him.

My cousin Killian is in the same category and possesses the emotional IQ of a goldfish, but at least he likes me, so I don't have to be on guard when facing him.

The same can't be said about Landon.

Not only does he not like me, but he also wouldn't hesitate to teach me a lesson just to get back at Kill and Niko.

His fingers tighten on my arm and I swallow the wince before it manages to pass through my lips. Dad always taught me to never show weakness in front of enemies, even when I'm in pain, even if every fiber of my being demands to release it.

Some monsters get off on your reaction to pain more than the fact that they're inflicting it, so never put yourself in a position where you're someone's source of entertainment.

My father's words echo in my head as I stare back at the monster of the day.

What? There have been so many of them in my life that I've stopped counting.

"I asked you a question." He squeezes again until pain pulses all over my arm. "Where's your answer?"

Fuck you, asshole.

But since I can't say that, or anything, actually, I just continue staring.

I could sign, but he'd figure out my identity immediately. Besides, it's not like he can understand me anyway.

So I purse my lips further and attempt to shake my arm from his grip.

Huge mistake.

His fingers dig in so hard, it's like he's attempting to break the bone.

My eyes widen. Wait…is that what he wants to do?

All of a sudden, he becomes taller and broader, nearly eating up the horizon with his build.

It's clear he has more height than me, but at this particular moment, he seems like a wall.

One that's covered by wires and glass shards. Was he always this muscular? Did his shoulders strain against his tailored tuxedo jacket a minute ago?

Or maybe I'm just becoming super aware of his presence to the point of hyperfixation.

Landon is a tall man, at least six-foot-four, with a lean, muscled body and a perfectly straight posture. To make things worse, those superior physical traits are topped by his natural charisma.

He carries himself with frightening assurance and a blinding ego. He's frustratingly confident, antagonistic to the point of bagging enemies everywhere he goes, and has an arrogance that could bring Narcissus to tears.

But there's another side of him I'm currently discovering.

He's…frightening.

And I don't mean in the way some wannabes try to look scary. He doesn't puff his chest out or raise his voice. He doesn't try to be terrifying by modifying anything in his demeanor.

All he has to do is let his true colors show through. The long fingers of his free hand wrap around his mask and he casually lifts it.

The moment I see the entirety of his face, my theory becomes fact. All Landon had to do was remove the mask so the real him could shine through.

His face is logically gorgeous, model-like in its symmetry. He has a high, straight nose, defined cheekbones, and a jaw so sharp, it could cut through stone.

Illogically, however, he didn't reveal his face to charm me into anything. It's a weapon he's using with the purpose of pure intimidation.

He willingly revealed his identity so that it's clear who has the upper hand here—him, the leader of the Elites and the host of the event at which I'm a mere invitee.

"Let's try again. Who are you and what are you doing in the men's room?"

My gaze meets his. Unwavering. Unblinking.

No fear, and certainly no change in demeanor, just because his face—that he doesn't deserve, I might add—is in view.

"You refuse to speak, is that it?"

I nod once.

"I see," he muses and eases his grip on my arm.

Is he letting me go?

I cast him a doubtful glance, but there doesn't seem to be any malicious intent in his eyes.

They're neutral. Amicable, even.

My heartbeat slowly returns to normal despite my alerted state.

Then, all of a sudden, something happens.

It's so fast and fleeting, I would've missed it if I'd believed in the fake safety he offered and dropped my guard.

In a heartbeat, he reaches for my mask, openhanded, as if he's about to suffocate me.

I don't think as I push his palm at the last second and it ends up on my breast.

My chest heaves and the weight of his hand on my breast makes it worse.

Instead of backing off, a smirk tugs on the corner of his lips and he squeezes the flesh over my dress. "So this whole charade was an invitation? You girls sure come up with the most creative ways to get my attention. Are you up for it here, where anyone can walk in and see you getting fucked senseless like a dirty, *dirty* girl?"

For a moment, I'm stunned into silence. Partly because no one's talked to me like that in the past.

No one's dared to.

I'm Mia Sokolov. The daughter of Kyle Hunter and Rai Sokolov. If anyone ever dared touch me and say those words to me, I would punch them to another planet. My parents would find them and have their balls for breakfast.

Don't even get me started on my brother. He'd resurrect them and slaughter them all over again.

In my stupefaction, his hand slides down my hip and over my ass cheek before he squeezes it and slams me against his front.

A wordless gasp falls from my lips as my stomach rubs against his semi-hard erection.

My temperature rises with pure fucking rage.

How dare he…? How fucking…

I don't think about it as I try to lift my knee and kick him in the balls.

Before I can do that, however, he tightens his grip on my ass, giving me no wiggle room whatsoever.

"Easy there, mouse. While I'm rather open to wrestling, I'm not sure you can take me on."

I'm going to take you to meet your fucking maker, asshole.

I attempt to slip sideways, but it's impossible to get rid of his fingers that are digging into my ass.

"You're a silent little thing." He grabs my other ass cheek with the hand he's holding his mask in. "You did your research, didn't you? I love them mute."

That's it.

I rein in my temper and let my body relax in his hold, willingly turning molten in his arms.

Then I lift a hand and stroke my index finger down his cheek to his jaw, slowly, flirtatiously.

His smirk widens and he doesn't seem to mind the touch.

That's it, psycho. Let your dick lead you like every other idiot.

I pull on his bottom lip, trying my best not to focus on the way he's taking the liberty of grabbing me.

He thinks I'm seducing him, but I'm just erasing that damn smirk so he'll stop looking like Lucifer's lost heir.

He strokes my ass and I resist the tingles that explode down my spine. I get on my tiptoes so that my mask-covered face is a few inches from his and then I punch him.

In the nose.

As hard as I can.

Damn. That hurts!

The motion is sudden enough that he freezes.

I use the surprise element to push against him, release myself, and run out the door.

Despite being disoriented and hot from the bastard's touch, I don't stop to look behind me. Not even for a second.

In fact, I run as fast as I can in case he's following me.

Even though I don't detect any steps, I don't let my guard down and keep running until I reach the control panel.

My heart nearly jumps from my throat, but I breathe deeply and push the button. I have no doubt that Maya succeeded.

Just as I expected, the timer goes on.

I go back through the garden—my plan B. There's no way in hell I'm returning to that bathroom, where Landon can ambush me again.

Note to self: Never be alone with the bastard.

He's a damn pervert, and a persistent one at that.

It takes me longer to return to the main hall, but I arrive at the back of the partygoers just in time.

After I join Maya, she signs, "What the hell took you so long? I was getting worried."

"A small complication, but don't worry, it was absolutely nothing."

I don't believe my words, even as I sign them.

That definitely wasn't nothing. It was everything but nothing. My body still tingles with both frustration and rage.

"What do you mean there was a complication?" Maya hisses under her breath. "What happened?"

I place a finger to my mouth when none other than Landon walks to the stage and taps his glass of champagne with a spoon.

Just in time.

He's wearing his mask, but it doesn't matter. After our encounter just now, I've developed the useless power to recognize the asshole from a mile away.

"Thank you for coming to our party," he starts in his suave, elegant voice that could be mistaken for a politician's.

That gorgeous British accent is lost on him. Just saying.

"We're delighted to open the Elites' doors for the people we consider VIPs. Tonight, we're going to have a personal meet and greet with yours truly, the man and the legend, Landon King."

Barf.

"He sounds and looks edible," Maya signs. "Too bad he's a dick."

"What's taking so long?" I sign back as the crowd goes wild for the potential future cult leader.

Did I somehow not click the right button in my haste? I was temporarily out of my mind after the bastard touched what he had no business touching.

No, I'm sure I did...

He raises his glass. "To the Elites."

"To the Elites," everyone else echoes.

Just then, the gates of hell open and pour right on top of him. Pig blood bathes Landon and his glass of champagne in an instant, turning him into a messy goo of ugliness right in front of the people who worship at his feet.

A collective gasp overtakes the crowd. I laugh behind my mask.

Take that, prick. You'll learn not to mess with me or my family ever again.

People and security rush to the stage, and Maya tugs on my hand. "Time to go."

I chance one last look behind me just to see the asshole looking like a fool, but he's already removed the mask and his eyes meet mine.

A wide grin lifts his lips, looking even more terrifying when he's covered in all the blood.

He does the universal 'I'm watching you' sign, and I don't know why I run the fastest I ever have.

THREE

Mia

"**Y**OU DIDN'T ANSWER ME." NIKOLAI'S VOICE BOOMS IN the room as he nudges me with a foot.

I lose balance, but I go back into position and don't open my eyes.

Anyone with any form of common sense would leave me to meditate in peace, but my brother and common sense have been fighting each other for his entire life.

He pushes me again, and this time, I fall to my ass and start to glare up at him, but I startle when I find him in my face.

Literally.

He's leaning so low, the bent position appears creepy at worst and awkward at best.

My brother is a year older than Maya and me, but he couldn't look any different. Where we take after our mom and her identical twin sister, he takes after Dad. They share the chameleon eye shade of turquoise blue, some of the same body structure, and dark hair—though my brother wears his long.

It's currently tied in a low ponytail at his nape, which highlights his unwelcoming, grim face. I love my brother, and he's actually handsome, but you have to look past his usual manic expression to see that.

Also, he's shirtless ninety percent of the time—now included.

And that puts all his hedonistic, scary tattoos on display for the world to see.

Add the fact that he's quite buff, and you have the perfect recipe for a disaster waiting to happen.

It doesn't help that he was brought up as the mafia heir for my parents' positions in the New York Bratva.

At times, he's like a psycho with a license to beat, maim, and even kill. Other times, he's just my brother who used to take me and Maya for ice cream and defend us in front of a deadly stray dog.

"I'm still waiting for an answer," he repeats his earlier words.

I can't help glancing at the bandage covering the base of his neck.

That's the reason I bathed that asshole Landon in pig blood a few days ago, and I would do it all over again in a heartbeat.

"I'm still waiting," Nikolai says again in his usual gruff, but now completely irritable voice. I swear he has the patience of a toddler.

"For what?" I sign, wearing my innocent face. "And rude, by the way. Didn't I tell you not to bother me when I'm meditating?"

"Blah fucking blah. You're not deflecting." He gets even closer so that I'm breathing mint off his breath. "Where did you take your sister the other night, and why were you laughing like evil maniacs after you came back? I know an adrenaline rush when I see it, and you two definitely had one. So out with it."

I play with the dozen blue ribbons in my hair, pretending to fix them. "What makes you think I took her somewhere? Maybe she's the one who took me."

"She's malicious, but you're the brains behind every disaster you two plan. I don't have all day, Mia. What the fuck did you do, and do I have to maim someone?"

I point a proud thumb at myself. "Your baby sister took care of it. Just rest assured, Niko."

He narrows his eyes and it looks maniacal, scarily so. He's not the type to be deterred from his inquiries, especially when Maya and I are involved.

Besides, although we live in a flat close to the mansion where he resides with the Heathens, he doesn't have access to us all day long.

Yes, there are bodyguards, but Maya and I made it clear that they were only for outside and would never come inside the house. Or, God forbid, follow us around.

We were unlucky the other day, because when we came back, we found Nikolai waiting for us.

He definitely didn't believe our lie that we were with friends. One, we don't have those. People have always been either scared or wary of us, so Maya and I became each other's best friend.

My sister has a huge following on social media and is in a clique with people who are similar to her, but even she wouldn't call them friends. She used to be super close with our nanny when we were growing up, and she often called her a friend, but that ended after the nanny left the state to be with her family.

Two, despite my and Maya's abilities to come up with an imaginary scenario on the spot and finish each other's lies effortlessly, Nikolai has been with us all our lives, and while he likes to pretend he can't differentiate between us when we dress the same, he actually can.

He can also tell when we're acting.

"What happened that night, hmm?" he asks, completely undeterred by my answer. "And don't tell me nothing, because I call bullshit."

"It's really nothing," I sign with a sweet smile.

I learned early on that I have a cute face. Maya does everything to make hers sexy. I'm using this shit to my benefit.

If you're cute and you smile, people will easily fall for your charms.

I just have to appear gullible until I find the chance to kick or punch them in the face. Like I did to Landon King.

A shudder snakes down my spine at the image of his manic smile that night. I actually had a nightmare about his bloodied smirk and the 'I'm watching you' sign.

He couldn't possibly know it was me. I never removed the mask, and I technically wasn't invited to that party.

My ally, the one who provided those invitations and let me in the Elites' mansion, wouldn't sell me out.

In fact, Brandon, Landon's twin brother and my ally, sent me a picture of his brother covered in blood with a text.

Brandon: Did you do this?

Mia: If I say yes, would you hate me?

Brandon: No. I actually like you more now. I'm impressed.

Mia: You're not mad that I used the invitations you gave me to do this?

Brandon: Not really. I figured you were up to no good when you asked for them.

Mia: What if you get in trouble with your brother?

Brandon: I know how to deal with him. Don't worry.

So it was a win on all accounts. I get to keep my fresh, new, and completely unsure friendship with Bran, and I also got revenge for what his psycho brother did to mine.

Still, I've been unconsciously watching my surroundings the past couple of days, expecting Landon to jump me from behind.

Or worse—drag me into some dark corner, where I would definitely be defenseless.

"Okay." Nikolai rises to his full height.

"Okay?" I repeat in sign language, not sure if I heard him correctly.

"Yeah, okay. You and Maya can have it your way." He tilts his head to the side. "In exchange, I'm adding two more bodyguards, and everyone on your bodyguard team will be following your every move."

I jump up and sign furiously, "You can't do that."

"You'll see proof of me doing exactly that first thing in the morning."

Oh crap.

If my brother says it's happening, it's definitely happening.

"Wait," I sign and release a sigh. "Okay, we lied. I actually met with a new friend of mine I don't think you'd approve of, which is why we didn't tell you."

"Name. Address. School."

"Brandon King. He lives in the Elites' mansion, and he goes to REU."

My brother pauses and his brows nearly reach his hairline. "Since when are you friends with someone from REU?"

"It just happened. You know, that time his brother, Landon, was bothering Kill and being rude, Brandon apologized on his behalf. Afterward, we played a game together and became friends."

"Killian never told me this."

"Not sure why." Because Bran actually asked him to, I think. And since Killian was trying to get on Bran's good side so that he could date his sister, he kept quiet about the whole incident.

"So you're telling me you and Lotus..." he trails off and clears his throat. "And *Brandon* are friends."

"Yeah. We meet for gaming and stuff. We keep kicking each other's butts. You should see it."

"Maybe I should," he murmurs under his breath.

"Does that mean you're okay with it?"

His bemused state completely disappears, and he narrows his eyes. "Absolutely not. You're not to get involved with anyone in the Elites."

"But he's really different, Niko. He's so nice and such a gentleman."

"Oh?"

"Totally! And he's nothing like his tool of a brother, Landon."

"So you and Maya were with Brandon that night?"

I nod.

"Where? In their mansion?"

"No. They had some sort of party there, so we met in a gaming café and played for a while."

"Maya. In a gaming café? The nerd hotspot, as she calls it?"

Shit. I miscalculated that.

Maya wouldn't step foot inside one of those places with her cheapest heel.

"She wanted to meet Bran because I've been telling her so much about him."

"So much about him," he repeats in a mysterious tone.

"Yeah. She totally likes him." Now, I have to actually introduce Maya and Bran. Yikes. They probably won't get along.

Nikolai fetches my phone from the floor and hands it over. "Call him."

I jerk. "What?"

"You said you're friends and spend time together. That means you have his number, no?"

I nod.

"Then call him. I want to verify your story."

I open my phone and type furiously. "This is ridiculous. Do you have that little faith in me? It's like you don't believe me."

"I don't," he says point-blank. "Call him."

"He's not used to me calling him."

"I'm sure he won't mind it this once since he's so *nice* and such a *gentleman*." I don't miss the way he stresses the words I mentioned.

Ah, crap.

I try to buy as much time as possible as I scroll to find Bran's name while hoping Maya will pop in here already.

She's always invading my space, but not this time. She's probably hiding so Niko won't grill her for answers. The little traitor.

When I take longer than necessary, Nikolai snatches my phone and types 'Bran' in the search bar. When the only contact with that name appears, he presses Call and hits the speaker button.

My heart nearly hits the floor as the ringing sound echoes in the air.

Don't answer.

Don't answer.

Please.

Please—

"Hello?" Bran's slightly husky voice sounds in the air as if he was woken up from a nap. "Mia? Are you okay with calling?"

I release a deep breath and catch a glimpse of my brother giving me the side-eye.

The horror.

"Mia?" Bran sobers up. "Is something wrong? Make any form of noise if you need help—"

"It's her brother, Nikolai."

Bran goes silent for a few tense beats and I nearly piss myself. This is going too bad too fast.

"Right." Bran clears his throat and sounds detached, cold, even. "What can I help you with?"

"My sister tells me she spent the night with you three days ago."

"Spent the night with me?"

"Is that not the case?"

Damn Niko. He makes it sound as if I slept with him or something.

"We met, but she didn't spend the night with me in that sense."

Yes, Bran. Thank you.

"What were you doing?"

"I'm sure you can ask your sister that."

"I did, and I'm trying to decide whether or not I'll lock her up based on your reply."

Silence again.

Poor Bran is being dragged into an unfair situation that he didn't agree with.

"We played a few games," he replies casually.

"Where?"

"In a gaming café."

"Which one?"

"The only one on the island. Play Dungeon."

"With who?"

"Alone."

I nearly stagger. He did everything right, as if I'd told him all the details, but he missed on the last one.

"Alone," Nikolai repeats with a sly smirk.

"Yes. We were the only ones who played. Maya was there, but she was too preoccupied with her phone most of the time."

My man.

I'm totally buying Bran the new *League of Legends* merch.

"If there isn't anything else…" Bran trails off and then hangs up.

I smile at my brother triumphantly and sign, "It's not good to distrust your own siblings. We need to work on these bad habits, Niko."

"You'll stay away from that bunch of little fuckers." He pushes the phone against my chest. "Brandon included."

And then he leaves. Gee. Talk about pissed off.

But oh well. This is still a win.

Now, I need to thank Bran personally and hope—no, pray—I never see his psycho brother again.

FOUR

Mia

SINCE MEDITATION IN THE HOUSE IS VIRTUALLY IMPOSSIBLE, I had to come up with an alternative.

The chess club downtown.

We have a chess club in The King's U, but they don't provide me with a challenge anymore. Besides, I might have kicked the club's president in the shin for calling Maya an attention whore.

So what if she likes to dress up and show off her body? It's none of his damn business.

As is obvious by now, I don't react well to people hurting or bad-mouthing my family. Besides, that damn president knows shit about our lives and the type of pressure and danger we've had to navigate through since we were kids.

Maya is an independent girl who loves dressing up and showing off her beauty. She definitely wasn't looking for that scum's attention.

Naturally, I was blacklisted from the club, despite being the best they had. Anyway, I was able to join the local chess club a few weeks ago after seeing a few flyers outside our dorm building.

There are some decent older players, but many of them come to gossip, as if it's some sort of knitting club.

Anyhow, since chess and meditation help me quiet down my demons, this is my last resort.

I also love looking after plants, but I've been hesitant to have any here. It'd feel like I'm cheating on my pretty flowers back home.

Point is, I really can't get myself kicked out again or I'm in trouble. In my family, I can only play chess with Gareth, but he's busy with studies lately.

I walk down the street, ignoring the looks everyone gives me. Today, I went back to my signature look—an ample black dress with a fluffy tulle skirt, chunky boots with chains, and matching ribbons in my hair. Oh, and killer blue-mirror sunglasses.

What? It makes me feel like the villain.

Many call this a goth look, but, really, it's not. Nor is it my Satan worshiper look—I'm out of that loser's league. I also don't wear black makeup. In fact, my only makeup is pink lipstick and mascara. If I'm in the mood for mayhem, like that day in the Elites' mansion, I add bold eyeliner.

I love being cute and deadly. It's my strength.

Once I'm inside, I remove my sunglasses and wave at the club's president. The other members look up, but upon seeing me, they either go back to their gossiping or their games.

Oh well.

Somehow, they figured out my origins and won't touch me with a ten-foot pole. They rarely talk to me either.

The only one who does is the president himself. He's usually my partner in the game as well. At my wave, he slowly stands from his sitting position by the reception and advances toward me.

Mr. Whitby is a nice old man with white hair, sagging wrinkles, and an impeccable posture for someone his age.

"How are you today, Ms. Sokolov?"

I do the okay sign that he understands by now. Everything else, I have to write in my phone's notes app.

After I type out my reply, I show him. "I told you to call me Mia. Just Mia."

He nods as the most perfect English gentleman I've ever seen. After my dad—who has a British accent but comes from a very complicated ancestry.

The only difference is that Mr. Whitby doesn't kill people for a living like Dad.

The old man smiles faintly. "I'm sorry I can't stay around for today's game. I have an urgent errand to tend to."

Oh.

"I'm sure one of the others would be thrilled to play against a bright young lady such as yourself."

No, they won't.

Mr. Whitby faces the other members. "Anyone?"

I hang my head. Seems no meditation or chess are on the table today. I do need to purge this energy before it consumes me, though.

This morning, I caught myself standing in front of the mirror, opening and closing my mouth. The disturbing part wasn't looking like a haunted, mentally-damaged goldfish. It's the fact that I haven't done that for years.

After I stopped talking at the age of eight, I tried to speak a few years later by standing in front of the mirror and opening and closing my mouth, attempting to turn the noises I sometimes release into words, but that only made me cry and even pushed me into a panic attack.

So I stopped altogether.

I'm just under a lot of stress lately or I wouldn't have done that today. It could also be because of the nightmares—

"I'll play against her."

My spine jerks and that familiar chill snakes to the bottom of my tight belly.

It can't be.

I must be imagining things.

I don't turn around to the source of the voice, though.

If I pretend I didn't hear it, that means it didn't happen. Who knows? Maybe my ears are catching up to my tongue and are also becoming dysfunctional.

A shadow stops in front of me, and this time, I do raise my head. My audible gasp nearly chokes me as my eyes clash with none other than Landon fucking King's.

For the second time in my life, I'm speechless. No, I'm stunned. Everything about this man is unsettling and none of his charm is able to camouflage it.

It's unfair that he always looks as if he jumped right off of a runway or out of a brand commercial. A crisp white button-down is tucked into his tailored black slacks, highlighting his sculpted waist. There's an effortless elegance in the way he carries himself, highlighted by a sharp presence and a sardonic smirk.

Unlike a few days ago, a slight stubble covers his cutting jaw, giving him a subtle ruthless edge.

The bastard sure knows how to use the weapons that are at his disposal. Beauty, style, and infuriating charm.

He cocks his head to the side, and the same grin from the other night curls his lips. Provocative, sinful, but most importantly, dangerous.

"Landon." Mr. Whitby clutches his shoulder in a friendly greeting. "Long time no see."

Long time no see? *Long time no fucking see?*

Please don't tell me this bastard is a member of this club.

"Frank," Landon greets the president with the familiarity of close acquaintances, his smile subtly switching to appear welcoming. "I missed this place and the people in it, so I thought I'd pay a visit."

Everyone, and I mean every single one in the hall, either smiles or stands up to surround the freak in a close-knit circle.

The women basically fight for his attention, and he acts like some sort of celebrity. Unlike a celebrity, however, he knows all their names and compliments one lady on her new haircut, another on her flattering glasses, and another on her cardigan. He also greets the men in a bro kind of way, and they all nod enthusiastically.

You've got to be kidding me.

I watch the show with my mouth agape. This must be what Bran meant by "You've never seen Lan in action. He can be the most charming or the deadliest depending on his mood and goals."

Now, I see it. The other side of Landon that I've only heard about but never had the misfortune to witness.

He captures people's attention with ease. It's clear that he's a natural at this and can't possibly be challenged at his own game, let alone beaten.

The worst part is that people flock to his presence with the suicidal tendencies of a moth to a flame. In no time, I'm the only one who's standing outside the circle, an outcast through and through.

Mr. Whitby clears his throat and manages to break the circle from around Landon.

Suddenly, I'm back in Prince Not-So-Charming's field of vision. Somewhere I definitely don't want to be after I single-handedly destroyed his party the other night.

"All right, everyone," Mr. Whitby says. "Landon came to play, so how about we let him do that?"

The man of the hour, as he probably thinks of himself, slides his attention to me while still wearing a destabilizing grin that could rival a serial killer's.

"Landon, this is Mia." Mr. Whitby motions at me. "She's unable to speak, but she can hear you just fine. If she needs to communicate, she'll write you a note on her phone. Oh, and she happens to be the best I've played in chess after you."

Did he just say *after you*?

Mr. Whitby, I was just building you an English gentleman shrine in my head, but how dare you place me after this asshole?

"After me, huh?" Landon echoes, and I swear a light glows in his eyes, making them brighter and more sadistic.

"Yes. She's such an intelligent young lady and a formidable opponent. I wish I could stay to watch you two play."

"Now, I'm intrigued." The bastard, who definitely doesn't resemble Bran in anything but looks, smiles again. How could he make something as simple as a smile drip with unhealthy charm and satanic voodoo?

I reluctantly sit at the vacant table in the corner. The biggest part of me wants to flee and reconsider devil worshiping to curse the man in front of me, but if I do that, it'll only look suspicious.

Besides, there's no way Landon knows I'm the one who humiliated him in front of his pretentious wannabes.

Still, my movements are stiff as I sit opposite him. So much for relaxing and shutting down my mind.

It's safe to say this whole situation is failing sideways.

I busy myself with pushing the white pieces exactly in the middle of the tiles.

"We meet again."

I slowly lift my head, only for my gaze to crash with his sardonic one and that taunting smirk at the corner of his lips.

Keeping my expression the same, I type on my phone, "Who are you again?"

The moment he sees the words, he bursts out laughing. "You're an interesting little mouse."

"My name is Mia," I type and show him.

"Mouse is a more accurate description. You love going unnoticed and leaving crumbs of havoc, no?"

Fuck this asshole.

What are the chances of me kicking him and not being thrown out by the fanboys and fangirls currently watching us from their seats?

Also, does this mean he suspects me?

Still, even if he does, he has no proof and, therefore, can't accuse me of anything.

I push my first pawn and stare at him. He stares right back as he glides his own pawn across the tiles. "I must say, you have above-average acting skills."

I raise a brow.

"To be able to meet me and stay calm and even pretend you don't know me should earn you a round of applause."

I type and show him, "I don't know what you're talking about. Did we meet? When? In your dreams, maybe?"

"My dreams?"

"Wow. I was really in your dreams? I know I'm pretty, but you can stop drooling."

His lips twitch. "Someone is certainly drooling here, but it's not me. And no, we didn't meet in my dreams. I'd have to give a fuck about you to allow you access to my subconscious, and I'm not known to do that. We did, however, meet when I ruined your cousin's car."

"Doesn't ring a bell."

"How about when you called me a fucking tool, then proceeded to teach me how to curse in sign language when I called you a mute? Do you remember that?"

My blood boils at the reminder and I'm tempted to flip him off again just because, but, instead, I move another pawn and then type, "No. I meet a lot of tools in my life and it's impossible to remember all of them. Good for you for having a strong memory for useless encounters, though."

There. K.O. The best way to get back at egotistical jerks with a god complex like Landon? Make them feel like they mean nothing.

"Hmm." His gaze slides from the phone to my face. "And here I thought I would apologize for the mute remark, but it turns out, there's no need."

I narrow my eyes but quickly conceal it. The damn prick nearly trapped me.

What is he playing at? Apologizing? People like him don't apologize.

If they do, they don't mean it.

And if they do mean it, there's an ulterior motive.

"Since you have a memory lapse." He wraps his fingers around the bishop's neck and meets my gaze. "I don't suppose you've been around my place lately, no?"

"I don't even know where your place is," I type.

"Funny." He leans forward. "Because I saw footage of my brother inviting you over."

Shit.

"Oh! I didn't know it was your place." I smile sweetly as I show him my phone.

"Just like you didn't possibly suspect that my identical twin—who literally looks like a copy of me—might be, I don't know, my twin?"

"I did suspect it when I met you just now, but it's rude to talk about someone's family, don't you think?" I smile again as I knock off his knight.

Guess someone will be right after me today, not the other way around.

"It is, which is why I prefer not to show footage of your twin sister making a fool of herself with one of my guards that night."

I freeze, my cheeks turning into hot flames.

"That's right, mouse. I know both of you trespassed on my property and bathed me in pig blood. Now that we've gotten the dull pleasantries out of the way, shall we discuss that further?"

FIVE

Landon

I'VE NEVER PLAYED WELL WITH OTHERS.

Yes, I might use my charm, but it's only so I can gain a favor here, a connection there, and a shag everywhere.

It's by no means to gather superfans and dreamy-eyed girls.

In fact, I've only ever played with others so they'd fall into the exact spot on the chessboard where I want them to be.

Force is for brutes who don't have the capacity to use their head. And while I relish the occasional bursts of violence, it's not truly my modus operandi.

Trapping a certain mouse in a corner, however, definitely is.

The insolent, insignificant little troublemaker who managed to bathe me in blood in my own house sits opposite me in a position that's an excellent imitation of a Greek statue.

Or, on second thought, maybe a Roman one. Those are more stilted and pack more of a punch in the details.

One difference, though—her eyes. They tell a different story from her posture. The muted blue is worlds apart from mine, nearly explosive in its color. Fierce, too, like a volcano that's buried in the depths of the ocean.

While it might remain dormant for years, it'll bring on a deadly tsunami the moment it erupts.

Or maybe they're the color of deep-blue wildflowers. Crushed by harsh nature but defiant. Proud and pretty yet temporary.

Her skintight dress offers a modest view of the curved slope of her round tits. Add the illegal amount of ribbons and the glasses on top of her head, and she looks like one of Satan's favorite fangirls.

A goth Barbie without the pretentious makeup.

The rook remains suspended in midair as if the world has hit Pause.

Only, it hasn't. And I get to watch the intriguing change in her expression from arrogance to absolute horror.

Taking my time to fully investigate the incident these past cou-ple of days was worth it. I could've gone a completely different route with this—which would have included violence and newsworthy mayhem. And while the thrill would've been enjoyable for a few seconds, it wouldn't have lasted. And it certainly wouldn't compare to the picturesque scene in front of me.

Plump pink lips, slightly parted, revealing a hint of perfectly white teeth. Rosy cheeks and neck. Eyes so stunned, I'm wondering if she can even still see me.

In conclusion, this round is a checkmate to yours truly.

"Hello?" I wave a casual hand in front of her face. "Are you still there, mouse?"

She blinks once...

Twice...

I see the exact moment she goes in for the attack. It's like when she had the audacity to hit me under my own roof. The only difference is that she's less guarded now and doesn't seem to be contemplating the option of amateurish seduction.

She balls her fist, but before she can punch me, I grab it in my palm and effortlessly twist it to the side.

"That's not very wise, now, is it? We both know I'm stronger than you and could squash you like an insignificant insect if I choose to, so don't let me choose to."

Her face contorts with either pain or rage—I'm not sure which. Hopefully, it's both.

I love watching people flounder in a pool of their spineless emotions before they wither and drown.

As rumor has it, I'm nothing less than a gorgeous anarchist with a penchant for sadism.

"We'll negotiate my terms now, shall we?" I drop her hand and it's only after I release her that I register how small that hand is. In fact, all of her is, from her tiny nose to her petite features. She's not short, but she's not that tall either.

A height that can comfortably fit in a casket.

Crikey. I've done it again.

Imagining people dead. If I get to witness her funeral, I vote for her eyes to be kept open. So what if it creeps everyone else out? As long as I get to enjoy it, the world can piss off.

The softness doesn't fool me, though. Despite her delicate appearance, this girl has over-the-top tendencies and has proven to possess balls bigger than some men.

The moment the little mouse is free, she signs furiously, her cheeks turning red with unmistakable rage. One of the perks of my genius neurons is being proficient in languages and picking them up from a very young age. I speak five fluently and a dozen more at different levels. Sign language, however, never really crossed my radar.

I don't understand a thing Mia is trying to communicate, but I smile and nod anyway. "I gather from your expression that you're not happy about the sharp turn of events. I'll find the capacity to empathize when I find some fucks to give."

She lowers her hand to the table and forces a breath in. It appears staggeringly ineffective and worse than a child's attempt to remain calm.

With a dramatic huff, she punches her phone's screen with nails that are painted blue—like her ribbons and sunglasses.

"Easy, tiger," I repeat what I told her the night she dared to provoke me and promptly signed her death certificate. "It's not the phone's fault you're losing in epic fashion."

She thrusts the phone in my face. "If you dare hurt my sister, I'll slice your throat and hang you out to dry by the balls."

My attention shifts from the text to her when she slides her fore-finger along her translucent neck that would look ethereal with a few marks. Then she squashes something imaginary—presumably my balls—in her palm and points at me.

I can feel my smile broadening as I connect my forefinger with hers. "Is this some telepathic method?"

She jerks her hand away and flips me the middle finger while wearing a sickeningly sweet smile.

One that's meant to look not only fake but also forced.

Interesting.

Seems that Mia Sokolov has no qualms about provoking me for the fuck of it.

Seems that I've stumbled across someone who's not particularly receptive of my godly personality and immaculate charm.

Then again, she wouldn't have bathed me in blood if she were.

She plays her rook, and I block it with my queen, then place an elbow on the table and lean my head against my fist. "I'm curious."

She types, "About how to be a better person? I can help with pointers."

"Don't be ridiculous. No one is curious about something that dull, and you're far from being the person to provide any pointers." I push my queen forward and she narrows her eyes at the unexpected move. "What I am curious about, however, is the reason behind your attack."

Her features contort in an "Are you kidding me?" expression be-fore she shakes her head with a huff. It looks as patronizing as a teacher who's fed up with her problematic student.

Her attitude is eerily similar to my sister Glyndon's whenever she tells me how done she is with my antics. But since I'm about to be twenty-four and she's only nineteen, I get older-brother privileges.

And I'm the second King grandchild to roam the earth. Each is a different superpower in its own right.

"What?" I tap my fingers against my lips. "If it's something I've done, you have to be more specific. I have no recollection whatsoever of my countless masterpieces. See, I have to delete some to leave space for the newer ones."

She reaches into her little dress that appears to be stolen from a gothic doll, retrieves what looks like a pen, and scribbles on the screen of her phone for longer than usual.

Her handwriting, if that's what it can be called, is tiny and messy, like a drunk ant that's trying to find its way home after a wild night out.

"You forgot about hurting my cousin Kill? Or kidnapping my brother, which directly resulted in his injury? How could you even kidnap my brother anyway? He's much bigger and stronger than you."

"Strength holds no importance when he was drugged. I slipped it in his vodka, and he was none the wiser. Word of advice, don't drink anything a stranger offers. But then again, your dear brother is a bit thick, isn't he?"

Her eyes blaze the color of hellfire. I counter it with a broad smile.

There's something intriguing about her murderous expression. Something I want to freeze into a stone.

Maybe transform her into one of my statues and stare at her spiky expression for eternity.

Huh.

That's actually the first time I've thought of sculpting someone into a statue just to stare at them. Usually, I'd imagine them as stone for the sole purpose of snuffing out their life.

"To clarify, your cousin Kill had the audacity to go after my sister—a sin I still haven't forgiven, mind you. As for your brother, he was part of a very elaborate plan that faced a few complications but still managed to be a fantastic success."

She starts to sign but then fists a hand on the table and scribbles with the other, "It couldn't have been as fantastic as punching you in the face and giving you a blood bath, asshole."

"Now, that's where you're wrong." I knock down her bishop and casually place it to the side. "Your attack the other night was directed at me, even though I've never targeted you."

She scribbles and shoves the phone in my face. "Targeting my family is no different from targeting me."

"I disagree. In fact, I see the assault as an invitation to a challenge, and I take my challenges very seriously, which is why the first step is to expose Maya as…easy, for lack of a better term."

She jerks up, both her fists balling and a vein in her neck popping with tension.

"Sit down before I decide that after her very public humiliation, I'll also fuck her and post the video for the world to see."

She lifts her fist as if she can punch me, but I continue staring her in the face. "Sit the fuck down, Mia."

Her lips purse, but she slowly lowers herself, even as her tiny frame shakes with her attempts to camouflage her reaction.

"What do you want?" she types on her phone.

"To be perfectly honest, I'm not sure yet. All I'm certain about is that I do want something in return for my nonconsensual blood bath and the punch that endangered my aristocratic nose."

She rolls her eyes. "You're an arrogant prick with not a decent bone in your body."

"I appreciate the unnecessary opinion, though it's pointless when I lack the fucks to give. Also…" I grab her hand that's holding out the phone, my fingers snaking over her tiny wrist. "You might want to stop calling me names and provoking me for sport, because you're starting to look very much like a challenge, and that's the last thing anyone wants to be when facing me."

My fingers glide up her bare arm, and I can feel the shivers that break out on her skin, whether involuntary or not, I have no clue.

Usually, I only touch women with the intent of seducing them into my blood-favored world. I don't intend to do that with this wild card.

Her destiny will see her broken against my edges. When I'm done with her, dust will be all that's left of her bull-like determination and troublemaking confidence.

Deep powder-blue eyes spark with fire. If I were petrol, I'd be burned on the spot.

She holds my gaze the entire time. When I channel my malicious, intimidating energy, people usually cower away after a second or two.

Even though I wear the charming mask so well, it's still a mask, and when I drop it, revealing the true entity of destruction lurking inside me, others avoid it—my family included.

Not Mia fucking Sokolov.

She stares me in the face with nothing short of a "Fuck you, how dare you threaten me?"

I seem to have forgotten that she is a mafia princess. She was probably fed pride, arrogance, and power in her baby formula.

All three will be smashed to pieces by yours truly.

The moment comes to an end when she snatches her hand away and types, "Show me your worst, asshole."

My dick twitches against my trousers and I grin. Wide. So wide that Mia's lips purse.

Lips that would look divine wrapped around my cock, trembling as I fuck her throat before I eventually smear them with my cum.

Well, well. I'm officially turned on by the little troublemaker.

"Are you sure? My worst can't be stomached by the majority of society. Also…" I move my rook forward. "Checkmate."

I stand up, and before she can study the board, where I already blocked all her exits, I'm beside her.

She smells of subtle magnolia imitating a breeze in the aftermath of freezing winter. I sink my fingers in the mass of her platinum blonde hair and ribbons, then push it aside to reveal her ear.

I lean forward, my lips finding the shell of her ear before I bite harshly, to the point that she jolts.

My dick thickens further, appreciating her reaction a bit too much. He's known to be whorish, but not this much. Besides, I'm not usually attracted to someone who poses a direct threat to me.

Another first. Interesting.

I release the shell of her ear and whisper, "Better close your windows at night. You never know what might crawl through them."

SIX

Mia

A WEEK LATER, I'M SITTING WITH BRAN IN THE GAME ROOM
in the Elites' mansion.

My relationship with this space is complicated at best. I
love the vibe, but I'm not a fan of how big it is. Low red lighting casts
a glow on our faces and around huge screens on the wall.

The chairs are comfortably massive, and sometimes, we opt to use
the sofa so I can hit Bran whenever we're playing opposite each other.

He's competitive, but he's not a sore loser.

Me? I don't have sportsman spirit whatsoever. What? I don't
take well to losing.

Bran, however, is a total angel, which is why it's no fun to win
against him. It's impossible to penetrate his walls or talk shit to him.

Then again, it's easier to lose against him since he doesn't really
rub his win in your face.

He's usually the only one who comes to this room since, I believe, he's the sole gamer in the house.

After numerous visits, I've come to the conclusion that many men
live in this mansion—Bran, his two cousins, his friend, and, most importantly, the devil himself.

My blood roars at the thought of that bastard and his gloating
"Checkmate" before he left me stunned in the club. But none of that

was as horrifying as the absolute skin-crawling sensation I felt when he touched me.

Not only did he touch me, but he also *bit* me like some freaking dog.

The shell of my ear is still in flames from when his teeth sunk into it like a starved monster.

It hurt, damn it.

But the pain paled in comparison to the pure terror that shot through my veins.

Even the thought of him now makes my spine jerk and goosebumps erupt on my skin.

I don't succumb to threats, but his were different. His included a vibrant image of my sister being used for his revenge. Worse, my sister would be used as his response to my hotheadedness.

Maya didn't initially agree to the plan of giving the bastard a pig blood makeover, but she's also my ride-or-die and refuses to let me go on these sorts of missions alone.

I wouldn't be able to forgive myself if she were in danger because of me. Over the past week, I've been trying to protect her and told her to be careful, but she has little to no self-preservation skills and can't be left to her own devices.

Maya and Nikolai take so much after Mom's go-getter personality. They slam in headfirst—either they get their way or they die trying.

I've always been like my dad. Silent but deadly. Appears sophisticated but could kill you with a smile.

That sense of confidence, however, seems to have left the building since my ill-fated encounter with Landon.

Not only have I been over-the-top paranoid, but my sleep has been plagued by malicious nightmares from a time in my past that I can't seem to forget.

I haven't spoken to Mom and Dad for a while out of fear that they'll see right through me.

And it's all because of the bastard who hasn't made a move.

Every night, I've been staring at my window, expecting him to jump through and murder me.

But people like Landon don't murder. They prefer to leave you hanging, waiting, and scared for your life. They prefer the mental torture and looming threats.

"Are you sure he's not here?" I show the typed words to Bran as we sit down for a dinner break.

He's opposite me on the sofa as we dig into Thai food takeout.

We've both been playing since we finished our afternoon classes. We're worlds apart in majors—he's an art student and I'm studying business management since I've always wanted to start something that only belongs to me. Not my parents, not my legacy. Just something that's purely mine.

Bran says he should be in the art studio, but he's been succumbing to 'one more game' for the past two hours.

He chews on the mouthful of rice and shakes his head. "He's out wreaking havoc and ruining someone's—or some people's—lives. Why are you asking? Are you scared?"

"He should be the one who's scared after my pig blood episode." I don't even feel the confidence as I show him the words.

Bran merely sighs. "I told you it's not wise to get on his bad side."

I wince and throw a piece of tomato in my mouth to mask my reaction.

Bran did warn me when I asked him stuff about Landon's Elite party that night.

I cock my head to the side and study him closely. He's the spitting image of his asshole brother. But I guess it's the personality that makes all the difference.

Bran is such a posh boy and what I imagine a well-bred and educated English youth to be like. His eyes are welcoming pools of pure blue, his jaw appears less sharp than Landon's, and his lips are neutral and by no means a weapon of terrorizing grins.

Oh, and their only real physical difference is that Landon has a tiny mole at the corner of his right eye. A small detail that I noticed the first time I saw them together.

I remember thinking Landon needed to be brought down a peg or two, and I can proudly announce that I'm still of the same opinion.

Hell, maybe he should be locked up for the travesty.

It's impossible to mistake the two brothers for each other, and I don't think that has to do with my being an identical twin myself and, therefore, skilled in the business of differentiating.

The truth remains, one is always calm, and the other is the definition of a shit-stirrer.

Besides, I don't feel threatened in Bran's company, whereas I'm always in fight-or-flight mode in Landon's presence.

"What is it?" Bran asks when I continue watching him. "Is there something on my face?"

I type, "I was just thinking how different you guys are."

"Just like you and Maya are different, no?"

"She's not a psycho."

"Touché." He laughs and takes a sip of a ginger lemon soft drink. "Still, I'm impressed with what you did the other day."

Thanks, but it's backfiring and causing me so much stress.

"He said he'll make me pay," I type and then show him my phone.

Bran gauges my expression. "Did you by any chance...challenge him?"

"How do you know that?"

"You shouldn't have done that, Mia. It's the easiest way to get on his shit list."

"Well, he's also at the top of mine."

He smiles, but it's sad at best and pitiful at worst. "Confidence is good, but no one has ever been able to win against Landon after he sets his sights on them."

"There's always a first. But hypothetically speaking, how far can he go?"

"You already know what he did to Killian because he pissed him off and to your brother because he was merely part of his plan. What you don't know, however, is that he was probably behind the fire that destroyed half of the Heathens' mansion, just because they proved to be an annoyance."

My lips part and I scribble furiously. "I thought the Serpents did it."

"They did, but he's the one who supplied them with the information they needed. Then he sat back and watched the entire show unfold from the sidelines. He's that dangerous."

That freaking bastard. Either I'm going to kill him or he kills me. No in-between.

I stuff my face with food and swallow without much chewing. I choke and start coughing, the obstruction blocking my windpipe.

Brandon reaches over and pats my back, then offers me a bottle of water. I gulp half of it down and do the "Thanks" sign.

He understands some of the basic sign language, and he's really been putting an effort into learning more lately. That's how much of a good person he is.

"You okay?" His eyes dip at the corners with genuine worry.

Why aren't there two of him instead of that evil Landon?

"I'm fine. Thanks, Bran. Not only for this but also for covering my back with Niko the other day."

He reads the words and I think I imagine a tic in his jaw before he nods. "I figured you could use some help."

"But how did you know to answer correctly about Maya?"

"I suspected that if he was asking about her, then it regarded the two of you."

"Smart."

"I know, thanks."

And there it is, a hint of his brother's overwhelming arrogance. Though Bran's is more subtle and definitely not overpowering.

"Were you in trouble with your brother?" he asks, looking at me from beneath his lashes.

"Nah. It was just Niko being Niko. He said not to get involved with you guys, considering the whole rivalry thing with the Heathens. He wasn't hearing it when I told him you're different, because he's a hotheaded mule. Anyway, these games and meetings will have to be our secret wherever Niko is involved."

His eyes flicker as he reads the text. "It's not like I'm acquaintances with your brother, so you have nothing to worry about."

Is it me or did he sound a bit too restrained just now?

"Bran!" A third presence barges through the gaming room door. "Have you seen my red Jordans? I swear to fuck one of these fuckers is hiding them and my lordship is going to break all hell loose…" He pauses upon seeing me and his expression transforms from annoyed to flirty. "Why, hello there. My day just got a whole lot better."

"You were literally just threatening violence," Bran retorts.

"Now, hush, Bran. Don't be rude in front of the lady." He offers me his hand and I shake it. "I'm Remington. Everyone calls me Remi, or your lordship for short. I have an aristocratic title and a fortune that can last for generations. May I know the name that goes with the beautifully graceful face?"

"Her name is Mia," Bran says to him. "She can't speak, but she can hear you just fine."

Usually, people's expressions either change to awkwardness, or most often pity, but this guy's smile remains the same.

He's a bit taller than Bran and has a straight nose and an easygoing, pleasant presence. "Why have you been keeping such beauty to yourself, Bran? I thought we were friends."

"Leave her alone," Bran says. "You're not her type."

"Unless she's a lesbian, I'm everyone's type."

I smile and type, "I like this guy."

"See?" Remi says with glee. "I'm the model of every girl's dream man."

It's arrogance, but, again, it's not the same as Landon's.

Why the hell am I searching for a type of egoism that fits his?

It hits me then.

I'm trying to find arrogance that's not equally intimidating and terrifying. Obviously, it's an epic failure.

"Get over yourself," Bran says with a shake of his head.

"That would be such a waste to the universe. Anyway, what are you guys doing here? Can I join?"

"Do you game?" I show him my phone.

"More in real life since I'm a basketball god, just saying, but I do play with Bran sometimes when he's being a loner."

"Join us, then," I type, then smile when he reads it.

"That's not a good idea," Bran tells me. "He's loud and a hopeless amateur who blames the game for his failures."

"Hey. Show some respect, peasant."

"Aren't you supposed to find your shoes?" Bran asks. "Lan probably hid them to mess with you."

Remi's disgusted face must match mine. I knew I liked this guy. "That little fucker is always out for trouble. He needs to chill for a second."

"More like for a lifetime," Bran mutters under his breath.

Seems I'm not the only one who's done with Landon's shit. His own brother and friend don't seem pleased with him either.

I offer Remi some of my calamari. He accepts it and scoots a chair over.

"Has he always been like that?" I type and show it to them.

"For as long as I can remember," Remi says, stealing Bran's drink. "This one was always the pacifist, and Lan, the anarchist."

That's such a stark difference. Maya and I have our own personalities, but we're both troublemakers in our own ways.

"He doesn't fit into a mold, and he's extremely proud of his twisted, individualistic view of life." Bran stares in the distance as if he's reliving a faraway memory. "He has antisocial tendencies that he tames enough to make him appear charming instead of threatening."

"Tell me about it." Remi sounds personally offended. "That little fuck keeps getting all the pretty ladies even though he has the attention span of a fly."

"He's a genius at what he does, so the girls make sense," Bran says. "What doesn't make sense is them knowing he refuses any form of commitment but still flocking toward him anyway."

I type, "A genius at what he does?"

"He's a sculptor and he's always been gifted," Bran says with a smidge of envy. "He's had many of his works exhibited since we were in secondary school."

Oh, right. I heard about that before. I did contemplate ruining his art studio, but it's thumbprint protected, so I couldn't get access.

"I still prefer your paintings. They're so relaxing and pretty," I type and show Bran.

A rare smile curves his lips and he pats the top of my head.

"But Lan hasn't sculpted in a while," Remi says after swallowing a bite of food. "The other day, he said it's just dull."

"Dull?" Bran echoes. "Sculpting is the only thing that reins him in."

"Maybe that's why he's been acting like a maniac lately."

That can't be a good sign, right?

We play together for another hour before I have to leave. Partly because I don't want my brother to question why I was out late and partly because I don't want to cross paths with Lan on my way out.

Still, I keep thinking about the conversation I had with Bran and Remi. How can I use the information I learned to get rid of that bastard Lan?

The answer is that I can't. At least, not yet.

But I can store the information for later, until I eventually come up with something.

The chill of the night prickles my skin as I walk to the car.

It's darker than I anticipated. I don't like being outside alone in the dark. It's where the monster lurk, waiting to ambush me.

The low yellow lights stacked between the trees do little to dissipate the claim of the night.

My skin crawls and I have to breathe deeply so as not to trigger the weak part of me.

I take large steps, but it doesn't help to dissipate my imagination.

A rustle swishes from the trees before large heads with big, ugly snake eyes rear through the branches.

My breath catches and I give up trying to stay cool, then run to where I parked my car.

You're not taking me today, assholes.

Not today.

The monsters flicker and grow in size until I can feel them spreading behind me like wildfire. They're running and I'm running, but I don't think I can outrun them.

My muscles scream with exertion and my breathing comes out chopped and unnatural.

I'm almost to the car.

Almost—

I jolt to a halt when a dark figure appears from behind a tree, wearing a mask.

A scream bubbles at the back of my throat, but I can't release it.

All I can do is stand there as it approaches me with the intention of swallowing me whole.

"We meet again, mouse."

SEVEN

Mia

"**B**AD GIRLS GET PUNISHED, AND THERE'S NOTHING I LOVE more than punishing."

No.

My feet tremble, and a pebble creaks beneath my foot as I slide one leg back.

I can still hear the creatures of the dark moaning, groaning, and whispering unintelligible words into my ears.

As much as they scare me, as much as my heart shrivels and splinters, that's nothing compared to the monster that's standing in plain sight.

Every year I survived up to this point, every illusion I painted about getting over the past shatters into tiny black crystals.

I'm back to being that little girl who ran and fell, then ran again.

And again.

And—

The man in the mask approaches me with steady steps. Calm yet firm.

He's slim but broad. Silent but lethal.

This is it.

I've escaped for so long, but I realize that was only an attempted escape. In reality, I'm stuck in the loop he created for me.

I try to summon the warrior inside me that I've been cultivating for over a decade, but there's no sign of my usual boldness or bravado.

There's just a girl. Cold, hungry, and absolutely terrified.

My legs aren't moving anymore. The creatures of the dark have managed to catch me and they're imprisoning me in place for their lord.

I open my mouth.

Mom.

Dad.

No words come out. Not even a tiny, horrified sound.

With both hands in his pockets, the masked monster eats up the space between us in seconds. Then he's right in front of me, towering over me, his height invading the horizon and murdering its stars.

Rough shadows fall on the mask, turning darker, nearly black in the dim light. The holes where his eyes should be are hollow, bottomless, even.

Sharp fangs of horror sink into my skin. It doesn't matter how much I tell myself to move. My mind has already turned against me and there's no way to undo the spell.

"Have you already come to your senses?"

His voice is deep, distorted notes of destruction, a mythical beast with an agape mouth and shallow breath.

"Strange. I thought I would need to scare you for a bit more. Push you into a tighter corner. Toy with you till you collapse."

The ringing in my ears heightens until all I can hear is my own heartbeat—high and torn to shreds.

"I love trapping misbehaving little creatures while they beg and cry. I might let them go or drive a sharp knife into their chests and watch them flounder and choke on their own blood. Metaphorically, of course."

Stop. Stop coming closer, stop…

"Why are you so frozen?" The monster pulls a hand from his pocket and reaches for my face.

My feet tremble, and every particle of my survival instinct demands I bolt out of here, but I can't.

Not when my mind has already checked out, leaving me as a defenseless eight-year-old. I'm thrown back ten years in time, with only myself as solace and company.

The moment his skin touches mine, I stop breathing altogether. Maybe if I pretend to be dead, he'll leave.

Maybe this is another nightmare.

Please let it be another nightmare—

He pinches my chin between his thumb and forefinger and tilts his head to the side, watching me closely, explicitly. Intimately, even.

His eyes grow behind the mask, no longer bottomless holes with a direct view of hell. But what greets me is worse.

A dash of sadistic blue stares me down, like my own custom-made curse.

My face doesn't feel like my own as he rotates it from one side to the other. "You look...positively stunning. A doll. No, a statue."

The ringing in my ears slowly subsides and reality settles in small but noticeable increments.

It's not the monster.

At least, not *the* monster from the past.

Now that I'm out of my self-inflicted panic, I can see the golden details on his Venetian masquerade mask. I can recognize the tall, broad build, the characteristically tailored slacks, and the tucked-in button-down.

I suck in a deep breath, but I only manage to inhale his head-turning masculine cologne.

"Where did you go?" He taps my cheek as if he's summoning another version of me. "Don't leave just yet. I haven't had my fill."

I finally snap out of it and push his hand away, my breathing shallow and fast.

The man in the mask, the asshole Landon, stares at his hand that I just knocked off with disturbing calm, then directs the same stare at me. He rubs his forefinger against his thumb. Once.

Twice.

As if he's reliving a dear memory.

"Hey." He advances all of a sudden, until his marble-like chest crushes my breasts. "Bring back the version from just now. I'm not done."

I place my hands on his shoulders and push, but I might as well be facing a wall. The power with which he preoccupies my space is nothing short of a barbaric invasion.

What in the ever-loving hell is this bastard's problem?

He wraps his fingers around my throat and squeezes hard enough to force all my movements to a halt.

My windpipe closes and all I can see is the shadowy side of his mask. "I said. Bring it back. Now."

My survival instinct kicks in again, and I claw and hit his arm with everything I have.

I can't breathe.

I can't...breathe.

I slap a hand against his mask in an attempt to deter his attention, even if momentarily.

"Don't be shy. Come out." His fingers tighten further until I think I'm dying.

No. I most definitely am dying.

I go still, my hands falling to either side of me, and I attempt to go into last-resort survival mode.

His grip slowly loosens and a wolfish grin lifts his lips and a striking light twinkles the deep blue of his eyes. It's like when the sun is kissing the surface of an ocean, light on the surface but will never reach any of the darkness beneath.

I slowly suck in a fractured breath but remain still so as not to encourage his choke-happy fingers.

"There," he marvels, his thumb stroking the pulse point in my neck. "Perfectly statuesque. Absolutely stunning."

There's something seriously wrong with this guy and he could use urgent professional help.

I don't like the shivers that cover my skin at his touch or the sensual intimacy in every stroke.

My body temperature rises and that can only be because I want to kick him in the nuts.

I contemplate doing that. I just need to push back—

"Don't even think about it." The rare light slowly fades from his eyes. "I'm on a high and that means I will react drastically to any provocation. Chivalry and I don't coexist and, therefore, I don't give two flying fucks that you're a woman. If you attack me, I'll choke the fuck out of you."

I try to reach for my phone so I can type a few choice words for the asshole despite being deeply disturbed and slightly terrified.

Okay, maybe more than slightly.

He shakes his head again. "I mean it, Mia. Stay like a statue before I snuff out your life."

"You need help, you sick psycho bastard. Go fuck yourself," I sign, even though he doesn't understand a thing. I just needed to get that off my chest.

He releases my throat, grabs both my arms and glues them to either side of me, then squeezes my wrists. "A statue doesn't move, now, does it?"

Then he steps back and removes his mask.

I nearly forgot how attractive Landon is. Probably because, weirdly, I don't see Bran as attractive. Well, he is, but I view it in a detached sense.

Landon, on the other hand, drips with charm and beauty. Both are muddied by his beastly nature.

He's definitely on the spectrum of either a sociopath or, worse, a psychopath.

My cousin Kill has antisocial tendencies as well, and if he's anything to go by, then Landon is a worse menace than I predicted.

I realize now that he's never really shown me his monstrous side before. Now that I've gotten a mere glimpse at it, I can't help feeling the need to turn around and run.

But I don't.

I really don't want to risk being strangled to death right now. Not when I'm still reeling from the earlier panic attack.

He throws his mask to the ground and takes a few more steps back, then tilts his head to the side.

A slow smirk lifts the corner of his lips. "I can make a brilliant masterpiece out of you. I can freeze you and sculpt you from the finest stone that ever existed. What do you think? But then again, a statue doesn't think."

I need out.

Now.

I don't ponder it as I calculate the distance to the car and run at full speed. I don't stop until I'm inside and the door is locked.

A bang sounds on my window and I gasp as I slowly glance at it.

Landon appears on the other side, tall and intimidating as he mouths, "We're not done."

I hit the engine with a shaky finger, and it takes me two tries for the damn thing to work.

Another bang. This time a fist against the glass.

I can hear the scream building at the back of my throat, but I press the accelerator all the way down.

The car revs forward, but as I speed out of the parking spot, I catch a glimpse of Landon in my rearview mirror doing the 'I'm watching you' sign.

Or maybe now, it's 'I have my eyes on you.'

This is the second time I've been this terrified in my life.

"Baby? What are you doing up so late?"

I stare at my mother's face on my tablet's screen and physically force myself to hold in the tears.

Rai Sokolov is not only my mother, the most beautiful woman inside and out, but also my role model.

Maya and I have her same shade of blonde hair and a carbon copy of her eyes, nose, and lips.

She and Aunt Reina—Mom's identical twin and Kill and Gareth's mother—used to joke by saying we're their mini-mes.

I've always known my mom to be a strong woman, undeterred and ruthless. Right now, however, there's a furrow between her brows.

It's late evening in New York, and I've caught her sitting at her vanity just after she's finished her workday as a leader in the New York Bratva. That's right. My mom is the only woman who's climbed the ranks within a male-dominated organization and snatched a chair at the decision-making table.

She's no less than my father in any way and made sure to teach us that being a woman isn't a weakness—it should be a strength.

I used to think I was as assertive and powerful as she is, but after tonight's incident, my confidence has taken a major hit.

Ever since I came back to the apartment I share with Maya, I've been blazing the lights in my room on the highest setting and lying in a fetal position on the bed, waiting for my parents to finish working.

My encounter with the new monster in my life has left a ball in my throat and a fire in my chest.

"What is it, baby?" Mom's voice softens. "Is something wrong?"

Everything is wrong, Mom. The fear, the strange arousal, and my heart that won't stop beating so fast.

Everything.

But I don't say that and, instead, sign, "I just wanted to see your face and hear your voice."

"Oh, baby." She smiles, but it's a tad forced. "I'm over the moon about being able to see your face after a long day."

I let my lips curve the slightest bit. Most of my smiles are either forced or fake. The day I lost my voice, I also lost my smile.

"Has Aunt Reina been watering and taking care of Amun, Iris, and their family?" I sign.

"I don't know what's weirder. The fact that you name your plants or that the head of the family has a demon name. Besides, your Aunt Reina doesn't need to come all the way here just to water them. The gardener or I could do it."

"Don't touch them, Mom. I don't want them to catch a case of early death."

"That's rude."

"Well, you really kill most plants you touch."

"I'm sorry I don't have the green thumb gene." She smiles and leans closer to her phone. "What's really wrong, Mia? Is there anything I can help with?"

Of course she'd know something is wrong. She always does.

"I feel a bit down," I sign.

"Is there a reason behind this?"

"I had a panic attack in a dark place. I wanted to scream, but I couldn't," I sign, then hang my head.

There's no way I can tell her about Landon. If I do, she'll come here herself and rip off his dick, and then she might get in trouble with his influential family.

Besides, if she fixes my problems for me again, doesn't that mean I will forever be weak?

"I'm so sorry, baby." Her face, tone, and demeanor drip with love. "I wish I were there so I could give you a mama bear hug."

"I'm fine." *Lie.* "I'll forget all about it in the morning." *More lies.*

"It's okay if you can't forget about it, Mia." She scoots closer. "Listen, I've been planning to broach this subject when you come back for a visit, but how about you give therapy another go?"

I link and interlink my fingers, then shake my head. "Therapy doesn't work. I can't speak."

"Of course you can, baby. You just have to find the will to do it again."

No, I can't.

That part of me is trapped in an unremarkable capsule that's hidden deep in the forest.

I've forgotten what my voice sounded like. But even if I do speak, puberty has already changed it. Sometimes, I think it's probably like Maya's, but deep inside me, a distant memory of it tells me there were some differences.

"We don't want to push you," Mom continues. "But have you considered that maybe you gave up on therapy way too soon?"

"We talked about this. Therapy was doing nothing for me and I hated it there. I hated dissecting myself in front of strangers and not getting any results." My movements are jerkier, angrier, and more disturbed.

Like everything inside me tonight.

"Fine, I understand. I just want you to know that the option is always on the table."

She's about to say something else when a tall figure appears behind her and says in a soothing British accent, "What's taking you so long, princess?"

My father's face comes on the screen and I'm struck by how much I miss them both. I'm eighteen going on nineteen, but I still want to hug my parents for comfort.

Kyle Hunter is tall, dark, and classically handsome. Where Maya and I take after Mom and Aunt Reina, Nikolai resembles him. But while Dad appears sophisticated and elegant but is secretly a menace, Nikolai is openly a menace. He's rougher around the edges and definitely doesn't have Dad's discreet modus operandi.

A wide grin illuminates his features when he sees me and speaks in a subtle British accent. "Mia, is that you?"

I wave.

"What a fantastic surprise. Wait. Isn't it late over there?"

"Yeah, but I just miss you guys," I sign.

"Which is why you should've stayed here instead of flying to the other side of the ocean," he says for the thousandth time since we got here. "Now I can't hug my baby girl whenever I want to."

"I'll have Niko hug me on your behalf," I sign.

"Doesn't count."

"Leave her alone." Mom swats him teasingly. "She's old enough to decide where she wants to be."

"Which should be beside me. Just saying." Dad leans forward. "Is there anyone bothering my little Mia? Should I go there and perhaps erase them from the records?"

"Kyle!" Mom protests.

"What? That's the least I can do to whoever is causing the perturbed look in my little girl's eyes."

He knows, too.

Of course he does.

My parents have always been the best and have made me feel

loved from a very young age, but ever since that incident a decade ago, they've become more attuned to me.

To the point of overprotection.

That's part of the reason why I wanted to leave New York and join Nikolai here. Maya also needed to do her thing without being supervised every step of the way.

"I'm fine, Dad. I'm feeling so much better now that I've talked to you guys."

"We love you, Mia," Mom says.

"I love you, too," I sign, and as I hang up, I catch a glimpse of my father kissing the top of her head.

I've always admired the fierce way they love and protect each other. They're a power couple and clash sometimes, but they still have each other's backs. Their relationship is one of my favorite memories from home.

As the screen goes black, the sense of safety that I got from talking to my parents vanishes.

The lights in the room are still on, but I can feel the darkness creeping in from the corners, about to suffocate me.

I grab my pillow and phone and sprint to my sister's room.

I fling her door open and flick on the light.

"Ugh, what?" Maya groans from the bed and covers her head.

I go to her side and she removes her glittery eye mask, grumbling. "Don't mess with my beauty sleep or I will cut a bitch..." she trails off upon seeing what must look like terror on my face.

She doesn't probe or push. She doesn't even ask.

Maya and I share a special relationship and she must feel the unease that's gripping me by the throat.

My sister pulls the cover back and taps the spot beside her. I don't think twice as I dive in next to her.

"Thank you," I sign.

"There's no thanks needed between us, idiot. Go to sleep. I'm here."

She pats my shoulder in a soothing rhythm like a mother who's putting her child to sleep. When I close my eyes, I can feel her sliding her sleep mask back on.

Unlike me, Maya can only sleep when it's pitch-black, but she doesn't comment on the strong light I blazed in her room or how I invaded her space.

Whenever I need an anchor, she's there for me without question.

I'm drifting to sleep myself when my phone vibrates.

After making sure Maya is out, I pull it out and stare at the text.

Unknown Number: Asleep?

Who…?

My phone vibrates again.

Unknown Number: You can't be asleep after you woke this thing in me. Come out. I need to recreate the scene from tonight.

My fingers shake around the phone. Landon?

How did he get my number? More importantly, what the hell is he still doing up past two in the morning?

My phone vibrates again and I nearly jump out of my skin.

Unknown Number: On second thought, sleep while you can. You have a very chaotic life ahead of you and you need all the energy you can get, muse.

EIGHT

Landon

THE IDEA OF A MUSE HAS OFTEN ELUDED ME.

I understand the concept and the general consensus, but the overrated obsession of artists with the existence of a muse has always left me in a rare state of bewilderment.

And that's coming from someone who used sand to sculpt at the age of two. It was a female devil with a long, pointy tail, inspired by a painting in Grandpa's house. I recall that first time I created a sculpture and the raw feeling of the wet sand slithering between my small fingers.

I also recall the unperturbed emotions that ran through me when I watched that she-devil get washed away by a wave.

It was only later that I found out my apathetic reaction to the destruction of my first creation wasn't the norm and that I was, in fact, the definition of neurodivergent.

My steady relationship with art in general, and sculpting in particular, has been persistent throughout my twenty-three years of life. My world-renowned artist mother calls it a natural talent. The world labels it as genius genes.

For me, it's been the sole method I could use to cope with my beast, his demon friends, and dull humanity without resorting to an extreme. Like transforming someone into stone, for instance.

Every artist has a muse—or so they say.

Since I'm a very important—if not the most important—member of a family of artists, I have come to the realization that I don't share Mum's, Bran's, or Glyn's over-idolization of their imaginary friends.

In my mind, that's what a muse is all about—an imaginary childhood friend whose constant chatter they couldn't lose during adulthood, so they decided to give them a fancy name.

The idea of a muse has always been redundant, useless, and categorically ridiculous.

But since I'm a master of blending in and fitting societal expectations, whenever someone has asked me about my muse, I've said geniuses don't talk about their muse, as if it's some sort of MI6 intelligence.

Now, don't get me wrong. There's no doubt that I'm the definition of an artistic genius who brings the sculpting community to literal tears. However, I've partaken in the absolute nonsense of the nonexistent muse and fake superstitious rituals to divert the horde's attention.

I also figured my muse manifested in the massive creative energy that's impossible to satiate.

She was the inner sadism of my outward charm.

The violence that burst at the seams whenever my plans faced an obstacle.

But that lousy half-arsed explanation lasted until yesterday.

Not in my wildest dreams did I figure that a muse could manifest at the most random time.

When I was facing an enemy, no less.

When I saw the youngest Sokolov running toward the car park like her little arse was on fire, I figured I'd toy with her and provoke those wildflower eyes—to tears if I felt like it.

After I left her tending to her crushed pride, I had a fleeting curiosity about how her eyes would look when she was crying and begging for my nonexistent mercy.

Since the blasphemous blood bath incident, I've been concocting a multi-phase plan, all dedicated to her demise. In a nutshell, I'd start by tormenting her and end with using her against her brother and cousins.

While those plans remain in the background, there's a slight hitch in the process.

The way she froze up when I approached her.

I've never seen a human go so completely still—professional art models included. There's always the rise of a chest here, the flaring of nostrils there, and micro-movements to remind me that the fools aren't really stones.

Mia, however? She was the definition of a lifeless statue.

It was my sign that it's never too late to find the perfect human stone.

I release a long puff of smoke and then stub the cigarette in the middle of the crowded ashtray. My cancer-inducing habit has been going on since my name started making the rounds in the art circles about eight years ago.

The prodigy.

The special one.

The gifted child.

It's by no means due to pressure. If anything, the sudden surge of marketing my name experienced has stroked my ego in all the right places and given me better pleasure than a pro choking on my cock.

Smoking simply gives me the right balance while I'm using both hands to produce people's next favorite sculpture.

My fingers hover over the countless pieces of clay I've created since I retreated to my studio after Mia ran away.

At that time, I had two options—follow her or purge the burst of inspiration that suddenly crashed into my skull.

I opted for the second, and ever since then, I've been modeling miniature sculptures in search of the right image of the inspiration I had at that exact moment.

A million mini sculptures later, I've exhausted my clay supply and I'm still not satisfied with any of them. I'm certainly not using them on a real sculpture.

If my art professors at REU were to see them, they'd fall arse over tits and call them masterpieces like everything I've made with my supremely gifted hands.

I don't.

Something is missing.

If that little fucking shit had just remained still for a few more minutes, I would've gotten the full image. But she was more pressed about escaping me.

Granted, I might not have stopped at just touching if she hadn't run away.

I grab the last miniature and throw it against the raw stone opposite me. My details were the sharpest in the first ones, but they dwindled as I made more.

The last ones are absolute rubbish and a staggering disgrace.

The first stab of inspiration that hit me has faded, and my mind is now the usual barren black.

Black used to be the standard for me. It was with black that I sculpted and with black that I continued to thrive.

But for the first time ever, this type of black isn't as satisfying.

I want the dash of colors.

The strike of lightning.

The sound of thunder.

None of them come.

"Lan!"

I stare up from my distasteful miniatures to find my brother standing in the middle of my kingdom. Brandon is a striking identical picture of me, who can't resemble my sublime character to save his life.

"How did you manage to get in?" I sound groggy to my own ears, so I pull out another cigarette and jam it between my lips.

My brother doesn't like the smell of cigarettes, but then again, he shouldn't be in my space.

"I helped." My cousin Eli flashes me a vicious grin as he appears from behind Bran like a horror cliché.

He's my second cousin, if we're being specific, since his dad and mine are cousins. Being a couple years older than me, he takes that as a pass to brag about the King firstborn privileges.

Oh, and he happens to be antagonistic for the fun of it. Yes, I'm the same, but I don't like competition in my own game. One of these days, he'll take it too far and they'll find his body mysteriously float-ing in the Thames.

"With what?" I deadpan. "Giving yourself a personality?"

"The only one in this building in need of a personality trans-plant is you."

"He found the master key so we could open the door," Bran says in his usual attempt at peacemaking. It's so disturbing to see him being Mother Teresa and spouting nonsense with my face.

I blow smoke in his direction. "And you trespassed in my space because…"

He closes his eyes for a beat, but, like a boring nun, he doesn't display any form of anger or even displeasure. "You weren't answering your phone or the door when I knocked for the past fifteen minutes."

And the hole of fucking strange keeps widening.

I'm usually more aware of my surroundings than a predator in a dark African jungle.

"I told you he's fine," Eli supplies like an arsehole. "As unfortu-nate as it might sound, nothing can hurt the twat."

"You, however, could accidentally end up on an MIA list." I match his grin with my wolfish one. "Don't worry, I'll console Uncle Aiden and Aunt Elsa after they receive the news."

"Not if you magically disappear first."

"Catch me if you can."

"Is that a challenge?"

"I don't know. Is it?"

"Can you both stop?" Bran shakes his head like a headmistress who's sick and tired of her most troublemaking students. "We're family."

Eli and I snort and then we burst into laughter at the same time.

Did I mention that my brother can be the sappiest plain Jane who ever walked the planet?

Eli pats his shoulder. "Family is what makes this more fun, dear cousin."

Bran doesn't appear the least bit amused, though his shoulders relax now that he's figured out Eli and I like to rile each other for sport.

He still wants to kill me for my plan that included his brother, but I'm sure he won't do it.

At least, not if he still wants to belong to the King family.

As in, the one that owns the UK and half of the world. My grandfather, Jonathan King, is a ruthless monarch with an iron fist and a sharp sense of business. He built the fortune his brother and father nearly eradicated.

My father, Levi King, and my uncle, Aiden King, have been transforming the business and making it more lucrative than oil princes' fortunes.

The future of the King empire falls on Eli, me, and probably Creighton. Bran and Glyn were never interested in business and prefer to be artists like Mum.

My art career is just a temporary ruse before I take over the world. Might need to study some business first, but who gives a fuck. I'm sure I'll excel at that like everything I've done thus far.

Nothing is permanent, and the world is a mere vessel to make my desires come true.

My every whim and want has been catered to, which tends to be boring, for lack of a better term. *Someone give me a challenge, for fuck's sake.*

"Is everything okay? You've been locked in here for over twelve hours..." my brother trails off when he sees the miniatures lying on the floor, and his eyes grow in size. "Wow."

Yes, wow. I've never made so many useless miniatures in one session.

"Wow for the murdered Smurfs he's been making?" Eli asks with a note of depleted sarcasm.

I side-eye him. "You're an uncultured swine with not an artistic bone in your miserable body. Don't pollute my studio with your lack of taste."

"I do have taste. It just doesn't include your ugly art."

"It's far from ugly," Bran says without looking at Eli, then lowers himself to his knees to inspect them closely. "These are some of your finest work. They're stunning."

"All of my work is stunning."

Bran stares at me. "You haven't sculpted a thing in months, Lan."

"These aren't sculptures."

"You haven't done any model miniatures either."

"They're doodles. They mean nothing."

"You're such an arrogant fool. If others… No, if *I* could make something like this while doodling, I wouldn't ask for anything else."

"You need to stop painting happy-go-lucky nature scenes and you'll be able to do better than this. You're welcome for the free advice from a genius."

"I told you not to meddle with my artistic choices."

"Cry me a river." I kill my half-finished cigarette and crack my neck. "What time is it?"

"Past your beauty bedtime," Eli says. "Dark circles look hideous on you."

"And that striped jacket gives you a fantastic grandpa vibe. Have better fashion sense before patronizing me about my looks." I point at the door. "Now, out of my space, and I'm going to need that master key so no one trespasses again."

Eli leans forward and whispers, "No," before he buggers off to make the world a worse place than it was an hour ago.

"You need some sort of an escorting service?" I ask when Bran lingers behind, still staring at the miniatures.

He reaches a hand to one of them but thinks better of it and retracts it. Good. That hand might have been accidentally broken if he'd put it on my possessions.

Though I might not be as murderous if he asks for permission. He's always wanted to touch my sculptures after I've given him the green light. Now, he doesn't even ask if he can.

My brother stands to his full height and faces me with a furrowed brow. "Are you going to sculpt any of them?"

"No. They're not worth it."

"Have you positively lost your mind? These are your…"

"Finest work. Stunning. A stroke of a genius," I finish for him.

"We obviously have a different definition of excellence. What you see as extraordinary is mediocre at best to me."

"Well, excuse me for not understanding the genius genes."

"Nonsense. You have them as well, but as I've mentioned a million times, you're shackling them to the best of your abilities." I prop an elbow on his shoulder and grin. "Want my help to bring out the side you buried so deep, you almost forgot it existed?"

"If by help, you mean to drown me in your blood-flavored activities, then no thanks."

"One day, you'll take me up on my offer."

"Not even if you're reincarnated as a saint."

"Bloody hell, Bran. Don't go manifesting pure torture over a small disagreement." I pat his cheek with the back of my hand.

It's a gesture he used to like when we were growing up. Now, however, he drops his shoulder, making me lose my balance, and steps out of the way.

"No disagreement with you has ever been small, Lan."

"Oh, for fuck's sake. Is this one of those times when you turn sappy on me as if I'm your imaginary therapist? If that's going to be the case, I get paid by the hour and in advance, thank you."

He releases a long breath and shakes his head with the surrender of an old man in the last stages of cancer.

"Just call Mum when you get the chance. She asked about you when I talked to her earlier."

Saint Bran.

The peacemaker who thinks he's holding our family together by a thread Bran.

Sometimes I wonder if the fact that he of all people happens to be my twin is some form of a calamity.

After one last lingering look at the miniatures, he leaves the studio as if his arse is on fire.

It's no secret that Bran doesn't like me. Might have to do with the number of treacherous, elicit activities I've been conducting over the years.

As Mum likes to say, we're like night and day, and while she means that as a compliment, the truth remains, it's impossible for us to meet halfway.

But Bran and his righteous shenanigans can wait another day.

I've already missed half a day in my attempts to retain the vision from last night. I don't have enough time or inspiration to resurrect it.

One thing's for sure. My next course of action starts with a certain little muse who's gotten herself into the deepest clusterfuck of her life.

To say I'm entering unfriendly territory would be an understatement.

Let's say The King's U college and I share the same level of disagreement of right- and left-wing politics.

In fact, I wouldn't be surprised if the Heathens have put a bounty on my head and a wanted poster at the entrance of every class.

My track record with Killian, Nikolai, and even Jeremy doesn't help. The only member I haven't harmed, at least not directly, is Gareth, but I doubt he'd be interested in having a cheeky drink and smuggling me onto their grounds.

Which is why I came in partial disguise.

The saving grace of being among the unpolished, rowdy Americans is that there are so many of them. Definitely more than the students at REU. Therefore, wearing sunglasses and a hoodie is enough to conceal me from the unholy masses.

According to my extensive research on the Heathens and, after the blood episode, on Mia Sokolov herself, I know she's studying business.

So I make my way to that school and wait by the corner outside her classroom like a perfect gentleman. Thankfully, her clone studies law, so they don't take the same classes.

I check my watch and count the seconds until she's out. After this, Mia still has one more class, but she's going to have to take a rain check on that.

The students buzz around me, their chatter clashing with the seconds on my watch.

I don't mind the wait. In fact, a sensation of calm overtakes me at the prospect of catching prey.

I'm good at camouflaging myself when need be and waiting for the right moment.

Like the night, I'm silent, overpowering, and—under the right circumstances—deadly.

Students start flowing like ants in a disorganized colony, but I'm not concerned about missing Mia in the crowd.

That won't be possible after the alien sensation I experienced during last night's meeting.

Sure enough, I catch a glimpse of her blonde hair and blue ribbons flying in the wind as she checks her cat-themed backpack.

She's wearing another black dress that's fit for a luxurious funeral, and a certain detail stands out. The upper half has a few straps that stop at a choker around her delicate throat.

My, my.

She even dressed for the auspicious occasion.

Mia Sokolov is a beautiful goddess without putting in any effort. She barely wears any makeup or tries to doll up like most girls. She also adopts a troublemaking personality that's designed to put a damper on her physical superiority.

I've barely seen her offer a genuine smile, and that includes all the footage I've gathered on her in my attempts to dig her a hole she'll never get out of.

However, she excels at offering fake socially accepted smiles and pretending to be a naive cute girl to draw the right people's attention.

And while she might argue that we're different, she's wearing the same version of the mask I do. Which means she might have a beast inside her, too.

And I will have to murder and cut it into pieces because I only need her as a statue.

Not flesh and bones. Thoughts and opinions. Words and existence.

Still rummaging through her bag, she walks in my direction as clueless as innocent prey.

There, little muse. I might give you a treat after I turn you into a statue.

"Mia!"

She's only a few meters away from where I'm lurking when she comes to a halt and turns around.

I curse under my breath upon detecting the last two people I need in this situation.

The first is none other than Killian—the guy who stole my sister's heart despite my explicit refusal of the damned relationship. The other is Nikolai, Mia's older brother, who might be out to slice my throat the moment he sees me.

Both needless presences catch up to her and I have to change my position to get a better view of the situation.

Logically, I should leave before those two catch a glimpse of me and choose to give me a taste of my own torture medicine. And it'll be much worse than I could imagine, considering I trespassed on their turf.

The risks I'm willing to take for the sake of my muse are irritatingly stunning.

She signs something to them that I believe means, "What are you doing here?"

I might have looked at some sign language videos—ASL, not BSL since there are significant differences. And by some, I mean dozens of them. It was enough to become proficient. What? It's not my fault that I'm not only an effortless polyglot but also a fast learner.

"I'm taking Niko on a stroll," Killian replies with an easy grin.

His cousin kicks his foot. "I'm not your dog, motherfucker."

Killian doesn't seem perturbed in the least. He's probably the one who resembles me the most from that bunch of little fuckers. The only difference is that I'm culturally superior and have a more prominent penchant for anarchy.

As I'm contemplating the best way to dump his body in the ocean without permanently losing my sister, something happens that derails my whole thought process.

Mia's eyes twinkle as her lips pull in a genuine, happy smile. It's the wildest look I've ever seen on her face. And, coincidentally, they've all happened around her family members.

As if they're the only ones who deserve this side of her.

"Wanted to check on you," Nikolai says and pushes a cup in her hand. "Bought your favorite Frappuccino. Double espresso shot with caramel syrup and cream on top."

"I, unavoidably, helped him," Killian says.

"You did not," Nikolai retorts.

"My presence was in itself a massive help. If I hadn't been there, you would've been kicked out by the cashier, who was scared to death by your grim, unconsciously frightening presence."

Mia signs a thanks and accepts the cup, then she leans in for a quick hug with both her brother and cousin.

A hugger. A blasphemous, absolutely distasteful habit with no practical meaning whatsoever. It's not needed for sex and, when used, can lead to an awkward angle.

But then again, I've never appreciated touching people when my cock isn't involved.

"Want to grab something to eat before we continue our stroll?" Killian asks her.

She shakes her head and signs that she has a class.

Nikolai pats her head as if she's still a child. "Don't make any trouble, and if you do, for all that's unholy, tell me about it."

"And me." Killian points a thumb at himself. "We can turn mere trouble into a tornado."

She signs an "Okay," then they finally part ways.

Thankfully, Killian and Nikolai go in the opposite direction, while Mia continues toward me as she slurps her drink.

She reaches into her dress pocket and retrieves her phone, completely oblivious to the trap she's walking right into.

I don't make myself noticeable when she's near. No.

I wait and bide my time for the right moment.

Once she passes me, I stand behind her and whisper, "So you do use your phone, and yet you left me on Read. Where are your manners, little muse?"

NINE

Mia

MY CAREFULLY BUILT ILLUSION SHATTERS INTO A MILLION pieces all around me. The shards prick my skin with the deliberate precision of a thousand cuts.

The straw falls from my lips and I sluggishly swallow the liquid trapped in my mouth as if it's poison.

A part of me is urging myself to run, hide, bury this episode in the tortured abyss of my soul where all fucked-up creatures reside.

And as much as I'd love to put up a brave façade, I recognize how careful I need to be instead. I've witnessed firsthand what it looks like to be in the middle of Landon King's orbit, and to say I didn't survive would be the mother of all understatements.

However, I abandon the flight option.

People like Landon get off on the act of chasing more than the finality of catching. If I run, I'll only provoke the insatiable and completely sadistic side of him.

So, against my better judgment, I gather what remains of my courage and turn around.

I'm not even fully facing him when he grabs me by the shoulders, his fingers digging into the flesh before he shoves me against the wall.

My back hits the brick and I swallow a wince as my Frappuccino shakes and swirls, almost asking for help on my behalf.

His marble-like body presses against mine as a stark reminder of last night.

Of the terror.

The helplessness.

The strange arousal.

All of it.

He's in an uncharacteristic hoodie today and his eyes are hidden by aviator sunglasses that give him a mysterious edge.

"I should've done this sooner." He tilts his head to the side, studying the length of me as if he's seeing me for the first time.

Why is he wearing the damn sunglasses? It's already hard to read his eyes without the added camouflage.

I search our surroundings for anyone who might be able to help, but I realize we're in a small nook in the corner that most people don't even notice.

Landon releases my shoulder and reaches a hand to my face. I tense, my body getting ready to fight, claw his eyes out and drink his brain through the sockets if he as much as hits me—

He strokes my cheek and I freeze, all my murderous thoughts coming to a sudden halt.

My breath catches and my lips part.

That's about the last thing I expected the psycho to do.

His long, lean fingers glide from my forehead to my brows, over my eyelashes, then swipe down the bridge of my nose. As I watch with a completely stupefied expression, his exploration continues under my eyes, over my cheeks, and down my jaw before lifting my chin.

Every stroke leaves a burning fire in its wake. No, it's an avalanche of tingles, goosebumps, and pent-up euphoria.

Like a blind person trying to discern someone's features, he lingers and strokes gently. Too gently, even.

My thoughts scatter when he slides his fingers over my upper lip, his middle finger swiping down my Cupid's bow, then moves to my bottom lip. This time, his thumb presses on the flesh with a breathtaking firmness.

I'm entranced, absolutely taken aback by the sight in front of me and the overwhelming feelings blazing through me.

It's like I've been transported to a different dimension where everything is bizarre and the merest touch provokes an extreme reaction.

"Stunning." His deep voice, the sound of dark lullabies, chains me further to the alien feelings.

I'm no different than a fly caught in the web of a spider, completely paralyzed as life is sucked out of my limbs.

"Five out of five," he whispers in words that have no business being so destabilizing. "As expected of my little muse."

He flexes his hand into an open palm and swipes it down my throat. The touch is intimately explorative and breathtakingly stimulating. His fingers latch onto the leather choker and he uses it to pull me flush against him.

I have to keep the Frappuccino to the side or he'd crush it between us.

A sly smirk lifts his sinfully gorgeous lips as he toys with the leather, his fingers skimming my skin as if he has every right to.

As if he claimed me in a different lifetime and is currently taking me back.

"I knew there was a wild side to you. Tell me. Do you fancy being strangled while a cock rams inside your soaking wet cunt? Or do you prefer having a cock choke your pretty little throat and fill it with cum?"

His crude words, delivered in the most sophisticated manner, snap me out of my drug-like haze.

And the worst realization is that another part of my body mourns the loss of that haze. There must be something freakishly wrong with me. How could I go so still when he touched me with the sensuality of a lover?

I push against him with my free hand, my face heating and my mind thinking of a thousand curses I can use to send him to the afterlife.

My attempts to free myself only manage to amuse him to no end.

So I scratch at his hand, but that doesn't erase the provocative smirk from his face.

He releases me, though he doesn't give my space back. "My, my. You're supposed to be a harmless tiny mouse, but you're fast upgrading to a kitten with claws. Such a feisty little one."

I hug the Frappuccino against my chest and sign, "I'm not little, you psycho asshole. Go fuck yourself."

"Calling me names won't stop me from referring to you as little. And I would rather fuck a hole instead of doing it myself."

My lips part.

No. He couldn't have understood every word. It's just impossible. This prick can't possibly—

"Surprised I speak ASL?" He grins. "I figured it'd be better than scribbling on your phone whenever you're about to burst with curses. Now, I understand all the curses, not just the fuck-you ones."

"How?" I sign, bewildered.

"I happen to be a genius. You're welcome."

"I didn't thank you, asshole."

"Which you should've. Again, where are your manners?"

"You're talking to me about manners when you have a tendency to corner people like a creep?"

"I prefer the word *observer*."

I sneer, my chest nearly exploding from the audacity of this damn man.

"Walk with me?" he asks like some sort of a medieval gentleman that he definitely is not.

I lift my chin. "You expect me to say yes to that?"

"No, which is why I asked politely. The next time won't be as polite, so I suggest you accept the offer before it's taken off the table."

"Go fuck yourself."

"As I mentioned, I prefer holes, Mia. Keep up. At any rate, we're moving to the second stage." His voice lowers. "Walk with me or I will ask Maya instead."

My spine jerks.

"She's finished school for the day and is probably filming herself for social media in the Pin Café, which happens to be her hangout. I suppose if I walk there, I'll find her within fifteen minutes. Should I?"

"I'll slice your throat before you talk to her."

"You mean, *walk* with her."

"Stop it."

He stands straighter, devouring the horizon and my air. "There's only one way for me to do that and it is, as I specified a few moments ago, if you fucking walk with me."

Every molecule in me demands I kick him in the face and send shards of the sunglasses into his damn eyes.

But I have enough access to logic to realize that if I do that, I can't guarantee Maya's safety.

She tends to fall for men's looks more often than not, and if this bastard pulls the charming card that he wields so well, he might convince her he never intended to hurt Nikolai. He might flirt and seduce her until she reaches the point of self-destruction.

Because that's what this asshole does. He ruins things and he ruins them thoroughly without allowing them a chance of survival.

My fingers tighten on the Frappuccino, the cold condensation doing nothing to alleviate the volcano raging in my veins.

"Let's do it later," I sign while offering him my worst glare. "I have class now."

"The class can wait." He grabs my elbow, fingers nearly breaking the bone. "I can't."

He pulls me with a strength that makes me lose balance. The Frappuccino falls and splashes on the ground, the cream and coffee forming a gruesome murder scene.

The ominous image lingers in my head as he drags me behind him with blinding strength.

I try to push at his hand, to claw the skin and cause pain, but then again, he's barely human and definitely inhumane, so his type doesn't really feel anything.

In my attempts to free myself, I don't notice we're already outside the campus. Landon has dragged me to where he parked his car in a secluded place a safe distance from the college.

I know it's his car, because I saw it at the Elites' mansion once. A special edition, matte black McLaren with a unique shine material on the side.

It looks as elusive as the asshole himself.

He releases me, then removes the hoodie and his sunglasses. I often forget how illegally attractive he is, even in casual wear. He has a regal presence. Toned body, broad shoulders, lean waist, and the right height.

Everything is perfection—from his tousled hair to the slight stubble on his strong jaw. Even his only imperfection, the mole on the corner of his right eye, adds more to his penetrating charm.

An illusionary charm that he wears like a permanent mask.

Or maybe it's not so permanent. He certainly didn't waste any time in coming after me and showing his true colors following my fabulous blood bath plan.

"Why did you bring me here?" I sign.

"I couldn't exactly stay in the Heathens' territory for long or some spy would point your brother and cousins in my direction and there would be carnage. For them, not me."

"Stop being delusional. You could never win against my brother, Kill, and Jeremy."

"But I already did. Countless times. I can do it all over again if you need tangible proof that I'm stronger than all the Heathens."

"And yet little ole me managed to give you a refreshing bath in pig blood." I smile sweetly, matching his savage energy with mine.

"A one-off."

"I can make it a two-off if you don't back the hell away from me and my family."

"Your provocations are a turn-on, so unless you're in the mood to get on your knees and choke on my cock, I'd suggest you refrain from making them so casually."

He points at the small tent in his pants as stark evidence of his words. My cheeks feel as if they've gone up in flames.

"You're a sick bastard."

"So everyone keeps telling me. Don't be part of the herd. It's both boring and pointless."

"Ever thought that there's some truth in it if everyone keeps saying that?"

"Definitely not. Everyone tends to be stuck in a neurotypical, empty cycle that I thankfully don't belong to."

I pause, my mind going back to the times all those therapists tried to mold me into a normal person. I refused to comply. I still do.

I fucking despise therapists and their holier-than-thou attitudes. I despise how I felt in their presence—small, abnormal, and not fit for society.

Is that possibly what Landon feels when he clashes with the world due to the way he's wired different?

Hating myself for thinking of his perspective even for a moment, I glare at him. "Are we done?"

"Far from it. We haven't even gotten started."

"You told me to walk with you and I kept my part of the bargain. So we're done here."

"Not yet." He unlocks the car. "I'm taking you somewhere."

"What makes you think I'd go anywhere with you?"

He appears disappointed as he tuts. "I thought you were smarter than this. Don't make me give you an ultimatum again. We've been there, done that, and it didn't exactly work out well for you."

I'm going to bash this bastard's head in and watch him bleed to death.

I shelf that thought for another day and say with fake mockery, "I feel sad for you."

"Sad?"

"You can only thrive by threatening and offering ultimatums. It must be so sad to be you."

"On the contrary, holding power over the herd is euphoric." His provocatively gorgeous smile remains in place as he juts his chin forward. "Get in the car."

"I don't want to."

"And I don't give a fuck. Must be so *sad* to be you," he repeats my words with that damn smile that I'm itching to punch off his face.

He pushes me forward with a palm on my shoulder.

I slide in with a grumble and a shove against him so he'll remove his hand. The psycho's only reaction is a grin and a shake of his head.

It's like I'm amusement material and he's enjoying every minute of pushing my buttons.

"Where are we going?" I ask once he's behind the steering wheel.

"You'll find out soon enough." He hits the engine and it groans loudly.

I instinctively hold on to my seat belt. What? I prefer smooth-sailing cars that don't make enough noise to wake the dead.

Sports cars and mayhem suit Landon to perfection, though.

As the car rolls down the road, his large hand falls on my pale thigh, touching the bare space between the hem of my dress and my knees.

His fingers squeeze the flesh. "Relax. I promise not to devour you. Yet."

I push at his hand, needing to get rid of the sudden attack of tingles and goosebumps. Now that I think about it, a variation of this foreign sensation happened the last time he touched me, too.

It must be a manifestation of my disgust. Nothing more.

"Let me go," I sign.

"What was that?" He feigns innocence. "Come closer? I know I'm irresistible, but I'm also driving, so you need to keep it in your pants for a bit."

I flash him the middle finger, to which he chuckles. "As I said, I'm open to fucking you, but not at the moment."

"You and I will never happen."

"Never say never." He tightens his grip on my thigh as if to cement his words.

I try and fail to remove his hand. It's like he's attached to me by an invisible string.

"Speaking of never, how come you've never replied to my text or followed me back on Instagram?"

He followed me on Instagram? I didn't notice that. Then again, I haven't been in the right frame of mind since yesterday. I'm also still sleep-deprived because even though Maya allowed me to share her bed, I couldn't relax enough to sleep after those damn texts and the images of his hand on my throat.

"Ever thought that maybe, just maybe, I don't like you?"

"Small detail that can be changed."

"Not even if you turn into a saint."

"Why would I do something so dull? Besides, you might fool the whole world, yourself included, but I'm well aware that you're not into saints. Not even a little. Not even close."

I swallow. "I don't know what you're talking about."

"Oh, my little muse. We're cut from the same cloth, you and I. Well, not identical cloth, but it's similar enough. And if I have to prove it, so be it."

The car comes to a halt and I stiffen in my seat as I look at the dark building in the middle of nowhere.

Landon's grip on my thigh brings me back to him. A terrifying smirk lifts his lips. "Welcome to my territory."

TEN

Mia

I KNEW I WAS IN TROUBLE WHEN LANDON'S PRETENTIOUS CAR pulled up to the abandoned house, its gates creaking open to reveal a nightmare I couldn't escape.

The goosebumps and tingles that snaked through my body shrivel to a slow death as the old castle-like building materializes in front of me.

It looks straight out of a medieval war—one that didn't go so well for whoever protected whatever this place.

The gray walls have nearly turned green with the smudges left by nature. Brittle leaves rustle in the wind, their jagged edges scraping against the blurry windows like the claws of a desperate animal.

The only new element in the property's immediate surroundings is the refurbished massive black gate that Landon drives through.

Even though the car remains steady, I can see the uneven, rutty road. The trees either have branches that resemble a witch's bony hand or contain so many intertwined leaves, you can't tell where one ends and the other begins.

The beds of flowers have withered to their tragic death, leaving gruesome skeletons in their wake. A grim stench reeks from every nook of this house that could serve as a den of ghosts and paranormal creatures.

The car comes to a slow halt near the front door. That is, if the old wooden shape with metal strips can be called a door.

"What do you think?"

I startle at the sudden appearance of Landon near my ear. The asshole moves like an evil snake, without making any sound whatsoever.

"About what? The poor imitation of a haunted house?" I pretend to be completely unaffected, although my stomach twists into a thousand knots.

"No imitation in sight." His hot breath skims along the shell of my ear as his hand grips my thigh tighter. "This is an actual haunted house. It is said that its previous owner became unstable due to the horrors of the war and cast a spell on the place. Ever since then, his family members have met tragic deaths, and anyone who enters never comes out of it sane."

"That explains your personality, then," I sign with a sweet smile.

He chuckles, his chest rumbling against the side of my arm. And just like that, the tingles and goosebumps resurrect from the ashes as if they were never slaughtered.

"Stop being so hot." He bites the shell of my ear. Like he did last night. Only, now, it's more intimate and provokes a throbbing between my inner thighs.

My nails dig into my palm, but I have no clue how to react to the strong physical reaction building inside me.

Then, as if to make matters worse, he licks the spot he bit and I have to clamp my lips shut to keep from making any noises.

As easily and fast as he touched me, he releases me. "Now, come out."

Just like that, he steps out of the car, leaving me in a heap of cryptic emotions.

It takes me a few seconds to gather my wits. I need to snap out of it. Since I've found myself in this situation anyway, might as well give Landon a taste of his own medicine so he regrets messing with me.

Armed with my new resolve, I push the door open and step out, chin held high and my nose nearly touching the sky.

The sudden chill causes more goosebumps to erupt on my skin, but part of that has to do with my company tonight.

Landon is waiting for me with that irritating smirk and amusement glinting in his deep blues. The color of an angry ocean and a midnight sky.

The color of my worst nightmares as well.

"You're not a delicate princess, after all. I'm impressed."

"Impressing you is the last item on my agenda."

"And yet you're doing it so well, I almost doubt it's on purpose. You know, like when you crashed my party and seduced me in the bathroom."

"That was only so I could distract you, and it worked." I sigh, shaking my head. "Men."

"What was that?"

"Men are so simple, no matter how grandiose they think they are." I jut my chin in his direction. "You're part of the herd, Mr. I'm Smarter Than You And Your Entire Bloodline."

"I *am* smarter than you and your entire bloodline, or you wouldn't be here, in the palm of my hand, exactly how I planned it."

"I'm in no one's palm. And the only reason I'm here is because you threatened my sister. I wouldn't have given you the time of the day under different circumstances."

"But you *are* giving me the time of the day."

"Unwillingly."

"Doesn't matter."

"My free will doesn't matter?"

"The excuses you offer your mind don't. I have no interest in participating in whatever lies you tell yourself to convince your brain that you're not remotely attracted to me. Unlike you, I don't sugarcoat the truth."

He reaches into his pocket and retrieves a key that looks like one of those enchanted treasure findings and uses it to open the door.

It creaks and squeaks like a dying person's attempt to resurrect.

My spine jerks into a line at the graphic noise, but I still wear the mask of indifference. Or I hope I do as I carefully follow the beast into his lair.

The inside isn't any better than the outside. Upon entry, I'm hit by the musty smell of the decaying building. The wind howling through the trees outside sounds ten times louder inside.

Grim, somber medieval stairs greet us in the middle of the foyer. There's a sofa and a few chairs that have lost their color, appearing pale pink instead of what I assume was once bright orange.

The wooden flooring is chipped everywhere, and the few intact pieces look older than the British monarchy. It creaks every time we take a step. While I'm careful, Landon walks with a sense of pride that's completely uncalled for.

My gaze strays to the open door to the left—probably a kitchen or a dining room. No matter how much I search for signs of life, this place seems more dead than my voice.

Whatever angle you look at it from, it's too shabby, messy, and underwhelming to fit someone as elegant and well-kept as Landon.

As much as I hate the asshole, he is illegally good-looking and has the charisma of a model in anything he wears. Even earlier in a hoodie and sunglasses, many stared at him, whispering to each other as if he were a celebrity.

Of course, the bastard basked in every second of the attention he got, despite trying not to get on my brother's and cousins' radar.

Landon is not only a psychopath but also a raging narcissist.

Psychopaths are born not made. I wonder what type of gene pool resulted in his existence and why he turned out like this when Bran is one of the best people I've met?

Wait…why am I curious about the asshole? I don't give two hecks about him and his warped psychology.

"It is said that the lady of the house fell down these very stairs and broke her neck." His sudden hot words in my ear make me shudder.

I jump away. "Stop doing that."

"Doing what?"

"Whispering in my ear from behind like a creep."

"How else will I have you tremble against me? I love your innocent reactions that are in clear contradiction with your bad-girl image. Heads-up, I will provoke it whenever I get the chance. Unless…" he trails off and tilts his head. "You're down for getting on your knees and closing those lips around my cock?"

"No."

"Worth a try." He kills the distance between us and places a hand at the small of my back close to my ass, probably trying to intimidate me with his physical presence.

"Can't you tell me to walk without touching me?"

"But you feel so perfect in my hand. It's a waste not to touch you."

I shake my head and choose to drop it. If I go down that road, it'll only get worse, and it's just not a battle worth pursuing.

He promenades me around the war-like foyer as if he's showing his most prized possessions. He stops by the pale pink sofa. "This is where the ghost sits. It's probably watching us as we speak and putting a curse on you."

"Why wouldn't it put it on you instead?"

"Maybe it already did and I'm a product of its curse that's tasked with devouring you alive and sucking you dry."

"Save it." I side-eye him. "I don't believe in ghosts."

"Oh? Why not?"

"Real monsters are scarier and a lot more common than invisible paranormal creatures."

"Interesting. Is one of those monsters the reason why you don't talk?"

I freeze and throw him a questioning look.

"What? You thought I planned your demise without looking into your past?"

I purse my lips. What does the bastard know? He couldn't have possibly dug up much since my parents are powerful enough to seal that part of my life.

He's bluffing. He has to be.

Landon seems completely oblivious to my reaction as he leads me down a long corridor. What must've once looked like flowery wallpaper is nothing more than a faded beige vinyl now.

"It's not that you're a mute, it's that you choose not to speak. I believe selective mute is the correct term. If you can speak, let me hear your voice."

I elbow his side, forcing him to loosen his grip on my back, then sign, "What do you know about my life? What makes you think I can speak or that I even want to? And just so you know, if I do happen to talk—which isn't possible by any stretch of the imagination, by the way—I'll never let you hear it, asshole."

"Never say never, little muse."

"I'm not little. I happen to be only five years younger than you."

"Aaaand your obsession with me continues." He smiles, but there's no amusement this time. Just the stark shadow of his calculation. "Tell me, what was the incident that took your voice away at eight years old? Your parents seem to have put a lot of effort into erasing it from everyone's memories."

I internally release a breath. So even Landon and his conniving ways haven't managed to get any information. For the first time, I'm thankful to be a mafia princess and in possession of the Bratva's and, most importantly, my parents' protection.

"Ever wondered if it's hidden because it's none of your business?" I smile with enough sweetness to give diabetes a run for its money.

"I can get that information anyway, even if it takes a bit longer than I'd like it to. So how about you tell me yourself now and save us both the time and effort?"

"I'd like to see you try."

His grin turns into one of demonic proportions. It's like I provoked the decadent side of him that definitely gets off on the mention of a challenge. Just like Bran said.

He nudges me forward again until we arrive at another shabby door that he shoves open, and then he pushes me inside.

I stop near the entrance, my eyes adjusting to the darkness of the room. It's a studio, I realize. Half-finished statues adorn the walls, some of them covered by white sheets. In the middle, there's a chair and a workstation with equipment methodically aligned in perfectly horizontal rows. Double glass doors hint at a balcony on the opposite side that looks creepy.

Still, this room is by far the cleanest and newest in the house. The stained-glass windows are tinted with church-like paintings of some guys who are probably important, but I can't name them to save my life.

The colorful lights cast a rainbow glow on the unfinished, disfigured statues. Some of them have faces and the others are missing features or even a whole body. Others are only torsos without a face.

"I thought you had a studio in the Elites' mansion that's protected by lock and key."

"Take it easy on your obsession with me."

My face heats, but I sign, "I only found that out in my attempts to sabotage you."

"An obsession is still an obsession, no matter the reason. The fact that you're stumbling to find an excuse is enough indication of the depth of your cute obsession. To answer your question, this is my second art studio, the third if we count the one at uni, but that one's only for show since it's shared with other students."

"And this one?" I sign, then turn to the miserable statues. I don't know why I feel sorry that they've been abandoned.

"This one is for the boring subjects that didn't make the cut. I have a theory I want to prove."

I turn to him with a questioning gaze, but my insides instantly knot into thick dread when my eyes lock with his.

Dark energy swirls in their depths, promising a taste of both danger and regret.

"Stand here for me and remain still. Like last night."

"Why would I do that?"

"For the same reason you came here with me. To protect your precious family."

I snarl and he merely smiles, then pats the top of my head as if I'm a pet. "Be good and no drastic measures will be taken."

He walks to a half-faced statue and strokes the unfinished part with careful fingers, as if he doesn't want to hurt a literal statue's feelings.

But why do I feel like, if given the chance, Landon wouldn't hesitate to erase that statue as if it never existed?

After careful inspection, he lifts it effortlessly. Or more like, he makes it look easy. I can see his biceps flexing as a translation of his smashing power.

Landon might appear lean and definitely has fewer muscles than, say, Nikolai or Jeremy, but he's still strong.

He deposits the statue on what looks like a sack of sand and sits on the chair opposite it.

He casts me a glance, throws a flirtatious wink, and then pulls out a cigarette and slides it to the corner of his lips. As he lights it, he fetches one of the countless tools and tosses it from one hand to the other as if testing its weight.

He puts it right back and retrieves another one that looks exactly the same to me, tosses it between his hands again, then inhales the smoke and releases a heavy cloud in the air.

I've never cared for the smell of cigarettes or smokers in general, but Landon makes it look hotter than it should be. It's the blasé attitude and the confidence of a god that drips from his every movement.

With the cigarette hanging from his lips, he again strokes the statue, which I notice has generous breasts. He runs his fingers along the slope and then taps the nipple once.

Twice.

My body burns with unfamiliar scorching fire. His hand slides to her throat and I can feel the choker tightening around my own neck as if it's his fingers.

What the hell?

His eyes flash to me and I stand still, scared to even breathe properly. The last thing I need is for Landon to think I find him attractive in any sense. He's already conceited beyond belief.

"There. You're such a good little muse." His hand is still stroking and groping the statue as if it's his lover.

"I'm just doing this out of necessity."

"Are those words directed at me or yourself?"

He grins, and without waiting for my response, he gets to work. His fingers slowly but surely shape part of the statue's head.

I'm struck by his expression when he creates. A stark difference from his usually mocking face. While sadism is still present, there's also something different. I've never seen his eyes so light and engaged. They're often half bored, as if the world holds no meaning to his immoral soul.

Now, however, he's so far into his task that I don't think he takes notice of how he seamlessly picks up tools or lights one cigarette after the other.

About an hour later, I'm getting tired of standing, so I attempt to lower myself into a sitting position.

"No." He shakes his head, even though he hasn't looked at me once since he started. "Don't ruin it."

"I'm tired," I sign, but he's still not looking at me. So I snap my fingers.

Nothing.

"Let's take a break. Do you have anything to drink?" I ask, but his mind seems to be busy focusing on his fingers and the unmoving object in front of him.

"I'm going to rest for a while." I start to sit down, but he stands up abruptly, making me stop dead in my tracks.

He's looking at me now, but I wish he wasn't. His dark blues are no different than a stormy ocean that's about to swallow me in its depths. "I said don't ruin it, didn't I?"

"You're not the one standing. It's tiring and boring," I sign with less bravado than usual.

"Come here."

"Why?" I sign cautiously.

"You said you're tired, so we'll fix it."

I remain rooted in place. I'd rather stay standing for another hour than get close to him.

"Don't make me come get you, Mia."

It's the first time he's said my name, and it sounds like a deep growl.

Slowly, I make my way to him, assuring myself I'll claw his eyes out if he hurts me. I can also break his dick for humanity's sake.

Once I'm next to the statue, Landon pulls me toward him so suddenly, I gasp.

The sound echoes around us as he pulls me down so I'm straddling with my back to his chest. I squirm when I feel the hard muscle beneath me. I've never made a habit of being this close to the opposite sex.

My previous encounters left something to be desired and the unshakable feeling that they were boys.

Landon, however, is all man. It's not about the age, it's the edge with which he carries himself. It's the unapologetic way he touches me as if it's his birthright.

"Don't move," he whispers in my ear, drawing goosebumps on my skin. "Don't blame me for what happens if you do."

His arm snakes around my waist and his palm cups the statue's breast, fingers stroking the nipple.

I shudder, then curse myself. "Why do you keep doing that?"

"Shh, not a word." He winks. "Unless you want to let me hear your voice?"

I give him the middle finger.

"That's the last time you flip me off. Do it again and I will take matters into my own hands. Literally."

He lights a cigarette and blows the smoke in my face like an asshole.

Soon after, his attention falls on the motionless statue. I'd feel sorry for her if she were a real person, but it's better if he focuses on his art rather than me.

But with the damned position, I'm forced to breathe him in, the scent of man and intoxicating cologne. This close, I can't help noticing just how well-built his face and physique are. Arguably as perfect as his beloved statues.

Too bad he's as cold as them, too.

About twenty minutes later, I start fidgeting. It's impossible to stay too long in one position. Unless I'm playing chess, and that's definitely not the case right now.

It doesn't help that I'm inexplicably drawn to Landon and keep telling myself I haven't gone crazy yet.

"Stop shifting unless you're trying to hump my leg. In that case, go for it."

"I'll hump your leg in hell, asshole," I sign.

"Fine with me, little muse."

"Why do you keep calling me that?"

"What?" he asks without looking at me.

"Muse. Why am I your muse?"

"Figures." It's a single word, but he says it with such nonchalance, as if it means nothing on his destruction curriculum for the day.

I lift my hand, but he gives me a look, to suggest I stop talking, no doubt. I'm so tempted to claw his gorgeous eyes out.

I try to remain still and chance taking out my phone. Landon doesn't seem to notice, or he probably does but doesn't care.

My attempts to relieve myself from the growing ache between my legs tether on the edge of failure with each brush of his arm against my side. The fanning of his breath against my cheek.

Inhaling deeply, I pull up Bran's number and find his text from last night that I wasn't in the right state of mind to read, let alone reply to.

Brandon: Have you gotten home safe? I'm here to help if your brother causes you trouble.

Mia: Hey! Sorry for the late reply. Yeah, I got home okay, and don't worry about Niko. I know how to handle him.

His reply is immediate.

Brandon: Good to know. I was worried something might've happened to you.

Something happened all right, and I'm currently paying the price for it in Landon's arms.

Mia: Hey, Bran. I know you've always mentioned I should stay away from Landon (not that I'm getting close to him or anything). Do you have any pointers on how to remove myself from his radar?

Brandon: The most important step is to never get on his radar in the first place. Once you're there, it's impossible to shake him off unless he willingly chooses to back off. Is he bothering you?

More like he's sucking the life out of me.

I'm about to tell Bran not to worry so as not to drive a wedge between him and his twin, but the phone is snatched from between my fingers.

I stare into Landon's displeased face and instinctively suck in a breath. The bastard has a mysterious power of making people feel uncomfortable with a single glance.

"Keep your attention on me when sitting on my lap."

I can feel heat flaring up my neck, but I lift my chin. "I would've if you didn't happen to bore me to tears."

"And yet I can feel you dripping on my trousers."

My mind goes blank. Did the earlier arousal somehow transform into something physical?

No, it can't be possible.

Landon is just trying to get in my head. If I let him, he'll swallow me whole and leave nothing but scattered bones.

"That's not true," I sign.

He methodically removes the cigarette from his mouth and stubs it in a makeshift ashtray made of clay.

Then he retrieves a wet wipe and cleans both his hands, enveloping me in an accidental hug.

He does it once.

Twice.

After the third time, he places the used wipe on top of the murdered cigarettes crowding the ashtray.

The arm that's snaked around my back grips my waist, strong fingers digging into the flesh.

His other hand slides across my dress before he bunches it up, using one finger at a time as if he's unwrapping a gift.

My heartbeat skyrockets and goosebumps cover other goosebumps on my flesh. The visual of his bigger, veiny hands—of course, the asshole possesses hands that are worthy of porn—on my paler flesh leaves me breathless.

Unlike earlier, his hand doesn't stop at my thigh and, instead, travels up and up, leaving a mayhem of tingles in its wake.

A part of me knows I need to stop this. Grab his hand and kick him in the nuts for daring to touch me so intimately.

But the other part is enamored. Completely and utterly taken by the monster who's triggering these emotions in me.

That part wants to see where this is going and how far I'll fall.

How hard it will be.

The closest I've been to this was with Brian from high school. He was nice and I convinced myself that I liked him, but the moment he touched me, I realized just how much I'd fooled myself into wanting something I didn't.

The brief encounter felt explorative, innocent, and mild. And that's when I discovered those weren't my flavor.

In contrast, there's nothing innocent about Landon. His touch is claiming, savage, and nonnegotiable.

I'm literally being held by a beast who wouldn't know what explorative or mild is, even if it hit him in the face.

And my body is reacting to it.

Damn me and my damaged brain.

"You're trembling." He buries his nose in my hair and ribbons, inhaling me while continuing his path. "Will you also be trembling while riding my cock? Or when I mess up these soft thighs with my cum?"

The temperature shoots up to three digits so fast, I'm whiplashed. I grab onto his shoulder to push him away, but I end up digging my fingers into his bicep as he slides his middle finger against my folds over my panties.

"So wet and throbbing, my little muse." His finger strokes again, this time finding my clit.

I don't know if it's because of all the time I've been sitting on his lap or the fact that his touch has awakened a side of me I don't recognize, but a needy sound leaves my throat.

"Impatient, too." He slaps my pussy over the wet panties. "Your cunt is so pleased to meet my fingers, it's soaking for my touch."

I can feel the wetness seeping through as he circles my clit, and just when I fall for the feeling, he slaps my pussy again.

A gasp echoes in the air, but it's interrupted when he pushes my panties to the side and thrusts two fingers inside me all at once.

The intrusion makes my legs shake so hard, I'd fall over if it weren't for his steel arm around my waist.

He drives in and out a few times with a calculated rhythm. "So messy. We're going to have to stretch this tight cunt a bit further so it's ready for my cock."

I don't reply. All I can do is hold on to him as he scissors his fingers inside me. And then he angles his thigh and adds pressure to my starving clit with his thumb.

An electric shock shoots through my limbs. My toes curl and my body spasms in a series of involuntary reactions. It's so sudden and powerful that I momentarily disconnect from my physical world.

As I'm coming down from the high, my limbs are numb, but Landon still has his fingers inside me.

He releases my waist and pulls one of my blue ribbons, forcing me to face him. I don't even want to think about what my face looks like right now. I just want to run away and hide from the intense emotions I just experienced.

Landon, however, doesn't seem to have the same plan. He licks the corner of my eye where involuntary moisture escaped and grins. "Now, you'll shatter on my fingers all over again while looking at me."

The bitter taste of panic fills my throat. What the hell did I just let him do?

Wait. Did I even allow him to?

You didn't say no, idiot. You didn't even push him away.

So I do. With all the strength I have, I punch him in the chest so hard, the chair squeaks beneath him. After I untangle myself from his hold, I do the one thing I should've done when I first saw Landon today.

I run.

His laughter echoes behind me like a dark, sinister promise.

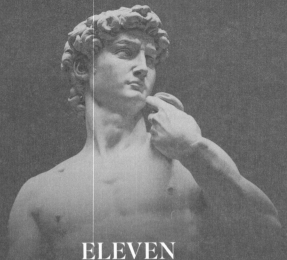

ELEVEN

Landon

"**A**RE YOU KICKING ME OUT OF MY OWN HOUSE?" REMI exclaims like the drama king he is.

Rumor has it he got dropped on his head as an infant and never recovered the lost neurons.

He's chaotic, and not in the good, anarchy-filled sense. But more like a caricature with nothing inside his skull but the need to shag and serve as the group's comedic relief.

He's a good support in certain situations, but this one definitely doesn't belong on the list.

He, Bran, and I are in the living room where they're waiting for *Match of the Day* and a much-anticipated premier league game.

My brother occupies the sofa, wearing Chelsea colors and a matching bandana. Our family members are traditional gunners, and my father used to play for Arsenal a long time ago, but Bran chose to root for a rival club. Out of all the important things he could choose to rebel on, he ended up with such a lousy one. And Dad actually chooses to be slightly offended, as if this whole thing means a fuck. Pretty sure King Enterprises owns shares in both clubs.

"You can't do that!" Remi jumps from his chair and points a finger at me, despite the fact that I dropped the subject ever so peacefully.

"What's with all the parties you keep throwing in the mansion?"

Bran asks as if he's my designated keeper. I happen to be fifteen whole minutes older than him and should assume that role if it were to exist, thank you very much.

"This is complete rubbish!" Remi throws his head back dramatically. "Back me up on this, Bran! We have to stop this overlord from occupying our space all the time."

Bran, who's definitely not as obnoxious as Remi, merely nods. Unfortunately for my childhood friend, he's missing his other ally.

A certain vexing presence who everyone else calls Eli. He's not around today, probably having fucked off to make other people's lives miserable.

Which is why I chose this perfect time to hold this type of meeting. If he were here, the state of affairs would be bumpy and unnecessarily draining.

"Give me a better reaction than that, Bran!" Remi calls out with his hurt, over-the-top voice that's begging for a few snips to his vocal cords.

Seems that tonight, they don't really have plans except for being a pain in the arse.

"Whether you agree or not," I say. "If I decide to throw a party, I'll just do it, so you better go ahead and cut your losses. You guys are invited if you'd like to join the mayhem."

"No, thanks." Remi gives me a look of disgust. "I become invisible to the ladies whenever you're around."

"Don't be jealous of my charm, Rems." I walk up to him and catch him by the shoulder. "To make it up to you, I can put you in a Jacuzzi with a flavor of your type."

He lifts a brow. "How many?"

"How many do you want?"

"Three."

"They'll be there."

"Then you'll disappear so they won't throw themselves on your dick instead?"

"Of course. What are bros for?"

"You got yourself a deal, Lan." He shakes my hand.

"Seriously?" Bran asks. "You were just whining about how he's always occupying our space, Remi."

"I just remembered his parties are fun. My lordship inhales fun."

"Which is why your lordship is such a good sport," I say with a straight face, despite internally cringing at how he calls himself that.

Mum also has an aristocratic title, but you don't see me flashing it and calling myself a lord for anyone to hear. I wouldn't shy away from using it as a plug in front of the right people, though.

At any rate, the mission is complete. There will be another mindless party, where I can invite the scum of the scum and crown myself as their leader.

It's one of my countless attempts to not get stuck in my head for longer than absolutely necessary. It's good for the art but usually bad news for everyone else. Especially for those who will be the target of my anarchy and their closest circle.

Lately, that's been a certain goth blonde Barbie that so inexplicably happens to be the only form of a muse I've ever had.

She's been trying to avoid me ever since she shattered all over my fingers a week ago, but I know how to smoke a mouse out of its hideout.

I'm about to go back upstairs, not really caring about football, when Bran catches up to me and grabs my arm.

I stare at his hand and then at his face. "Something on your mind, little brother?"

"Mia."

I pretend to be unaffected and suppress the instinct to narrow my eyes at him. I know she's somewhat friends with my brother. That didn't particularly bother me before and that shouldn't change now if I'm being logical. But for some reason, I don't like it.

"Who's that?" I ask while tapping an index finger on my mouth.

"You know exactly who she is, considering you've been going after her."

"Did she tell you that?"

"I don't need her to tell me anything. I've known you all my life, and I can recognize when you're up to no good, which is, unfortunately, more often than not lately." He releases a long, frustrated breath. "Haven't you done her brother enough damage already?"

"She's not her brother, now, is she?"

"No, but he'll kill you if he finds out you're targeting his sister."

"Not before I kill him." I pat his head. "Don't worry about me, little bro."

"That's the last thing on my mind," he mutters, his face harder than usual.

Hmm. Does he really care for Mia? Maybe in *that* sense?

Too bad she was soaking wet for me, not you, Bran.

"Surprise!"

Three girls with different hair colors—blonde, white, and chestnut—swarm through the front entrance, carrying what looks like takeaway boxes.

Ava, the one who announced the unbearable surprise, grins as she dumps the armful of what I assume is Indian food, judging by the smell, on the coffee table.

She's blonde, loud, and has little to no concept of personal space. In short, a mellowed-out version of Remi but nineteen.

The white-haired one, Cecily, is more like the mother hen of the group, a position that she's been fighting Bran for.

But considering the repressing shit my brother is into, I'd give her the crown any day. Where Ava is too loud for anyone's liking, Cecily is soft-spoken and likes to baby everyone around her.

She carefully places the contents in her arms on the table and nods at us.

The third girl abandons some drinks beside all the Indian food and walks in my and Bran's direction. Her chestnut hair with natural blonde highlights falls to her mid-waist.

Glyndon is the only one in our family who got some of Dad's glorious blond Viking hair, as Mum calls it. She's over four years younger than me and likes to pretend that I barely exist.

She hugs Bran and he wraps his arms around her in a sweet, mushy, and absolutely unnecessary show of affection.

I don't understand why neurotypical people vie so much for

validation and find it vital to display care and love. It's not that they can't possibly survive without the tedious emotions.

"What a nice surprise," he says when they break apart. "Why didn't you tell me you were coming?"

"Ava said she needed to confirm something first."

As in, she had to make sure Eli wasn't within the perimeter before she decided whether or not to come over. Don't ask how I know that. One, it's far from being a secret at this point—even the gardener and his extended family probably know about their strange foreplay. Two, I happen to hold everyone's lives and secrets in the palm of my hand in case of possible future use.

Glyn nods at me as if we're colleagues in a stuck-up law firm. "Lan."

I nod back with the same energy. "Little princess."

Since Dad calls Mum a princess, Glyn has assumed the title of 'little princess'.

My sister stiffens, probably thinking I'm up to no good, including, but not limited to, eradicating her boyfriend from the face of the earth.

I laugh and ruffle her hair. "Relax. You're too uptight."

Bran shakes his head, more in resignation than anything else, but Glyn releases a breath. She likes to pretend that her unhinged boyfriend is different from me just because she fell for him harder than a moth to a flame. But oh well. I did cause her some minor discomfort. By minor, I mean I never really showed her affection like Bran does and, instead, preferred to watch over her.

One of us had to be the symbol of austerity, and Bran definitely can't be stern to save his life.

Besides, she never really needed that from me, and I prefer not to pretend when it comes to my family. It's exhausting and feels empty enough as it is with the rest of the world, and they certainly don't belong to the same category as my family.

"What do you mean there's no fish and chips?" Remi asks Ava, then pokes her. "Are you even British? Bring out the imposter in you."

"You brought it the other time. We wanted a change. Besides, Indian food is delish!" She pushes him away. "And stop poking me."

"You should be honored that my lordship is even touching you, peasant."

"I'm going to bite your head off."

"I would like to see you try."

I walk to them and nod at Cecily, who's bringing out the take-out boxes. She nods back and focuses squarely on her task. She used to be in love with me—like everyone who's had the honor to meet me. Well, not *in* love, but she had a major crush on my unmeasurable charm, but like every girl with a brain, she soon realized I have nothing inside me she can reach.

It's no secret that I'm an empty entity of anarchy and destruction. A vessel for uncharacteristically violent tendencies and artistic genius.

In fact, when those personality traits disappear, I'm nothing more than odorless air. It's part of the reason why I've made mayhem the purpose of my existence. Without that, I'm an endless void.

I don't delude myself about those facts. Some girls—including the old Cecily—do. They like to think they can fix me, and I let them hold the illusion while I break them into irreparable pieces.

What? I'm a no-strings-attached type of man who likes the adventure of new holes. It's not my fault they think of baby names after I fuck them into oblivion.

I didn't fuck Cecily, though. I contemplated it once but then thought of her super strict father, Uncle Xander, who would dismember me and drink my blood as the soup of the day if I were to ever go near his precious princess.

And while I possess the moral compass of a shark, I don't like stirring the waters too close to home. My folks have been friends with Ava's, Cecily's, and Remi's parents since way before we were conceived, and I supposed it wouldn't be practical to be chased with a golf club by their parents during family dinners.

That doesn't mean I can't mess with them, though.

Keeping Bran and Glyn in my peripheral vision as they catch up on their cringeworthy relationship, I lean against a pillar and smirk at Ava. She pauses her childish back and forth with Remi and narrows her eyes on me.

"And what do you want?" She huffs. "Going to bitch about fish and chips, too?"

"Nah. I couldn't care less what type of food I consume." After all, its only purpose is to keep the machine going on and on and fucking on.

Until I inevitably drop, that is.

"Then why are you grinning like Satan's wannabe?" Ava asks, completely oblivious to Remi, who's already digging into the food, despite starting drama about it two seconds ago.

"You wound me. I thought Satan wanted to be me."

She rolls her eyes and crosses her arms, the long mermaid sleeves of her pink camisole a whole character on their own.

"You came because you thought Eli wasn't here, no?"

Her gloating expression falters. "Eli who? I couldn't care less about his presence or the lack thereof."

"In that case, you'd be okay knowing he's coming back home in about…" I trail off and check my watch that's worth more than a dozen of her Louboutin heels. "Fifteen minutes."

Her face pales and she clears her throat. "You're bluffing just to fuck with me."

"Am I?" I fetch my phone and send a quick text to my cousin.

Landon: Ava is here with delicious food. Yum.

He doesn't disappoint and his reply comes in a matter of seconds.

Eli: Be there in fifteen. You better make the earth swallow your hedonistic form before I arrive.

I tap the last text so it blurs the background, then show it to Ava. She swallows and narrows her eyes. "Did you tell him I was here?"

"Whatever makes you think that?"

"You being a twat, maybe?"

"Is that another word for Cupid?"

She growls like a cornered animal and I grin, contemplating how to play with them further before he actually arrives.

That is, if Ava doesn't run away or disappear like a ghost since she happens to be a coward.

Speaking of cowards, I re-check some of the texts I sent to Mia over the past week that she had the audacity to leave on Read.

If you weren't in such a hurry just now, I would've given you a ride as soon as I was done licking your taste off my fingers. I never thought of pussy as a five-star meal, but I'm quickly changing my mind.

Text me back when you're done trying to bury your head in the sand. If I were you, I'd save myself the trouble. It won't work.

If you stop running away, we might have a redo and I'll let you suck my cock.

I'm curious. Do you usually make that expression when you come? If you don't answer, I might track down your ex-lovers and confirm a theory. Are you interested to know what it is?

Apparently not, because you're into this weird hard-to-get foreplay. I'm sure you figured out by now that I'm not exactly normal and these tactics don't work on me.

Patience isn't my forte, little muse. Don't make me come after you.

That was my last text and it met the same fate as its predecessors. Mia doesn't know this yet, but she's playing a dangerous game. The more I'm tempted, the more drastic the reaction.

Ignoring the rampant chaos around me, I open my Instagram app. Her profile appears on my home screen before I even attempt to search her name.

Usually, it's Remi's antics that greet me first. Looks like my algorithm has found me a new source of entertainment. It might also have to do with the fact that I've been checking her socials like a seasoned stalker.

The picture that appears on the feed is a carousel captioned *They Call Me Baby Satan.*

The first one shows her staring down, wearing her brother's yellow stitch mask. The look is enhanced by her tulle black dress, boots with chains slithered like snakes, and her platinum blonde hair that's held in ribboned pigtails.

In the second picture, there's no mask as she leans an elbow against Nikolai's heavily tattooed naked shoulder while they both glare at the camera.

The third includes her and her flashy twin sister, who seems to be seducing the camera while Mia makes peace signs from the side.

The fourth is of the three of them, both girls hanging on Nikolai's arms.

In the fifth, she headlocks both Nikolai and Killian and laughs. Gareth is in the background, head thrown back in laughter. The image is blurry and seems to have been taken on a whim, probably by Maya.

I zoom in on the so-called Baby Satan, studying her free expression. I've never seen her laugh, not even during my admittedly limited stalking sessions. I wonder how she sounds when laughing.

She does gasp and groan when overwhelmed by pleasure. My fingers twitch in remembrance of her welcoming cunt swallowing me whole.

I suppose there are other sounds she can make, and I will pull them out one by one.

Seems that Eli and Ava are safe for the day because I prefer a much better target for my dose of mayhem.

TWELVE

Mia

MY FEAR OF THE DARK IS A TALE OF MISSED OPPORTUNITIES and a different life whose ultimate development I'll never know.

It tastes of bitterness and hollow emotions. It reeks of piss, vomit, and the promise of a horrifying death.

Despite having a determined, no-bullshit personality, I'm terrified of death. For me, death is the look in the monster's eyes when he silenced me forever.

Death is living in the dark for eternity.

I've been holding on to life with broken fingernails and desperate, cracked hope, just to assure myself that I'm still alive.

And yet every night, when I'm alone in my room, the rancid breath of death rasps at the back of my neck to announce the presence of the monster. His groans and growls echo from the corner like a trapped animal that's waiting for me to go to the bathroom so he can ambush me.

It's why I don't like being alone for long. One problem, though. I'm not exactly a social person. I don't get off on nightlife or drunk crowds who are just 'out to have fun.' I'm never out to have fun. I'm usually out to survive.

That's why I visit my brother and cousins, go out with them, or cling to poor Maya like an annoying second skin.

I did all of the above today, but none of it managed to push away the darkness of the night or scare the monster back into its hideous cave.

I ended up performing a thousand routines just so I'd be able to fall asleep peacefully.

It started with meditation and a foot bath to help blood circulation, and then it was playing online chess, followed by finishing my entire school project.

It's one in the morning, and there's no sign of drowsiness. Not that my method is bulletproof, but I can only hope that when I do fall asleep, I won't have a nightmare about his hideous face.

I lie on my back and stare at the artificial stars adorning the ceiling. They'd look better in the dark, but I'd rather lock myself up in an asylum than turn off the lights at night.

My options are to toss and turn all night or go ruin Maya's beauty sleep again. But considering I've been overdoing that the past week, I go with the former.

Flipping to my right, I retrieve my phone, and my finger hovers over Mom's number, but then I think better of it and shake my head.

She's still asking me about the real reason I called the last time and if there's anything she can do to help.

If I do that again, Dad will definitely fly here to ship my ass back to New York.

So I open Instagram and check the comments from my last post.

the.maya.sokolov: *Slay, queen.*

killian.carson: *Superior genes show.*

gareth-carson: *I'm here for Kill and Niko making fools out of themselves.*

nikolai_sokolov: *The scary guy in the pic who looks ready to snap some necks is me. Think about that before touching my baby sisters.*

I smile to myself. He's extra as hell and the worst part is that he doesn't think he is.

I also spot comments from Bran and my recent friend from the Elites, Remi. Despite being a certified clown, he's fun to talk to. It helps that he turns everything into a joke.

lord-remington-astor: *Pretty lady with an even more beautiful personality.*

brandon-king: *Beautiful.*

I like Bran's comment and hit the little icon of his profile. My stomach clenches in uncomfortable intervals when I see the last picture Bran posted captioned *Chelsea, anyone?*

It's a group picture in the Elites' mansion, where they seem to be watching European football and enjoying some food. I recognize the familiar faces, namely Glyn, Killian's girlfriend, Cecily, whom I met once when Maya was being unreasonable, and, of course, Bran and Remi.

I'm not familiar with the blonde girl who's scowling at her food as a tall, dark, and handsome guy stands beside her, smiling at the camera.

The reason for my stomach acting out is none other than Landon, who's grabbing Remi by the shoulder and pointing at the TV.

I zoom in on the picture to get a better look at him. He's laughing, seeming to almost match Remi's enthusiasm.

Almost.

Because where Remi seems genuinely excited, Landon is merely mirroring him. I've seen Killian do that often in the past, especially when he was younger. Since emotions don't come from inside him, he's perfected the art of emulating those around him, namely Gareth and Nikolai.

Landon is the same.

Maybe it has to do with the fact that I grew up in the presence of someone with antisocial behavior, but I can see the show he's putting on so clearly.

It might also have to do with the fact that I haven't been able to purge the asshole out of my thoughts ever since he flung through my walls and touched a part of me that's been dormant.

I don't know what came over me that day. I blame it on the haunted gothic vibe of the art studio dedicated to imperfections. But most of all, I blame it on the man himself.

The absolute enigma of a man who's merely projecting an image onto the world, and they gobble it all up. It makes sense that he thinks of himself as an arrogant god. If they can love him for a personality he specifically created for them, why wouldn't he become conceited and prideful?

The asshole probably thinks of his existence as a gift to humans.

I click on the tags and then go to his profile. *landon-king*. He actually has over a million followers. Wow.

Part of that must be due to his flourishing art career, and the other part is because he's one of those annoying people who's effortlessly popular.

His pictures are a translation of his posh rich boy/genius artist status. Some are taken at parties, others are with what I assume are family members. He has one picture where he's kissing a statue on the mouth.

Jesus. The man is a lost cause.

And yet I can't help but look at his expression, the euphoria in his mystic eyes, as if he could breathe a soul into the cold stone.

Which is ironic since he obviously lacks a soul.

He has pictures with what appear to be world-renowned artists, professors, mentors, business people, and half of the British aristocracy.

It's like he has a hundred hours in a day.

The devil works fast, but Landon King works faster.

I scroll to the top of his profile and read the caption.

Landon King. The Prince Charming your nana told you fairy tales about.

More like the monster.

I wonder if he's always been in control of the image he projects onto the world and what gave him the incentive to invent this image.

If he was born this way, like my cousin was, then there must be some form of a process that led him to where he is.

Not that I'm interested in his story. I am not.

I'm about to click the link to his website, but I accidentally follow him back.

Shit.

Jumping up into a sitting position, I unfollow him, hoping he doesn't notice. Then again, an account like his must receive thousands of notifications, so he probably won't pay attention.

With a sigh, I fall back against the bed and exit Instagram altogether. My phone lights up with a text and my breath catches.

Devil Lord: Playing hard to get?

What the hell is he doing up this late? But monsters don't really sleep. What's worse is that he actually noticed.

My cheeks heat and I curse internally. There goes my attempt to escape this shameful situation.

My phone lights up again.

Devil Lord: You make a cute stalker.

I lose my grip on the phone and it falls on my face. Pain throbs in my forehead and nose and I groan.

I can't believe I'm being chastised by none other than Landon.

When I look at my phone again, there's already another text from him.

Devil Lord: Stalker is a better and more decadent description than a coward.

Mia: Who are you calling a coward?

Devil Lord: Why, hello there. Here I thought my texts were for some reason being written with invisible ink.

Devil Lord: But I digress. Good to know you're still awake. I planned a little something.

Mia: I'm not going anywhere with you.

Devil Lord: There's no need.

I narrow my eyes. He's surprisingly not threatening me with my sister or offering ultimatums, and while that should be good news, it actually isn't.

From my unfortunate interactions with him, I've come to the conclusion that he's the type who'll go the extra mile to make sure he gets what he wants, come hell or high water.

So the fact that he gave up so easily is suspicious at best.

I continue staring at the screen, expecting him to bombard me with another series of texts, but none come.

Maybe his body finally gave out on his evil brain and he fell asleep or—

The lights go out.

My heartbeat skyrockets and I grab my phone in a tight grip as I study my surroundings.

All I find is black and more black.

Pitch-black darkness spreads around me, smothering my skin with a coat of the monster's sticky scale-like skin.

No.

No...

This can't be happening. Why would the lights go off?

Don't tell me the monster has finally come for me...?

I will my leg to move. My best option is to run to Maya's room, but I can't even stand up.

Terror comes in different shades. Mine has always manifested in turning completely frozen.

Maybe I don't want to leave the room, because I'd go to Maya first. A part of me vehemently refuses to get my sister involved in this.

What if he targets her this time and scars her for life like he did me?

No. I'd kill him before he touches her, or I'd die trying.

Still, I can't move.

So I screw my eyes shut. If I pretend not to see anything, maybe this will pass. Like the thousands of nightmares I've survived over the past decade.

His breath reverberates in the corners of the room and wraps an invisible noose around my neck.

My fingers tighten on the phone. I can't call the police, because this isn't real. And I can't call Mom, Dad, or Niko, because I'll look like the unhinged, paranoid version of myself and they'll be the ones to lock me in an asylum.

I let the phone fall to the side of the bed so I'm not tempted to do that and pull my knees to my chest, then hide my face in my crossed arms.

This isn't real. It's only my mind playing tricks on me.

I chant even as tears sting the corners of my eyes and sweat covers my brow and upper lip.

My entire body trembles under the sheer pressure of my own thoughts. My mind chooses this moment to tune in on memories I've tried to erase, to no avail.

I'm trapped in a small dark and humid place. Blood drips through the cracks like a haunting song, and empty eyes stare at me the whole time.

A distorted voice whispers in my ear, "This isn't over."

I can still feel his rancid breath against my nape, shoulder, and ears. Like a deadly lullaby, he keeps whispering those words again and again.

And again...

"I clearly warned you to keep your windows closed, no?"

The overpowering emotions of terror slowly wither into colorful bursts of...confusion? Excitement?

Both?

I slowly lift my head and stare at the dark figure standing by my bed like the Big Bad Wolf. It's a monster, all right, but it's far from being the terror of my life.

Landon's face is barely visible through the shadows, but I know it's him.

The new monster who won't leave me the hell alone.

"Though perhaps you did it on purpose because you wanted me to jump inside." He runs his fingers through my hair and pulls on the only ribbon I wear at night, then uses it to wipe beneath my eyes. "Are these tears, muse?"

I slap his hand away, ashamed of my weakness and the fact that none other than Landon is witnessing it.

"Is that a challenge?" He grabs both my wrists in one of his hands. "Because I love those."

I don't know what comes over me next. Maybe I'm still on a high from the emotions I experienced just now or I always wanted to give this asshole an actual taste of my temper.

I kick him the hardest I can. I aim for his dick, but I think I only hit his thigh. He jerks back, but he doesn't release my wrists.

I pull and push him with my leg, but it's like he's securing them in stone.

"Well, well, looks like I got myself a fighter. I love it when they fight." His amused voice is laced with subtle sadism as he pushes me down on the mattress.

My back bounces, but before I can sit up again, he's on me. Landon slams my wrists on the pillow above my head, still securing them with his hand. His knees rest on either side of my stomach, locking me in place.

"There, much better." He hovers over me like a tyrant king who's expecting all his demands to be met.

I snarl up at him and wiggle. My wrists hurt from how much I've tried to pull them from his grip.

"It's utterly pointless to fight against me, so how about you relax and enjoy the process?"

I still kick my legs in the air and try to hit his back or anywhere where it'll hurt. Badly.

"But then again, you did punch me after I made you cum. Do you get off on violence?"

My cheeks heat and I sneer at him.

"I'll take that as a yes." I can hear the grin in his voice. "What am I if not a good sport? I'll let you fight me before you return the favor for the orgasm."

As soon as he releases my wrists, I headbutt him and punch him in the chest, then I kick him, not sure where, but it sure feels so damn good.

He's the one who falls on the mattress this time, and I mount his hard body and punch him in the shoulder, collarbone, anywhere my hands can reach.

Fuck you fuck you fuck you.

I chant in my head as I take out all the frustration, fear, and completely unhinged emotions on him.

It isn't until I'm partially spent that I realize he hasn't even attempted to stop me or hit back.

So I direct my fist at his face. This time, he grabs it in midair and tuts. "Not the face. It's actual real estate that's worth more than you reincarnated a hundred times."

All of a sudden, he flips us back so that I'm beneath him and he's on top of me. He does it so effortlessly, as if he's mocking my earlier enthusiasm and the short-lived feelings of victory I experienced.

"Now that you got your violence kink out of the way..." He slides up so his knees are on either side of my head and unbuckles his belt. "It's time for *my* kink."

My eyes widen as he pulls out his hard cock, which looks huge despite the lack of light. And for some reason, my inner thighs tingle at the sight.

"Your fight is such a turn-on." He slides his fingers from my forehead over the slope of my cheek and then down to my mouth before he pulls on my lower lip. "As expected of my little muse."

I grab on to his thigh over the lowered pants, my chest squeezing, as is the case whenever he calls me that. His muse.

Why?

Just why did he pick me as his muse?

Is this my curse?

"What's the meaning of this? Playing hard to get again?" He wraps his fingers around my throat and squeezes. "We both know you want me. You're shuddering at the prospect of sucking my cock. Deep down, you're begging for all the cum I will spill down your throat.

I dig my nails into his thigh and shake my head. I refuse to think that I'm by any means attracted to this enigma of a man whom I barely know.

A man who's only tormented me.

But it hits me then.

The reason why my panties are slick with arousal even as he chokes me.

I'm in pitch-darkness and I'm not thinking about the monster. I'm surrounded by black, and yet I'm not scared for my life.

I've never felt like this, not even when I invaded Maya's room and hugged her to sleep.

"Just for your information, I have girls falling arse over tits and begging to choke on my cock like seasoned pros. I'm not interested in your reluctance." His voice turns deeper, more menacing.

"And yet you're here instead of going to those girls," I sign, not sure if he sees much of it in the dark.

But even if he doesn't see it, he must sense it from my tightening grip on his thigh. I'm no one's second or third choice.

I'm the first. The one and only.

"Touché." He squeezes my throat one last time before he releases me. "So how about you do us both a favor and open those lips."

I don't. Instead, I wrap my hands around his cock. And yes, I need both of them to be able to take all of him.

After two jerks, I slowly slide it into my mouth. I'm completely relying on instinct here, having no clue what the hell I'm doing.

I've never found the prospect of sucking cock appealing, but I do want to give him the feeling he gave me that day.

I hope he's as confused and mind-blown as I was. I hope he thinks about me for days to come.

Darting my tongue, I take tentative licks. He tastes the same way he smells—like an edge of danger and forbidden fantasies.

He groans, the sound sexually raw. I clench my thighs as if his vocal cords are vibrating against my most intimate part. Landon is the only person I know who oozes such powerful erotic energy without even trying.

"I knew you were a creature of the dark." He slides his fingers over my hair. "Just like me."

I'm in no way like him.

"But enough foreplay." He pulls on the ribbon, releasing my hair just so he can grip it in a merciless hold. "This is about my kink, after all."

Keeping my head in place, he thrusts all the way in. It's sudden and brutally mesmerizing.

Everything about Landon is enchantingly dark and effortlessly gripping.

His rhythm escalates until I can hardly keep up. All I can do is let go and feel his feral strength. I'm like a doll, an object he uses to get off without caring whether he hurts me or not.

And for some demented reason, I'm entirely captivated.

"Your mouth is made to be fucked." He thrusts all the way in and I gag. Tears fill my eyes and I gasp, grappling for nonexistent air.

Does that stop Landon? Deter him?

Not even a little.

Not even close.

If anything, he goes harder, faster, as if he's on a high and I'm a mere vessel to get him there.

Once I think I'll faint, he pulls out. His sadistic eyes remain on mine as I suck much-needed air into my starved lungs. Barely a few seconds pass before he grabs my chin and thrusts in again. "That's it. Choke on my cock. Show me how much you love this."

His grip on my hair sends throbs of pain to my skull. Not to mention the manhandling that should revolt me to the core, and yet my clit throbs and my panties are soaking wet.

If I could just touch myself for a second…

My thoughts come to a halt when he thrusts with unprecedented intensity. I grab on to his thighs for dear life as he—there's no other expression for it—uses me to get off.

It's fast, ferocious, and completely vicious.

I've never been this turned on in my whole life.

Finally, he slides his dick out of my achy mouth and I feel a warm liquid on my face. Did this asshole just come on my face?

I'm still reeling from the throat-fucking and delirious with my own arousal, so my reaction is delayed and all I can do is watch.

Landon smears his cum on my face, massaging it on my lips before he whispers, "My own piece of art."

I blink, still unable to believe the sight in front of me. He definitely looks elated, but there's also a dangerous purse in his lips.

"You really shouldn't have caught my interest. Now, I'll have to swallow you alive, little muse."

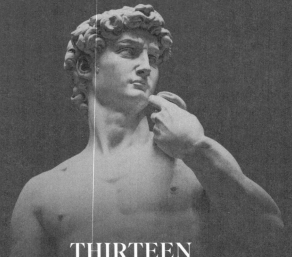

THIRTEEN

Landon

I HAVE NINETY-NINE PROBLEMS, BUT POPULARITY ISN'T ONE OF them.

Due to my charming personality, mouthwatering looks, and genius skills, I happen to attract a lot of attention.

But not all attention is good.

As is pointed out by my vice president of sorts in the Elites. Nila. And by vice president, I mean the one who does my bidding. I only gave her a title so I could manipulate her to the fullest. Like all the other members, her role is to be used as a dutiful pawn.

She's short, packs more of a punch with her words than her fists, and likes to believe she has a spot on my small list of prodigies.

Now, don't get me wrong. Nila was probably a good fuck, which is why I remember it happened, although it's been a few years, and she's the only one I've fucked more than once—as in, once and a half because I couldn't be bothered to finish the second time around. But that's about it.

She's standing at the entrance of my college art studio, wearing a camisole that's only held up by a flimsy thread around her neck.

Her brown hair falls to her naked shoulders and she likes to consume chewing gum more than air. There's nothing I want to do more than dump her and her cheap habits into the dirtiest part of the Thames.

However, she's relaying important information and it's in my best interest to listen to her. The brilliant Thames idea has to be unfortunately postponed.

I abandon the piece of clay I've been working on, stub my cigarette in the ashtray, and lean against the wall opposite her.

"You were saying? And make it quick, because my tolerance for people in my space is below zero."

She bats her fake eyelashes. "Including me?"

"Especially you."

She juts her lips in an immature pout but quickly recovers. "So yeah. Apparently, you pissed off the wrong people. The Heathens and the Serpents are, contrary to your plans, speaking together and possibly plotting against you."

"More fun. Who cares?"

"Uh, I don't know. The rest of us who will be caught in the aftermath? We're not trained mafia men like those guys."

"You signed up for this knowing full well about the possibility of turning into collateral damage."

"So…you'll let us fend for ourselves?"

"For fuck's sake." I retrieve another cigarette and light it. "You're not kids, last I checked. Besides, if there's something major, I will interfere and stop it from affecting the group."

I can't be arsed, if I'm being honest, but an attack on the club is a direct threat to me, and that's simply not an agenda I support.

"Rory said you're not paying much attention to the club."

Rory, the second in command with Nila, and someone I only gave the co-vice president position to because he can be molded like clay, has started to think he could have his own opinions. I don't appreciate that in my domain, and I will certainly have to nip it in the bud before he turns into a worse problem.

"Tell Rory everything is under control. I'm sure you'll help me convince him, Nila. You know you're the only one I trust."

I don't mean a single word I've said, but I'm convincing enough that I'm rewarded with Nila's heart eyes.

"Of course!" She approaches me with a sultry look plastered all over her above-average face and places a hand on my chest. "Now that we got that out of the way..."

I stare at her mud-green eyes, so big and muted and terribly boring. The only eyes I'd like staring back at me are those of powder blue and tarnished innocence.

Mia kicked me out of her room last night after she signed that if I cut off her light again, she'd slice my throat in my sleep. Since then, I've been in the uni studio for the sole reason that it was the closest.

A burst of creative energy rips through me every time I touch Mia. It's strange, powerful, and, to my dismay, unexplainable.

I don't tread in unknown territory. And when I do, it's only after I've studied all variables. That doesn't seem to be possible with a certain blonde who's messing up my patterns, habits, and, most importantly, my equilibrium.

It doesn't matter that I spent the whole night here. That energy started to slip soon after I left Mia.

There must be a way that I can contain this energy. When I was coming all over her petite face, I figured the only solution would be to lock her up, but she's literally a menace and would snip my balls the first chance she gets.

Now, there's another option that I don't particularly care for, but it could be the only one on the table.

"You look gorgeous today." Nila's annoying voice brings me out of my reverie.

"I'm gorgeous every day." I grab her wrist with two fingers and throw her hand away.

Touching is one of the most revolting things humans ever invented. I tolerate it out of necessity and only indulge in it when my cock is involved.

"Now off you go." I push her in the direction of the door.

"But—"

"I won't fuck you, Nila. Go find yourself another dick. Though it won't be as satisfactory as mine, I'm sure you'll survive the downgrade."

"You're such a prick."

"Being obsessed with my cock won't get you on his Ten Favorite People list. Fortunately, he's not turned on by desperate holes." I slide the studio door closed in her face and make a note to ask the janitor not to give her the keys again.

Though that would be talking to his dick she obviously seduced and won't be an easy task.

Men, as a general rule, are guided by their lower parts, and while I belong to the disgraceful gender, I don't share their mindless animalistic instincts.

Fucking, like everything in life, is a power play. A means to take what I want and fuck off.

Just like last night.

Then why did you want to stay afterward, Lan? the voice inside my head that I thought I'd murdered for his blasphemous suggestions whispers.

To get more from my muse, I reply back—in my head, of course, because I'm not a lunatic. *Oh, I'm sorry. You don't have that, so you don't know what that means. Throw a pity party for yourself and don't invite me.*

That shuts him up.

Good.

Hope he chokes to death on the sentimental bollocks that he wears like a charm.

I'm about to leave the studio to execute my next diabolical plan that may or may not include a certain goth Barbie when my phone vibrates on the work table.

Now, I won't be winning a Son of the Year award anytime soon, but I don't usually ignore Mum's calls.

I pick up the video call with a grin. "Morning to the most beautiful queen."

Mum laughs, her face radiating. Bran and I inherited the shape of her eyes, while Glyn has her facial structure.

Astrid C. King, as per her paintings' signature, is the reason all three of us have artistic genes, though I have the strongest, mixed with a dash of chaos.

She soon narrows her eyes. "Why are you buttering me up first thing in the morning? Are you hiding something?"

"Just the fact that you're the best mum ever, maybe?"

She laughs again.

It's easy to deal with my parents because I just unleash my inner boy who actually appreciates them.

Mum is a tad better than Dad, though. He, for some reason, still holds a grudge that I pushed Bran and called Glyn unnecessary when we were kids.

So I veered to pretending that I love them to death and that seems to work wonders.

"Stop it, seriously." She sobers up. "We haven't spoken in a while."

"A while being two days."

"Still too much. All three of you are living far away from home and I just miss you."

"We miss you, too, but Bran and I have been away from home for over five years now."

"Still doesn't get easier." She sighs with enough drama to rival soap opera actors.

And my mum isn't even the dramatic type.

"We were never meant to stay," I say while staring at my collection of clay statues that lie around like ghostly puppets.

"Drive that knife deeper, would you?"

"I wouldn't dare knife my own mother." I grin. "We'll visit soon."

That's literally the whole point behind her terrible act.

As expected, her expression lights up. "Bring Bran and Glyn. Kill, too."

"Only if Killian gets to be brought chopped to pieces and shoved in a freezer."

"Landon!" She gasps, her eyes chastising me all the way to Sunday.

"What? It's no secret that I don't like the twat."

"Your sister loves him."

"One more reason to dislike him. She often has terrible taste. Like that time she painted all over my statue."

Mum winces. "People express their artistic abilities differently."

"And some people repress it to death, like your dear Bran."

Her brow furrows and her lips part the slightest bit. So she knows that his ridiculous attempts at painting nature is a camouflage. Seems she's more in tune with us than I previously thought.

Interesting, and not for the right reasons. I need to be more elusive so she doesn't see what's inside me and decide I don't belong to her little minion prodigies.

"Bran is…" she trails off and wipes the sweat on her upper lip. "Different. He just needs time. When he's ready, it'll all work out."

"It makes sense for him to be delusional, but you don't even believe what you're saying. I suggest you practice your acting skills in front of the mirror before you broach the subject with him."

"Don't speak to me in that tone, Lan." She's pretending to be stern when she can't do that to save her life.

Mum is all about love, peace, and a million colorful, useless slogans that revolve around harmony. Since we were young, she's tried to create this picture-perfect family, where we all get along and no one pokes the other member the wrong way.

The result of that effort is obviously the fluid relationship between Bran and Glyn. Me, however? I love poking more than breathing. I can't survive a day without rubbing someone the wrong way and making them question their entire flimsy existence.

My siblings and parents aren't excluded. What? It's not my fault they like to be a cheap reincarnation of Little Miss Ostrich. I don't like them burying emotions, repressing, or acting like something they're not. So I shove them here and give them a slice of reality there.

They hate me for it, except for my mum, who still tolerates my shenanigans, but they still need the wake-up call.

I accept thanks in the form of tough love, thank you very much.

"I'm just offering innocent advice, Mum." I grin at the screen. "I've got to meet a professor. Say hi to Dad and everyone."

"Will do. Don't cause trouble, Lan."

"Never."

More like I absolutely will.

I don't cause trouble; trouble caused me.

On that note, I end another successful phone call with my mother.

When I was younger, I didn't realize that letting one's true nature out was taboo and could be categorized as social suicide. Especially when it's full of antisocial bollocks.

And while I was completely fine being my beautiful, destructive self, I soon realized I was the reason behind my mother's distress and my father's case of epic confusion.

He tried to rein me in by being stern, which failed miserably and backfired. Then he attempted to become my friend, and that only bit him in the arse, because I thought he was giving me the green light to use him. In the end, he was left with no practical solutions to deal with me.

As a last resort, when I was ten and I nearly burned down my school, my parents took me to professionals. The group of pretentious psychiatrists and psychotherapists plugged wires to my head and asked me dumb questions.

My answers to those questions landed me the diagnosis of antisocial disorder, and a brain scan showed mine wasn't wired like everyone else's.

I remember the stony expression on my parents' faces so well. They didn't show it openly, but I could tell the news upset them beyond words.

They still took me for ice cream afterward and treated me the same. They still considered me their son, despite the fact that I felt alienated.

I was around twelve when I realized the house was in a state of shambles due to my fuck-the-world attitude. I couldn't possibly let that state fester, now, could I?

So I've worn a mask since. I took the useless therapy and pretended that I could be fixed. I convinced myself, while trying not to gag, that all I needed was peace, love, and family.

That's also when I realized people, including your own family, don't really like you for what or who you are. It's all about how you make them feel.

Ever since I started wearing the mask of societal standards, the few wrinkles I added to my parents' faces have eased a little, and I'm, in a way, their favorite—when Bran isn't channeling the saint he thinks lurks inside him.

My siblings, however, didn't get the merciful version of my otherworldly transformation. I don't like them making fools out of themselves, and I might have taken drastic measures to make sure they're not acting like idiots.

What? It reflects badly on my pristine image.

I leave the art studio, and even though I'm running on more sleep deprivation than a seasoned hooker, I greet my colleagues, comment on their atrocious edgy clothes, and make small talk with my current and previous professors, who would worship me if I started a cult.

All the social interactions are a strain, painfully empty, and hold the importance of a used napkin. And yet I'm an excellent conversationalist and the holy messiah of charming others.

It all comes down to wearing the appropriate mask in the right situation and with the right people.

It still bores me to tears, though.

People as a concept have only one merit—the ability to be used. Other than that, they're a brainless, rotten species that I like to pretend I don't belong to.

Finally, I leave the charade of pretending I give a fuck about their fangirling and fanboying.

I grab a coffee from the nearest coffee shop, making sure I

tell the owner she looks like Princess Diana on her wedding day. Complete nonsense that she gobbles up without a hint of doubt.

Then I consume my three-shot espresso in one go and dunk the cup in the bin.

My brain restarts in quick overdrive, ready for whatever I dish his way. Yes, I know too much caffeine isn't healthy, but I'm not beneath using crutches when I need an extra boost.

Whether it's cigarettes, coffee, or sex.

I slide into my McLaren and check my phone. After I left last night, I sent Mia a very sweet good night text.

Landon: My cock is pleased to make the acquaintance of your wet little mouth and he can't wait to meet your cunt after my fingers made a compelling recommendation.

Landon: Oh, and good night. Have an erotic dream of me plowing into your tight little hole.

Unsurprisingly, she didn't reply at the time.

Now, however, I find a text from her. She sent it about fifteen minutes ago, during the time I was playing my Prince Charming role to perfection.

Mia: Oh, I did dream of you all right. You were hanging from a tree by the balls and I snipped your dick off *scissors emoji* I'd be careful if I were you. My dreams usually come true.

I throw my head back in genuine laughter. This girl is, by all accounts, the most entertaining thing since playing chess with Eli or Uncle Aiden.

Maybe even more so.

Landon: Point is, you still dreamt of me. You like me that much, huh?

Her reply is immediate. Something rare.

I'm breaking that wall, brick by each brick. Once I'm done, my muse will be fully mine.

Mine to own.

Mine to use.

Mine to destroy.

Mia: The delusional police called. You're under arrest for spreading fake news. In case that wasn't clear, you're the last person on earth I'd like.

Landon: And yet you choked on my cock like a good girl.

The dots appear and disappear, but her reply doesn't come.

Landon: Lost for words?

Mia: More like I'm deciding which voodoo doll of you should I bake in the microwave.

Landon: You're even making voodoo dolls of me. The obsession is cute. Speaking of cute, are you up to sucking my cock again? I loved your little licks and amateurish attempt at blowing me. The innocence show was such a turn-on.

Mia: No.

Landon: Does that mean you prefer I stick my cock in one of your other holes? Perhaps both?

Mia: Seriously, you need to chill for one fucking second.

Landon: Is that a no?

Mia: Of course it's a no.

Landon: Pity. You're missing out on my porn-worthy sex drive. Will try again tomorrow when you're in a better mood. In the meantime, want to come over?

Mia: To your funeral? Sure. I'll wear my worst black dress and throw a dead rat in your grave when no one is looking.

I laugh again. I can almost imagine her doing exactly that with a sly grin on her face.

She's definitely a menace, and I'm loving every second of it.

Landon: That's tempting, but I meant to come over to the haunted house and model for me.

Mia: No, thanks.

Landon: Your resistance is amusing to a degree, but don't overdo it, because I could and would crush you once the right circumstances arise. Don't make the mistake of provoking me again. We both know how it ended up the last few times.

Mia: *Middle finger emoji*

Landon: Very well.

Looks like we're doing it my way, after all.

I'm about to throw my phone away when she sends another text.

Mia: Just what the hell do you want from me, Landon? Leave me alone.

Landon: No can do. And as for what I want, the answer is simple. I want your soul, little muse.

FOURTEEN

Mia

I TIPTOE TO WHERE A FAMILIAR FIGURE IS STANDING BY THE corner of the kitchen, the only sound is the swishing of my boot chains.

Maya is completely oblivious to my presence, despite having the advantage of our twin instinct.

Her fingers clutch the wall as she hides her body and peeks around the corner, spying on God knows who.

We came over to the Heathens' mansion for dinner and I just finished catching up with Niko and Kill, but that ended when my brother threw us out of his room so he could sleep.

On the balcony.

With his body on the chair and his feet on the railing.

Half naked.

He's my brother, but he's weird as fuck. I don't remember the last time I saw him sleeping properly in a bed.

But then again, he does have trouble sleeping and can only do it in odd places and in odd positions.

I came down to tell Maya we shouldn't wake him up for dinner if he actually falls asleep, but I found her spying in what's considered our second home on the island.

At first, I contemplate scaring her, but I think better of it and lean sideways to see who got her attention.

Jeremy and his new senior guard, Ilya, stand by the kitchen counter. Jeremy is a few years older than us, is Nikolai's best friend, and is possibly the only person who can stop him from launching into a full-on suicide mission.

He's huge, handsome, grumpy, and serious to a fault. His father is a big deal in the Bratva, and Jeremy is the heir to that legacy like Nikolai is expected to take over my parents' duties.

Mom said Maya and I can definitely have our place at the table if we want to. Maya said, "No, thanks. I have better things to do with my life." I also prefer to be a businesswoman with my own company.

Back to the present and Maya, who's spying on Jeremy, the Heathens' leader and the one she's had her claws out for. Since we were children, she's always thought she'd make him her husband. One, she likes to vie for the strongest man in the room. Two, considering his father's influence and wealth, he's, in my sister's words, a catch.

The fact that he has a girlfriend has never deterred her. When we heard about that, Maya just flipped her hair and announced—smugly, I might add—that he'll realize his mistake and come begging at her pedicured feet.

But there are two points that contradict the fact that she's spying on him.

One, Maya never hides. A few weeks ago, she put on her favorite perfume, walked to Jeremy with a sway in her hips, and asked him when he was going to stop making a mistake and pick her.

She tried to run her red nails down his jaw and flirt with him, to which Jeremy respectfully pushed her away. Not only is he painfully not interested, but he also knows that if Niko catches her hitting on his best friend, there'll be carnage.

Two, she's not even looking at Jeremy and actually seems more interested in following the movements of the guard, Ilya. A tall, silent blond guy whose voice I've only heard a couple of times.

I know because Jeremy is leaning against the wall, but Ilya is the one who's moving around, getting some ingredients from the cupboard and adding them to the pan on the stove.

They're talking in Russian—something about the Serpents and the Elites and retaliation. Maya doesn't give a fuck about any of that.

But I do.

Especially when I catch a name in Jeremy's dialogue.

"...Landon needs to be put in his place."

My heart rate skyrockets and I hide myself, mimicking Maya's criminal-like behavior.

I glare at my chest as if I can see my heart floundering and getting on a metaphorical high.

Seriously, what the hell is wrong with me? Just the mention of his name and I'm immediately in this state.

My cheeks flame at the reminder of last night. Punishing darkness, a sinister voice, and unapologetic lust.

I was more confused about the strength of my reaction than his psycho self. Landon is who he is, but I'm not him.

How could I be attracted to an unfeeling narcissistic psychopath who'd eradicate me and everyone I care about in a heartbeat?

"What did you have in mind?" Ilya asks while still focused on the pan.

"We'll discuss it with the others later, but one thing's for certain. Once I get my hands on that motherfucker, I'll break his hand and destroy his little sculpting hobby."

It's not a hobby, though.

I've read articles about his first exhibition a few years back, and I've seen the disturbingly beautiful statues he won multiple awards for. He's a global talent, and while it's annoying that he knows it and even gloats about it, that doesn't take away the fact that he's an actual genius.

A psycho genius, but oh well.

"I need someone to follow him at all times without drawing suspicion," Jeremy continues.

"I will do it," Ilya says.

"No. You're too obvious, and he's too smart for his own good."

I walk out from my hiding place, catching the two of them—three if we're counting Maya—by surprise.

She has no choice but to clear her throat and follow me out as if we were just walking past here by chance.

"I happened to overhear your conversation," I sign to Jeremy since he understands. "I'll follow Landon around."

He straightens. "Out of the question."

"I'm going to do it anyway, so either you back me up and get whatever information I'll gather, or you don't."

"Nikolai will kill me if he finds out about this."

"Which is why he won't." I smile at Maya. "Right?"

Her face is red as she fiddles with the strap of her Chanel bag. Maya never fiddles. Seeming to sober up, she releases it and shakes her head. "No way in hell. You're not getting in the middle of this."

"I already am."

"Mia." She grabs my shoulders. "The whole pig blood thing was reckless enough as it is. You don't need that guy's attention."

I already have it anyway, so might as well use it for the greater good. Including, but not limited to, bringing the asshole down.

Besides, I need to find an explanation for my strange attraction to the bastard. I'm sure the more I find out how amoral he is, the less attractive I'll find him and then I'll be happy to throw him to the wolves—aka the Heathens.

"I'll be fine," I sign to my sister, then disengage from her hold to face Jeremy. "Do we have a deal?"

"No, Mia. I'm not pushing you into his lethal orbit."

"I'm already there." I lift my chin. "He thinks I'm his muse or something like that, so I'll use that to my advantage."

Jeremy's eyebrows shoot too close to his hairline. "Since when?"

"Since I'm getting revenge for what he did to Nikolai."

"We're planning that. Seriously, stay out of it."

"Too late. Remember the blood bath he got at his own club's party?" I point a thumb at myself. "That was me."

"Jesus fucking Christ," he says with more bewilderment and pride than anything.

"No god can stop the psycho but I can." But let's ignore the fact that I'm hiding in my brother's mansion because this is the only place where he won't be able to pull any shit.

I brought Maya along, too, so he won't be able to threaten me with her either.

"Be careful and retreat the moment you sense any danger," Jeremy says.

"You can't possibly be serious?" Maya directs her attention to him.

"You and I both know we can't stop her once she puts her mind to something."

I grin like a Cheshire cat and nod approvingly.

Maya points at Ilya, who turned off the stove and is about to leave. "You, talk some sense into him."

Ilya looks at her as if she's nothing but the dirt beneath his shoes. That's the first time I've seen anyone disregard my sister's bigger-than-the-world presence.

"He's not a *you*," Jeremy says calmly. "His name is Ilya."

"He's not important enough for me to recall his name, but he has a job of advising you not to make stupid mistakes, like throwing Mia in the middle of a war."

"Hey." I push her. "I decided this. Don't overstep, Maya. Neither you, Jeremy, nor Nikolai get to tell me what to do."

"But…I'm worried about you." Maya's brow furrows.

She's always been overprotective of me since that incident, even more than our parents and Niko, and that says something since those three could've been mistaken for my wardens the first few years following what happened.

Still, Maya needs to learn that I'm capable of making my own choices—mistakes included.

"I can take care of myself." I shake hands with Jeremy. "Apologize to Ilya on Maya's behalf."

He nods silently, but Maya releases an exasperated sound. "I have nothing to apologize for."

I grab her by the shoulder and push her into one of the guest rooms. She wiggles free from my hold and faces me with an epic frown.

"You had no right to do that. And what's with apologizing on my behalf lately? You're making me look like a bitch."

"You can manage that on your own without my interference." I cock my head to the side. "Besides, you were just being overly defensive to hide your actual reaction. Why were you spying on Ilya and why were your cheeks red?"

Her lips part and she goes a deep shade of red before she stomps her Hermès heel on the ground with the impatience of a toddler. "As if I would pay that loser any attention. I was just keeping an eye on Jeremy because he's going to be my future husband."

I give an "Uh-huh" look and she goes berserk, trying to convince me—and probably herself—that there's nothing to the earlier episode.

She doesn't realize that the more she defends her metaphorical position, the less plausible she sounds.

When I continue to stare at her, she pretends that she's gotten an important call and runs out of the room as if her ass is on fire.

Maybe it's because we're twins, but Maya is more readable than computer chess. While it's fun to mess with her sometimes, she's really flustered beyond saving this time, so I leave her be.

I go to check if dinner is ready. I'm starving and need my calorie fix.

Sure enough, Nikolai didn't manage to sleep. He's lounging in the living room, still half naked, and listening to Gareth.

Jeremy, Ilya, and Kill head to the table and call everyone along.

My brother flicks Gareth on the forehead so he'll shut it, then he headlocks him and drags him to the dining area.

There's no trace of Maya.

I pull out my phone to call her, but she's already hurrying in from the patio, cheeks kissed by the cold.

She avoids my gaze and breezes past me to the dining room. I narrow my eyes on her back. There's something wrong with her and I need to figure out what.

I'm about to join them when my phone vibrates in my hand. I would ignore it, but then I catch a glimpse of the name of the man who refuses to be ignored under any circumstances.

It doesn't help that I've kept myself busy the entire day, just so I wouldn't think about the next thing his defective mind might come up with.

Devil Lord: I'm outside.

I read the text and tilt my head. That's it? He spent the whole day doing fuck knows what just to say he's outside?

Devil Lord: That was an invitation to come and see me if you didn't notice.

Mia: I'm not at the dorm.

Devil Lord: I know. You've developed this annoying habit of hiding in the Heathens' mansion. Didn't take you for the type who needs other people's protection.

The damn—

Wait a minute.

Mia: Please tell me that by outside, you mean you're outside the dorm.

Devil Lord: Why would I be there if you aren't?

He sends me a selfie of him cocking his head to the side and grinning like a little suicidal idiot. Behind him, I can see the gate of the mansion and the lights from where we all are. A dash of panic explodes at the base of my stomach and I inhale deeply.

Mia: Have you lost your damn mind? Everyone is here. Niko, Kill, and Jeremy included.

Devil Lord: Why, yes, the holy trinity that's out for my head due to dreadfully childish reasons.

Mia: Kidnapping and assault are childish reasons?

Devil Lord: They're not dead, now, are they? Matter of fact, they're enjoying your company while I'm being hugged by the cold, merciless wind.

A doctor needs to dissect this monster's head and see if he has anything normal in there.

Mia: Just leave before they find out.

Devil Lord: Not without you.

Mia: Are you serious?

Devil Lord: A million percent. You can either come out and spare everyone the drama or you can let them find out, or tell them yourself if you're in the mood for some mayhem, then watch as they come out and maim me. Of course, you'll have to live with the fact that Glyn will break up with Kill and Cecily will leave Jeremy, because I will definitely make it look as if I were kidnapped and lured here. I'll convince them that their men don't love them enough to spare me for their sake. So what do you say, little muse? Peace or havoc?

My hand shakes around the phone. I have no doubt that he'll do exactly what he said. Someone like Landon isn't afraid of getting physically hurt for the sake of chaos.

I'm starting to suspect that it runs in his veins instead of blood. "Who's that?"

I freeze when Nikolai stops in front of me, eyes narrowed. Shit. I was so focused on Landon's antics that I didn't notice my brother approaching me.

With a smile, I tuck my phone into my dress's pocket. "No one. I just got a reminder that I have a school project I forgot about."

"Is Brandon a school project now?" he asks.

My brow furrows. "What? What does Bran have to do with this?"

"You're still friends with him despite my clear order not to be."

"Well, he's a great guy."

"He's one of *them*."

"Not all of *them* are bad. Kill, Jeremy, and Annika are dating people from there and you seem to be okay with that." I pat his shoulder. "Anyway, I have to go."

"Have dinner first."

"I'm not hungry." I don't wait for his or the others' comments as I slip out the front entrance and jog for about five minutes to reach beyond the gate.

I'm out of breath, but I search on the sides, where I assume he could be hiding.

Maybe he thought better of it and left. Though I doubt it. His go-getter personality resembles a hunting dog. It's highly unlikely that he'd leave without securing prey.

I veer farther into the bushes, then stop when it gets too dark and retrieve my phone.

Hot breath swarms my ear as a hard body glues itself against my back and a strong hand wraps around my throat. "You made the right choice, but I'm afraid it's too late. We're going to play a little game, muse."

FIFTEEN

Mia

Turns out, Landon was being literal when he mentioned a game.

We're sitting in the haunted house that could be used as a sequel of *The Nun*. Landon and I are on opposite tall Victorian chairs that were covered by sheets and there's a table between us.

To make matters worse, we're surrounded by candles of different colors and shapes, representing a mismatched symphony of chaos.

The shadows dance around us like demons, casting an ominous edge on Landon's already fucked-up existence.

"Your turn." He motions at the chessboard with a provocative smirk that will get him killed one day.

I narrow my eyes as I grab my knight. His smirk widens as if celebrating my next move, which he probably thinks is leading me to my doom, but I still make it anyway.

The worst thing possible is letting someone like Landon access my head. He's already affecting my body in a way I don't care for, and I'm simply not allowing him more space.

That would be no different than lying around waiting for the predator to pounce and devour me.

"The game you wanted to play is chess?" I sign.

He doesn't even look at the chessboard as he moves his rook into an extremely vulnerable position.

"What else did you have in mind?" he asks with a strange gleam in his empty eyes. "Perhaps something kinky?"

"As if."

Though I can't deny that those thoughts actually passed through my head after he ambushed me in front of the Heathens' mansion and brought me here. He definitely made it sound like there'd be something more to this game of his.

Or maybe that's another method to mess with my head and I need to stop being on edge.

"Here's a piece of advice for you." He strokes the knight that he killed off a few minutes ago between his fingers. "It's not mandatory to fight me about everything. While it's a turn-on during sex, I don't care for it the rest of the time."

"Here's a news flash for you. I don't care for your preferences."

"You should. Considering they'll be front and center in your life going forward."

"Arrogant much?"

"Just the right amount, in my opinion."

"Your opinion, just like your whole personality and existence, is awfully flawed and in need of a desperate revamp."

"Oh?" He strangles the knight between his index and middle fingers. "I thought I'd survived just fine until now."

I knock down his rook with an innocent grin. "You thought wrong. But hey, it's never too late to start being a decent human being."

"The thought of decency bores me to tears, so I'm inclined to disregard the suggestion."

"Why?"

"I don't subscribe to the righteous notion most people strive for."

"Don't I know it. You're more interested in chaos and mayhem."

A smile stretches his lips and I'm momentarily distracted from the board. All I can do is stare as light twinkles in his normally dead eyes, sending streaks of brightness within. It's not his usual taunting smirk with a dash of sardonic irony. This is possibly the closest thing I've seen to a smile on his sculpture-like face.

And I don't mean he has a sharp jaw but that he's really as frigid and emotionless as his statues.

"Touché."

I clear my throat and then sign, "How about you do something different for a change? You can start with small steps."

"Such as?"

"Stop kidnapping people and taking them to places against their will, maybe?"

"But how else will I have your full attention that's not muddied with either babysitting Maya or following the Heathens like a lost puppy?" He pushes his second rook, again putting it in an obviously volatile position. "Not to mention the unnecessary time you've spent with my brother. Spoiler alert, the girls prefer me over him."

"Well, they've made the mistake of their lives. Bran is much more likable than you. In fact, you're on different planets and don't even compare." I narrow my eyes on the rook.

What's he playing at? There must be a secret move that he's trying to pull, but what is it? He already lost his other rook, and it's downright reckless to sacrifice the second one just after.

"And yet it's my fingers you came all over and it's my cum that decorated your pretty little face."

I jerk up, my attention flying to him. His features are overshadowed by the candles' dim light and pure sadism. The cocky smirk slips back onto his face with a vengeance. All of a sudden, he seems bigger and darker than I recall, as if he gained a few inches of height in the span of seconds.

"Stop talking to me like that," I sign.

"Like what?"

"Like I'm your toy."

"I prefer my future fuck doll."

"More like your Grim Reaper, because I'll slice your throat while you sleep."

He laughs. "You're such a menace, I want to gobble you up."

"I'll give you indigestion, asshole."

"Worth it, muse."

"Not sure you'll think the same when you're drowning in a pool of blood."

"Blood. Yum. You just keep ticking all the kink boxes today." He pretends to be shocked. "Did you do your research on me, after all?"

"Not even if you were the last man available."

"Last man available to everyone? No. To you? Highly likely."

I shake my head even as I make my move, choosing not to knock off the rook so that I won't fall for his possible trap.

My body hums with inexplicable energy, a type I've never had while playing chess, even with the most skilled players I've had the honor to face.

The strong emotions nearly burst at the seams with every passing second, and it terrifies the shit out of me.

I haven't had such a visceral reaction since that doomed day. Only, now, it's fundamentally different and confusingly exciting. In fact, this feeling is similar to when I gasped, recoiled, and rode his fingers to orgasm.

Or when he thrust in and out of my mouth and used me to reach his peak.

It's an addicting frenzy that I want more of, but I'm also judging myself too hard for wanting this from psycho Landon.

"Don't flatter yourself," I sign. "Also, what's with all the candles? Are they for your demon friends who are sitting on your shoulders and whispering nasty things?"

"They're for my foul-mouthed demon lady."

My brow furrows. "I don't like candles."

"But you don't like the dark—a piece of information I discovered last night when you momentarily lost your marbles. I suppose that has to do with the reason you refuse to let the world hear your voice."

My lips part and I stare at him as if he's an alien who came with the sole purpose of wiping out humanity.

"Your face says you're wondering how I know. Reading people comes naturally to me; they're rather predictable and dreadfully boring." He pauses, lips thinning as if he doesn't want to admit what follows. "You're not. Predictable and boring, I mean. Because even though I desiccated your fear, I'm still unable to figure out the reason behind it. I'm impressed. Others wouldn't have lasted more than a few hours in your position, but you're still going strong. I applaud the determination."

"Should I feel honored?"

"Preferably." He leans his elbows on his knees and steeples his fingers near his chin. "But first, let's work on that mystery."

I knock down his knight. "If by mystery you mean the missing ball situation you'll suffer from by the end of tonight, then sure. Let's go for it."

"Stop having violent thoughts for a second." He advances his queen to protect his rook. "I'm more interested in the incident that stole your voice. Tell me more."

"No."

"Please?"

"No."

"How about *pretty* please?"

"Still no."

"Pity. I thought you'd crumble for my carefully crafted charming persona, but you don't like nice and charming, do you, little muse? I have a feeling that you prefer being chased and cornered while you fight for your life."

I knock down his queen with a huge grin, then throw it at him. He catches it with a sly tilt of his gorgeous lips.

"Let's try again, and I need your mind to be open to other options aside from no." He strokes his dead queen like he does his unfeeling statues. "You can tell me the reason behind your mutism, or as a second, less preferable option, we can discuss your kinks."

"How about no to both?"

"Let's make a bet," he says, completely ignoring my words. "If I win, we'll talk about the silence situation. If you win, it's the kinks."

"Nice try. But that's not how it works, you narcissistic psycho.

When you give a choice, you have to give up something when you lose."

"Like."

"If you win, we'll talk about perverted kinks." *That I don't have.* "If I win, you become my slave boy."

"Oh?" He raises a brow. "I didn't realize you had that kink you naughty, *naughty* girl. I do refuse, however, as I'm too dominant to ever be a slave to anyone, including the devil himself. I'd rather strap women up and tie them down as I fuck them to within an inch of their lives."

"I don't mean sexually, you pervert. I meant that you'll have to do everything I tell you and serve me until I'm satisfied."

"For how long?"

"A week."

"Hmm. You got yourself a deal."

"Your queen is dead and so are you." I push the first of two pawns protecting his king. One more move and he's done for.

Of course, he'll move his king out of the way, but if he does that, he'll be cornered by my bishop. It's over on all accounts.

Landon's annoying smirk remains in place as he moves that damn rook right next to my king and out of reach of my queen and bishop.

"Checkmate."

I stare at the board, refusing to believe what I'm seeing.

It couldn't be.

"You thought sacrificing the queen was blasphemy, but you forgot a significant anecdote. The queen's job is to die for the king."

I glare at him. How could he be so hateful, even when talking about chess?

"Now. For that kinks discussion, care to elaborate?"

"Joke's on you. I don't have any kinks." I grin back, matching his psycho energy with my wild and determined one.

"Don't be ridiculous. You got off on being ambushed in the dark and choking on my cock, so that means you have a submissive streak. One kink down, more to go." He leans his head on his fist. "Don't be shy. I don't bite."

"You want me to believe that?"

"Fine. I don't bite outside of sex."

Perverted asshole.

I busy myself rearranging the chess pieces. What the hell am I supposed to say in this situation? He's not the type who'll be satisfied with half-truths, and I can't exactly go with the 'I'm a virgin' confession, because then he'll possibly become more insistent about claiming me.

Or worse, he'll mock me for being such a closeted prude, since he probably lost his virginity the first time he got a boner.

"You're far from innocent," he comments dryly. "You must've had your fair share of painfully unexceptional dicks—a problem my cock will fix, by the way, so let's hear it, what do you enjoy when you spread your legs?"

"Missionary."

"Too vanilla for someone who's anything but vanilla."

"Well, I like simple stuff and caring lovers. Sorry my kink isn't as exciting as your extensive experience."

"Which is why we have to fix that. You're in desperate need of the excitement that comes with the unknown. Sex is supposed to be a fun indulgence, not a boring technical task." He narrows his eyes as if he's seeing me for the first time.

I stare back, glaring, even though my insides are crumbling. What is he thinking now? He couldn't have possibly figured out that the only clue I have about sex is some porn videos.

Yes, I was curious, but not enough to give it to the first boy who came knocking at my door.

"What are you looking at?" I sign.

"I'm trying to think of the experiments we can perform to determine your possible kinks. For a start..." he trails off. "Strip. Leave the boots on."

"No, thanks," I sign, even though I can feel my cheeks turning hot.

"Don't be a prude. We already saw each other half naked."

"An experience I wouldn't wish on my worst enemy."

One second, he's sitting leisurely like a lion in his den, and the next, he's on me. The whole thing happens in a flash and I don't even register when he hovers over my chair. One hand lands on the arm-rest and the other wraps tightly around my throat.

Oxygen dries out of my lungs and I gasp for nonexistent air.

"You don't seem to grasp the situation, Mia. My patience has limits and I don't appreciate mouthy brats." His thumb presses on my pulse point. "But perhaps this is part of your kink repertoire, too. You love having that control taken from you by force, don't you? You love not being able to think about what will happen or how. You prefer just being there, like when your tight little cunt creamed my fingers."

He eases his hand enough to offer me a breath, but not so I'll be able to kick him in the balls.

I still try to claw at his fingers as he reaches his free hand out and gropes me over my dress. My nipples instantly harden and he finds them, slowly flicking them over the material with lazy ease.

"See? Your body is welcoming me, so how about you follow the example?"

I glare at him. This is only a bodily reaction that could happen even if I were with someone else. I refuse to believe that my skin's rising temperature is because of him.

Landon plunges his hand into the front cut of my dress, beneath the built-in bra, and twists my nipple. A zap of pleasure shoots to my groin and I bite my lower lip.

This definitely didn't happen when Brian touched me in high school.

"So responsive." He strokes my pebbled nipple and my pulse point at the same time, then twists the other one.

My toes curl in my boots as pressure builds in my most intimate part. I can feel myself wetting my panties, and the embarrassment makes me curse myself and him.

The man who's using me and offering me pleasure I never thought available.

He toys with my nipples, his powerful calloused hand twisting, flicking, and pinching so hard, I gasp and try to bury my face in the chair.

He doesn't allow me that, though. His hand around my throat

tightens, keeping me firmly in place as his fingers torture my nipples and his eyes drown mine in a pool of chaos.

"You want this to stop?" he asks with dark, sinister words.

I nod once.

"Then do as I said earlier and strip."

I reach behind my neck and he does release my super sensitive nipples, but that doesn't stop my thighs from getting sticky and wet.

The position is awkward, but he doesn't even help me as I lower the zipper and shimmy out of my dress.

The material pools on the ground in a silent whoosh, and just like that, I'm in only my panties and the boots. Landon's somber gaze measures me from top to bottom, darkening and gleaming as if I'm a meal he's looking forward to consuming.

No, possibly eradicating off the face of this earth.

I've never felt both naked and desired in my life.

"You look like my new possible addiction." He slides his hand from my neck, over my sore nipples, and down to my belly. "Addictions don't survive me, little muse."

Goosebumps erupt on my skin like a fiery explosion.

He said he'd make it stop, but he's taking it further. And I'm not even trying to put an end to this.

Could be that I'm enchanted, or, more likely, it's because I've never reached this level of arousal in my life.

His long, powerful fingers linger on the band of my panties before he slowly, crudely, and so deliberately glides his middle finger over the soaked cloth.

An evil grin curves his lips as my wetness shamelessly seeps onto his hand.

He lifts it up and massages the sticky evidence of my arousal between his fingers. "Choking and manhandling. Check."

I look the other way and wish I could disappear into a hole and never crawl out for the rest of my life.

"Perhaps we can also add the kink of being given an ultimatum." His face gets so close to mine that I can only breathe his intoxicating scent and minty breath. "You would never admit to wanting me unless you were in this position, would you?"

I'm about to snarl at him, but he strokes my own arousal down my nose, over the slope of my cheek, then presses his middle and ring fingers on the cushion of my lips.

My mouth parts and he slides them inside, forcing me to swallow my own arousal. He thrusts in with a power and control that turns me delirious. He presses on my tongue, then curls his fingers around it, rolling and smearing my arousal. It explodes on my taste buds like an aphrodisiac.

"Lucky for you, I'm very well equipped to play the role of your villain. I will drag out your kinks one by each bloody one."

He pulls out his fingers all of a sudden and steps back with casual ease.

The loss of his touch leaves me cold for some reason.

"Now, to unlock other kinks." His voice drops with a chilling edge. "Run."

The challenge in his eyes strikes me in my bones and a shudder spreads through me for a different reason other than cold.

I don't know what's come over me or why I'm even entertaining his crazy.

Maybe it's my own crazy.

Slowly, I stand on unsteady legs, wearing nothing but my panties and boots, and I do the exact opposite of what's logical.

I run.

SIXTEEN

Landon

MY MUSCLES TENSE AND RIPPLE AT THE PROMISE OF A hunt.

Blood rushes to my limbs and pumps my cock with extra attention.

The prospect of a chase makes me nearly come in my trousers like a pubescent.

Problem is, I've never had this feeling before.

Yes, I get off on hunting, just like I indulge in a thousand other kinks as a sexual outlet. However, it never used to be this thrilling and…positively riveting.

I inhale, filling my lungs with the smell of candle wax and the faint, gripping scent of Mia's pussy.

However, I don't move.

My little muse has been such a good sport, though reluctantly and only after I relentlessly pushed her buttons, so I'll give her the courtesy of a head start.

My gaze remains locked on the back door, where she ran to the back garden—or more like a mini jungle.

The candlelight casts an ominous shadow on the makeshift living area, subconsciously creating my favorite mood.

I bring up my fingers that are still sticky and lick them one by one.

Pussy as a concept has only ever served as a hole to be fucked. Despite the different colors and shapes of cunts I've seen in my lifetime, I've never relished touching them. Never gotten off on giving oral and have always made it a point that I'd only fuck. If they wanted something else, I was not the guy for it.

And yet, my lips are twitching for a taste of Mia's sweet little pussy. My blood definitely chose my cock as its preferred organ when I was toying with her just now.

Her little gasps still ring in my ears. Her widened eyes and parted lips will be masturbation material for a few days.

That is, if I don't trigger another more interesting reaction out of her. By the end of tonight, I will have done the devil's work in converting another soul to the dark side.

Though Mia has never been innocent and definitely scores high on the darkness scale. Let's just say I'm unleashing her full potential.

Sliding a hand in my pocket, I follow her trail. The back garden is like an unkempt jungle, with huge old trees, half-dead branches hanging like skeletons, and suspicious mushrooms lying around.

Pretty sure a few aimless ghosts fly overhead, moaning about having a subpar location and few to no visitors on a daily basis.

The moonlight plays hide-and-seek with the clouds and night owls scream in the distance, adding some DJing to the whole creepy vibe.

Four out of five. Would recommend it for satanic rituals.

I slip through the fallen branches and the broken trees that were probably brought down by malicious lightning. Murdered leaves crunch beneath my designer shoes and I don't make the effort to conceal the sound of my approaching steps.

The best way to smoke out a mouse? Scare her to fucking death.

I want to see the fear mixed with excitement on her delicate face. Just like a moment ago when she squirmed and gasped and soaked my fingers even when she was horrified about the prospect of being choked.

My cock is suggesting we try that again with him inside her cunt this time. I shelve that idea for later as I shove unruly branches out of the way.

To say I'm taking my time would be an understatement. However, I'm plotting, listening, and searching for any signs of my prey.

The lack of light might, at first glance, seem like a handicap, but it's far from it. Due to my vision's limited field, my ears prickle at the tiniest noise, and my hunter instinct kicks into full gear.

It's for that reason that I stop in the middle of the jungle of possessed trees and study my surroundings. Too dark.

Too hollow.

Too…creepy, by societal standards.

Even though I could sleep here and welcome demons to try and possess me, Mia wouldn't.

She slept with the lights on last night, and while I might have suspected that to be a one-off after my impromptu visit, her threatening me with bodily harm if I ever cut the lights off again means she was terrified at the prospect.

Not to mention, she didn't deny it when we spoke of the candles earlier.

Conclusion: She wouldn't wander this far, not even to throw me off.

I make a U-turn and run. This time, I silence my steps and control my breathing. I prefer the option of hunter, not the one being hunted, so it's imperative that she doesn't figure out my location when I'm not sure where she fucked off to.

I stop at the entrance of the back garden and sniff the air. Sure enough, there's a hint of her perfume—magnolia.

Two options come to mind. She hid in the corner of the garden and then went inside when I left.

Or two. She ran around like a headless chicken, then came back here.

At any rate, she has the option to retrieve her dress and run away from the property.

Sure enough, I catch a shadow leaning down near the coffee table, probably to pick up the dress. Most of the candles have died down, so it's hard to make out her profile.

"Is that you?" My low, whimsical whisper echoes through the old walls.

The shadow jolts and Mia abandons the dress and rushes to the stairs.

"Hide, little muse. If I find you, I'll swallow you whole." I follow after, taking the stairs two at a time. I can hear the creaking of the wood under her small frame.

Old houses are the best snitches that ever existed on the planet.

My smirk widens the closer my feet lead me to where she's scurrying around like a literal mouse.

Again, I give her a bit of a head start, igniting her hope that if she runs fast enough and gives in to the adrenaline, she'll be able to escape me.

Humans, by nature, can't live without the promise of hope, as false as it might get. It doesn't matter if the doomed reality of their situation hits them in the face. If they believe there's a light at the end of the tunnel, they'll go for it. Over and over again.

There's nothing worse than hope.

Hope is the medicine of all fools, which is why I make complete use of it in any possible situation.

The wood creaks under my weight as I make my way up. Judging by the noise, Mia is close to the top, at the second and final level that consists of an open bedroom.

There's a smaller third level that serves as an open roof, but it's half destroyed and the makeshift stairs that lead to it are partially gone.

Soon, the creaking stops. Only the amateur symphony of the owls filters through. There isn't even the faint sound of breathing that most humans can't conceal.

But Mia isn't just any human. She already sealed her voice and is probably able to suppress so much more.

"I know you're here." My voice drifts in the darkness. "Your hiding abilities are feeble at best and your running skills are categorically nonexistent."

I expect her to jump me and make her favorite threat about snipping my balls—or kicking them—a reality. Although she's a menace with the same boldness level as her brother, she's also, like him, easily provoked.

She does have some of Killian's characteristics as well. Which is probably why, contrary to the possibility I entertained, she doesn't show herself. She doesn't even make a peep or an indication of her location.

Smart little minx.

"Do you honestly believe your little attempt at hiding will succeed? I'm Landon King and you're nothing but prey, waiting to be eaten."

That should've done it, but no.

She's definitely not falling for my provocations.

This is both bothersome and, surprisingly, more gripping than I'd previously anticipated.

My eyes scan the area for a possible hideout. There's a closet, but considering her nyctophobia, she wouldn't go for something that terrifies her the most.

All the other options—under the bed, on the small balcony, and behind the half-torn curtains—come up empty.

My eyes narrow on the closet. She couldn't have possibly gone in there. Unless she's in the mood for a panic attack.

Just in case…

I move in that direction, but the moment I open it, a creaking noise comes from behind me. On the opposite side of the room.

Right on the broken stairs.

She can't possibly—

I run to the stairs and, sure enough, Mia has managed to climb through the available stair skeletons. She hid under them, waiting for me to be far enough away so that she could pull this stunt.

While I don't catch the whole climbing up process, I do see her lifting the weight of her entire body on a broken step.

Fuck me. Now that's an impressive athletic body.

She jumps up on the makeshift roof, rising to her full height, and stares down her nose at me and flashes me two middle fingers.

A fucking goddess under the full moon.

The silver light bathes her glistening naked skin and the generous slope of her breasts, highlighting the tips of her soft pink nipples.

The knickers and boots add an edge to the ethereal view.

I throw my head back in laughter. "I'm impressed."

She lifts her chin and holds the middle fingers higher. As if telling me she couldn't give a fuck about what I think of her.

I grab the stairs with both hands. "I am impressed, but you're not the only athletic one here."

Easily, probably as easily as she did, I lift my entire weight with my hands over the few available stairs.

Mia's expression turns from triumphant to frantic. Her eyes dart around as if she's looking for a certain weapon, but it's too late.

I'm already close to her.

As a last resort, she attempts to jam her boot against my face. I duck at the last second before she smashes my head in.

Knowing she has no reprieve from my imminent and very real chance of catching her, she abandons her position.

I jump up, a step breaks under my weight, and I land on the not-so-sturdy rooftop.

Mia runs to the only other available escape—the destroyed part of the roof.

My muscles burn from the effort I made, but the view that greets me is worth it.

Mia runs around, almost entirely naked, her breasts bouncing and her nipples hardening. My dick bulges and presses against my trousers with the need to touch.

"I advise you not to go any farther." I jam a hand in my pocket and walk toward her unhurriedly. I even stop to shake the dust off my previously-pressed trousers and shirt. "That part is as hazardous as a nuclear weapons field."

Does she listen?

Of course not.

She swings around all of a sudden and the floor gives out from underneath her. The creak of the wood echoes in the air and her shriek follows.

That's the first time I've heard a terrified sound come from her pretty lips. Then Mia slips and falls into a hole of her own making. The only thing keeping her from hitting the second floor is her elbows on either side of it.

I stand above her and grin. "Found you."

Thankfully, they haven't invented a murder weapon that can be triggered by a glare. Otherwise, I would've become cooked meat by now.

I offer her my hand.

She doesn't take it.

Instead, she attempts to lift herself up.

"Don't be suicidal." I jerk my chin in my hand's direction. "Take it."

She steals a glance at me, then, as if possessed by her stubborn demons, she tries to lift herself up again.

The floor shakes beneath me as the hole swallows her. I catch her extended hand at the last second and pull her out with all my strength.

We both tumble back, falling in a heap on the floor. So much for dusting off my clothes.

My hand flexes on Mia's back since I made sure she'd fall on top of me.

And they say I'm not a gentleman. The blasphemy.

Mia's chest rises and falls frantically above mine, like a war that's about to happen. I glide my hand across her back and to her side, then over the slope of her breast.

It's intoxicating to have her on top of me, naked, ready for my cock to plow inside her tight little cunt.

In fact, my cock is making non-subtle hints and bulges against the bottom of her stomach.

Mia lifts herself and hits my shoulder, then signs, "Stop groping me, you pervert."

"I'm just making sure you're not hurt anywhere. We can't be too careful when it concerns my little muse's health." I flick my finger on her nipple and she flinches.

Then she hits me across the chest.

One moment, she's on top of me, the next, I flip us so that she's underneath me. Her gasp echoes in the air, but it morphs into eerie silence when I settle between her legs.

I slap them apart, enjoying the sound of her groan as I lick the inside of her thigh, then bite. Hard. Until she squeezes me between her thighs.

I'm not done, though.

Far from it.

I rip off her panties and bask in the sight of her milky white skin that appears bluish under the midnight moon.

My first taste of her leaves her trembling and my cock begging for a go. So I do it again, running my tongue all the way to her clit. As I suspected, she's soaking wet. Maybe even more than before.

"Chasing kink. Check." I speak against her folds and she squirms, turning her head to the side, but she's not trying to push me or show me her favorite middle finger. "I'm sure going to have my hands full with you."

And then I feast on her pink little pussy. I swipe my tongue along her folds all the way to the slit, feeling her shudder.

As she trembles, I flick my tongue on her clit. Once. Twice. Then I suck and toy with the bundle of nerves.

Mia's back arches on the shambles of destruction. Only, there's no such thing as escaping me.

When her hips jerk, I thrust two fingers inside her. She coils and sinks her nails into my hair, then pulls hard enough to cause pain in my skull.

I'm not one to lose a challenge, though.

Still thrusting inside her, I expose her sensitive bud and nibble on the skin around it, then circle and flick my tongue.

Mia's hips jerk up and down as her gasps and moans mix and echo in the air.

It's the most beautiful sound I've ever heard.

And surprisingly, I want more.

So I up my rhythm until she's riding my face and drenching it with her sweet taste.

Best pussy I've had in…ever.

And that's a complication, because I don't get attached to pussy. Ever.

Not even an addictive one like Mia's.

I lick her through the orgasm as she shudders and hisses like a damn sex goddess.

When I lift my head, I make a show of licking my lips, but I don't feel the sense of triumph I set out for when I started this game.

And it's all because of the way she's watching me.

The innocence. The awe.

There's no hatred, glares, or middle fingers. As she props herself on her elbows, Mia looks at me as if I'm a god.

And while I could be in some obscure religions, I'm certainly not *her* god.

I'd crush her in no time.

I'd decimate her before she could take her next breath.

I let a smirk lift my lips. "You might want to wipe that look off your face or I'll be inclined to think you're falling in love with me."

She blinks once, then she narrows her eyes and flips me off.

Now, this is a territory I can play in. Whatever that look was has to be eradicated and not revived for a lifetime.

"I thought I told you what would happen if you flipped me off again." I grab her hand and then thrust that middle finger inside her with my own middle finger.

Poetic justice of sorts.

"You're going to come for me again and then you'll use this same energy to choke on my cock, little muse."

Once I'm done with Mia Sokolov, there will be no pieces left to pick up.

What a pity.

SEVENTEEN

Mia

HOPE IS THE WORST EMOTION TO EXPERIENCE WHEN THERE'S no light at the end of the tunnel.

You wait.

You pray.

You even try to delude yourself that it's not happening to you. That it just *can't* be you.

But that's the problem with hope.

The false positive. The feeling that the horrible situation can end any moment, when that's far from the truth.

It's the falsification of reality.

The yearning for a different dream.

A feeling of being on the cloud that can't be reached in real time.

Once again, I'm back in the pitch-darkness. Tendrils of black slither across my hands and feet, swallowing me deeper into the clutches of nothingness.

My lungs choke on the dying hope of ever seeing light again.

"Mom…Dad…" My haunted whisper echoes in the dark silence like an eerie lullaby.

My limbs tremble and my heart shrivels. Tears sting my eyes again and I sniffle as quietly as possible.

If I trigger the monster's wrath, he'll throw me against the wall and laugh at my loud crying.

He laughs when I say Mom and Dad will come to get me.

He laughs the hardest when he unleashes the weight of his wrath on me. When he kicks and throws me against the wall as if I'm the punching bag in our home gym.

Again and again.

And again.

Until I wish it would end already.

It doesn't, though.

The monster is here again, his fangs visible through his sardonic smile. His eyes are as dead as the boogeyman from Dad's bedtime stories.

I crouch further, eyes squeezed shut, and I cover my ears with my sweaty palms.

Don't touch me.

Please.

Daddy! Mommy! Help!

"You'll never escape me, you little rascal."

No!

I startle awake, sweat soaking my whole body and my hair sticking to my neck. My breathing comes in long, chopped inhales and my heart palpitates in my chest.

No, no, I can't be back there, I can't—

"Welcome back to the world of the living, sleepyhead."

My attention swings to the source of the voice, and it's none other than the second monster in my life.

The one who barged in without knocking or even announcing his presence.

Landon sits on the half-torn chair opposite me, working on a medium-sized statue. Only, it's not made of stone. Judging by the dark material that's seeping between his fingers like butter, he's using clay.

The scene slowly comes into focus. We're in the haunted house that could be used to scare misbehaving children. Some of the candles have gone out, and the remaining ones surround me as if I were the object of a satanic ritual.

Considering Landon's extremely unhinged nature, I wouldn't be surprised.

Earlier, he showed me a part of myself I didn't know existed. Yes, I suspected it, but I never dared to try it. And maybe, if the psycho hadn't forced me, I never would have.

All I know is that I enjoyed it more than I'd like to admit. I enjoyed it to the point that I'm completely ashamed.

But another part of me, the part that fell apart due to his rough touch and psychopathic tendencies, is still humming at the recent memory of his and my fingers inside me.

As if that wasn't crazy enough, Landon pushed me to the edge of the fragile stairs and fucked my throat. The fact that we could have fallen at any second did nothing to diminish the pure animalistic way he touched me.

In fact, the louder the wood creaked, the harder he thrust in and out of my mouth. It didn't matter that I'd already come twice, seeing Landon's lusty gaze under the moonlight made me hot and bothered again.

I can still smell him—a fatal combination of cedarwood and male musk.

After he came down my throat and made me swallow every drop, he helped me down the dangerous stairs. I should've gone down myself, but I was too lethargic to do anything.

It's probably why I must've fallen asleep after I put my dress back on. I remember thinking the sofa looked nice and mindlessly walking toward it.

Something must really be wrong with me, because I felt safe enough to fall asleep around the bastard.

A bastard who's the definition of a life hazard.

Said bastard is now half naked as he watches me from beneath his lashes with that smirk of je ne sais quoi and blows a cloud of smoke in the air. Smudges of clay cling to his muscular abs dusted with fine hairs that lead to a place I prefer not to think about.

It doesn't help that his pants hang low on his lithe hips, revealing the defined V-line and leaving practically nothing to the imagination.

I catch glimpses of snake tattoos slithering up his side, one of them is shaped into an infinity symbol, eating its own tail. It's an ouroboros, I realize—dark, striking, and gives off deadly vibes.

A third nipple would've been so nice, but no, the asshole had to be physical perfection.

His middle finger that's all gray with clay wraps around his belt's loop and pulls. "Want a closer look? My cock would certainly appreciate a second round. Maybe make the acquaintance with your cunt this time?"

My gaze snaps back to his sardonic face I suspect has never known what happiness looks like. And I don't mean his makeshift joy or the feeling of accomplishment that he fakes so well. But real happiness that the likes of him can probably never feel in this lifetime.

"Why are you half naked, pervert?" I sign.

"You were shivering."

I look down at myself and sure enough, I'm wearing his shirt and it has nothing to do with an action I've taken.

No wonder I've been smelling him on me. I chalked it up to earlier, but turns out, he's actually *on* me. Well, his shirt is.

"And they say chivalry is dead." He grins like a hedonistic lord. "You should thank your lucky stars for ending up with a well-mannered gentleman like yours truly."

"More like cursed stars."

"Don't be so negative. Life has brighter sides—namely me."

I physically roll my eyes, and I don't usually do that. "You're so full of yourself."

"For all the right reasons." He stubs his cigarette in the ashtray, letting it join a dozen others lying about, and motions at the coffee table where there's a takeout box. "Eat."

I lick my lips. "How did you know I was hungry?"

I didn't get to eat earlier because of this same bastard, so the sight of food makes my stomach growl.

"Because of that. Your stomach was making itself noticeable, even when you were slumbering away." He chuckles and I inhale deeply, but I smell him more than the food.

He's all around me, and even metaphorically inside me. It's a mismatch of colors and emotions that leaves me hopelessly chaotic. I'm unable to process anything when he's everything I see, hear, and breathe.

I can even taste his cologne on my tongue.

So I choose to focus on something I understand. Food.

It's Italian—my favorite. But it's not really that weird that he got it since most people love Italian.

I dig into my pasta without bothering to glance in his direction.

"Your manners must've left the building." His voice echoes around me like the Grim Reaper's favorite lullaby. "The least you can do is express gratitude for my thoughtful behavior."

I swallow the mouthful of pasta, put the fork down, and sign, "People who have thoughtful behavior don't expect gratitude."

"I do."

"Thank you."

A grin lifts his lips. "You're welcome, little muse."

"This doesn't negate the fact that you interrupted my actual dinner."

"It was totally worth it, and if you weren't drowning in absolute nonsense, you'd admit it as well."

I lift my hand to give him the middle finger and he raises a brow. "Just think about where that finger will be if you flip me off."

I snarl, because I know he absolutely delivers when it comes to threats, and choose to dive back into my pasta.

At least this makes sense.

He definitely doesn't.

Silence stretches in the living room, minus the sound of the fork against the cardboard plate. It's strange that he didn't grace me with one of his over-the-top mocking replies.

I chance a glance in his direction only to find him studying me so closely and coldly, I feel as if I'm being dissected by a mad scientist.

"What?" I sign after I gulp loudly.

"I was just thinking that you look edible in my shirt, possibly more than the food you're consuming. Want to consummate your push-pull relationship with my cock?"

"No."

"Doesn't hurt to ask." He lifts a nonchalant shoulder. "But mark my words, Mia. You'll welcome my cock in your tight little cunt, whether by choice or after we do another discovery journey of your kinks. One thing's for certain, though. He'll be your favorite flavor."

I really can't believe him.

He could easily bag an award for the most arrogant and impossibly unbearable man.

"What about your kinks?" I ask in an attempt to turn the tables on him.

He uses a tool to sculpt the face of the clay statue, his movements smooth and elegant. The discarded pieces fall on the floor, forgotten and without purpose, probably like everyone in Landon's life.

"What about them?" he asks.

"What are they?"

"My, muse. I know you like me, but you might want to tone it down a bit. Here's a tip, don't be obvious."

"Here's a tip. Don't be ridiculous. I asked you about your kinks just like you asked about mine."

"That's the thing. I didn't ask for your kinks, I took you on a discovery journey. You're welcome, by the way. There's only one fair way to tell you about my kinks." His lips curl in a sardonic smile. "Demonstrate them."

"No, thanks."

"You sure? Mine are a lot more colorful and fun."

My lips part. He got hard as he chased me earlier; I felt it, and he didn't attempt to hide it, so that means he enjoyed that. The whole scene was already too far out of my comfort zone. What could he possibly mean by *more colorful*?

But then again, why am I interested?

The 'like what?' question lingers on the tip of my tongue, but I swallow it back down and focus on the food that I've been pushing around on the plate.

"Not interested," I sign.

Landon abandons his statue and I stiffen as he walks toward me. Or more like waltzes, like a large cat who appears lazy but would snap you in half if given the chance. As he approaches, I notice a scar at the bottom of his stomach. I wonder what happened to cause that then curse myself for being interested.

It was so easy to just hate him to death a few weeks ago, but that's, unfortunately, not the only feeling I have anymore.

After he destroyed my defenses and stomped over my limits, there are other morbid feelings lurking through me. I don't understand most of them, but I definitely recognize the curiosity and the need for more.

Not to mention that I have to spy on this bastard for a long time if I want to gather anything about him.

My fingers tighten on the fork as he approaches. The light of the candles casts ominous shadows over his ethereal face.

His abs flex with every step, adding another edge to his cutthroat presence.

He stops in front of me and chucks me under the chin, then lifts it with a thumb and a forefinger. "Too bad you don't get to decide, little muse. I'll enjoy every second of discovering all of your kinks. Don't try to run, you know exactly how much I enjoy the chase."

I've fallen deep into a version of myself I don't recognize.

It's been two weeks since the day Landon unleashed a side of me whose existence I never imagined the magnitude of.

Since then, he's shown me exactly how far I can go. How much I can do. How hard I can take it.

He started by threatening to show up while I'm with Maya or Niko, then he kidnaps me to the haunted house. So lately, I just text him that I'll be there, which is usually met by Landon's over-the-top gloating response.

You like me even more, don't you?

Are you that excited about reuniting with my mouth and fingers?

My cock got in touch recently and he'd like to have a go. If you'd leave the prude nun act at home, that would be great.

Every time, he hints or tries to go further, but I either shove him, punch him, or simply say no.

Surprisingly, Landon doesn't push after that.

He's fine with the word no. He doesn't get threatened or provoked by it. He's definitely toxic and has red flags galore, but while he toys with the line of consent, he never crosses it.

He does like to play with me, though. He likes to chase me and see how far I'll go into the cursed forest. I've been getting farther every day, despite the darkness. It has to do with the fact that I know he's right behind me.

After all, only a monster can crush another monster.

We sometimes wrestle and I hit him. He doesn't hit me back for some reason, but he does trap me beneath him, disable my movements and show me that his power will always be superior to mine, and if he chooses to, he could easily smash me to smithereens.

He loves playing with me, baiting me, making me think I'll win (whether in chase or chess), then he pulls the carpet from beneath my feet with a sardonic smirk on his face.

It's insane how intense the pleasure he gives me is and how it keeps getting worse, not better. I'm scared that one of these days, my heart will jump out of my chest or completely give out on me.

Still, I love the lustful, glorious look on his face when I wrap my lips around his cock and suck the life out of him. I'm a fast learner and have been training my gag reflex so that I can take him as far as possible. The more I make the effort, the harder he comes down my throat or decorates my face.

But most importantly, after we're done, he wraps me in his shirt, hoodie, or jacket and buys me food, namely Italian and Turkish since he discovered they're my favorites. He likes to sculpt while I'm munching on my food or working on my new mini garden opposite his art studio.

Landon is definitely a sight to behold when he's working on art. A heart-stopping image no one could look away from—least of all, me.

The other day, after I was spent from wrestling with the asshole just so I'd lose and suck him off, he got out a brush and used a water-color—blue, like my favorite color—to paint all over my face.

Then he stared at me for over a minute and nodded to himself.

He went to sketch something in his notebook, so I looked at the mirror and was horrified beyond measure. It looked like the kind of lines someone would make on the face of a patient for reconstructive surgery.

But then again, I shouldn't be surprised anymore about anything that's related to Landon. The more time I spend with him, the more I realize he truly is a narcissistic sadist and an insatiable anarchist.

I haven't been able to get more information about the Elites, because we often meet here and he's not the type to be milked unless his dick is involved.

Jeremy, who's in a 'we'll murder Landon' phase, told me he's up to something, but I can't figure out what exactly that something is.

So, my other option is going into the lion's den.

Yes, I've been in the Elites' mansion before, but only for Bran, and aside from doing some thorough research to pull off that blood bath episode, I didn't snoop much when it came to Landon.

Time to change that.

So here's the thing. My plan is fairly simple, but it requires a certain level of cunning behavior—without my actually looking the part.

I got Bran to invite me over—*sorry for using your good hospitality so shamelessly, Bran*—and we spent the last hour playing, but I said that I need to use the bathroom.

Obviously, that's a blatant lie.

Because I'm heading to Landon's room.

Snooping much? Absolutely. This is the only chance I'll have since his studio is locked with his thumbprint and I'm not in the mood for dismemberment today—might change my mind the moment I see him, though.

Apparently, there's a spare key for the studio somewhere, but neither Remi nor Bran is willing to disclose that information. Besides, I don't think there's anything different in his home studio compared to the haunted house one.

He probably doesn't like having others look at his creations before

he's done with them, which is why he has all those half-finished statues in an unsuspecting place.

He didn't seem to mind when I watched him, though. So who
knows? Maybe, like with everything else, it's up to his ever-changing
mood.

At any rate, this is the perfect place to launch an investigation.
Figuring out which one is Landon's room is easy. The other day when
I came over, Bran said he'd pick up something from upstairs and I
followed. As we were passing by, he pointed at this room, "Stay away
from that one. It's where the evil twin hibernates before plotting everyone's demise."

Apparently, I'm blind to red flags, because I slip inside and slowly
close the door behind me.

Landon's room is as meticulous as his haunted house art studio.
There's an air of great detail put into the positioning of the furniture
and the elegant masculine color scheme.

One corner is occupied by a tall platform bed with a leather head-
board that's as black as his soul. In the center, there's a matching sofa
and two elegant standing lamps.

What catches my attention, however, is the desk in another corner topped by a few books.

I tiptoe in its direction and read the titles of books mostly written by artists and professionals in the sculpting scene.

Out of the corner of my eye, I spot a notepad. After casting a
fleeting glance on either side of me, I open it.

The pictures that greet me rob my lungs of their last breaths.

3D statues lie in front of me, glorious in their details and absolutely stunning in their elegant disposal.

One pattern that exists throughout the notepad strikes me.

None of them have faces.

Some are half finished like the statues in the haunted house, as if
he couldn't find the right image to draw, but most of them have been
left blank.

As I go farther, I notice a few silhouettes of absolute chaos—intertwined circles, crossed lines, and meaningless figures.

The stark difference between these objects and the perfect statues is so jarring that I double- and triple-check them. It's impossible to believe both were made by the same person.

Maybe he was in a different state of mind when he sketched these.

I run my fingers over the intertwined lines. What was he thinking of when he drew these? Usually, he's focused to a fault during the creation process—posture erect, eyes like a hawk, and lips slightly parted.

Art mode looks brutally elegant on him.

I have no idea why I want to see him when he's making these loops of nothingness. Maybe it's because this is the first time I've noticed a break in his perfectly perfect façade.

Landon can get petty, antagonist, and absolutely insufferable, but I've never actually seen him angry. Maybe he doesn't even know what anger is.

Movement comes from behind the door and I return the notebook to where I found it and frantically search the room for a place to hide.

Shoot. None of the furniture is able to camouflage me.

The door opens and I jump behind the tall curtains and catch my breath. The balcony door behind me is open and the chill seeps into my bones.

Footsteps shuffle into the room, and I don't have to guess. It's Landon. I couldn't mistake him for anyone else when my lungs are filled with his delicious smell.

Other footsteps follow. "You haven't been around."

A feminine voice.

And it's not Ava's, Cecily's, or his sister Glyn's. I've heard all their voices and they don't sound snotty like this one.

"Didn't feel the need to be around," Landon replies in his signature sarcastic, bored voice.

"You can't do this. We agreed about our next hit."

I notice that I've been balling my hands into fists ever since I heard the girl's voice and slowly release them.

I need to be calm. After all, this is my chance to do what I came here for—spy on the asshole.

"Our next what?"

"We agreed we'd slash their tires this weekend."

"We did?"

"Yes! Everyone is waiting for their orders. We need to sit down and plan this thoroughly."

"Ever heard of free will, Nila? It's a curious, liberating feeling that you should engage in sometime."

"Don't even think about pushing me to the sidelines again, Lan. You don't want to cross me."

"Already have, countless times, including when you were begging for it on your knees."

My face heats and my fists ball again until my nails dig into my palms.

"Is that what you want?" Her words come out as a purr. "Me on my knees?"

"Not particularity, but if you're in the mood to bow down to me, by all means. Don't let me stop you."

My foot falls back and I slip behind the open door and onto the balcony. My steps are silent and careful despite the red-hot fire that blows through me.

I have to leave, because if I stay, I'll definitely jump in the middle of the room and punch them both in the face.

It's me who I should punch. Why have I thought that I'm the only one he plays with for sport?

Of course he has side pieces like Nila to tend to his stupid kinks all day, every day.

I breathe heavily as I climb over the railing of the balcony and jump to the next one—Brandon's.

Another factor that I forgot about in my attempts to spy on his psycho brother.

I have to make an excuse to Bran and leave, because if I see Landon again, I might accidentally kill him.

And I don't like these strong emotions I have because of the bastard.

More importantly, I want my chest to stop aching.

EIGHTEEN

Landon

I'M DREADFULLY, EXCEPTIONALLY, AND CATEGORICALLY BORED out of my fucking mind.

It's no secret that I'm prone to lose interest in all objects, people, and concepts. The world, by definition, is a dull place that's shackled by economic and political expectations and run by societal standards. Once I perfected the art of fitting in, existence turned into splashes of black on gray.

Sometimes, the gray is more prominent and I thrive on the prospect of injecting chaos into the world's bloodstream.

Other times, like now, black ink dots overflow from my brain cells and invade every inch of my sporadic, hazardous existence.

The party blares in full swing around me, doing a fantastic emulation of a world I don't belong to by any stretch of the imagination. Ironically, I reign over it.

Loud music shrieks from the speakers, bathing our mansion in tacky, mindless mayhem. Students from REU jump and move to the beat like drunken ants. Despite the designer clothes and the stench of old money, they all blur into one tedious existence.

Once upon a time, when I was young and senseless, I wondered why I couldn't be bothered to fake joy or pretend like I gave two fucks about people.

Turns out, I actually don't, and that allows me to make use of their miserable emotions. The world would be much better with fewer people getting in touch with their feelings.

Just saying.

The members of the Elites, whose names I couldn't be bothered to remember, sit on the sofas on either side of me or join the crowd.

We have our signature Venetian masquerade masks on, which my members use like a get-out-of-jail-free card.

Nila and her imaginary rival, Bethany, have been hanging on either of my arms, begging for my nonexistent attention.

Rory has been glaring at me from beneath his half-mask for the past hour as if I suffocated his nana with a pillow. Fact is, I merely told him that if he doesn't stop getting high and sabotaging my work, I'll discard him faster than a used condom.

He said he's trying to quit, but apparently, not hard enough, judging by his bloodshot eyes. Truth is, I score high on the apathy scale and can't be arsed about his addiction habits. I just despise wiping up after anyone's mess.

Nila brushes her half-naked tits against my arm and Bethany does the same. They're starting to piss me off, or more like, I've been pissed off since they each took an arm.

I refuse the mere notion that this black state of mind has anything to do with a certain muse. It's been exactly four days since I last saw her—three if we count the day she snooped into my room and ran away like her tiny arse was on fire.

Mia's been doing a spectacular job of avoiding my vicinity. It's a whole ritual that started with ignoring my texts and ended with avoiding our cocoon of mayhem.

She also hasn't met up with Bran and, instead, has been making a point of being surrounded by Jeremy, Nikolai, and Killian—often at the same time. And while I'm open to suicidal missions, I can't exactly hate-fuck her when I'm nursing broken limbs.

Seems that I underestimated Mia's ability to play dirty. She's anything but docile, which is my cock's flavor of fucked up, but it's difficult to tame the wild-horse spirit that's hidden behind cute ribbons and fake smiles.

But then again, I've never shied away from a challenge.

I pull out my phone for the third time in the span of five minutes and stare at the texts she hasn't graced with a reply.

Running late tonight?

I'm not the punctuality police, but you're over an hour late. My cock is developing a serious case of blue balls that can be easily fixed with your pretty little lips.

If you weren't coming, you could've sent a text. Your manners are 404 not found.

Then the next day.

Are you in the mood to witness blood spilling on your edgy boots? Because I don't mind some petty knife crime with your Heathens.

Your ghosting efforts are proving to be both vexing and irritating. Believe me, you don't want to push me. Come over tonight and I won't hurt you.

Okay, I lied. I won't hurt you much while I punish you for the insolence.

She didn't show up. Not that night or the one after or the one after. My string of threatening texts went completely unanswered as if she couldn't dignify me with a reply.

So I referred to my second preferred method of gathering information, also known in pop culture as stalking.

These days, she's been posting pictures with her gang for the day. Today—as in, an hour ago—she posted a selfie, where Jeremy is in the background, leaning against a sofa and watching TV.

Mia is pouting at the camera, face leaning against her fist and her other hand pulling at a blue ribbon.

The caption is *Bored.*

My fingers tighten around my phone and I glare at Jeremy in the background. She's been spending more time with him than necessary lately—the necessary amount is zero.

She's vindictive, yes, but I'm not sure if she's petty enough to try and provoke me with Jeremy's constant presence around her.

Who am I kidding? Of course she is.

She possesses the hotheadedness of a bull on crack.

Seems I have to take matters into my own hands.

I send her a text she can't ignore.

Landon: You didn't only make the mistake of ignoring me, but you also went the very wrong way about it. Challenge accepted, little muse. If I have to effectively and personally wipe out your newest boy toy, that's exactly what I'll do.

Half an hour later, I physically check myself out of the party and drive to an unassuming place no one would think fits my plan.

In reality, everyone and everything does. Like a chess piece on my board.

Mia included.

She just doesn't know it yet.

The only difference is that I'm alarmingly relying on her presence to create or, more accurately, finish the failures that didn't make the cut. Before she came along, I used to shape this convincing façade that I was able to sculpt at will. Unquestionably, I made some stunning pieces of art, but I often found them underwhelming, like getting to a physical climax, but the mental side doesn't live up to the intensity.

Ever since Mia's ghosting, I've spent time in the studio staring at the miniatures I've made or the statues I've finished since she came along. I've created unquestionable masterpieces that I'm too possessive to show to the world. Not even Mum, who's been my number one art guide and cheerleader wrapped in one.

The process is even weirder since I made those while she was slumbering, watering—and talking to—plants, or eating like a weirdly adorable food monster.

At this point, it's veering dangerously close to an unhealthy addiction and I don't allow those. Even smoking is an indulgence I can quit if I choose to. In fact, I've been cutting down on the cancer sticks lately.

Mia needs to be like cigarettes. Something I revel in but

can discard when I'm bored. And I *will* be bored. It's a fact, not a speculation.

After I park my McLaren in plain sight for anyone passing by to see, I stroll through the animal shelter's door.

It's late o'clock even for people who worship at animals' feet, but that doesn't seem to deter our resident Goody Two-shoes from coming here at this ungodly hour of the night. It smells rotten, just saying.

Some cats hiss at me as I pass by. Dogs growl, but I glare at them and they hide behind their tiny cages.

It's no secret that Bran is the twin who's a lover of all things animals and sunshine. I never cared for these creatures. Humans are enough of a headache as it is.

Besides, I can't really use animals if they're incapable of being manipulated, now, can I? Unlike popular psychological bollocks, however, I've also never considered hurting them like wannabe psychopaths.

Only mentally weak psychos with mummy issues hurt helpless beings, and I refuse to be lumped in the same category as the idiots.

I barge straight to the storage room, where Mother Teresa—sorry, I mean *Cecily*—is organizing pet food on the metallic shelves. Her silver hair is held in a messy chignon, making her look like a wise figure.

Leisurely, I remove my mask, casually hold it in my hand, and clear my throat.

Cecily glances in my direction with a slight jump, then pushes one sack of food in place. "What are you doing here?"

I stroll inside, taking my time and basking in the plain surroundings. "I'm wounded in my little heart. No hi, how are you?"

"I don't think you came here for any *his* or *how are yous*. I'm surprised you even know this place exists."

I park myself against the shelf beside her and summon Mia's dramatic pout. "You've become so cold, Cecy."

"Doesn't feel good to be treated the way you treat people, does it?"

This, of course, is because she helped me, though indirectly, to set off the Heathens' mansion like fireworks. Apparently, Cecily isn't a fan of how I used the information she freely provided.

"Aww, you still mad about that other time? That happened centuries ago in human years."

"You might be able to hurt others and forget about it, but that's not me, Lan."

"They allowed themselves to be hurt. Who am I not to indulge them?"

"You're impossible, and there's no reasoning with you." She heaves out a sigh. "I honestly don't know what I liked about you."

I grin. "Oh? Is this a confession?"

"No, this is me calling myself daft. I think I liked the idea of you, but when I got close, I realized you're like your statues. Gorgeous on the outside." She taps my chest. "Empty on the inside."

"Did you say *gorgeous*?"

"Just leave, Lan. I have some work to finish up."

"Not so fast." I step in front of her, blocking her exit. "See, I know you swapped me for Jeremy, and while I'm wounded in my little black heart, I let it happen because you can help me bring him down."

"You...knew?"

"About your feelings for me? You couldn't have been more obvious, Ces."

"Why didn't you say anything?"

"You didn't; why would I? Besides, it was only a phase, no? Because you somehow got on Jeremy's radar and you grew to like it. I rooted for you. I even encouraged it. In that fight, I noticed he was looking at you and I wanted to test him, so I said, 'How does it feel to fancy someone who loves me?' Kind of got beaten up for it, but confirming he has feelings for you was worth it. The mighty Jeremy in *luuurve*. Isn't that poetic?"

A gasp falls from her lips.

That's it, Cecily. Get the fucker back and leave a certain muse with no other choice but me.

And, yes, I knew about Cecily and Jeremy's unorthodox relationship for a long time, which is why, during an underground fight, when I got the chance to push Jeremy's buttons, I went for it in spectacular fashion and succeeded with flying colors.

My childhood friend slowly regains her composure and looks at me as if I'm a cardboard cutout of a human—which isn't entirely wrong. "I don't love you. I never did."

"That's what he thought, though." My grin widens. "Sorry, I mean *thinks.*"

"Doesn't matter." She pushes past me, choosing to focus on the boring task of organizing shelves. "We're no longer together, and even if we were, I would never help you hurt him."

"Are you sure? Because he has a blonde bombshell hanging on his arm and pasting herself to his side like superglue. There's her mute clone, too. The Sokolov sisters are vying for his attention, and if you don't do something about it, one of them will have him."

She stiffens, but soon, her shoulders drop. "He can do whatever he wants. And don't call her a mute. That's not nice."

"I'm not nice."

"Shocker." Cecily rolls her eyes. "Also, Mia is only around to watch her sister. She didn't look to be interested in Jeremy."

"Or that's what she wants you to think while she slithers around him like a snake."

Maya is flirtatious by nature. Mia wouldn't know how to flirt even if she took a lesson in the art. Despite her attitude and extensive kink flavor, she's actually closed off and a bit clueless. So the fact that she's purposefully spending more time with Jeremy is a red flag in every dictionary.

"Point is, get Jeremy back. This is the last courtesy I'll offer you before I slice his throat open and sculpt him into the ugliest stone."

"I'm not helping you, Lan."

"I don't want you to help me. Just take him off the market."

She pauses and cocks her head to the side, mimicking an arrogant shit she definitely is not. "Oh. I get it. Is this about Maya? Maybe Mia? Both?"

"Don't worry your pretty little head about that and just resume whatever weird thing you had with Jeremy."

Her shoulders droop and she sighs like an old lady who's gone through both world wars. "I can't."

"Why not?"

"He's not interested in me anymore."

I look at her intently. Is this a distasteful joke? People, my friends included, are a fucking headache. Seriously, what would everyone do without me in their lives?

"Not interested in you? On what planet have you been living, Cecily? The guy stalks you like a creep and actually smiles while he does it—honest to fucking God thought he didn't know how. He's also developed some bizarre fetish about removing anyone who poses an obstacle to you. That teacher who was giving preferential treatment to his friend's kid? Jeremy was the reason he asked to transfer. Those American football players who stole and slashed your textbooks? Jeremy eliminated them. Those guys at the club who danced with you? Jeremy beat them the fuck up and put one in a coma. Oh, and news fucking flash, he tortured Jonah to near death by waterboarding him and threatened to kill his parents, brothers, sisters, and everyone he cared about. Then he proceeded to tell his family about all the scandals he could get them into by airing some of their dirty laundry. That's the only reason Jonah turned himself in. He still gets beaten up in prison every day because Jeremy and his whole fucked-up entourage have the ability to pay off people who can do it. Inside England's prisons, which should be far away from their territory, but isn't. You still think that's not called interest?"

Cecily's mouth hangs open for several beats before she sobers up. "How do you know all of that?"

"I have someone who follows him, just like he has someone who's following me."

"Following you?"

"Yeah. You think he knows by now that I'm here?"

Panic slithers in her light eyes like a highly contagious disease. "Lan, whatever you're planning, stop it."

"I need you with him, Ces. I'm not asking." I slide my fingers on her cheek and time my reaching down to the moment I sense movement behind us.

In a pure emulation of a caricature, I'm shoved off Cecily with a force that I could fight but choose not to.

Jeremy punches me in the face. I let myself fall to the ground when I spot a very tiny and very familiar boot. Mia stares down at me like she did that day on the ruined roof, her eyes resembling fractured midnight rain and crushed nightmares.

My own fucking fallen angel.

She lifts her boot and kicks me in the balls.

I grunt, suppress a smile, then roll onto my back. My lip has doubled in size and I can taste metal, but I still grin.

"Hi, mouse. Miss me?"

She glares harder, as if I'm at the top of her murder list, and flips me off—which will get her fucked like a dirty whore in a few. Then she signs to Jeremy, who's grabbing Cecily's elbow and staking a claim I couldn't give two flying fucks about.

"He's all mine. Don't interfere or tell Nikolai or get in touch. I'll deal with him on my own as we agreed." Mia places a hand on her hip when she's finished, her face and body emanating more attitude than should be allowed.

"He's all yours," Jeremy says.

"Oh?" I jump up and secure the mask around my neck. "I'm going to have to decline whatever deal you two have." I snatch my childhood friend's other hand. "Cecy and I have a date."

I stare at Mia, who's flat-out aiming metaphorical lasers at where I'm holding Cecily.

Should've thought of my retaliation before the ghosting galore, muse.

"The only date you'll have is for a funeral." Jeremy pulls Cecily and I release her so that she lands against him. I'm such a good cupid and should be rewarded for the effort.

"Necrophilia. Yum." I lick my lips at Mia.

She lifts her leg, no doubt to annihilate the family jewels once and for all, but this time, I shove a hand against her forehead, stopping her advance. "Jesus fucking Christ, calm down, and stop acting like a rabid dog."

As expected from the spitfire, she kicks, punches, and tries to shove against me, but all of it mostly ends in the air. I easily block her and offer Jeremy my most provocative grin. "Let go of Cecily."

"No."

My friend wrenches herself free. "You have no right to touch me."

They glare at each other in a ridiculous play of hard-to-get. But it's no worse than Mia who's still trying to kick me while signing that she'll kill me.

"What she said." I tsk. "How does it feel to be the second choice to me? In fact, you wouldn't have even been on her list if you hadn't stalked her."

Jeremy storms toward me with all his demons carrying machine guns. Provocation success rate? One hundred percent.

Cecily jumps between us, her back to me as she stares at her nemesis, who ironically happens to be the man she's in love with. "Stop it."

"Step away."

"I said stop it."

"And I said to step the fuck away."

Time to let them do their thing. This carefully concocted plan could grant me a seat in the UN if I ever think highly of world peace as a career choice.

"We're out of here." I drag Mia by the arm as she struggles, elbows, and uses every trick under the sun to release herself from my grip. And while I contain her crazy, I can't resist throwing over my shoulder, "Remember, Ces. You loved me first."

Jeremy strides toward me, but Cecily stops him again.

Soon enough, Mia and I are outside. She kicks up the aggressiveness a notch and tries to kick my knee.

I swing her tiny body and shove her against the wall under a faint streetlamp. The light casts a soft glow on her petite face and adds a subtle shine to her blonde tresses intertwined with blue ribbons.

Her dress is short, exposing her slender long legs, and I like to think she dressed up for me. It doesn't help that it's been longer than I prefer since she's graced me with her infuriating presence.

My fingers dig into her shoulder. "Calm the fuck down. What's got your knickers in a twist?"

"You." She points at me, her eyes blazing a darker blue like the color of murdered roses. "Go to hell, you fucking bastard."

"Only if you come along. I'd appreciate the company."

Her murderous state only seems to rage further as red splashes her cheeks. "What the hell do you think you're doing? Why were you trying to kiss Cecily?"

"Aww, jealous, are we?"

"More like I don't want to see Jeremy hurt."

"Your dear Jeremy loves Cecily, so unless you're in the mood to become a third and very unwanted wheel, I'd suggest you give up." I jam my knee between her legs. "Besides, I can keep you satisfied."

She lifts her chin. "One cock isn't enough, I'm afraid. I like variety."

Now, it's my mood that takes a sharp dive to a black inky well of nothingness, even worse than when I saw her selfie with him. "What the fuck did you just say?"

"You understood me just fine." She pushes me away. "Now, if you'll excuse me, I'll go find some fun for the night."

"Don't turn your back on me, Mia. You know perfectly well what I'll do if you run."

She flips her hair and flips me off.

A sadistic grin lifts my lips.

Mia will run, and not only will I catch her, but I'll also fuck her until she can't move.

Until she understands there's no other cock that'll be inside her but mine.

NINETEEN

Mia

THE ASSHOLE IS OUT FOR BLOOD.

There's no other civil way to describe whatever the hell is going on in the psycho's head.

He's the most unpredictable, lethal person I've ever come across, and that might or might not include the monster from my past.

And this is coming from me, who was literally raised within the New York Russian mafia.

Landon is downright insane, but I'm not entirely sane either, because I'm baiting him. I'm flaunting my tail in the same provocative language he speaks, waiting—no, *needing* him to come after me.

Chase me.

Inject my veins with that shot of ecstasy only he can provide.

I drive at full speed down the empty streets. Lights blur in my peripheral vision, adding a mystic vibe to the dangerous night. For more reasons than one.

My nostrils flare at the image of Landon attempting to kiss Cecily.

We have a date. That's what he said, even though he doesn't do those, even if he were held at gunpoint. He prefers the thrill of the unknown, the intensity, and sexual preferences that are socially frowned upon.

He's all about the carnal and never about the emotions.

But then again, Cecily is soft and posh. His childhood friend, no less. He probably wouldn't touch her crudely and whisper filthy words as he fucked her mouth.

He wouldn't strip her down and build her back up again just so he could do it all over again.

A black car appears in my rearview mirror, looking larger than a vengeful crow.

I hit the accelerator as hard as possible, but while I love my Mercedes SUV, it doesn't compare to the power of a sports McLaren.

Landon catches up to me in seconds and slows to my speed as he drives parallel to me. We're definitely *not* on a one-way road.

I look at him with a "What the fuck are you doing?" gaze.

"Chasing you, muse." His grin could only belong to Satan himself.

I release the accelerator, letting myself fall behind, but he does the same, so I hit it again and speed up all of a sudden until my body glues to the seat.

Once again, Landon keeps my pace, still smirking with unmasked sadism. I've come to recognize that look as savage lust. It's the look he sports whenever he chases me or chokes me to within an inch of my life.

My thighs clench, and I blame it on muscle memory. It can't be anything else. I refuse to believe it is.

Headlights flash on the other side of the road, as in, the side that Landon shouldn't be driving on.

I glance at him.

Move.

Go.

"Move!" I sign with one hand.

He doesn't.

What the hell? Is he really planning to kill himself?

"The ball's in your court."

"What?" I sign with one hand.

"My decision will depend on where you drive. Here's a hint, go to where you were supposed to be yesterday!" he shouts over the blaring honks of the other car.

I do the "Okay" sign with a trembling finger. Right in the nick of time, he hits the brakes and swerves back behind me.

My forehead and back break out in a sweat, my fingers shake on the steering wheel, and my foot is unsteady on the brakes as I lower my speed.

I can't for the life of me drive normally when my whole body is in a state of shock, but I do the best I can, and Landon follows me, not attempting to overtake me or ride beside me.

As soon as I arrive in front of the haunted house, I'm surprised by the lights illuminating the hideous garden with snake-like leaves and ghost trees that have fallen to their imminent death. But then I catch a glimpse of my newly planted flower beds, still alive and slowly growing compared to the last time I saw them.

They're the only thing I missed about this place.

Or are they?

I step out of the car on shaky legs. Landon takes his time to climb out of his stupid McLaren, his demeanor detached at best.

I get in his face and sign wildly, "What the hell did you think you were doing?"

"Bringing you back where you belong." He slowly and leisurely removes the mask from around his neck and slides his fingers across the golden decoration. "We wouldn't have gotten to this stage if you weren't playing a pointless episode of cat and mouse."

I shove at his chest with all my might. "My choice to come here or not is mine, not yours or anyone else's."

Strong fingers wrap around my elbow and he tugs so that I fall against his chiseled chest muscles. "Your choice ended the moment you walked into my life. Your thoughts, your temper, and the very marrow of your existence belong to me now."

I shake my head vehemently.

"Denying the truth doesn't make it any less viable. I advise you to get used to my role in your life, because it won't disappear any-time soon."

I punch him across the chest. A rumble rips from deep within him and he imprisons my hand, then crushes it so the fist is flattened against his pectoral muscle.

"Don't. Your adorable fight turns me on, and that's not a wise idea when I'm already bursting with unfulfilled energy." He releases me and steps back. "Now, do as you promised. Run."

"Go chase one of your other girls," I sign with more energy than needed. "I'm too special to be lumped in with your side pieces."

There, I said it.

Finally. The words I've been thinking about for days are out in the open. The ache I felt when I overheard him with that Nila. The absolute rage and pain I experienced when I saw him on the verge of kissing Cecily.

I wasn't even supposed to be there, but one of Jeremy's men called and told him that Landon was with Cecily. Jeremy had this terrifying expression when he left. My anger must've matched his when I hopped in my car and followed along.

An inexplicable urge flows through me. A rush that's impossible to shake off or ignore.

And it goes by the name of Landon freaking King.

It doesn't matter that I've been avoiding him. I've been thinking about him and his texts and his damn presence every second.

This is what it feels like to be addicted, doesn't it?

But no matter how attracted I am to the slimy bastard, I'd cut off my own legs before I'd let him step all over me.

"Side piece?" He approaches me, his eyes darkening to the color of ravens and crows and expelling the same ominous energy.

He stops in front of me and lifts my chin with his curled forefinger. "I can sleep with anyone on this planet. Hell, I have an extensive repertoire of women begging to suck my cock if I were to so much as look in their direction. But I don't even acknowledge their existence. These lips are the only lips I want to be wrapped around my cock. This face is the only face I want to be marked with my cum. You think I would put all this effort into someone as difficult as you if you were only a side piece?"

"You won't touch anyone but me." Not a question, but a demand.

And yet he answers, "I won't."

Simply. Without any of his infuriating conditions, bets, or ultimatums.

"You won't touch anyone but me either, or we'll have a very serious, very bloody problem."

"Stop being so psychotic."

"Stop being so cute."

My mouth falls open and the skin he touches explodes in a thousand tingles. I sink my teeth into the cushion of my bottom lip in a hopeless attempt to control my reaction.

His weird acceptance of the situation is enough to wash away the doubts I've been drowning in for the past few days.

It's enough to fill my muscles with a foreign need. A need so empowering, it hums beneath the flesh.

Landon leans forward and whispers in dark words against the shell of my ear, "Run, little muse and run as fast you can. Tonight, I'll fuck all the other cocks out of your memory."

He doesn't need to tell me twice.

The moment he releases me, I speed inside the house. Despite it being dimly lit, some yellow bulbs cast shadows on the worn-out sofa, the chairs, and the unfinished chess game we were playing the last time I was here.

Landon's steps ring right behind me, sure and unhurried, as if he knows he will catch me. I quicken my movements and rush to the highest floor. I hop on one of the ruined steps, but a strong grip catches my ankle.

I gasp as I stare behind me.

Landon looks like a devil in the darkness, complete with imaginary horns and a hellfire agenda. "The same trick won't work twice."

I try to kick him away, but he tugs me down so hard, I yelp as the world is pulled from underneath me. Before I hit the ground, Landon reaches for my waist, but I slip past his grip and hop away at the last second.

I run down the hall at full speed. Landon's heavy steps follow me in no time. My heart races and my temperature rises until I'm delirious.

A startled sound leaves my lips when I hear his breathing, but I don't look back.

Excitement and thrill intertwine and grab me by the throat. Every fiber inside me hums to life the faster I run and the longer I hear the creak of his steps behind me.

I descend the stairs three at a time and skip a few, then hold on to the railing when I nearly fall. I slip into his art studio and hide behind one of his unfinished statues. He stands in front of it.

Our chests rise and fall in a frantic rhythm, but while I'm struggling for breath, Landon has a hand in his pocket.

"Give up, little muse. Your cunt is mine to fuck. Mine to own. The sooner you accept that reality, the better."

In a flash, I make for the right, then change direction to the left. Landon does the exact same. I release a gleeful sound as he catches a few of my ribbons, pulling them free from my hair.

The statue rattles on its base as I push past it and run to the balcony attached to the studio. I realize my mistake the moment the floor creaks beneath my boots.

I'm trapped.

I turn around to escape in the opposite direction, but Landon's already blocking the entrance.

He grabs the top chipped frame of the balcony door. His shirt rides up, revealing a hint of his hard abs and the fine hairs perfectly positioned in the middle of his glorious V-line.

His mocking, slightly raspy voice comes from behind me. "Someone is trapped."

Not yet.

I climb up on the unsteady railing, but before I can jump down from it, I'm greeted by the sight of thorny bushes.

Landon's scent fills my nostrils and he quickens his steps behind me. I turn around so fast, I lose my footing and fall backward.

A scream bubbles in my throat and I jam my eyes shut.

A strong hand wraps around my waist and warmth flares at the base of my belly at the feeling of a solid body against mine.

I slowly open my eyes and find myself caught by Landon's soulless eyes.

The reality of my situation clears as slowly as a fog. My upper half is hanging outside and the other half dangles inside the balcony, my feet not touching the ground.

The only thing that's stopping me from falling and being cut by a thousand thorns is none other than Landon.

My sweaty hands wrap around the metal railing for dear life as my chest rises and falls in irregular intervals.

"A pretty view to welcome me." Landon slides his free hand along my thighs, stroking, pinching, and leaving a trail of goosebumps in his wake.

That's when I realize my dress has risen up to my middle, revealing my fishnet stockings and my royal blue panties.

"Pull me up," I try to sign with one hand, then point at him and me.

"You didn't listen to me when I sent you all those texts. Why should I listen to you?" He glides his hand between my thighs and forces them apart. "Besides, I love the fear and lust in your eyes. It's making my cock rock fucking hard."

He's a sick asshole.

The most dangerous psycho I didn't know existed, and yet my body hums for what he's promising.

My temperature rises to an alarming level and all I can do is burn in the intensity of Landon fucking King.

He strokes me roughly over my panties. "You know what I'll do now?"

I shake my head.

"No? Well, let me clarify it for you. I'm going to fuck you, Mia. Hard. Like you've never been fucked before. I won't go easy on you or stop when it becomes too much. Not even if you're breaking and shattering to fucking pieces."

My lips fall open. Why am I...so turned on by that?

He drags me so my upper back rests on the ledge, gathers the material in his hands and rips it so powerfully, my breath hitches. My panties and stockings fall in shreds, some still hanging off me, and the rest scattering on the ground.

I can't help catching a glimpse of the fading sucking and bite marks he left on my inner thighs the last time he touched me. I might have looked at them in the mirror every day and stroked them every night.

My thoughts fly out the window as his fingers dig into my slippery folds. "Your greedy cunt is so wet for my cock. You're going to let me use your hole like I used your mouth, aren't you? You'll writhe and moan and show me your erotic little face as I pound that defiance out of you, won't you?"

My only reply is a muffled sound.

He slaps my pussy and my hips jerk. Ferocious tingles spread over my sensitive skin.

Still holding my waist, he makes quick work of unbuckling his pants and pulls out his very hard, very engorged cock. I've never seen him this aroused, to the point where the veins are turning purple and angry.

He slams me against him and releases my middle. My legs automatically wrap around his lithe waist so I don't fall back into the bushes. The soles of my boots sink into the backs of his thighs as the railing digs into my spine.

Landon grabs my thigh and digs the pads of his fingers in the soft, sensitive flesh near my core. "You made the mistake of assuming that there are any other dicks on the table for you. I'll teach you the valuable lesson that, as long as I breathe, you are only mine to chase. Mine to own. Mine to fuck."

Why?

I want to ask, probe, reach beneath the metal armor that he wears as a sophisticated façade and tear it apart.

I want so much more, but I can't say anything as he thrusts inside me. Resistance meets him and I sink my teeth in my bottom lip to not shriek.

Landon pulls out a little, then drives back in. "Your cunt is custom-made for me, little muse. Can you feel it choking my cock?"

More resistance greets him and he wraps his fingers around my throat, choking me until all I can see is his face. Looming, overpowering, and in complete control.

"Relax, Mia. It's not like you're a virgin."

My inner walls crack and shatter into a thousand shreds. My lungs burn and my womb contracts in frightening intervals. I choke on a gasp as a warm liquid seeps between my thighs.

Landon's pace finally slows down as he stares at the space between us. His eyes narrow on what I assume is my blood as his fingers tighten around my throat.

"Either you conveniently got your period now or you lied to me. Which one is it?"

I lift my chin even as the pain sears inside me. I need him to do something to stop this feeling.

"You're a virgin?" His voice sounds darkened and distorted in my ringing ears.

I sink my nails into his hand that's around my throat and squeeze.

"Finish what you started, you fucking bastard," my eyes communicate, and although he can't possibly understand that, a sadistic light shines on his brutally beautiful face.

In a flash, he gathers me in his arms and I grab onto him as he kicks off his shoes, pants, and boxer briefs.

Then, while still inside me, he walks inside the studio. He does it effortlessly, as if I weigh nothing, his powerful steps eating up the distance in no time.

While carrying me, he pulls down my dress's zipper and I help him push it over my head, then the bra follows right after.

My nipples brush against his shirt and I suppress a groan of pleasure. Despite the pain throbbing between my legs, I can't deny the attraction that beats deep inside me.

I've never been as turned on in my life as I am in Landon's embrace.

I'm in a beast's arms, wearing nothing but torn fishnet stockings and boots, but I feel strangely safe.

Wanted.

Enveloped in a lusty cloud.

Certainly needed.

Landon pushes a huge blank canvas from the corner of the room and lays me on top of it so that he's hovering over me.

My legs are still wrapped around his thighs, refusing to let him go for some reason. I've been thinking so much about this, imagining and playing it in my head that the thought of it going wrong gives me anxiety.

Both his hands wrap around my throat as he thrusts deeper but at an unhurried pace. The sound of his cock smeared with my blood and arousal echoes in the air like an aphrodisiac.

"Bleed for me." *Thrust.* "Break for me." *Thrust.* "Make me your one and only."

My thighs tremble and pleasure knots my belly. The pain slowly but surely explodes into a thousand pleasurable sparks.

I hold on to his muscular arms, not so I can remove them but because I need the anchor. Or maybe I want the connection, as heartless as Landon is.

Not in my wildest dreams did I imagine sex would be this tantalizing. Landon dragged out my most animalistic side and stroked it, literally and figuratively.

The harder he chokes, the stronger the flood of my arousal. The deeper his thrusts, the quicker my breath hitches.

My intelligible sounds echo in the air and he rolls his hips, pulls out, then slams back in again. My back arches as my mouth opens and closes soundlessly.

"Your body is a temple for mine, little muse. I love the feel of your pussy when you're struggling for air. It clenches and milks my cock so tightly. You're quickly becoming my favorite fuck hole."

He pulls out again, only his crown staying inside, and then thrusts back in. "You'll take every last inch, won't you?"

I don't know if I'm too demented to ever be cured, but my hips jerk with every thrust. With each look into his cold, empty gaze, I drown deeper.

For a fraction of a second, I think I see some semblance of emotion, but it's fleeting and soon disappears as if it was never there.

It probably wasn't.

I'm the one who's chasing an impossible notion, hoping, even as I'm torn apart by this beast, that there's a corner in his soul I can reach.

I'm being devoured by a cold, merciless monster and I don't want it to stop.

My thighs shake and the orgasm washes over me in long bursts. His thrusts turn animalistic, painful, even, but I revel in each and every one.

Landon looks like his favorite Greek statues when he's coming—an absolutely stunning god, but cold and cryptic.

I'm nothing but a warm hole he's using for the physical climax.

Just like he's nothing but a dick I'm using for my own pleasure.

It's absolutely nothing more, I tell myself even as I feel the tears gathering in the corners of my eyes.

Landon lifts one hand from my throat and wipes the wetness, then brings it to his lips as he whispers, "You're becoming a dangerous addiction, little muse."

And then he comes inside me in long, hot spurts.

I can take being an addiction. After all, that's what I think about him as well.

A lethal, irreversible addiction that might or might not push me to my downfall.

TWENTY

Landon

CONTRARY TO COMMON BELIEF, PRIMARILY TOLD BY MY haters and those who had the misfortune of being collateral damage to my chaos-thirsty soul, I'm not a beast.

I know, I know. It's hard to believe that notion, considering my anarchy plots that could and would bring Satan's edgy worshipers to tears.

My beast is different from the general consensus most people have about me, my ex-therapists included.

It's not me. It's part of me.

My beast has been hooked to my bones from the moment I was conceived by my parents. Pretty sure my and Bran's beast got split and I received the louder one. His can be easily kept in chains. Mine would kill me before I were to attempt such blasphemy.

This may shock the antisocial disorder police, but I actually don't relish hurting people for the fuck of it—though everyone, my family and friends included, would tell you otherwise.

Truth is, the individuals I hurt just happened to be in my path.

I don't react well to obstacles. The moment I see one, I come up with a hundred and one solutions to eliminate it, and because I need anarchy, I usually go for the most difficult resolution that will cause the most damage just so I'll feel somewhat accomplished.

Real.

Alive.

I also take immense pleasure in bringing others to their knees in front of me. It's an addictive power that I need to satiate as much as my need for chaos.

My beast is easygoing. All I have to do is offer him some violence, anarchy, and possible blood and he'll be golden, lounging around like a lion in his cave.

My beast is also quite pragmatic. Deep down in his black soul, he wants to murder à la serial killer style and look into people's eyes as they turn lifeless. He wants the power of holding other people's existence in the palm of his hand like their custom-made god.

He ranks high on emotion and catastrophe control and would be a perfect candidate for a wanted murderer—famous but would never be caught.

However, that thought never has and never will come to fruition for a very simple reason. A moment of gratification isn't worth the damage that could be inflicted throughout my lifetime in the 0.01 percent chance I'm caught.

Imagine—me behind bars? The blasphemy.

And yet right now, my beast is far from being rational, peaceful, or relaxed. I've been standing here for the past…fuck knows how long. An hour? Three? Five? It's probably close to dawn and I haven't been able to sleep a wink.

I sculpted a stroke of genius, then shoved it at the back of the other statues with the canvas that has Mia's blood all over it.

Virginal blood.

Summoning Satan using that is a tempting idea, but I'm opting for something a lot more devilish.

Something that defies reality and puts everything I've done thus far to shame.

I light a cigarette and exhale a cloud of smoke under the shadows of early morning slipping through the window whose cracks I filled with clay after Mia was shivering a few weeks ago.

Sucking on my cigarette, I stroll to where Mia lies on the sofa, her small body wrapped in my shirt.

Only *my* shirt.

It's become a habit now. Even when her dress is intact, she also puts on my clothes before she falls into slumber.

The fabric rides up her pale thighs, revealing my fading marks and the fresh ones I added today. Earlier, her inner thighs were smudged with proof of her innocence, but I smeared every drop on the canvas and licked the rest clean.

I needed to devour the evidence even when she looked mortified by the attention. I licked and nibbled on her soft core, then sucked on her thighs, stomach, and mound. Everywhere I could leave a hickey of ownership.

The whole time, she watched me with a bizarre fascination bordering on both lust and confusion.

Mia might act righteous, but she's also harboring a beast. It's different from mine and has irregular codes of conduct, but it's a beast all the same.

I inhale the cancer stick into my lungs and release a trail of smoke in the air as I circle the sofa on and on as if that'll make sense of the sheer chaos brewing inside me.

Mia was only supposed to be a temporary muse, an outlet through which my creativity climaxes—literally and figuratively.

But as I look at her soft features, lips slightly parted and thick lashes fanning her cheeks, I realize how sorely mistaken I've been.

A fuck has merely whet my appetite for more of her taste, more of marking her flesh and swallowing her into my kink-flavored world.

And I don't fuck the same woman twice. Have never wanted one again as soon as I was done with her. Have never watched one while my beast concocts plans to have her writhing beneath me while her cunt milks my cock. Soon.

Now, even.

Her presence is starting to influence my thoughts and decision-making process. I need to put an end to this and sabotage the very marrow of her being before she becomes the bane of my existence.

Mia stirs as she usually does when she has her naps. For some reason, she sleeps a lot around me, something even she finds weird. The other day, she accidentally told me she doesn't sleep much, even with the lights on.

What lines did the dark cross to turn you into this?

I narrow my eyes as I blow smoke in her face.

A part of me knows that I don't care about people's circumstances. Never have and never will. The only reason I'm having these thoughts is so that I can gather more information about her and use it to prey on her. I'd shatter her into minuscule pieces so that no one would be able to put her back together again.

Contrary to what I anticipated, Mia doesn't wake up. She pulls her knees to her chest and wraps her hands around them so that she's lying in a fetal position.

Unintelligible shaky noises fall from her mouth. Sweat beads on her upper lip and forehead, and her disheveled blonde strands stick to her skin.

My hand wraps around the back of the sofa as I lean down to try and decipher the noises.

There's a lot of whining, gasping, and moans of pain, but something else slips in between.

When I finally make out the sound, the cigarette falls from my hand and hits the floor, releasing a spark of orange light, then it dies out.

"No…"

That's what she's saying between trembling noises. It's not much, but it's without a doubt something she's never said before.

A word.

I was right. She sounds nothing like the pretentious Maya. Her voice is lower, softer, and possibly the only voice I'd listen to on repeat.

Over and over.

I fetch my phone and hit record.

"No…" she repeats, a bit stronger, even though she's still shaking like a bird caught in a storm.

All my blood rushes to between my legs. My cock bulges against my boxers at a speed I've never experienced before.

The sound of her voice explodes somewhere behind my rib cage and I find myself leaning farther down so that my ear is nearly glued to her luscious lips.

"No…please…"

Please.

Who is she begging if it's not me?

She has no right to beg anyone but me.

More moans. Gasps. Whimpers of pure twisted pain.

I push back to stare at her anguished face, furrowed brow, and the tears that pool in the corners of her eyes and then cascade down her cheeks.

Not only is she having a nightmare, but she's also suffering more with every passing second.

A better person would wake her up, but if I do, she won't speak again. This is her subconscious talking, and she probably won't even remember the words she's just released.

Besides, how dare she dream of someone else after the explosive introductory meeting between my cock and her cunt?

Fuck it. I'm waking her up anyway.

After I throw my phone on the table, I tap her cheek with the back of my hand. She doesn't even stir.

"Open your fucking eyes," I say not so nicely and fail to recognize the reason behind my darkened tone.

Mia doesn't reply or show signs of acknowledging her surroundings.

Don't blame me for what I'm about to do.

I clearly asked her to wake up, but she didn't seem keen on the idea, so I have to resort to other measures.

And yes, I'm deeply disturbed by the fuck mode situation my cock easily slipped into. I might be known as someone with an immense sex drive and an extensive repertoire of paraphilia, but I don't actually get turned on easily.

Or I didn't. Mia obviously changed that.

Earlier, Nila and Bethany were practically humping me and offering a fuck-one-get-one-free deal, but I couldn't muster an ounce of interest.

Mia speaks two words in her sleep and I'm ready to impregnate her with my fucking child so she'll have no way out.

Fuck. What was that thought all about?

I pull down my boxers so that I'm fully naked, then hop on the sofa.

My knees rest on either side of her as I throw one of her legs over my shoulder and bare her swollen pink cunt.

She's most definitely sore, and the last thing she needs is another sexual adventure.

Someone else would probably leave her alone.

Good thing I'm *not* someone else.

I lift my shirt up to expose her pink nipples and tease one then stroke her folds, sinking my fingers into the pink flesh. A shudder goes through her tiny body. The creases of discomfort slowly disappear from her face and the groans of pain quiet down.

Just like magic.

My fingers find her clit and I circle, then tap it slightly. Her hips jerk and a moan of pleasure falls from her parted lips.

I keep doing that until I feel her sticky arousal welcoming me and the intoxicating scent of her pussy fills my nostrils.

As she writhes, I release her cunt that should just be called *my* cunt at this point. I wrap my fingers around her throat, digging my thumb into the red fingerprints I left earlier.

I jerk myself a few times, using her stickiness on my palm as lube, then slowly slide inside her welcoming heat.

Mia moans, her head falling back and her body shivering.

Fucking fuck. She's perfectly tight.

I thrust at a moderate pace, relishing how she clenches around my dick as if she's conscious. The fact that she's not makes this a lot more erotic.

My cock is seriously considering a longer subscription for the first time in his hedonistic life.

Mia's nipples harden as her hips meet me stroke for stroke. I've never believed in fate, but I'm so sure this little muse was made for me. Her body's memory of mine kicks in and she jerks her hips and arches her back in welcome.

"Your cunt is so greedy for my cock. You're going to take my cum deep inside like my favorite little fuck hole whenever I want, aren't you?" I groan and pick up my pace, going from zero to one hundred in no time.

Mia's eyes pop open, and for a second, she appears disoriented as she blinks the tears from her eyes.

My gaze captures her wild one as I ram into her, owning every inch and leaving no scraps.

I don't stop.

It's too late to stop.

Her frantic gaze goes from my face to where we're joined.

I expect her to try and push me away, but she tightens around my cock, her arousal offering the best lube I've ever had. Okay, it's tied with her blood.

Mia is a piece of art when she's orgasming. Her brow furrows, her mouth opens in a silent *O*, and she jerks her hips.

I'd expected myself to last longer, and I usually do, but the view of her shattering on my cock brings me to the brink in no time.

Fuck.

My balls tighten and I come in long spurts over her bare stomach.

I nearly came inside her. *Again.*

I don't know what the fuck has come over me. I have rubbers all over my person and place, but for the second time, I forgot to put one on.

Or maybe, deep down, I tricked myself into forgetting. It's no secret that I needed to feel her bare skin against mine as she came undone.

Mia mentioned a week or so ago that she had an appointment to change her birth control shot, but still, this is a considerable slip on my part.

We remain there, basking in the aftermath of the lust haze. My mind is a fog of unanswered questions and dangerous possibilities, and yet my cock is still, for all intents and purposes, half erect.

Mia recovers first, pushes my hand from her neck, and scoots away on her elbows.

"What the hell was that?" she signs.

"Your attempts at looking angry are an utter failure. Might want to try again when your face doesn't look freshly fucked—and pleased, if I might add."

She glares.

"To answer your question, that was, as we agreed, demonstrating one of my kinks." I grin. "Somnophilia for the win."

Her lips part and she swallows thickly.

"Oh?" I tilt my head. "Judging by your reaction, it might be your kink as well."

She shakes her head harder than needed, but her cheeks flush a deeper shade of red.

"No need to be ashamed when you just came because of it. But I digress, only until the next time I wake you up with my cock."

What am I saying? There shouldn't be a next time.

She starts to get up, but I grab her by the hand. Mia pauses, wearing a bemused expression. I snatch a few tissues from the coffee table, where her dinner waits, and wipe the evidence of our fuck session from her translucent skin.

What am I if not a caring gentleman?

It helps that I get to trace my finger marks on her flesh. These irregular hickeys and bite marks are fast becoming my favorite creation.

Mia remains still and watches me with eyes that resemble half-crushed, barely surviving wildflowers at the edge of volcanic lava.

It's definitely not because of the sex, considering the smidge of lust still shining through them.

"What were you dreaming about just now?" I ask as I finish cleaning the space between her legs, then wipe her stomach.

"Nothing."

"You were crying and gasping."

"Nothing," she signs the word with more attitude this time.

"A long time ago." I take extra care in cleaning the rim of her belly button. "Bran came into my room without light in his eyes, and when I asked him what had happened, he also said nothing. And yet he hasn't been the same since. So I have deep trust issues with the word *nothing*."

She swallows and hangs her head. I can tell she's close to breaking, and all I have to do is push a bit further.

My voice softens. "Is it related to whoever took your voice?"

Mia nods once.

That's a good start.

"Is he still alive?"

Another nod.

So it's a *he*.

"Did your parents make him live as a cripple?"

She shakes her head and then signs, "No one knows who or where he is."

Not even her mafia parents.

This must be why she's often looking over her shoulder and only sleeps when there's a light on.

Someone stole not only her voice—her beautiful, melodic voice—but also her peace of mind.

Someone who took the major risk of attacking a mafia princess, not caring about the consequences, is of a different caliber.

"Not even you?"

Her eyes, the color of sheer determination, meet mine, looking a bit lost. "What do you mean?"

"You said no one knows where he is, which makes sense, but what about who he is? You've seen him, no?"

The air crackles with tension so thick, I could possibly cut through it with a knife. All color drains from Mia's face and a tremor twitches her parted lips as she shakes her head frantically.

Interesting.

"But I will find him," she signs after she partially recovers. "Either I get my voice back or I die."

I push a tangle of blonde hair and blue ribbons from her face.

Mia stares up at me with a struck expression, her plump lips parting and begging for my cock between them.

But that's a thought for another day.

"Complete nonsense. The only ultimatum is that you'll get your voice back *and* kill him. I can make it happen. All you have to do is ask."

I don't even know what the fuck I'm doing. For the first time in my life, I'm prioritizing someone else over my own schemes.

Maybe, just maybe, I'm irrevocably bewitched by that soft voice and I refuse to believe that was the last time I'll hear it.

TWENTY-ONE

Mia

THERE'S AN ERROR IN THE MATRIX.

A miscalculated equation.

A hopeless, absolutely disfigured view of reality that's impossible to fix.

And it all has to do with a certain Landon King.

The current monster of my life.

The demon who's ushering me to hell with decadent smirks and a hedonistic view of reality.

Never in my wildest dreams would I have thought I'd be into the demented things Landon keeps showing me. It started with mere curiosity, but now, I'm proficiently fluent in his crude kinks.

That morbid curiosity is morphing into something a lot bigger and more intimidating. He's cutting each of my self-imposed limits with sharp, bloodied claws.

And the scariest part is that I can't put a stop to it. Every day, I go to the haunted house, which Landon is slowly renovating, with the resolve that tonight will be the last hit.

And yet each night, I keep going back again and again like a hopeless addict.

My excuse is that a deep part of me has been yearning for this feeling of complete abandon and being slightly forced into giving up control. That black hole in the corner of my soul has been dreaming about unleashing this darker side of unbound lust—the side I wouldn't even tell Maya about.

A side that's frowned upon by all societies and their religions.

I often felt an itch in high school. Where Maya loved the attention, I realized early on that none of the boys I knew could satisfy this itch, not even other mafia leaders' sons who thrive on violence and asserting their place in the world.

So imagine my surprise when I found that in none other than a posh British guy.

A psycho artist with a taste for everything forbidden and wrong.

The truth remains, I've never felt so stimulated as when he takes me unapologetically, uses me thoroughly, and manhandles me.

I've never been as thrilled as when he chases me and lets me think I've gotten away with it, just so he can tackle me to the ground and hate-fuck me.

It's an aphrodisiac. A hit better than any drug.

The worst part is that I feel safe in his company. Two weeks ago, after he woke me up from a nightmare in the most pleasurable—and sick—way ever, I didn't feel violated. Not in the least.

In fact, I was thankful that he was able to wrench me out of that loop. He's done it again a few times since—I'm pulled right out of a horrific nightmare to find myself in blissful pleasure.

I never told him this, but yes, considering I've experienced an explosive orgasm every time he's done that, I'd say somnophilia is safely one of my kinks as well.

Perhaps the reason I'm so addicted to Landon is either the sense of gratefulness or the rawness of emotions he triggers in me. Maybe it's the ease with which he slid into the middle of my life. Even though we usually meet at the house, he still challenges me to the occasional epic chess game at the club, and because he spends so much time with me, the other members are gradually warming up to me.

Whenever we get together, he has my Frappuccino waiting for me, just the way I like it. He also helps with my presentations sometimes, even though we have completely different majors. In his words,

"I think we already established that I have a superior IQ and school projects are child's play to me. Besides, I'll eventually study business so I can take over my family's company."

Every night, after he fucks me to within an inch of my life, he makes sure I'm well-fed and hydrated. He also has a surprisingly consistent aftercare routine where he wipes me clean and even massages my whole body as I fall into a deep sleep.

Nevertheless, I shouldn't have disclosed bits of my past to him.

Landon might be in lust with me, but that's the extent of his attention. None of his caresses and fake grins can fool me. He's still a narcissist through and through and he'll use my weaknesses against me when the time comes.

If I want to survive him, then I need to bubble-wrap my fragile, amateur heart that keeps being touched by his calculated gestures. The moment I comment or even show a bit of discomfort about something, he gets it done.

First, he installed new lights in the house so that it no longer looks dark and grimy. He replaced the cracked glass in the windows, ordered new furniture to replace the old pieces, and he's been buying me gardening equipment.

He also employed a landscaping company to clear the premises of any fallen branches and hazardous objects. I asked him about the reason behind that and his answer was amazingly simple.

"I can't have my muse injuring herself when she's running," he said while lifting my chin with his index finger. "The marks on your body can only be inflicted by me."

He's cutthroat and viciously emotionless, but maybe that's all I need. I'm not in this game for feelings, after all. When push comes to shove, I'd still side with my people.

It's much better this way. At least I don't feel guilty spying on an unfeeling monster.

And yet as I stare at my face in the mirror that's in the middle of the guest room in the Heathens' mansion, I painfully realize that I put on more makeup than I usually do. My cheeks are rosy, matching the pink color on my lips.

I'm not dolling up for him, right? It's for myself because I feel beautiful—

My phone vibrates in my dress pocket and I pull it out.

Landon has attached a picture of bags of fertilizer in the cleaned-up gazebo in the middle of the garden.

Devil Lord: Will these satisfy your green-thumb kink?

I smile. He's been calling me an amateur gardener with an unlikely hobby. Truth is, I always loved tending to the garden back home. Neither Mom nor Dad liked the task, but I take after Aunt Reina—Kill and Gaz's mother—in that regard.

We each have a beautiful little garden on our bedroom balcony that we often compare notes about. Let's just say Aunt is winning, so the dead garden at the haunted house is my practice until I can go back to New York and personally greet my plants.

Lan always busies himself with his unfinished statues as soon as he's cleaned me up and thrown his shirt or hoodie at me. And while I'm thankful for the downtime, he can literally go on sculpting for hours—once, it was over five hours.

So I've started bringing my homework, but I finish that in no time. We play chess, but that's normally a bet on what kink he's going to indulge in for the day. I usually lose and when I win, it's only for a harmless bet on his side.

Therefore, I came up with the compromise that I'd plant my flowers and he could watch me from the tall windows of his studio. That way, we can both be productive.

I sit on the edge of the bed and type my reply.

Mia: They'll do. Have you gotten me the seeds I asked for?

He sends another picture of a bag of seeds.

Devil Lord: At your service, my lady. I am, after all, your favorite gentleman.

Mia: You're the furthest thing from a gentleman. Don't be delusional.

Devil Lord: Don't be ungrateful.

Mia: Thanks. But then again, this is the least you can do for all the inspiration I've been giving you.

He finished three statues in a short time and showed pictures of them to his professors. I think the director of some gallery is offering to exhibit them, but Landon refused.

"Not yet." I heard him talking on the phone. "They're not exactly perfect."

I thought he was being sarcastic or exhibiting a false sense of modesty. But one, Landon is so arrogant, modesty would shrivel and die before touching him. Two, he looked serious and was frowning as he said those words.

It's true that I'm not an artist, but even I can see why he's labeled the genius of his generation. The level of detail he puts in his sculptures can only be described as otherworldly. The lines in the fingers, the creases around the eyes, the dip of flesh beneath a harsh grip. Everything is simply a perfect piece of art.

And yet he just pushes those sculptures to the back, then brings out new subjects to work on. I feel bad for those abandoned ones. They must feel lonely and unwanted.

My phone vibrates, bringing me out of my thoughts.

Devil Lord: I've been doing my due diligence by bestowing you with my cum every night.

Mia: And I've been giving you the honor of touching me.

Devil Lord: Does that mean I'm lucky?

Mia: Uh-huh. Thank God for it.

Devil Lord: Nonsense. He has nothing to do with what I made happen. See you in an hour.

I trap the corner of my lip between my teeth and type.

Mia: I can't tonight. I'm having a mandatory dinner at the Heathens'.

Devil Lord: Mandatory? What is this? The sixteenth century?

Mia: Niko and especially Maya are suspicious about all the disappearing I do. I've spiraled into a bad mental state when I've done that in the past, so they're freaking out a little, thinking I'm relapsing. I just need to assure them that everything is okay.

Devil Lord: Then tell them you're seeing someone.

Mia: They'll want to know who.

Devil Lord: Then just say it's me. In fact, I don't mind coming over to introduce myself.

I study my surroundings to make sure no one is around before I type.

Mia: Have you lost your mind? Niko will kill you.

Devil Lord: You won't let him, right?

I chew on the corner of my bottom lip as I read and reread his words.

Devil Lord: Right?

Mia: Just stay away. Do something productive with your time and water the plants.

Devil Lord: I'm many things, but a background character isn't in my repertoire of functions.

My eyes narrow. What the hell is that supposed to mean?

"What are you so concentrated on?"

I startle, but soon regain my composure upon seeing Nikolai at the doorway of my room. I didn't even hear him coming close.

His long hair is loose, stopping at his shoulders and giving him a more rugged look. He's wearing only sweatpants and a grim expression.

Subtly, I slide my phone back into my pocket, then leave the guest room and sign, "It's a friend."

Nikolai follows after and stops me in the middle of the reception area. "Brandon King?"

"No."

"What other friends do you have?"

Touché.

"It's really not him." *Just his infuriating twin.*

Besides, Bran has been keeping his distance from me lately. Whenever I ask if he's up for a game, he says he has exams coming up or that he's focused on a project.

The excuses have become so similar that they stand out. I wonder if he found out about me and Landon. Last week, I finally managed to meet up with him and Remi for a game and Landon happened to come by.

I made a show of ignoring him, but he barged right in, teamed up with Remi against me and Bran, then proceeded to kick our asses.

So I sent him an article-length text with a few choice words, at which Lan laughed, shook his head, and whispered something to Bran before he fucked off to make other people miserable. I wondered if Lan had told him something, but then again, Bran was being distant before that incident. Which has been making me feel weird.

Nikolai is right. Brandon is the first friend I've made outside my family.

Jeremy is Nikolai's best friend, not mine. His younger sister, Annika, used to be friends with Maya, not me—that is, until they fell out of each other's graces.

Not only am I too difficult to get along with, but I also make it a habit to never let anyone close. I developed severe trust issues after that monster stole my voice. And yet Bran put in the effort and made me feel precious. Until lately, of course.

Maybe I can't have both, after all.

Either the nice twin or the evil one.

"The more you defend him, the higher he gets on my hit list." Nikolai's harsh tone sends a dash of panic through my veins. "I'll see to this myself."

I grab onto his arm and then shake my head.

Bran is so drastically different from Lan, if they didn't share identical looks, no one would believe they're twins, let alone brothers.

I would never forgive myself if I put him on Nikolai's merciless radar just because I'm selfish enough to want a friend.

"Listen," I sign. "I'm old enough to choose who I spend time with and who I don't. I appreciate your protectiveness and I adore you more than you'll ever know, but you don't get to tell me who I talk to and who I don't. Bran did nothing to you or anyone in the Heathens. So this animosity is uncalled for and I won't allow you to hurt someone innocent just because of his last name."

Nikolai's eyes narrow to threatening slits, but his face soon returns to its normal grumpy expression as he grabs my shoulders. "I don't like the secrecy in whatever you're doing lately."

"Everything is okay." I stroke his arm like Mom used to do whenever he got too into his head. "Trust me."

He narrows his eyes again. Thankfully, I catch a glimpse of Maya, who must be boring Kill to death, considering his near-murderous expression.

I wave them over.

As soon as they're within reach, I jump on Killian's back and headlock him in a not-so-friendly greeting.

He elbows me and when I get back to the ground, he ruffles my hair. Not to brag, but I'm probably his favorite Sokolov, maybe even more so than Niko.

"I was talking, Mia." Maya gives me a look and taps her shoe on the floor and hikes a hand on her hip. She's done that since we were toddlers and it's never changed.

"About insignificant fashion topics that could result in someone's accidental suicide," Killian says.

"That's rude." She glares at him.

"What's more rude is your indulgence in these shallow topics that make you look like an airhead."

"Hey," I sign to him.

Maya's never really cared about Killian's—or anyone's—opinion of her. She's a diva and wears it like a badge while flipping everyone the middle finger.

And yet her face reddens. "I'm not an airhead."

"Then develop more interests that aren't confined to some boring Paris catwalk show." He pauses. "Considering our blood relation, your clear tendencies of being a stereotypical brain-dead blonde reflects badly on my perfect image."

All psychos are arrogant assholes who think the world revolves around their inflated egos.

However, I've never felt resentment toward Killian. Granted, he's never hurt me or my siblings. Even now, he's not really being malicious to Maya. He's just trying to provoke her on purpose or something.

"Try harder, Kill." She flips her hair. "Your arrogance used to rival mine, but I'm only looking at you through the rearview mirror now. It would reflect badly on my goddess image."

"Stop drooling. Your bullshit is splashing on my fifty-grand shoes."

"More like *your* bullshit is polluting the air around my special edition LV dress."

I get between them and look at Niko so he'll help break up the verbal fight.

My jaw nearly hits the floor when I see him sprawled out at the bottom of the stairs, eyes closed. I didn't even notice when he left the scene.

Truth be told, Nikolai has never been good in these situations. Not that he can't break up fights, but if it doesn't involve his fists, then he loses all interest.

Thankfully, Gareth walks in, recognizes what's going on right away, and joins me in breaking up the two most volatile cousins—in the ego department.

"You're officially blacklisted from my next birthday party," Maya tells Killian.

"Be right back. I'm going to cry into my pillow."

Gareth and I manage to take each of them to the dining room. Then I go back to wake up Nikolai so he'll join us.

He still looks at me weirdly, and for some reason, I can't suppress my fear for Bran's safety. Maybe I should warn him just in case?

The problem with Niko is that he appears aloof and only interested in violence, but, in reality, he can be secretive and impossible to read if he chooses to.

The five of us sit down for dinner, with Maya and Killian still bickering like children.

"Where's Jeremy?" she asks as the food is served and points a fork at Killian, who's taking Jeremy's usual place at the head of the table. "I certainly didn't come for your face."

"Desperate doesn't look good on you." He smirks. "Besides, is it really Jeremy you're asking about, blondie?"

"W-who else would I be asking about?"

All of us, aside from Niko, who's busy eating, look at her.

"What?" she whisper-yells.

"You just stuttered," Killian taunts. "I would've sworn you didn't know how."

"I did not."

"I'm afraid you did," Gareth says.

"See? Even Mother Teresa's lost son agrees," Killian replies and makes a show of smearing a piece of meat in blood.

Maya, a vegetarian, scrunches her nose at him and then focuses on Gareth. "Jeremy?"

"He said he has something to do."

"Without me?" Nikolai finally gets into the conversation.

"Who knows?" Gareth lifts his shoulders. "Tried checking your phone?"

Nikolai does just that and his eyes light up. "I'm out of here."

"Where are you going?" I sign.

"Nowhere you need to worry about."

"I thought you insisted we have dinner together."

"Dinner finished." He gulps his glass of beer and kisses the top of my head. "Stay out of this, Mia."

He kisses Maya's head as well. "Don't cause any trouble."

Killian stands up as well and I meet his gaze with my questioning one.

He smiles a little. "Not your scene, baby Sokolov."

And then they're out the door, leaving the three of us alone.

"Were you left out, Gaz?" Maya asks with a dejected tone as she stabs her salad over and over again.

"I opted out. I have exams coming up." He chews leisurely, not even bothering to check his phone.

I have a bad feeling about this.

We put on Maya's favorite movie, *Clueless*, but I barely focus on it. I contemplate going to the haunted house, but Lan is probably entertaining his band of posh Elites.

Wait. What the hell?

Since when did I start to call him Lan?

This is so hopelessly disturbing.

By the time the movie ends, Maya is already fast asleep on the couch. Gareth offers to carry her to one of the guest rooms, but I shake my head.

She'll wake up and will find it hard to fall back asleep.

So I cover her, sit on the floor, and continue staring at my phone.

If there's one thing I've learned about Lan, it's that he doesn't know how to take no for an answer. It's not in his DNA, vocabulary, or code of conduct.

The fact that he didn't send any other texts or threaten to barge in doesn't sit well with me.

He won't do anything stupid, right?

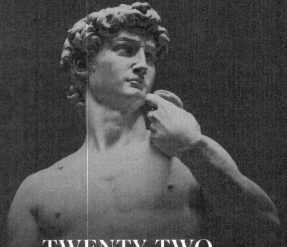

TWENTY-TWO

Landon

DUE TO THE NOTICEABLE ABSENCE OF MY NEWEST FAVORITE toy, I had to content myself with beating up her brother. What?

It's not my fault she's exceptionally bad at reading the room and keeping my beast satiated. It's no secret that the situation morphs into absolute carnage whenever he's left to his own devices.

His weapon for the night is undiluted violence. While it's not particularly my favorite method, it does get the job done, and for a long time, it could've been compared to the physical climax shagging holes provided.

Small problem, though. I've been going at this for about ten minutes, and I'm closer to dozing off than any form of climax.

I'm being beaten up all right since, well, Nikolai is this huge motherfucker with a grudge about a certain incident that I might have caused.

Don't expect me to keep track of all the chaos my superior brain conjures. I'm under the obligation to archive those files to allow my neurons space to create worse anarchy.

Nikolai Sokolov, the eldest in the Sokolov family, that fucker Killian's cousin, and, most importantly, Mia's older brother. They look nothing alike except for a faint resemblance due to their sibling blood.

They do, however, share some aspects of a brute persona, the need for violence, and the thirst to cause trouble.

Must be because of the Russian mafia blood running through their veins.

There's one major difference, though. Nikolai has the type of face that's begging to be beaten. Mia's face, on the other hand, is the definition of an aphrodisiac.

Lately, the situation has become so dire that just imagining her naturally pouty lips and the blue wildflower color of her eyes is enough to make my cock jump like a fanboy.

Ah, fuck. I'm getting a hard-on in the middle of a fight. Well, the referee just called a break, but I still glare down at myself.

Way to read the room, dick.

My gaze strays to Nikolai, who's on the opposite side of the ring being prepped by none other than Jeremy—the recent president of my anti-fan club.

The mere look at the brute is enough to kill any erotic thoughts. I definitely have no qualms about destroying his features and giving him the incentive to go through a desperate reparative surgery.

"You okay, Lan?" Remi asks from outside the ring and passes me a bottle of water.

He's the only one of the guys who loves accompanying me on these bursts of violence. There's also Ava, who loves to come cheer for me. She must be in the crowd somewhere as the president of Fighter Landon Club.

Ava and I have an easygoing relationship. I help her in bringing Eli down and then she helps me with all my gossip needs. What she doesn't know is that I also help Eli sometimes. What? He's still my cousin. The King men might fight and see the world through different lenses, but we'll always be family.

Or that's what Grandfather Jonathan says.

At any rate, I've been taking part in underground fighting since Eli first took me to one—behind our parents' backs, naturally.

After his first years in uni, my cousin gradually pulled out from these scenes, but I found a much-needed venting outlet in the adrenaline this provides.

The crowd.

The screams.

The fuck fest that usually takes place after.

REU's students' shouts surround me in a halo, a drug that shoots through my bloodstream and shoves me toward the sky.

I grab the bottle from Remi, down half of it and pour the other half on my head, then shake it out like a dog. Girls swoon and I offer them my usual charming grins that would make them drop their knickers if I as much as asked. The only difference now is that I couldn't give a fuck about their attention.

I don't even have the right motivation to finish this fight.

"Do you have to do this?" my clone asks from the side of the ring.

Brandon is about the last person one would expect to attend fight clubs. He's more squeamish than a sheltered prince and he looks the part of an upper-class, preppy boy with his groomed hair and snobbish face. He came dressed in a white shirt, a beige cardigan, pressed trousers, and classic Prada loafers.

Still, the fact that he chose to offer his support is a rare event that I plan to make full use of.

My lips curve in a sly grin. "Do you have to be here?"

He slides a hand in his pocket, posture straight and voice calm. "You're the one who texted me."

"Oh? Since when do you come running after I inform you of my fights?"

"Mum asked me to keep you out of trouble."

"Didn't think you listened anymore."

"You're my brother. I won't like seeing Mum cry if you somehow get yourself killed."

"Aww." I jump down from the ring and ruffle his perfectly styled hair, sending it into irreparable chaos, then smile.

He pushes me away. "Stop it."

"I knew you loved me." My grin disappears as I grab him by the collar of his shirt and whisper in his ear, my voice hardening, "But try again, Bran. You're a terrible fucking liar."

As I pull away, his eyes widen a little, not enough to be noticed by Remi, who's busy trash-talking Nikolai's fans. However, Bran can't hide from me and just unconsciously proved one of my grim theories. The one I was contemplating when I sent him the text about my fight with Nikolai.

"I don't know what you're talking about." For all intents and purposes, he does sound unaffected.

"I'm talking about your recent fascination with Nikolai. Care to explain yourself?"

He lifts his hand to the back of his neck, but upon seeing me staring at it, he drops it before he can indulge in his stress-relieving habits.

But the fact that he had to do that and hide it in the first place is telltale enough.

I'm about to get in his space, when the referee announces that the fight is resuming.

I narrow my eyes on my brother and he narrows his back.

When I jump back in the ring, I find Nikolai glaring down at me with a bloodied nose—that was my doing, by the way—and a tight posture.

"What's got your knickers in a twist?" I ask casually, then point a thumb at myself. "Want a piece of this?"

As soon as the referee gives the go, Nikolai pounces on me with the vengeance of a thousand ghost warriors.

I manage to stand my ground for the first few hits, but then he backs me into a corner and nearly jeopardizes my Greek god looks.

Thankfully, the referee manages to break us apart.

"Jesus Christ." I spit out a mouthful of blood and grin. "I know you're jealous about your inability to ever reach my superior looks, but tone it down a notch, would you?"

"You're going down, motherfucker." He punches his bandaged fists together.

I suppose that's a no about breaking the news about my cock's unorthodox relationship with his sister's cunt.

But then again, his cousin took my sister, so this could be seen as fair payback. Just saying.

When he charges again, I punch him in the ribs as hard as I can. Nikolai recovers faster than lightning and knocks me down on the canvas, then hails me with fast, sharp punches.

Fucking fuck.

"Hey, twat," I manage between groans. "That hurts."

"Exactly the point, motherfucker."

I block some of his hits, but some of them land straight on my rib cage.

I wonder if I'm bleeding on the floor. Perhaps my ending won't be as glorious as I thought it would be. Preferably in the middle of my studio, surrounded by my masterpieces that come to life à la Pygmalion style.

"Is this the best you can do, mafia prince?" I taunt with a barely audible voice. "You punch like a girl."

A certain girl comes to mind whenever erotic violence is involved.

Only, I don't mind if she shatters my ribs as long as she rides my cock and chokes on it for redemption right after.

"Stop!"

The voice filters through my haziness, and I pause. Please don't tell me I lowered my standards and asked Nikolai to stop.

It's then I realize it does sound like mine. Only one person has the audacity to be so chaotically emotional while sharing my otherworldly physical traits.

Surprisingly, Nikolai jerks back, putting the episode of "Punching Bag Landon" on hold as he stares at who I assume is my brother. His eyes narrow and darken and his nostrils flare.

What. The. Fuck?

I'm going to kill this bastard. How dare he look at Bran—my fucking twin brother—like he's his next bitch?

My. Fucking. Brother.

The Landon King's identical twin.

I slam my fist against his cheek so fast and hard, he falls sideways, and blood explodes on his face.

My ribs ache, and I can feel my own blood decorating my features, but I manage to stagger to my feet in the midst of roaring cheers.

"King! King! King!"

I kick Nikolai in the ribs before he manages to get to his knees, then I jerk him up by a fistful of his hair and whisper in his ear, "This is your first and last warning. Keep your fucking eyes off my brother or I will claw them the fuck out."

He kicks me back, but I dodge at the last minute, letting the hit fall to the edge of my leg. Then I jump out of the ring.

Fuck the fight.

Fuck the lot of the Heathens. I'm going to set their lives on fire before they get another one of my siblings. I'm not even over the fact that my sister defected to Killian, and now, this fucker thinks he can set his sights on my brother.

Remi and Bran rush toward me and I grab my brother by the collar and drag him out while Remi dabs at my lip and tries to stop the bleeding.

"What did you say to him?" Bran asks, not bothering to fight my grip.

"None of your fucking business."

"It is if it was about me."

I stop in the middle of the tunnel that leads to the changing rooms. "Do you want it to be about you, Bran? Is that it?"

This time, he pushes me away and stands toe to toe with me. "I didn't say that."

"You don't have to for me to get the message. What's with you lately?"

"As you so eloquently said earlier, none of your business."

"Now, now." Remi steps between us. "No need to fight when my lordship is here. Drinks on me?"

"Take him." I flick my finger in my brother's general direction. "He's obviously in desperate need of a wake-up call."

"And you're not?" Bran gently pushes Remi away and gets in my face. "What Nikolai did just now will look like a warm-up once he finds out about your recent fixation on his sister."

"His sister?" Remi asks, sounding as lost as a lamb. "Mia?"

I grin, purposefully putting my bloodied teeth on display.

Naturally, when I found her having fun with Bran and Remi, I was under the obligation to set the record straight and hint, not so subtly, that she was off-limits.

Bran shares my genes and, therefore, is intelligent enough to put certain pieces together. But Remi seems to have perfected the fool's image, even though it's mostly that—an image. Now, however, he's connected the dots and looks at me as if I've completely lost my marbles and will actively cause a third world war.

"He won't be able to hurt me in this lifetime. I, on the other hand…" My voice drops. "Can finish what I started with his meaningless life."

"At the expense of losing Mia for good?" Bran delivers the question with disturbing calm.

"Utter nonsense. If anything, she should kiss my feet for taking on the tedious task of removing the unnecessary oaf from her life."

"Just because you think so little of your own siblings doesn't mean everyone else shares your sentiments." He jams his index finger against my shoulder. "If you cared to know more about Mia, you would've found out that she loves and, more importantly, *respects* both her siblings. They have a tight relationship, ask about one another all the time, and make sure to meet several times a week. But then again, you've always faked your way through those feelings, so of course you wouldn't know what they mean, even if they were to splash your precious car's windshield. So, by all means, attack her brother and cousins. Burn down their mansion and sabotage their existence. Destroy whatever saving grace she sees in you so she'll send you packing. The way I see it, you don't deserve her and never will."

"If you're done preaching like a hypocritical pastor…" I push past him and control the limp in my step.

I'm nothing less than the personification of physical perfection, and the world won't see anything else, not even if I'm drowning in my own blood.

Bran's words keep ringing in my ears like an unholy prayer. Or maybe it's holy, because the more I think about it, the more pissed off I get.

After washing up in the locker room and changing into casual trousers and a hoodie, I head to the half-deserted car park.

My whole body aches as I slowly slide into the driver seat. That fucker Nikolai got me good and probably bruised several of my ribs.

I pull out my phone and find a few texts.

Ava: I can't believe you lost after I bet on you. What the hell, Lan?

Rory: If you don't give me my rightful place, you'll deeply regret this, Landon. Remember, you're not immortal.

Bethany: I miss our good times. Can I watch if I bring you one of my friends?

Nila: You're belittling us at this point, Lan. Who's getting all your attention?

Definitely not you.

I ignore all of them, except for Ava, whom I tell that I'll pay her back the next time we meet.

Usually, I tolerate people, but at this point, they're becoming my least favorite chess pieces that I'd much rather kill off instead of seeing them on my board.

I scroll to the text that Mia obviously read but didn't reply to. When she said she was abandoning me for some stupid family dinner, I personally sent a fighting invitation to Nikolai that I knew he wouldn't refuse.

He's wanted to fight me ever since the incident that sent him to the hospital, but due to being busy with his sister, I haven't really had time for the fight club.

So yes, I might have ruined her family night, but then again, I clearly stated I'm not to be shoved aside to a mere secondary role.

I tap the back of the phone, contemplating how to drag her out of her ivory castle. I suppose I could light it on fire again, but the thought that she might accidentally get hurt promptly removes that thought from my mind.

There's the option of going home and calling it a night, but my beast rebels against the very foundation of that idea.

I've been keeping him entertained by chasing, biting, choking, and fucking Mia in the most acrobatic positions. Not to mention the bursts of creativity caused by her mere presence.

Forget being able to sculpt after she's gone. That's impossible now. My muse only manifests itself whenever Mia is around and is at its peak after I've fucked her to several powerful orgasms.

So I can't possibly get to work now or I'll only produce mediocracy. After being used to glimpses of perfection, I can't allow myself to slide back down to the peasant category.

I just refuse to work on anything but finishing touches when she's not around.

The addiction I feared is now flowing in my veins and turning into a nuisance. The worst part is that it's probably too late to cut it out without suffering the consequences.

So what should I do now?

Maybe you can just water the plants as she asked?

I'm about to reach for that sappy part of my brain and strangle him to death, but I catch a glimpse of three masked men standing in front of my car.

Well, well.

Seems my beast won't go home empty, after all.

They are, of course, the Heathens. The one wearing a yellow stitch mask didn't even bother to put any effort into hiding his identity. Nikolai is still wearing black shorts from when we were fighting. His distinctive tattoos, which could give an artist a stroke, are on full display.

A baseball bat hangs nonchalantly on the shoulder of Red Mask, who's none other than Killian. The reason I know is disgusting at best and involves seeing Glyn wearing it before making out with the bastard in his car when they came to visit my parents.

Naturally, I emptied his tires of air the moment he went inside. All four of them.

What? I managed to blame it on wild animals.

The orange mask is Jeremy, judging by the height and unnecessarily bulky build.

His weapon is a metal golf club that could possibly shatter someone's skull. The target in this case being me.

But I do have a car that could crush a few legs. Preferably all three pairs of them. I grin as I rev my engine.

This baby can go from zero to one hundred in a few seconds and will teach them a lesson or two.

Nikolai approaches first, not giving a fuck about my McLaren's loud engine.

He hits the bonnet with a fist. "Come outside."

The tasteless brute dared to touch my car.

All I need is to hit the accelerator and he'll join his family's graves.

One second passes.

Two.

Three.

I don't hit it.

As annoying as Bran is, he was right. If I hurt Nikolai, Mia is out of the picture faster than a rocket. Hell, she might hurt me back for revenge like she did with that blood bath.

In fact, that would be mild compared to what she'd do to me this time. And while I don't give a fuck about violence, I do give two fucks about her pulling away from me.

Truth is, I give more than a few fucks. A dozen of them, to be more specific.

I push my gear stick back to Park, shut off the engine, and step out of the car. *Motherfucker.*

Pain spreads through my limbs. It takes me more effort than necessary to stand by the car and paint a mocking smile on my face.

"To what do I owe this unpleasant surprise?"

"Do you want us to start counting all the shit you've stirred?" Jeremy asks while tapping his golf club on the ground.

"We'd probably be a while if you do that, so how about I take a rain check on that and this entire Halloween-esque encounter?"

"You think you can get away with it?" Nikolai steps in front of me.

"Already did. Also, the masks look hideous, so you should consider an urgent makeover of the brand. You're welcome for the free aesthetic advice."

Killian steps beside Nikolai and swings his bat. I don't move or flinch as he stops it a mere inch away from my face.

"Hi, Killian. Glyn has been wishing that we'd spend some time together. Should we FaceTime her and show this beautiful scene? Or maybe you'd rather she finds out after you're done with beating me up for sport?"

"You'll have no proof."

"There's no need. She'll know it's you." I motion at Jeremy. "You, too. Cecy might have gotten over her crush on me, but I'm still her childhood friend. A peaceful soul like hers would shatter to pieces if she finds out you touched a hair on my gorgeous head."

Jeremy lifts the club, but he doesn't even swing it in my direction.

Fucking fools. This is what happens when you submit to inferior emotions like love. You become weak and eventually lose.

I will always, without exception, reign supreme over these idiots.

Nikolai grabs me by the collar and punches me, sending me flying against my car. "I, however, can break your bones and eat them for breakfast."

"Did I miss the memo where you're a dog?"

"You think I'm joking? I will end you."

"Oh?" I straighten and make a show of wiping the fresh blood that exploded on my already split lip. "Are you sure? Think about who you're trying to impress and what role I play in their lives."

So no, Nikolai won't get within a mile radius of my brother—at least, not with a functioning dick—but it doesn't hurt to make him believe I'd allow it for my ulterior motives.

His fists clench, but he doesn't move.

"What are you doing?" Jeremy asks him. "You wanted this, no?"

Nikolai's growl fills the air and he kicks one of the cars. The loud alarm fills the otherwise silent car park as he continues growling like a cornered animal.

I pat his shoulder and whisper, "Bran is nice, but I'm not. Keep that in mind when you attempt anything funny."

"Fuck you."

"Fortunately, you're not my type." *Your sister is.*

But I don't say that in an attempt to remain civil and, most importantly, keep my balls in one piece for today. Besides, I'm already beaten up as it is.

I leisurely slide back into my car and drive away with loud revs of the engine while watching the three fools in my rearview mirror.

There will never be a day when I'm lumped in with them. Not even if I have to cut off my own arm to prevent it.

TWENTY-THREE

Mia

"**W**HAT HAPPENED?" I SIGN AS I FRANTICALLY TAKE in Nikolai's bloodied state.

He's half naked, his face a map of purple bruises with a split lip and a swollen eye. What's worse is the manic, detached look in his darkening eyes.

"Just the usual fight," Jeremy offers diplomatically, not bothering to hide the fake tone.

Killian leads Nikolai to the living area and throws him on one of the sofas with zero softness, then goes to a cabinet and retrieves his first aid kit.

"More like he got beaten up for nothing." My cousin jams an alcohol gauze against Niko's blood-coated nose. "I didn't become a med student to fix your fuckups."

"Is someone going to tell me what's going on?" I sign at the three of them.

Ever since Maya and Gareth fell asleep, I've been pacing the mansion's entrance and imagining all sorts of scenarios. I just didn't think it'd be this bad.

Imagine my reaction when the three of them come back after one in the morning. Killian's wearing an annoyed expression and Nikolai looks to be on the verge of murdering an entire village.

Jeremy is the only one who seems grounded enough as he says, "He fought with Landon."

My heart jolts so hard, I have to swallow a few times to catch my breath.

"Who invited the other?" I sign.

"Landon," Jeremy says. "He sent the four of us texts, inviting us to watch him make a fool out of Niko."

That *motherfucker*.

That's why Kill and Niko abandoned the dinner without a backward glance.

How dare he ruin my dinner with my family? To beat up my brother, no less?

I stand in front of Nikolai and force him to look at me. "Did you lose to the bastard?"

"I beat him to within an inch of his life."

"Good," I sign, and yet a strange spark of pain slithers its way to my heart.

"He only won…" Killian applies ointment without practicing any form of gentleness. "Because Landon forfeited."

"I would've won anyway," Niko growls. "You've seen how I used him as my punching bag."

"Then you let him go because someone happened to shout for you to stop." Killian clicks his tongue at him.

My brother's hands ball into fists and he fishes in his pants for a cigarette, then jams it between his lips. "Temporary lapse of judgment."

"Was the parking lot also a *temporary* lapse of judgment?" It's Jeremy who asks. "We had him in our claws and could've buried him alive then and there, but you chose to let him go."

"You also let him go." My brother points his cigarette at Killian, who's finished cleaning the blood. "And you, too, motherfucker."

"I'd love nothing more than to cut him to pieces and use his body as my forensic practice, but there's a small problem." Kill slams the first aid box shut. "He's Glyn's brother, and no matter how much she says she doesn't get along with him, she worries about him and never stopped seeing him as her brother. I'd rather the mosquito stays alive, as annoying as he is, instead of risking losing her. Besides, he's never satisfied with the lengths he goes to or the chaos he inflicts. In order to keep the same level of entertainment, he has no choice but to increase his diabolical plans. He can't possibly get away with it for eternity and will eventually self-destruct. When that happens, I'll make sure to offer Glyn a shoulder to cry on."

"Kill is right." Jeremy runs a hand over his face. "I'd love to punch him to death, but the better choice is to watch him dig his own grave. Maybe even help him dig faster without being directly involved in his demise."

I stare between them as the ache in my heart blossoms and spreads throughout my chest. What is this all about?

Why am I completely taken aback by their animosity toward Lan, when I shared it until recently?

My lips part as the weight of my own words crashes against my chest.

The keyword being *shared*. Past tense.

Not too long ago, I hated Lan with a passion and personally orchestrated his downfall. Hell, I went on that spying mission for Jeremy so I could participate in Landon's destruction.

And yet that plan has morphed into something carnal and utterly unrecognizable. It's a haze of dangerous lust and intense desire. A red mist that I can only see him through.

I still hate the bastard's guts, but I can't seem to come down from the high he knows how to drag out of me so well.

What am I supposed to do in this situation? It's only a matter of time before he targets my family or they target him. There's just too much bad blood to ignore.

When that happens, I'll be stuck in the middle and will be forced to break this new version of myself into irreparable pieces.

"Fuck that." Nikolai kills his cigarette on one of the dirty gauzes. A black and orange hole forms in the middle before it's smothered by the blood. "I'm going to kill that bastard. I don't care how, but his life is mine."

No, it's mine.

I catch myself before I sign that. Thankfully, Nikolai goes up the stairs, not bothering to say good night.

He's in a foul mood, worse than when he's on one of his usual bursts of violence.

"You're welcome," Kill shouts at his back and gets a half-hearted wave from my brother.

"You need to keep him in check," I sign to Jeremy. "No one knows what he'll do when he's in that state."

"I'll try, but I can't promise anything." He pauses as if trying to weigh his words. "How should I put it...? On the way back, he crashed his bike against a tree."

My lips part.

Kill circles his index finger near his temple. "He's going whacko."

"And it'll only get worse," Jeremy supplies.

After years of constant observation, he, of all people, recognizes Niko's off mode more than anyone else. Usually, he's able to put the brakes on it or propel Niko into diluting his intense mania.

It helps to present him with fights and people to punch. However, not even Jeremy's methods work when Niko slides down into the black hole of his brain.

I don't like it when my brother loses grip on his mind and falls into the mindless, animal instinct side of himself.

"It's all because of that waste of space Landon." Killian clicks his tongue again. "If that asshole is out of the picture, I'm sure Niko will return to being himself."

He's right. It's all because of Landon and his stupid provocations and tendencies to cause trouble with every breath he takes.

It's also because I chose the normal option of having dinner with my family. If I hadn't pushed him aside, he probably wouldn't have challenged Niko and yanked out this side of my brother.

My phone vibrates and I flinch and then cautiously check it. If it's Landon, I'll kill him—

My murderous thoughts pause when I see the name on the screen.

Bran: Can I see you for a minute?

I reply in the affirmative and agree to meet him at the beach. Kill goes upstairs, but Jeremy stays behind.

"What?" I sign as I slide my phone back into my pocket.

"The mission about spying on Landon is terminated. Effective immediately."

"But—"

"Not another word, Mia. If Niko finds out about this, I'll lose him for good and that's not a risk I'm willing to take." He pats my shoulder. "Landon asshole King isn't worth it."

I nod, for once feeling his words instead of hearing them.

Jeremy's right. Landon isn't worth it.

His enigmatic presence and his intense touch and safe company are not worth jeopardizing my brother's mental state.

Metaphorical darkness lurches in my chest during the whole drive to the beach. The decision I have to make is loud and clear, but my heart still resists, floundering and twisting in its binds and refusing to submit to its fate.

When I arrive, I find Bran leaning against the hood of his car, absentmindedly looking at his phone.

I park behind him and step out of my car. Goosebumps erupt on my skin at the night beach breeze, and I taste the salt on my lips.

The waves crash against the rocky shore, creating a wild, turbulent chaos similar to the clash between my heart and mind.

Bran is scrolling through a familiar IG, but before I can figure out whose, he notices me and makes his phone screen go black.

We briefly hug in greeting before we lean against the car's hood so that we're both staring at the angry sea. Under the headlights, he appears pale, unsettled, even.

It's disturbing how much he looks like Lan but doesn't share any of his characteristics or intensity. They're the same on the outside but completely different on the inside.

"You wanted to see me?" I type on the phone.

"I want to tell you a story," he says with his usual calm.

I nod, even though I'm not sure where he's going with this. Especially since he's been avoiding me lately.

His eyes appear as bottomless as the ocean when he speaks. "When I was in secondary school, high school for you Americans, I was targeted by a group of three excruciatingly rotten guys. They made it their mission to not only ridicule me, but to also spread nasty rumors about me, including, but not limited to, my mental state and sexual life. I ignored them because they're not worth it, and usually, these types of rumors die out when they find a fresh target.

"Landon used to hang out in their circle and actively participate in the mayhem they brought to other people's lives. In fact, he could've even been their leader and the instigator of the chaos they caused. However, after I became their newest toy for the week and he found out about it, the situation quickly escalated to absolute carnage. He beat them up and broke enough bones that they had to be admitted to the hospital. But do you think he stopped there? Not even close. As soon as they started recovering, he planted drugs in their lockers, spread rumors about their sexual inadequacies, and turned them into the joke of the school.

"Just like that, they became the outcasts and the targets of bullying. Then he threatened their parents with incriminating pictures of their adulteries and tax evasion proof. He shattered their reputations, jeopardized the foundation of their families, and completely destroyed their minds. At some point, one of them lost it and attacked Landon. He stabbed him in front of the entire school and got arrested. He's still serving time for that. The second guy had a mental breakdown and is in the psych ward as we speak. The third one hasn't left his house in six whole years."

I cup my mouth, unable to control the shock that rattles me to the bone. So the scar on Landon's stomach is a result from that stabbing.

Brandon continues in the same tone, "I'll never forget the look on his face when he was stabbed. He was smiling triumphantly for driving someone to the edge and giving them the final shove over it. He didn't even care about the pain as long as he got what he wanted."

He tilts his head in my direction. "Do you think Lan did that because he cares about me or my well-being? No, and no. It was for himself. Due to my being his identical twin, Lan has always seen me as his property and an extension of his being. He considers any disrespect toward me a direct attack on his person. Which is why he likes to keep me on a leash. He did the same to Glyn, which is why he hates Killian with a passion. Not only was he not intimidated by Lan's antisocial tendencies, but he was also the first boyfriend that she chose on her own. All her exes were personally picked by Lan and threatened with bodily harm if they touched her inappropriately."

"What are you saying?" I sign, not sure if he understands it.

Apparently, he does, because he releases a sigh. "Landon suffers from an antisocial and narcissistic personality disorder. Like Killian. The only difference is that Killian makes an effort to care and I have no doubt that he treats my sister right. Lan would never care or try to. He sees everyone as pawns or possessions. It doesn't matter what effort he puts into a relationship, he only makes it for egotistical reasons to benefit himself. I like you, Mia, and I don't want you to be one of the people he destroys."

I stare at my boots that are covered by the sand, then type on my phone, "How did you know?"

"He likes announcing his possessions. Besides, you're a bit obvious when he's around."

"And here I thought I was discreet."

He smiles a little. "If it's any consolation, I'm probably the only one who could pick up on it."

I smile back. "You're right. Tonight, I had two wake-up calls. The first was him hurting my brother and the second is this."

Bran straightens. "Is your brother okay?"

I shake my head.

"Was…he badly hurt?"

"Physically? No. Mentally, however, it's highly debatable."

"And it's because of Lan?"

"The one and only devil lord." I smile sarcastically as I type, "I almost forgot that he nearly killed my brother with his shenanigans. And now, he's done this. I should really stay away from him, shouldn't I?"

"You should." His brows dip. "I don't even know what you see in him."

Danger.

Thrill.

Illusion.

The monster who can fight the other monster.

"I know, right? You're a good guy, Bran. I should've totally fallen for you."

"But you didn't."

"Unfortunately."

He smiles. "You have terrible taste, but if it's of any consolation, I understand why girls flock to him. They're attracted to his charm and, most importantly, to the prospect of being the chosen one who can fix him."

I shake my head, but I don't type anything.

Never have I thought about fixing Landon. If anything, I slid down his rabbit hole as if it were where I always belonged.

In the thrilling darkness.

The animalistic chasing.

The explosive fucking.

But now, I realize with clarity that some desires are better left unfulfilled for everyone's greater good.

"He's too set in his way of thinking," Bran continues. "After years of futile clashing with our father, Dad gave up trying to correct him and eventually left him to his own devices. It's hard to speak reason to him and impossible to change him."

"And yet something tells me you're not giving up?"

"I'm an idiot and stuck with him for life. Everyone else should save themselves while they have the opportunity."

"You're not an idiot, Bran. You just care." I show him my phone and then pat his shoulder.

"One of us has to." A bitter smile crosses his lips. "I'm sorry if your acquaintance with me has caused this trouble—"

I put a hand on his mouth and shake my head, then I type, "Don't you dare blame yourself. I made this choice about Landon and I'll handle the consequences. Besides, meeting you is one of the best things that's happened to me, so don't avoid me again. We should probably meet outside, though."

"Why?"

"Because I'd rather not cross paths with your psycho brother."

"No, I meant why do you still want to see me if Lan is out of the picture?"

My lips part and I type furiously, "Don't tell me all this time you thought I was befriending you to get close to Landon?"

"Weren't you?"

"Of course not. I liked you and hated the asshole from the beginning."

He grabs the back of his neck, a shy smile appearing on his lips. "Thanks. You're the first girl who's actually liked me and didn't fake interest in me just to get close to Landon."

"They do that?"

"Yeah. Apparently, I'm the boring twin and he's the hot one."

"I'm going to need names so I can teach the blind bitches a fucking lesson." I punch the air, then kick it.

Bran throws his head back and laughs. I laugh, too, even though no feelings of joy penetrate my heavy chest.

After Bran and I part ways, I drive to the Heathens' mansion. My screen pings with a text from Landon and I hit the brakes, coming to a sudden halt.

The ache in my heart spreads and causes my throat to restrict as I tap the screen.

He attached a half-naked mirror selfie, showcasing the dark purple bruises on his chest and his bloodied lips.

Devil Lord: Your brother did this. Come kiss it better?

While I saw glimpses of his manipulation tactics before, I had a veil over my eyes. But now, I can distinguish it loud and clear. Landon has the fascinating ability to use his own pain as a weapon to make his will a reality.

Just like when Bran said he was smiling while being stabbed.

Still, I can't control the pulsing pain in my chest as I type.

Mia: I'm bored. We're done.

Then I block his number and his IG.

Best way to get rid of a rotten limb? Amputate it. Even if it hurts like crazy.

I don't know if it's because I've lost the safety illusion, but as I drive past the gate, I sense the monster's eyes following me and his breath trickling down my neck.

TWENTY-FOUR

Mia

A FINGER SNAPS IN MY FACE AND I STARTLE AS I MEET MY identical eyes. Only, the ones in front of me are framed with glittery eyeshadow and have two neon hearts on the corners.

Maya gesticulates in my direction while holding a massive coffee cup. "How dare you ignore my very important ramblings about our birthday preparations!"

"Sorry," I sign, then take a long slurp from my Frappuccino as I stare out the cute coffee shop's tall glass windows.

"You don't even mean that." She nudges me under the table with her pointy toe.

"Here. Let me take your picture. It's good lighting."

"Yes!" She passes me her phone and then quickly retracts it. "You're not changing the subject or bribing me, Mia."

Epic failure.

I wince and play with the blue straw of my reusable cup. In a further attempt to disperse Maya's hawklike attention, I take pictures of her using my phone.

She poses for a few, but then she snatches my phone and glares at me. "What's the reason behind the sudden reappearance of the emo?"

"I'm not going into an emo phase."

"Bitch, please. You've been eating ice cream à la cheesy chick flicks, and lately, you wear so few ribbons, it's a bit disturbing. Also, you haven't been nagging me about all the sneaking around I've been doing lately."

"Wait. You weren't with your fashion club?"

"There!" She slams her cup on the table. "The old Mia would've made sure I was with the fashion club, not just take my word for it."

I groan into my hands and busy myself with slurping intensively.

"Don't ignore me," Maya warns. "Unless you tell me what's going on, I won't know how to help you."

I inhale a deep breath. It's been three days since I blocked Landon out of my life.

Three days of restless sleep.

Faceless monster nightmares.

And excruciating emptiness.

The type that lurks in the background, no matter how much I keep myself occupied.

It doesn't help that the marks Landon left on my body are taking their sweet time in fading away. Almost as if they got past the barrier of my flesh and are lingering in my soul.

To make things worse, he didn't just take the hint and leave me alone. Of course not. In true Landon fashion, he texted me from a different number the same day I blocked him.

Whatever got your knickers in a twist better untwist sooner rather than later. I hate to break it to your pretty little head, but we're not, in fact, done.

I blocked him again.

Then I spent the past two days ignoring my phone and pretending I'm at full capacity, when, in reality, I'm barely surviving.

It took some time to realize that I was so deep into Landon's world that I needed the distance to see things clearly. My eyes were covered by a mist of lust and chaotic emotions and now I have the chance to see the world without it.

A world in which Landon is the definition of every decadent emotion and the hallmark of unapologetic psychos.

"It's just a down phase," I sign to Maya and mean it.

I really believe that I'm an addict and rehabilitation takes some time. First comes the excruciating withdrawals and then I'll be immune.

Maya abandons her seat and crowds my bench to envelop me in a clingy hug. "I was thinking your nightmares had gradually disappeared, but the past few days, you've been having screaming nightmares."

My lips part and I gently push her away. "I was screaming?"

She nods. "I was so scared and tried to wake you up, but you never acknowledged me."

"I'm sorry for scaring you."

"I wasn't scared of you, idiot. I was scared *for* you." Tears shine in her eyes. "I feel so helpless whenever I want to ease your pain but can't. If I could...I would take all your nightmares."

I stroke her cheek and wipe away her tears. As much as I love and appreciate Maya, I'm well aware that no one can take away these nightmares.

For a foolish moment, I thought Lan would with his crazy kinks and evil character. And yes, his presence helped, but the nightmares never completely vanished.

It's me who desperately needs to acknowledge these tangled-up emotions and ideally find solutions for them.

"I'm fine, idiot," I sign. "And, seriously, stop crying or you'll ruin your makeup."

"Don't care." She hugs me again, burying her face in my neck. "Promise you'll tell me first when you're ready to talk about ten years ago."

I nod against her, even though I don't plan to talk about it. Not now, not ever.

My shoulders lock together at the thought of mentioning the monster again. I barely managed to escape the first time. I won't be able to make it out alive the second time.

Subtly, I pull away from Maya and tell her I need to use the bathroom.

Once I'm inside the stall, I lock the door and lean against it to catch my breath.

It's all going to be okay. I've survived worse states of mind, so why does this one feel fundamentally different?

Cheerful female voices reach me from outside, then disappear. So I open the door and force a brave façade.

The moment I step out, a hand wraps around my throat and shoves me back inside the tiny stall.

My back hits the flimsy wooden separator with a thwack as a tall frame looms over me with the horrifying aura of the Grim Reaper.

It's insane how someone's presence can take the form of a hurricane, but that's exactly what I feel as I stare into Landon's darkened eyes. There's no trace of his permanent taunting smirk, as if he's done pretending to be the charming god whose altar everyone worships at.

Right now, he looks nothing short of a beast who's out for mayhem.

He kicks the door closed and slams his other hand beside my head. The *thwack* reverberates at the base of my belly as he imprisons me in his grip.

"Hi, muse. Miss me?"

I plant a hand on his chest and attempt to push him. All of a sudden, his firm yet loose hand on my throat tightens. The breath rushes out of my lungs in one whoosh and tears form at the corners of my eyes. I claw at the collar of his shirt, scratching the skin in a desperate effort to remove his grip.

Landon, however, doesn't waver. Not even a little. Not even close. "Don't fight me, Mia. Not when I'm *so* close to fucking you all up."

Slowly, and against my better judgment, I drop my hand from his chest and stare at his monstrous face through my blurry vision. He means it, and I know that not only is it futile to fight, but if I do, I'll also provoke his uglier side.

His fingers ease on my throat, but they're not completely gone. "You're intelligent enough to recognize my beast's cues, so whatever gave you the impression that blocking and ignoring me was such a brilliant idea?"

I lift my shaky hands and sign, "I told you. I'm bored."

"Nonsense."

"I don't want you anymore."

"More fucking nonsense."

"It's not my problem that your ego is bigger than the earth and can't take the reality."

"What reality?"

"The fact that you're not all that. I got a taste and the high only lasted for so long." I glare at him, then shoot him his favorite sardonic smirk. "I'm fucking bored."

It's one moment, a fraction of a second in time, but I think I catch the subtle clenching in his jaw. The dark blue of his eyes morphs into a bottomless ocean where thousands of ships would meet their demise.

I'm not sure if I'm the ship or the storm that's sinking it to the bottom. Maybe I'm both.

"The fucks I have to give about your feelings are nonexistent."

"And yet you're acting as clingy as a desperate ex."

"Mia…don't push it. You're starting to piss me the fuck off."

"Oh my. I'd be affected if I could care less." I push him again. "As I said in that text, we're done, Landon. Go find yourself another toy."

"I never agreed to that and, therefore, it's not happening."

"You know what? This is your problem. You're so conceited and up your own ass that you don't even notice when others are bothered, suffocated, or completely miserable due to your presence and actions. You don't care about the well-being of people close to you and even go out of your way to hurt them and sabotage their lives just because they happen to cross your path. If you look up the word asshole in the dictionary, you'll find your picture on it."

"Are you certain the word *asshole* is in the dictionary?" he delivers with unbothered calm.

"Is that all you heard from what I was saying?"

"Was I supposed to hear something else? Pretentiousness laced with a sense of victimization, perhaps?" He pushes his thumb against the pulse point in my throat. "Don't act as if I forced you into anything, Mia. You begged for my cock on your fucking knees before you proceeded to choke on it. You ran so I'd chase you. You fought me so I'd wrestle you down. Spoiler alert, just because you pretend it was all me doesn't take away your share of responsibility."

"I'm not you. I take full responsibility for my actions. I admit that I made a mistake in falling into your trap, which is why I'm rectifying it. Let me go, Landon. Unless you're ready to force me and unavoidably get your throat slit."

The corner of his lips pulls in one of his taunting smirks. "You think the prospect of a slit throat would stop me?"

"No. But the possibility of losing my fight would. You want me because I challenge you every step of the way. I make you work for that fuck, unlike many of your previous dolls who opened their legs or dropped to their knees willingly. You reach a climax because, as you previously stated, I'm difficult. What you didn't say is that you can only feel alive when there's a certain level of provocation or defiance. You're so empty inside that you need chaos to feel alive. You're so emotionally stunted that anarchy has become the soul of all your relationships. So if you're in the mood, go ahead and force me, Landon. I'll become as lifeless as your countless statues until I get the chance to kill you."

There, psycho. You think you're the only one who's perceptive about others?

I lift my chin, waiting for the smirk to be wiped off his face. My spine jerks when not only does it stay in place, but it also widens, so much so that he looks like a demon lord on his way to a war.

My body tightens, ready for a spar, though I really can't take anything physical right now. Despite my big talk, I'm still not immune to his touch. Hell, the place where his fingers spread burns and sends a rush of tingles throughout my starved body.

I expect him to push further, to taunt and ridicule me with his brand of sarcasm, as is the norm for the asshole. However, he swiftly and easily releases me and even steps back, allowing me my first breath without his intoxicating scent and overpowering presence.

"You want me to let you go? There, I let you go."

I stare at him, not believing what I just heard. Is Landon giving up? That's just unfathomable. I expected resistance. Hell, I thought I'd be in this limbo for a while before he finally got bored and gave up.

I also thought he'd go the brute route and try to keep me by force or threaten me as he's done countless times before.

This completely unbothered version was never, not even for one second, on my list of expectations.

"Mia?" Maya's voice filters in from somewhere outside. "What's taking you so long?"

"Go," he whispers with that smirk still in place. "Run, muse. Try to hide. If you let me catch you again, I'll fuck up your barely put-together life."

My spine jerks and my fight-or-flight response surges to the surface in one overpowering go. I've always opted for a fight, even when I was an underdog and could be beaten to death.

The only exception is when I'm faced with Landon. I can't fight. If I do, I'll just slide back into his trap.

And he looks absolutely venomous and positively ravenous for another bite of my flesh.

I don't give him that.

With one last look at his taunting grin and clenching jaw, I pull the door open and do what I should've done the first time I met him.

I run.

My birthday has always been a weird event. One, I've never really liked to be the center of attention, and that situation can turn from mildly weird to full-blown awkward.

Unlike me, Maya thrives on being the star of the show. She's wearing a white chiffon princess dress with high heels that add unnecessary height to her already long legs. Perfect blonde curls fall down her back, teasing at the bare skin beneath it. As is customary on our birthday, I'm wearing the black version of her dress with knee-length leather boots. My hair is tied in pigtails intertwined with blue ribbons.

This is the first year we're celebrating our birthday without our parents. Mum and Dad offered to come, but Maya said she wants to celebrate with friends. I didn't encourage them either, because I could and would blurt out everything about the chaos that's been happening in my life lately.

Still, Mom and Dad sent us gifts and were the first to wish us a happy birthday. They told us they loved us and that we were the brightest stars of their lives.

Niko, Kill, and Gareth threw us a massive party in the Heathens' mansion. Everyone from TKU and their next of kin have flocked to the extravagance of money and blinding power.

They look up to my brother, cousins, and Jeremy as if they're celebrities. The Heathens' nonnegotiable power and untouchable vibe are everything they want to be. Mom has always told me that power is a dangerous game if you don't know how to play it.

The Heathens, led by Jeremy, definitely do.

And that type of charisma attracts people like a magnet. This is why the hall downstairs brims with people, alcohol, and loud trendy music

Maya is dancing with a group of her fake friends of the week, taking pictures, and chugging alcohol. Technically, we're supposed to wait until we're twenty-one, but we've been drinking since last year. Besides, it's the UK, and the legal drinking age here is eighteen.

Niko doesn't seem to mind either. I'm sitting between him and Kill on a sofa on the upper floor. From our position, we can overlook the entire party while being detached from it.

I'd rather go to the chess club or have a birthday talk with my plants instead of taking part in this mindless celebration.

Worse, a part of me sees it as an anniversary of being a powerless mute. It's been nearly eleven years already and there's still that dooming thought that I'll never be able to speak again.

Here's to another year of complete silence, I tell myself as I take a sip of foul-tasting beer.

I don't particularly like alcohol, and I'm such an embarrassing lightweight, but I need to shut off my brain tonight.

Especially since it's been on high alert ever since last week when Landon declared that he'd let me go. He hasn't tried to contact me from a thousand numbers, hasn't cornered me again, and hasn't even gone to the chess club.

I've been there almost every day to play against Mr. Whitby, but I was told Landon hasn't been coming to the club at all lately.

Not that I care.

In fact, I'm glad he's out of my life. I suspected the brief, tension-charged meeting in the bathroom wasn't the end of Landon, but maybe I'm reading too much into it.

Maybe he's finally done with me.

Good.

I don't need the definition of toxic drama in my life.

And yet the beer tastes even more bitter and disgusting. Everything does.

I'm convinced it's just a phase. It *has* to be.

"Why aren't you dancing down there with your less pleasant clone, baby Sokolov?" Kill yells over the music and nudges my arm with his.

I lift my shoulder and don't say anything.

Besides, one—or two—of us needs to keep an eye on Niko.

I steal a peek at my brother, who's been chain-smoking for the past thirty minutes. One after the other, as if he's on a mission to give his lungs cancer.

He's been getting worse, not better, despite the coping methods Jeremy has been dishing his way. It seems that no amount of violence will drag my brother from his state of mental self-destruction.

I tap his hand and he looks at me, but like this morning when he hugged us and wished us a happy birthday, he's not really seeing me.

After abandoning my can of beer on the coffee table, I sign, "Wanna dance?"

He shakes his head.

"For me?" I blink my eyes innocently.

He shakes his head again.

Kill throws a pillow at him. "It's her birthday. Do it."

"I'm going to fucking murder you, motherfucker." Nikolai throws back the pillow, hitting Kill square in the face.

My cousin doesn't do it again, because he might have provoked Nikolai's trigger-happy fight response.

I grab my brother's hand and pull, but since he's a specimen of pure muscle, it's impossible to move him.

Finally, he stubs out his half-finished cigarette in the overcrowded ashtray and lets me tug him to a standing position.

I hold on to his hands as I jump to the music. At first, he's completely unaffected, but then Kill joins us and pushes Niko to make more of an effort.

The whole dancing thing happens due to them shoving each other and spinning me around.

For a moment, I get to unwind, laughing and giggling at how they're so close to fighting while pretending to dance.

Then, all of a sudden, Kill comes to a halt.

The reason is none other than Jeremy walking in our direction, an arm wrapped around the small of his girlfriend Cecily's back and accompanied by Glyn and Bran.

Glyn envelops me in a hug and pushes a bag into my hand. "It's small gifts from the three of us. Happy Birthday."

"Thank you. You didn't have to," I sign and look at Bran, who's unusually stiff, then type on my phone, "I didn't think you'd come."

"You personally invited me. I wouldn't miss it," he says with a polite smile, keeping his eyes on me.

"What the fuck are you doing here?" Nikolai pushes me behind him and gets nose to nose with Bran. "Another elaborate plan from your brother? What is it this time? Arson? Assault? Murder, maybe?"

I grab onto Nikolai's arm, and when he doesn't move, I stand beside him and sign, "Bran is my friend. I invited him to my birthday."

"It's okay, Mia," Bran says to me, even though his eyes, disturbingly similar to Landon's when he's angry, remain on Niko. "I couldn't care less about your brother's opinion of me, but it's probably better that I leave."

"No." I shake my head a few times.

"Mia is right," Jeremy says. "You're our guest."

Killian, who just finished kissing Glyn—or more like eating

her face in front of her brother—releases her and grabs Niko by the shoulder. "If you can accept Glyn and Cecily, you'll have to accept Bran, too. He has nothing to do with Lan, despite the creepy physical resemblance."

"He's right," Glyn says in a soft voice. "Bran is completely different from Lan. I promise."

Nikolai continues glaring at Bran as if he wants to seep inside him and destroy whatever he finds in there.

This side of my brother is eerily frightening, and the worst part is that I don't think I've ever seen it before.

I grab his hand and pull him back so that he looks at me. "It's my birthday. I get to invite whomever I please. Don't ruin it, please."

He grunts and snatches his pack of cigarettes, but before any of us can release a breath, the hairs on the back of my neck stand on end.

Oh, no.

Please tell me I'm overthinking—

My hopeful thoughts come to an end when a very familiar, effortlessly taunting voice echoes in the air.

"What's with the tense atmosphere? I thought this was a birthday. Also, did someone mention the word 'ruin'?"

My eyes widen upon clashing with none other than Landon's.

I was wrong.

He doesn't look one bit done with me.

TWENTY-FIVE

Landon

DIFFERENT DAY, SAME IRREPARABLE NEED TO FUCK UP THE world and watch it crash and burn.

A wave of hostility shoots in my direction, attempting—and failing—to penetrate my skin from every side. Glares and sneers bounce off my outer layer like rubber arrows.

None of them mean shit to me.

The only one I honor with my undivided attention is the girl in a hot black dress that hugs her curves in all the right places. A leather collar is wrapped around her delicate throat and my favorite blue ribbons snake through her pigtails.

Defiant, proud eyes the color of blue wildflowers stare at me. For a moment, during the fraction of a second when I made my spectacular theatrical entry, those eyes were stupefied, then those emotions morphed into being horrified, but now they're pools of disapproval.

I can work with disapproval.

Hate, even.

I'm proficient in antagonistic situations and won't be leaving until I'm back in my muse's good graces. I didn't realize how much I missed her until I listened to the recording of her voice on a loop.

And I didn't know I was capable of *missing* someone.

Now, the method I came up with might be controversial at best and suicidal at worst, but I need to set certain records straight in front of the whole world.

"What the fuck do you think you're doing here?" Jeremy, the waste of space bulk of a man, tightens his grip on Cecily and sharpens his entire body for an attack.

In fact, all of them do, including my own siblings. They don't have a loyal bone in their bodies. The only one who's subtle about their need to maim me is Killian, but he does hold Glyn close, as if he needs to protect her from me—her own flesh and blood.

Glyn and Cecily look more aggrieved than old ladies who've lost their pensions and are seriously considering the option of burying themselves alive. Bran's expression turns to that of full-blown pain like when he watched me get stabbed for his fragile honor.

At the other extreme stands none other than Nikolai. In the myriad of conflicted and absolutely stunning reactions to my godly presence, he's the one who fails to hide an ounce of hostility and lets it flood his body language and manic expression.

"I thought this was a birthday and everyone was invited," I say lightly, ignoring the world war that's brewing in the distance.

"You're not," Killian says point-blank.

"Seems that I am now." I step toward Mia, who's been watching me the entire time as if I'm a statue, not its maker. "Happy Birthday. Aside from the gift of my attendance, I have something else for you, but I'd rather give it to you in private—"

I don't manage to take my second step before Nikolai slams his fist square into my beautiful face.

Coughs escape my clogged throat and I spit the metallic liquid that's filling my mouth on the floor. My first instinct is to spew it in Nikolai's fucking face, but that won't do me any favors for the case I'm trying to make.

"Lan..." Glyn releases herself from her boyfriend and comes running to me.

Maybe I was wrong and she does have some semblance of loyalty to me, after all.

She stops a few paces away as if she's scared to get any closer. "Just…go."

I take it back. She just doesn't want any drama in her lowlife boyfriend's place and is probably scared for his cousin's life.

Which is legitimate since if he weren't my muse's brother, he'd be driven up the wall with my fist as we speak. Then probably shipped to a mental institute that he so desperately needs.

"I didn't go through all the trouble of bribing incompetent security guards just to leave." My gaze meets Mia's horrified one.

She's taken a step forward, and one of her hands is balled into a tight fist. A part of me soars at the idea that she's worried about me, after all, but it soon crashes and burns when she grabs onto her brother's arm.

"He's not worth it, Niko."

That's what she signs—with a straight face, I might add.

Did she just say I'm not worth it? *Me?* Landon fucking King?

Nikolai obviously disagrees and definitely thinks—like everyone else who isn't Mia—that I'm well worth it since he raises his fist again.

Killian subtly pulls Glyn from the middle of the action so that she's once again in his overrated protective cocoon.

"Time out." I lift a hand in front of Nikolai. "Before you proceed with your attempts at rearranging my features, allow me to clarify an important element. I happen to be in the process of courting your sister, and any attempts at ruining my face will not play in the favor of said task."

Everyone is stunned into silence, including Nikolai, whose fist remains suspended in midair. I like to call this the Landon effect— quite powerful and pleasing to watch.

Mia is the first one who recovers and graces me with the glare of all glares; lips pursed and eyes blazing with fire.

She's the holiest view I've ever stumbled across, and I'm not a religious person by any stretch of the imagination.

"I'm going to fucking kill you before you lay a hand on her." Nikolai flings forward.

"Oh, that's already done."

Another pause.

Another myriad of beautiful, stupefied expressions that are a product of my words.

"What the fuck did you just say?" This time, Nikolai has enough patience to speak slowly.

"I said." I close the distance between us so we're eye to eye. "The touching part already happened. In fact, our rendezvous included more than touching, but I'll spare you the details since you're her brother."

"You fucking—" He pushes into me and I'm about to let him pummel me to the ground for Mia's difficult sake, but Bran moves in front of me and takes the punch.

My brother staggers back and falls against my chest.

The change of events is so fast-paced that everyone takes some time to come to terms with the new variable in the equation.

My idiotic fucking brother.

I grab him by the arm so that he doesn't fall sideways and inspect the cut on his lower lip and the blood that's gushing from it.

The motherfucker who would be dead if he didn't have a blood relationship with Mia got him good. Bran shakes his head a few times as if he's fighting a concussion. While I'm fine with violence and do strive for it whenever possible, Bran is literally squeamish about blood.

I pull out a tissue and help him wipe the shit off his lip as he struggles to remain standing.

Nikolai doesn't move, his jaw ticking and his muscles tightening until the veins bulge. Killian, Jeremy, and Mia pull him back and, unlike what I expect, he doesn't fight it.

Instead, he points his glare at his sister. "Is it true?"

She freezes, and any attempts to calm her brother down come to a staggering halt.

"Is what the fucker said true, Mia?" he asks again, his voice filled with enough tension to start a nuclear war. "Have you been sleeping with him?"

An expression I've never seen on Mia's face greets me. An expression I now realize I don't ever want to see on her delicate features again.

Shame.

First, I'm not worth it.

Now, she's fucking ashamed of me.

She slides her gaze to me, and even though I've been busy trying to stop the bleeding on Bran's fucked-up lip, I meet the eyes that have been haunting my every waking moment.

Go ahead and lie, Mia. Go ahead and deny yourself and pretend it's all a fucking illusion.

"It's not what you think," she signs.

"And what does he think?" I slap the tissue against Bran's mouth and shove his hand on it, then step in front of him so that I'm facing Mia.

"You shut up." Her movements are jerky, uncoordinated, and hint at a complete loss of control.

Good.

Maybe this way, she'll be able to understand the frustration of being cast aside and discarded like a used condom.

"I'm happy to shut up, but only if you tell the truth and nothing but the truth."

Liquid eyes the color of a stormy sea glare me down as if I'm the next target on her hit list.

"What is he talking about?" It's Killian who asks this time, his expression darkening.

Considering his pseudo-brother relationship with Mia, his distress brings me great satisfaction. *How does it feel to walk in my shoes, motherfucker?*

Mia glares at me again before she signs, "It was just a ruse that meant nothing. It's all over now."

I'm going to choke the little shit to fucking death.

But then, in the still-functioning logical part of my brain, I realize she's saying all these demeaning things on purpose.

I let my grin show through, hoping the blood makes it more gruesome. "I disrespectfully disagree. It was more than a ruse and is far from being over. Mia and I came to a slight disagreement about priorities and my notorious penchant for anarchy. Despite my dramatic entry, I'm not here to stir up any shit. On the contrary, I came to propose a long-due truce between our clubs."

"Not even when you're buried six feet under," Nikolai snarls.

"I wouldn't be so quick to rule it out." I meet Mia's gaze. "This rare chance will work out so well for both of us if you just give it a go."

"My sister is not for fucking sale."

"I never suggested that. Unlike what she said, Mia came to meet me every night. There was no coercion involved in our nighttime rendezvous."

Nikolai's eyes slide to her again and she looks hotter than a ripe tomato before she meets my gaze. "Whether the truce happens or not, I'll never go back to you."

"Never say never." I was going to add *muse* at the end, but I'm not in the mood for the extended audience to have their nose in my business.

It's enough that I've made this very public display of affection.

Her chin trembles. "You're insane."

"Guilty as charged."

"You won't have me."

"I had you once."

"Won't be happening again."

"We won't know until I try."

"Stop being delusional."

"Stop fighting the inevitable."

Nikolai steps between us, accompanied by his dull sidekick Jeremy, and puts a sudden halt to our harmless banter. "Leave before I fuck up your face."

"Last I checked, that's not a good starting point for a truce, no?"

"Let's just go." Bran pulls on my arm, but I don't move.

"I won't be taking a step outside unless, one, you give me your word about the truce." I meet Jeremy's gaze. "You know this is for everyone's benefit. Cecily and Glyn included."

"Not happening," Nikolai grinds out.

"It can be for your benefit, too," I say casually. "In return, I will refrain from breaking your face for the damage you inflicted on my brother."

"Forget it, Lan." Bran pulls harder, his fingers digging into my arm. "I'm fine."

"No, you're not." I tilt my head in Nikolai's direction. "I don't like it when others harm my family."

"Funny coming from you." He tries to free himself from Kill's grip. "Once I'm done with you, nothing will be left for anyone to recognize."

"Please stop," Glyn pleads with him and I realize that she's also on my side now, her hands slightly shaking. She looks at her joke of a boyfriend. "Lan isn't the type who offers truces, so can you take it?"

My baby sister knows me, after all. Because she's right. Truces don't exist in my vocabulary of fucked-up anarchy.

But then again, drastic measures need to be made to trigger a considerable change.

"Even if we agree to the truce," Killian says, "Mia is off the table."

"That's not for you to decide, is it?" I smile and meet her gaze.

"She already told you no," Jeremy says.

"I can work with a no." I step toward her, followed by Glyn and Bran, who install themselves as my amateur bodyguards.

Mia keeps watching me with that tense expression as I slip a small box into her palm, then say so only she can hear me, "Happy Birthday, little muse. Remember, a future where you don't belong to me doesn't exist."

Nikolai shoves me back so hard, I half fall on Bran and Glyn, who wince at the brute's animalistic force.

The fucker is pushing it, and I will make him pay. Just not today.

"I'll take that as you said yes to my offer. As for the Mia issue, I'll leave that to her. Just know that I won't take lightly to any censorship or attempts to keep me away from her. You can torture me if you fancy. I'll also leave my door open in case you want to kidnap me and exact revenge for past travesties, so let me know your plan. Or don't. I'm open to surprises." I stare at Killian. "You and I are even, considering the whole Glyn situation."

He steps forward, but Glyn and Bran are already pulling me back.

"I'll be out of your hair," I call. "For some reason, it feels like I'm not welcome here. I wonder why."

"You motherfucking——" Nikolai comes for me, but Killian, Jeremy, and Cecily drag him back.

Mia stands there, one hand balled into a fist around my gift and her eyes blazing with inextinguishable fire.

I physically have to stop myself from running back there and kidnapping the fuck out of her.

Then it hits me.

The reason behind the horrible feeling I've been experiencing ever since she fucked off out of my life.

The peculiar emptiness.

The absolute lack of motivation for anything but creating schemes for how to get her back without fucking up what she cares about.

I've become categorically obsessed with Mia Sokolov. My mind has filtered the whole world out and all I see is her defiant face.

In every corner.

On every statue.

Every-fucking-where.

And now that I've seen her again, the last thing I want to do is leave.

"What the hell is wrong with you?" Bran asks as soon as we're out of the pretentious Heathens' mansion and in front of my car.

I shake myself out of the strange phase I've been trapped in and focus on the disapproving faces of my siblings.

Glyn crosses her arms. "This is ballsy even for you."

"I'm nothing if not full of surprises." I grin and wince at the pain that explodes in my mouth. "That being said, I love your loyalty and the feeble attempts at protecting me."

"More like we were trying to protect people from you." Glyn releases an exasperated breath. "Can't you just stop?"

"Stop what?"

"This whole thing with Mia."

"No."

"But you don't care about girls."

"She's not just a girl." *She's my muse.* There's no other explanation for this need to possess her until she wholly belongs to me.

The inexplicable urge to have her with me at all times.

It's getting to the point where I don't recognize myself when I'm not with her and that's a serious problem.

"You mean to tell us you won't discard her the moment you're bored, which is due to happen very soon?" Bran asks.

"If I were going to get bored, I would've been so weeks ago."

"But you will, Lan," Glyn says. "That's what you do. You get bored and you hurt people to feel a form of pleasure."

"Thanks for the amateurish psychotherapy, little princess. But if you want to make your psychological endeavors more realistic, you should've inserted your boyfriend as a plug. Doesn't he get bored easily as well?"

"Kill is different."

"In what sense? You've managed to understand him because he's similar to me, so why, suddenly, is he the love of your life while I'm the forever devil?"

"Because you've never made an effort to love us, Lan!" she screams. "I know you're wired differently and no one can change your nature. I understand that. What I don't understand is why you expect us to behave according to the lines you trace, and when we act out, you squash us until we fall back to where you want us to be. You protect us because of your sense of possessiveness and the fact that we make you look good. Bran and I protected you just now because, despite everything, you're our brother and we care about you. We don't calculate in our relationship with you and we certainly don't use you just because we're bored. All we want is for you to make an effort and stop following your narcissistic instincts when dealing with your own brother and sister."

Tears gather in her eyes and Bran holds her by the shoulder, his expression as wretched as hers.

As the scene plays out in front of me, I recall the conversation I had with Uncle Aiden right after I cornered Mia in the tiny bathroom stall.

I'd intended to pretend to let her go just so I could sweep in again and remind her that I'm her only option.

But then I called Uncle Aiden. He's Eli and Creighton's father, but we've always been close because I'm that loveable.

Well, that's a lie. He's one of the few people who doesn't judge me, despite my extreme chaos-oriented nature.

He also encouraged my dad to just let me be when I was developing my holier-than-thou personality.

Uncle Aiden has always treated me and Eli with respect, even though we're different from everyone else.

Possibly because he shares some of our traits.

I put in my AirPods, fingers splaying on an unremarkable piece of clay that will definitely make it to the bin collection.

Uncle Aiden picks up after the first ring. "Why, hello, Landon. Is it just me or have you been avoiding me?"

"Me? Avoiding you? Not in a million years."

"And here I thought you were reflecting about your recent reckless involvement in Creigh's incident."

"You know I didn't mean to, Uncle."

"Doesn't mean it didn't happen." He pauses, then sighs. "You might think yourself a god, but your clear disregard for consequences will catch up to you sooner rather than later."

I stroke the hip of my creation, then pause. "Maybe it already has."

"Oh?"

"Hey, Uncle." Stroke, swipe, stroke. "You always told me it's okay not to be like the other kids and that I'm not broken. You said that just because my mind is wired differently doesn't mean I'm any less than them. In fact, it means I'm more special."

"That's true."

"So why the fuck doesn't she see that?"

"She?"

"A certain thorn in my side who's accusing me of being empty and a disaster to the tedious emotion called empathy."

"And you care about her opinion?"

"No...I don't know."

"Then you probably do."

"How do I stop caring?"

Uncle laughs.

I narrow my eyes. "This isn't funny."

"It is to an extent. You sound childlike with your emotions. But at any rate, if you want to keep her, you need to practice empathy."

"No, thanks."

"Then let her go and go back to your shallow encounters with people you barely remember come morning. That way, you won't have to care for the rest of your life and will be able to wear the emptiness she previously filled as a badge."

My movements stop, fingers resting on the hip. "How do you know she filled the emptiness?"

"Your Aunt Elsa does that for me. In fact, so does your mother for your father."

"Really?"

"Yes. Your father wasn't always put together, which is why he was a bit strict with you growing up. He didn't want you to make the same mistakes he did."

I didn't know that. That must have been what he meant when he once said that he didn't want me to regret my decisions after I grew up.

To which I naturally replied that I don't do regrets.

Uncle Aiden continues, "That feeling of emptiness is a morbid emotion that eats you alive more and more the older you get, and unless you find someone to fill it, you're irrevocably fucked. Sooner or later, you'll succumb to higher felonies to reach that temporary reprieve that never lasts and will eventually self-destruct."

I retrieve a cigarette, stuff it in my mouth, then light it. "I'm entirely uninterested in practicing empathy."

"That makes sense since it doesn't come naturally to you. But you have to think about whether or not you're ready to succumb to a fundamentally bleak path just because you refuse to change."

"I don't know how the fuck to practice empathy."

"Did you ever find yourself refraining from ruining or hurting *something or someone she cares about because you understood that it would hurt her?"*

"Maybe."

"That's a small step forward. You need to see the situation from her perspective first, not from yours. You have to shackle your instincts as much as possible."

"You mean like I did whenever I wanted to hurt Bran and Glyn while growing up and directed that energy toward punishing those who hurt them?"

"Something like that. In fact, it's best to have Bran give you advice on your relationship with her."

"The prude who barely has any sex? Pass."

"A relationship isn't about sex, Lan. That's a physical need that I'm sure you excel at. The emotional side, however, is your biggest weakness."

"And Bran's strength." It's not a question. It's a statement.

"Remember what I told you when you were younger?"

"Bran feels too much and I feel too little, which is why we balance each other out."

"Exactly."

"He'll never help me, Uncle."

"Did you ask?"

No, I didn't.

But as I look at my brother and sister, I fully understand the meaning behind Uncle Aiden's words.

I, Landon King, lack something my siblings have in excess, and while I've always seen that as a power, maybe I need to reshuffle my cards.

"It's pointless telling him all this, little princess," Bran says. "He'll never get it."

"I do."

Both Bran and Glyn look at me as if I'm being possessed by a demon who's been expelled from hell for his friendly behavior.

"Is this a joke?" Glyn asks cautiously.

"When have I ever joked?" I grab both their shoulders. "I'll make the effort."

"Why?" Bran asks.

"Because you're my family." I smile. "In return, I might ask you a couple of things during the day."

"Couple of things?"

"About how to practice empathy."

Bran smiles. I don't.

I know I won't like this one fucking bit. In fact, my beast roars at the idea of being shackled, even if temporarily, but if it's the price I have to pay for my little muse, then so be it.

TWENTY-SIX

Mia

"**G**OOD ONE. YOU'VE SOMEHOW MANAGED TO TRAP ME." Mr. Whitby—Frank, as he insisted I call him—nods in approval at my move.

We're sitting in the empty club, only accompanied by the howling wind outside. Since it's early afternoon, I'm safe from encountering the other members' snobbishness.

Let's say the women became even more dismissive of me after they saw me coming here with Landon. Apparently, I'm the 'snob' who doesn't deserve the 'exceedingly charming' Landon's company.

He's got them all buying into his act. Hook, line, and sinker.

At any rate, to avoid any inevitable confrontation, I texted Frank and asked if he was free for a quick game. Since he's the perfect gentleman, he agreed. Pretty sure I hauled him from his very important gardening class, considering the smudge of dirt on the edge of his cuff.

"It's much safer to give up now. This game has already been decided and it won't be long before the checkmate," I type and then show him my phone.

"I wouldn't be so sure. It's a mistake to underestimate one's adversary."

"Too bad for you that I came here fully intent on destruction."

He smiles like all polite British people do, when I'm sure, deep inside, he wants to call me crazy. I've been in this peculiar mood since Landon made his spectacularly catastrophic appearance at my birthday party a week ago.

Not only did he advertise our relationship to the world, but he also had the audacity to announce that he was *courting* me.

In front of my family.

To say Nikolai hasn't been taking it well would be an understatement. His manic state deteriorated from bad to worse in just a couple of days. Usually, he's able to go back to normal in a week or less, but that's obviously not the case this time.

Killian shook his head at me and said he was disappointed in me. Those words hit me worse than I could've imagined. Gareth and Jeremy didn't have to say it, but I felt the crushing disapproval through their patronizing gazes and excessive sighing.

Maya naturally found out about the recent talk of the town and has been acting butthurt. Unlike the others, she didn't judge me, but she was mad that I hid something so monumental from her.

The only support I had was from none other than Bran. He texted to apologize on behalf of his 'twat of a brother' and asked if I was okay.

I definitely wasn't, but I also didn't want to bother Bran, who was clearly distressed throughout the whole night. On top of nearly being shown the door by Nikolai, he also got punched by him, although accidentally.

Glyn later came back and apologized as well before Killian whisked her away. Bran never returned. He probably kept Landon company so he wouldn't try something crazy again.

Did that stop the asshole? Absolutely not.

He's been showing up near my classes, without a disguise, as if he's begging for his face to be beaten and crushed to minuscule pieces.

Naturally, I've avoided him and have even sent my bodyguards over so he couldn't trespass into my space.

Though I should've known better. Landon and giving up apparently don't see eye to eye, because he's been in my vicinity every day over the past week, carrying my favorite Frappuccino.

I don't take it, but that doesn't deter him from his morning ritual.

Then, in the evening or whenever my classes finish, he offers to give me a ride in his show-off car. He's always blocked by my bodyguards, who accompany me home instead.

It's clear he doesn't like that, and I often expect to be reintroduced to his ugly side, but he surprisingly just leaves. Yet not without telling me he'll be back or that this push-and-pull only manages to turn him on.

In order to escape his vicinity, I've also been avoiding the chess club unless it's an unplanned game with Frank. The last thing I want is to be alone with or in close proximity to the bastard.

While that might be perceived as cowardly, I don't care. Landon threatens the very foundation of my being and, more importantly, he's a danger to my family. Even if a part of me longs for his touch and intensity, I'm well aware that it would only end in peril and destruction.

We started as the epitome of a toxic relationship, and those never end well. So if I have to crush these nuisance emotions and my heart in the process, that's exactly what I'll do.

His inability to give up isn't helping. He's practically a stalker at this point, and that's creepy, to say the least. His birthday gift was even more disturbing. In the box he gave me, there was a golden QR code with 'Happy Birthday' engraved in the middle. When I visited it, I found an image of a half-blurred statue face that looked so much like me.

On top of it, there were the words, 'If you want to see the whole thing, all you have to do is come to our haunted house. P.S. The plants seem to miss you.'

His attempts at getting me alone again were clear, and no matter how much I wanted to visit the plants and see the entirety of that statue, I didn't go.

I'd have to be insane to willingly go to Landon's den.

The door opens and I go still. Please don't tell me I accidentally conjured him…?

A chill shoots down my spine and my entire body tightens, ready for the inevitable meeting. I don't have my bodyguards with me right now, though if I send them a text, they'll be here in fifteen. Maybe less…

My thoughts scatter when a new face strolls inside, his features closed and his pressed suit suggesting a certain level of control. He looks to be in his thirties and carries the aura of a wise, formidable opponent.

"Welcome, Professor Kayden," Frank greets, his eyes softening.

"Kayden is just fine, Frank." He speaks in a distinctly American accent that's similar to mine. His gaze slides to me and he pauses for an uncomfortable beat. "I didn't realize you have company this time of the day or I would've come another time."

"Don't worry about it. I'm sure Mia doesn't mind."

I nod, then push my rook forward and grin.

"Looks like you got a checkmate, Frank," the newcomer, Kayden, says with a slight rise of his brow.

"Oh my." Frank looks at the board as if he can't believe his eyes.

It's useless to try to find fault in my plan—or little tricks, so to speak. I might have picked up some bad habits from the time I spent in psycho Landon's presence.

As much as I hate the bastard, he's an absolute genius and a master of chess. He's the type who believes in playing the player instead of the game, and when I complained that it wasn't fair, he chuckled and offered to teach me. I have no clue why he disclosed his tricks when he's not the sharing type, but I'll definitely use them whenever possible.

What? I don't like losing.

"I didn't see that coming," Frank says. "Nice game."

"Thank you," I sign.

"Is the young lady by any chance interested in playing against me?" Kayden asks.

"As long as you're willing to lose, sure," I type and show him.

He smiles a little, but it doesn't reach his eyes. I pause. For some reason, he seems oddly familiar, like I've met him.

But when? Where?

He couldn't have come to one of the Heathens' parties, right?

"I'll leave you my place." Frank slowly stands. "Professor Kayden is one of our newest and rising-star members. He teaches criminal law at your university, Mia."

Oh. That must be why I find him familiar. I must've seen him around campus.

Kayden removes his jacket, revealing a muscular build that doesn't fit a stereotypical professor. He sits opposite me, wearing an easy but entirely disingenuous expression.

"Nice to meet you," I type and show him.

"Likewise. It's rare to find young students who are interested in chess."

"It's my favorite hobby and my number one coping mechanism."

His attention slides from the phone to my face. "Interesting."

I internally cringe. That was definitely too much information for a person I just met. What is it about this Kayden that seems awfully familiar?

"My sister is in pre-law. I also have a cousin who's studying law at TKU. Maybe you know him? His name is Gareth Carson."

Kayden's eyes skim over the text, pausing for an uncomfortable beat again, then he says, "Could be."

"He only joined The King's U this year," Frank says from beside him as if he's his designated butler. "He can't possibly know all the students."

"You'd be surprised," Kayden deadpans. "How close are you with this cousin of yours?"

"Very. We were brought up together, so he's like a brother."

"I see." For a fraction of a second, I think I see a smirk, but I must be imagining things since it quickly disappears.

I play white as usual and the start goes well. In no time, I manage to use the tricks Landon taught me, but unlike Frank, Kayden isn't completely oblivious. He counters each and every one of them and drives me into a corner.

The last stage of the game is basically me fighting a hopeless war against his relentless and highly strategic attack.

"Checkmate," he finally announces with emotionless coldness.

I purse my lips and study the board to try and figure out where I went wrong.

"You want to know your fault?" he asks, the question obviously rhetorical since he continues, "Instead of playing chess, you're playing a treacherous war-like game with no codes of honor whatsoever. Instead of focusing on the pieces, you were too busy trying to out-smart me."

"Chess is all about playing the player, not the game," I type, then wince. Those are that bastard Landon's exact words.

"You need to be psychologically stronger than your opponent before you can attempt to play him."

"I tend to agree." The low, deep voice catches me completely by surprise.

I was so caught up in my tragic loss that I momentarily let my guard down. None other than Landon ruthlessly used that gap to come into my vicinity.

He strolls inside wearing nonchalance like a second skin and psychopathy as a personality trait. Pressed black ankle-length pants add elegance to his long legs, and the crisp white shirt that's tucked in them outlines his lean waist and broad shoulders.

His hair is styled and I can smell the expensive cologne that seems to be made exclusively for him.

A chill spreads down my spine as my flight response zings through every fiber of my being.

I need to run.

Run…

Landon stops beside my chair and wraps a casual hand around my shoulder as if it's the most natural motion in the world.

His fingers dig in the bare skin of my upper arm, keeping me completely immobile. My temperature rises and, to my horror, it has nothing to do with rage and more to do with an outrageous sensation.

Like how good his touch feels.

How much my body is starved for the intensity.

The manhandling.

The unknown.

It's been so long since he's been this close, and I'm unable to put a halt to the volcano brewing deep inside me.

"And you are?" Kayden asks with a less welcoming tone than the one he used with me.

"Landon King," he says as if everyone is supposed to know his identity.

The sense of narcissism in this man is absolutely mind-blowing.

"Mia's boyfriend. Though she might prefer the term lover."

I stare at him with an open mouth, but I quickly recover and sign, "You're not my lover, asshole."

"We can define our relationship in due time, little muse."

"We can't be in a relationship since, wait, that actually requires someone who cares."

"I would've shown you my utmost care if you hadn't shoved me into a nonconsensual relationship with your bodyguards. In case you failed to notice, they're far from being my type."

"Oh, I'm sorry. I'll make sure to employ female bodyguards who are your type. Maybe that way, you'll finally stop the stalking behavior and leave me alone."

"Unless you're in the mood to be a bodyguard yourself, that plan is doomed to fail. I've been developing a new type that only you can fit."

My lips part and my hands remain suspended in midair.

Why the hell would he say things that he definitely doesn't feel or believe in? What does he have to gain from lying at this stage?

"I assume he's the one you learned those stratagems from. Am I right?" Kayden asks.

Shit. I completely forgot he was right opposite us and listening in on our conversation.

Well, on Landon, since he couldn't possibly understand what I was saying.

"Indeed." Landon's grip tightens on my shoulder. "Now, if you'll excuse us, we're going to play. You can go to Frank."

Kayden doesn't move, silently refusing to comply. "Why don't you play against me instead?"

"Not interested." He drops a kiss on the top of my head and goosebumps erupt all over my skin. "Mia is the only one I'm willing to spend my precious time with."

Kayden remains still for a beat, but then he unhurriedly stands up. "Very well."

I expect him to play against Frank, but he merely exchanges a few words with him at the entrance. He throws one last glance at me before he leaves.

My chin is suddenly jerked up so that I'm staring into Landon's merciless eyes. "I'm over here, muse. You should know by now that I don't appreciate not being the center of your attention."

"You should know by now that I couldn't care less. Aren't you supposed to have gotten bored already?"

"I am, but I've come to the bitter realization that this is different."

"Different because I keep telling you no and you don't like that word? Or is it different because for the first time in your life, you won't get what you want?"

"Different because I'm taking drastic measures I've never entertained before."

"Such as?"

"One, being patient. You've been pushing it for a while now. In fact, you're so past my limits that I don't see them anymore. Two, playing nice with your brother and cousin despite the countless death threats they dropped in my inbox. Three, not kidnapping you the fuck away so you and the world will finally admit that you belong to me. In conclusion, I'm being such a good sport, and not only is it unlike me, but it's also a first. Isn't that absolutely fantastic?"

"Finally being decent isn't fantastic. It should've been a given."

"It's not a given for me, Mia." His tone darkens. "What you think of as normal isn't in my repertoire of reactions. In fact, I learned social cues so I could emulate normal, but it remains a foreign concept to me. It's fucking torture to go against my instincts and nature to placate you."

"Why?"

"Because you're so fucking difficult, it pisses me off."

"Why would you take all these drastic measures for me? I'm sure you'd prefer kidnapping and forcing me to do your bidding until you're done with me. So why didn't you do that?"

"Because, according to Bran and Glyn's amateurish empathy classes, that means I have to risk losing you."

"And you care about that?"

"Apparently, I do."

"Why?"

"Figures."

"That's not an answer."

"It's the only one I have."

I see it then. In the depths of his mystic eyes that have a personality of their own. Landon himself doesn't understand the full extent of his strange obsession with me.

And for some reason, that makes me feel triumphant and absolutely elated.

I like that I'm the first who can provoke this side of him. That, somehow, he's not the only one of us who has power over the other.

"I still won't get back with you, Landon," I sign. "You're anarchy in fancy clothing and will eventually ruin me and my relationship with the people closest to me."

"I won't."

"You can't stop your nature."

"I've been doing it just fine for a week."

"A week is nothing."

"Considering I used to fuck your tight hole multiple times a day, I would say this period of abstinence is fucking something."

My cheeks heat and I clear my throat. "I still can't do this."

"Why? Is it because you're scared?"

"I'm not scared."

"It looked that way the night of your birthday. You weren't ashamed of me. You were ashamed of your reaction *to* me. To the fact that you want me despite the galore of red flags. You still do, Mia."

"Leave me alone."

"Never." His words are whispered in my ear before he releases me and sits opposite me. "How about a bet? If you win, I'll leave you alone. If I do, you'll do something for me."

"No, thanks."

"Is that the coward in you speaking?"

"I'm no coward, asshole."

"Then you won't mind this harmless bet."

There's nothing harmless about Landon King. I know exactly what he's doing, but I still sign, "If I lose, you can't ask for sex."

"Cruel, but okay."

I narrow my eyes. "Really?"

"You want me to disagree with your condition?"

"No, but I expected you to demand it."

"I have no interest in your reluctance, little muse. When I fuck you again, you'll be begging for it." A smirk tilts his lips. "Now that we got that out of the way, are we doing this?"

"You're on."

His wolfish grin makes an appearance again and I regret agreeing to the bet.

I'm being lured into his den again.

The worst part is, maybe I don't want to resist it anymore.

TWENTY-SEVEN

Mia

I EXPECTED MANY DEMANDS FROM LANDON, INCLUDING TRYING to trick me into having sex, forcing his way into my life, or suggesting we get back together.

Surprisingly, he does none of the above.

In fact, he merely asks me to go on a date with him.

A date.

No kidding.

Landon King, who would be elected as the leader of psychopaths if given the chance, actually wants to do something as normal as a date.

Not only that, but he invited me over to the Elites' mansion, where he set up an extravagant setting on the open terrace on the roof.

Dim yellow lights hang above the table like a halo.

Two blue candles sit on the aesthetically pleasing tablecloth, casting a soft edge on the otherwise sharp atmosphere. A few dishes lie on the table and I lick my lips at the mouthwatering smell.

Lentil soup, Mediterranean salad, pasta with meatballs, and a delicious-looking lamb tagine. Landon definitely picked up on my favorites and the fact that I love eating everything at the same time without the common order of appetizers, a main course, and a second course.

A large hand lands on the small of my back and the smell of

intoxicating male cologne fills my nostrils as Landon leads me to one of the chairs.

He pulls it out and helps push me forward once I'm seated, like he's some sort of chivalrous prick. He looks the part, too, dressed in a casual black sports jacket and pants with an off-white shirt.

He sits opposite me with infinite elegance and pours me a glass of cola and himself a glass of wine.

He often offered me that, but alcohol and I don't vibe very well, so he learned to get me cola whenever I came over to the haunted house.

I can't help studying his face in search of a sign of deceit. Considering he's possibly the definition of the word, it's strange that I find no trace of it.

My gaze skims over his outwardly peaceful expression. His usually dangerous lips are set in a neutral line, and even the mole beneath his right eye that usually looks menacing is now just a welcoming beauty mark.

"What's with all of this?" I sign.

"I told you." He swirls the red liquid in his glass with the elegance of a demon lord. "A date."

"Why here and not in a restaurant?"

"You find them tedious and less personal, so I opted for a more intimate experience where you can have all your favorite dishes instead."

I mentioned that several weeks ago and he still remembers it so well. Seriously, I'm starting to think he has an elephant's memory.

In my internal musings, I nearly forgot I was staring. To which Landon smiles broadly with a perverse sense of satisfaction.

I clear my throat. "Why are you taking me on a date? It's not like you believe in normal."

"I don't, but you do."

"But—"

"Can you stop asking pointless questions and just eat? Look at what I cooked for you."

My lips part and I pause before I grab the spoon. "You cooked these?"

"Of course."

"Of course? Why are you saying that as if it's a given? You never cooked before."

"As I've mentioned countless times, I'm a fast learner. You're welcome."

I cast another glance at the food and then take a tentative sip from the soup. The rich taste explodes in my mouth like a home-cooked meal. Before I know it, I'm done with it.

I move to the pasta, and it tastes even better than the soup. The lamb is a knockout, but I choose to take my time with it, partly because I'm almost full and I want to savor what I'm eating.

A sudden breeze ruffles my hair and goosebumps erupt on my naked arms. For some reason, the sensation doesn't seem to be entirely related to the cold. I lift my gaze, and my mouthful of food gets stuck at the back of my throat.

Landon, who I assumed was also eating, is not. His undivided attention is dangerously focused on me, head on his fist as he swirls the wine glass with his free hand.

I swallow the contents of my mouth with effort and slowly set my utensils on the table. "What do you want?"

"Should I want something?" he replies with disturbing nonchalance.

"You always do."

"Hmm. Maybe you're right and I do want something."

"Which is?"

"To get my fill of you, which I've been doing spectacularly."

The temperature rises in my chest and forms knots at the base of my belly. I try and fail to control the unconscious reaction as I sign, "You want me to believe that the great Landon King would settle for such a trivial thing?"

"I couldn't believe it myself, but I also wouldn't categorize it as trivial."

"You mean to tell me you're content with this very normal date and wouldn't trade it with chasing or choking me?"

"What type of blasphemy is that? Of course I would. But,

apparently, it's better to go against my instinct in situations like these. I don't really get the hype about emotions, but I'm trying."

"Trying to what? Have them?"

"Nonsense." His lips lift in clear disgust and he drowns it with a sip of wine. "I'm trying not to use my understanding of emotions in a destructive manner. At least, not with the people who matter."

Thump.

Thump.

Thump.

My heart nearly explodes from behind my rib cage. I breathe in and out slowly, attempting, no, refusing to be caught in the web of Landon's chaos-driven world again.

"Does that mean you didn't consider your other options?"

"What other options?"

"The girls who throw themselves at you ready to satisfy your wildest kinks."

"The only girl I want to satisfy my kinks is you, so everyone else is redundant."

I swallow thickly, my heart rate still refusing to go down. "Are you telling me you weren't tempted? Not even a little?"

"No. I quit going to the sex clubs after you came into my life."

"You went to sex clubs?"

"All the time. I used to go there mostly to satisfy my exhibition-ism kink."

"And you don't need to now?"

His eyes darken. "Absolutely not. The thought of anyone seeing you naked turns me murderous."

I clear my throat. "I don't know what caused this change, but it doesn't matter. If you hurt my family again, Jeremy included, not only will I never share space with you again, but I'll also make it my mission to destroy you."

"Oh?" A sardonic smirk lifts the corner of his lips. "Did you mention a form of destruction?"

"Do you think I'm joking?"

"Far from it. Which is why I'm taking the risk."

"Risk?"

"I told you this whole sentimental gibberish doesn't come naturally to me." He takes another sip of wine and stares into the starless sky in the distance.

"Then how do you intend to learn it versus merely emulating it?"

"As I've continuously mentioned, I happen to be a genius."

"Intellectual IQ is worlds apart from emotional IQ. You might score two hundred on the former, but you're minus two hundred on the latter."

He clicks his tongue, the first sign of annoyance peeking through the creasing lines around his eyes and mouth. "I'm far more superior and efficient than fools who let their feelings dictate their actions. What's so high and mighty about having emotions?"

"You really don't get it, do you?" I sign without any sense of anger or disappointment. I've always thought of Landon's condition in the clinical sense, or maybe as I blamed him for all the shit he keeps stirring, but this is the first time I've realized he probably doesn't know anything else.

He's never experienced any of the normal emotions many of us do. No genuine love, sadness, heartache, or anything of sentimental value.

The fact that he can emulate them doesn't mean he can feel them. It's why he's lethal when he gets hold of other people's weaknesses.

His lack of both empathy and guilt makes him the ultimate mental weapon.

It's also why he gets irritated when forced to act opposite his nature.

"Get what?" he asks in an unfamiliar tight tone.

Landon's strength is his ability to not get agitated or ruffled, like an ancient, untouchable god with thousands of followers.

He's right. It's different now.

He's definitely trying to go against his fundamentals and it's throwing him off. For some reason, a part inside me softens and I can't help feeling a tinge of joy that he's trying to act different.

For me.

Not anyone else. Just *me*.

I shake my head and choose to focus on something else instead. "If you want to learn emotions, I can help."

"Oh? I thought you were a self-proclaimed emotionless bad bitch."

"Bad bitch, yes. Emotionless, no. I just enjoy teaching those who mess with me or my family a lesson. Anyway, let me ask you." I take a sip of my cola. "From your family and friends, who do you think of when you hear the word love?"

"What is this? Amateur therapy?" He scrunches his nose as if he smells something foul. "Why does everyone seem to have an imaginary license lately?"

"Just answer the question, Landon."

"Mum and Dad. Next boring question."

"Why do they come first?"

"Ever since I was young, they've always respected, worshiped, and taken care of each other. They've never had a fight that lasted more than a day. They love each other to the point of obsession, if you ask me. Too much PDA for my liking."

"Have you ever thought about having a relationship like theirs?"

"No. Because I don't see the hype about the love and compromise strategy they employ in their marriage."

"Who have you felt closer to between the two?"

"Dad in the beginning. Then Mum because of our shared artistic values and because she said I'm a better artist than her or anyone she knows. Neither now. I realized my personality and theirs are so different, I might as well not have been their son. I don't hate it. I don't like it. I simply understand it the way every individual should instead of transforming into a drama queen...why are you looking at me as if you pity me?"

"I don't." I just feel inexplicably sad for him. He might not feel it, but the fact that he realized early on that he was so different from the people he was closest to must've been so confusing to him.

He narrows his eyes. "Are your wannabe shrink questions over?"

"I'm not trying to be a shrink. I just want to understand you better."

"Why?"

"Because that's how interpersonal relationships are made."

"Huh."

He appears genuinely pensive and I wish I could take a trip inside his brain and see how he processes information. This is the first time he seems so open and not attempting any form of manipulation.

Landon finishes his glass of wine and pours himself another one. When he offers some to me, I nod. The first step of establishing a bond is to build common ground around something. I'm ready to sacrifice my disregard for alcohol to get him to open up more.

He raises a brow, but he pours me a glass anyway, then takes a sip of his. "Tell me more about how these so-called interpersonal relationships happen."

"Well, first you have to be interested in getting to know the other person."

"I'm clearly interested in you. Next."

I nearly choke on the tentative sip of wine I've taken. The heat from earlier rises to my ears again, but I choose to believe it's because of the alcohol.

"Then you'd want to learn as much as possible about them. Like their interests, favorite color, favorite movie, hobbies, and so on."

"Despite wearing black all the time, your favorite color is, in fact, blue. I suppose you don't wear it as much because you hold it in high regard and don't want to waste it on everyday activities. Your favorite movie is a tie between *Mad Max* and *Fight Club* because, unlike your prim and proper anti-chaos talk, you do enjoy watching violence and anarchy, which is why you often complain about Maya's romantic comedy movie nights. Your favorite food is Italian, mostly pasta, specifically carbonara. Your interests include chess, meditation, working out, and, of course, growing plants and then talking to them as if they possess a soul and feelings. Oh, and you definitely have deviant sexual tastes that fit mine like a glove."

My lips part and I have to catch myself before I start drooling or something a lot worse.

Landon is perceptive to a fault, but I never thought he'd pick up pieces and stitch them together this efficiently.

"Did I miss something?" he asks when I don't reply.

I clear my throat and sign, "Yeah, one thing. I'm not as deviant as you."

"Highly debatable. Care for a bet?"

"I'm done betting with you."

"I wouldn't be so sure. The temptation will arise sooner or later."

I narrow my eyes but soon relax. "I see what you're doing."

"What I'm doing?"

"Trying to rile me up so we'll slip back into your territory, and you'd have complete control over the outcome of the situation. I'm telling you it won't work, so you might want to give up."

A slight smirk lifts his gorgeous lips. "My territory is more fun. Just saying."

"It's also more destructive and causes strain to anyone who's not you."

"If by strain you mean coming a few times a night, then sure, it's a massive strain."

I glare. He stares back, still smirking.

Then again, it's impossible to make him abandon all bad habits in one go. The fact that he's willing to listen without imposing his threats and ultimatums is progress as it is.

Small steps, right?

"Moving on," I sign. "Another method is to tell the other person something no one else knows."

"I will only do that if you reciprocate."

I narrow my eyes. There he is back to the choices. But this one seems fair enough, so I nod.

"I've never considered any of my statues a masterpiece."

I straighten in my chair. "Are you joking?"

"When have I ever?"

I stare at his face, but there's no hint of a lie. He means it. He actually thinks all his absolutely gorgeous, though often disturbing, pieces are not all that.

"But you always say you're an untouchable genius and God's gift to the art community and humanity."

"That I am. I just still haven't produced the piece I've been wanting to since I was two years old."

"What defines a masterpiece for you?"

"It's just a feeling. I'll know it when I experience it." He points his glass at me. "Your turn."

I bite the corner of my lip and then release it. He really did tell me something special, so I can't just hide from this.

Maybe it's because of my inexplicable need to build up the bond between us, but I go for it. "I never told anyone about my kidnapper, because they said if I mention anything, they'll know and will kill that person in front of my eyes."

My limbs tremble as I sign the words. The words due to which my entire world has been flipped upside down leave me like a whoosh of icy air.

"Is that why you stopped speaking?" Landon asks in an eerily calm tone.

I nod. "My family thinks it's because of the trauma and I let them believe that."

Why am I telling him all of this? Why am I digging my fingers into the old, infested wound even though it hurts?

It's alcohol. Must be the alcohol.

Landon stands up and I'm too slow to follow his movements. Before I know it, he's beside me. He removes his jacket and places it around my shoulders, then presses down gently.

It's then I realize that not only my hands are shaking, but my whole body is.

Landon lowers himself so his face is level with mine. The scent of his cologne sends a strange calming effect through me and I inhale him, breathing in as much as my lungs can take.

Isn't it mad that I find peace in a monster?

My eyes meet his darker ones, but for some reason, they appear lighter, shinier, like the sky before sunset.

"I'm drunk," I sign. "Forget everything I said."

"On the contrary, I will remember every word." He slides a stray strand behind my ear and I lean my cheek against his warm hand. "No one steals from you and gets to breathe, little muse. I'll make sure you regain your voice even if it's the last thing I do."

My breathing comes in short intervals, but before I can think of anything to say, Landon lowers his head and nips my bottom lip.

Then in one swooping motion, he dips down and claims my mouth with a ferocious passion. He doesn't only kiss me, he feasts on me. His tongue curls around mine, sweeping, tasting, and biting.

Landon has always been more interested in sex, but he's rarely kissed me. This one, however, is more than a kiss.

It's a whispered promise.

A nonnegotiable claim.

A new beginning.

Because I know, I just know, Landon and I will never be the same after this.

TWENTY-EIGHT

Landon

THIS ENTIRE CHARADE OF PRACTICING EMPATHY HAS BEEN proving more tedious than my sexual frustration.

And that's saying something, considering my cock has been a literal dick ever since we've been closed for business.

Forget trying to shag other women. I can't even look at them without imagining Mia's soft face, pouty lips, and bright eyes looking at me like my own sex goddess.

Once upon a time, before she came along, I used to go to deviant sex clubs to find women who are into the unholy kinks I like to dish out. But after making the acquaintance of Mia's sweet cunt and ferocious fight, the mere thought of touching someone else brings a foul taste to the back of my throat.

So now, I'm nothing more than a tension-filled entity of irritation and violence. An existence that can neither be measured nor contained and that keeps growing bigger with each passing second.

My beast has been scratching and clawing at the walls of my sanity, demanding a purging outlet. The crazier the better.

I would love nothing more than to give him a taste of euphoric anarchy. But the downside is, if I let him loose, Mia won't give me the time of the day ever again. I'll turn mental and could and would revert to drastic measures to have her.

And believe it or not, that would—according to Bran, who's up for a sainthood—ruin everything and make me lose her for good.

There wouldn't be any late-night roof dates like a few days ago. She wouldn't meet me for chess or for a boring walk along the beach like some Victorian couple.

She wouldn't open up to me or try to understand me. There would be no more magical laughs, bashful smiles, or pointed glares that only manage to tease my cock out of his hibernation state.

That mere possibility hovers over my chest and sanity like a dangerous brick wall that threatens to crush everything I've been building.

I'd be empty again like Uncle Aiden said.

And while I was completely comfortable with my supreme emptiness before—proud of it, even—that option isn't on or under the table anymore.

So I'm dedicating my energy to something a lot more productive or, more precisely, *on* something that I've been considering for a while now.

"So?" I ask as Glyn stands in the middle of my room like a lost lamb.

Bran gives me a look from his position on the sofa beside me. Let's just say he's been enjoying this 'let's teach Landon emotions' mission a bit too much.

He's a glutton for righteousness and likes to think about other people's emotions. All the time. Like a psycho.

I honestly believe he needs urgent apathy lessons from yours truly. But that's a topic for another day.

Glyn releases a long sigh and slowly sits on the chair opposite us and pushes strands of her hair behind her ears. Her movements are wary and a bit awkward, like when she couldn't figure out where she belonged in our extremely artistic family.

She often felt like she was the least talented, no matter how much Mum told her that art manifests in different manners for different people.

I taught her how to sketch for the first time when she was maybe three years old. For some reason, as I watch her now, I'm hit by the magical look that she had in her big green eyes when she looked at me back then.

The awe, the wonder, and the complete enchantment that was there when I used her little fingers to doodle on some paper. Of course, that was my creation, but Glyn took that paper and went running to Mum, screaming, "Look what Lan taught me!"

I realize with a sense of slight discomfort that back then, I experienced these bursts of pride and joy for reasons unknown. Naturally, those moments were few and far between and diminished the older I got, but they did exist.

It's like a reminder of how largely the emptiness staked claim inside me. I refuse to lose any more of my agency to the demons lurking in the dark corners of my soul.

"Are you sure this is the right thing to do?" Glyn asks Bran instead of me since he's the morality police around here.

"He doesn't want to hurt her," Bran says with the calmness of an ancient monk.

"Still. Isn't it a breach of privacy to talk about something the family has kept hidden?"

"Not if I have information they don't." I take a sip of my beer in a failed attempt to hide my grin.

I happen to be quite proud of the fact that Mia told me things she's never spoken of to her family. Prick Nikolai and pretentious Maya included.

Have you ever thought she told you that because she believes whoever knows will be killed by her kidnapper? part of my brain that's wishing for a bullet whispers like a stage-five twat.

Besides, I could've asked Mia about the rest of the story and she would've eventually told me, but I didn't want her to relive her kidnapping incident when she already gets nightmares about it.

"But…" Glyn trails off and plays with the zipper of her tiny backpack that I'm surprised can fit anything bigger than a mouse.

Speaking of which, I would rather I was in the company of my own little mouse, but, apparently, we're not supposed to meet often.

When I asked her if she was hiding me from her family, she didn't reply, and that was enough of an answer. She's still ashamed of me, possibly refusing to tell her brother and his band of meddling fools that she's seeing me.

And will be for a very long time.

But that's okay. Everything will fall back into place. Not because I'm a hopeful romantic—disgusting—but because I'll make it happen whether she likes it or not.

I'm open to anything, including relearning the entire world fucking history and seeing it in rosy colors instead of human greed, but letting her go is not an option.

Not in this lifetime or the next, or the twenty after.

"You don't like lying to Killian?" Bran finishes for Glyn, bringing me back to the present moment.

Of course he'd figure out what she was about to say just by looking at her. I figured it out, too, but mainly because I'm nothing if not brilliant at linking patterns.

Glyn is somewhat of an empath, so she's partially fine with exposing Mia's secret if it means she'll participate in helping her. What she's not fine with, however, is going behind that twat Killian's back to help me.

And I happen to be her brother, for fuck's sake.

"He told me what he knows because he trusts me," she says. "I don't want to lose his trust."

"You won't, because none of us will tell," I say in a calmer tone than I feel. "Think about it this way, the good outweighs the bad in this situation. Do you think he'll be mad if what you disclose will help his beloved cousin?"

"Well, I don't think so." She releases her bag's zipper and straightens. "Okay, so Kill has always avoided this subject whenever it comes up, but a few days ago, after the show you put on, something changed."

Thank fuck.

I don't say that out loud, though, or my attempts at rehabilitating my image with my siblings would take a sharp dive toward the worst.

I actually like that they don't wear expressions of dread or disgust whenever I'm in their field of vision. They actually come to hang out in my room without me forcing them to—in Bran's case it's more to keep an eye on me.

They're tangible proof that, yes, I controlled them over the years, but despite my godly logic, that process never produced a great relationship. This softer version, while not my favorite, is able to generate better results.

"In what sense did it change?" Bran asks.

Glyn leans forward in her seat. "So he was livid, understandably, since you apparently called her a mute upon first seeing her."

"An ancient mistake," I say.

"Killian doesn't see it that way. He feels that you're unable to respect that part of her. So I probed a bit more and he told me what he knows. The story happened when Killian was nine and Mia was about eight years old. Maya and Mia were being driven home when they were attacked in the middle of the road. One bodyguard got killed, but the other managed to protect the girls. However, one of the assailants reached in and took both of them. Mia struggled, kicked, and bit his hand until he released Maya. In the end, she was the only one who got kidnapped. The other bodyguard managed to get Maya home safely. For three days, they didn't have any news. Her parents expected a ransom call, but they didn't get one in the beginning.

"Killian said that was the darkest time for their family. Her parents mobilized the entirety of their resources in the Russian mafia to find her. They closed New York and flipped it upside down in search of the assailant, but they came up empty. Just when they were about to go crazy, they got a call. The kidnapper wanted twenty-five million sent to an offshore bank account, and only when they made the transfer would he tell them her location. If they didn't agree to his demands, he would've still told them her location, but she would have been dead. Naturally, they made the transfer, and he sent them a GPS location. They found Mia balled up in a fetal position inside a dark, humid basement. She was starved and had a bloody lip and welts on her body, but she wasn't crying. The doctor said that while she was hit, thankfully, she wasn't sexually assaulted. But ever since then, she's never spoken a word, and the professionals ruled it as mental rather than physical."

My fingers tighten on the bottle so hard, I'm surprised I don't crush it to pieces and watch my blood spill on the ground.

Just listening to what happened to her triggers an avalanche of feelings I know so well. It's similar to when those twats made Bran the joke of the school, but these emotions are a lot stronger in intensity and could only be categorized as black rage.

Someone had the audacity not only to terrorize my Mia but also to threaten and traumatize her enough to steal her voice for a whole decade.

"She went through a lot," Bran comments with a hunch in his shoulders.

"What else?" I ask in a slightly tight tone that even I don't recognize.

Glyn watches me carefully. "That's all. Mia's parents searched all over the world for her kidnapper but found no trace of him. They suspected it could have been one of the bodyguards who disclosed the route since only they and her parents knew about it, but one of them died and the one who survived brought Maya home while badly injured, so if he had been in on it, he would've had Maya taken as well. They've been at a stalemate since then. It doesn't help that Mia never disclosed any details about what happened."

Because she was threatened by the fucking bastard who'll wish he was dead the moment I find him.

"Does her family have any theories? Suspects?"

Glyn lifts her shoulders. "Not really. They definitely suspect it was an enemy of either or both of them, but that's apparently a given in the mafia. Even Annika, Jeremy's sister, was nearly kidnapped a few times. This is the only time they've gotten away with it, though."

No, they haven't.

If my calculations are correct, there's one possible theory that none of them seem to have considered. But in order for that possibility to work, I need to confirm a few things first.

"Not sure if that helps..." Glyn trails off.

"It does." I abandon my beer, then stand and ruffle her hair. "Thanks, little princess."

She stares up at me with a parted mouth before she nods and lets her lips pull in a smile. "Sure."

I head to my walk-in. "Feel free to hang out with the drama king, Remi, or Creigh if he's around. I'm going out."

"I'll ask the girls to join me," Glyn throws back and I hear her footsteps retreating from the room.

Other footsteps, however, approach me. I remove my shirt and dunk it in the laundry bin, then stare at my brother.

Bran leans against the doorframe, arms and ankles crossed. A rare gleam and subtle smugness shine through his eyes.

"What?"

"You just thanked Glyn for the first time ever."

"Don't be ridiculous. I must've thanked her before." I click the wardrobe button and watch my crisp, ironed shirts roll before me.

"No, you haven't. You're too egotistical to thank others or even see merits in them."

"The only people whose merits I refuse to honor with even a glance are incompetent fools. Glyn doesn't belong on that endless list."

"Because she shares your genes?"

"Precisely." I snatch an off-white shirt. "And she's also never been daft. Just a bit too hung up on emotions for my taste, but oh well, as you constantly remind me, not everyone is built from the same genius clay you and I are made of."

"You...think you and I are the same?"

"We're identical twins, Bran."

"Not in thinking."

"Not one hundred percent, no." I put on my shirt and start to button it as I look at him with a tilted head. "But you're suppressing something, and as long as you're doing that, we're not too far off in hiding our secrets, are we?"

A somber look passes in his eyes, and if I weren't in such a hurry, I'd explore it with more vigor. "I don't know what you're talking about."

"You never do, Bran." I grab his shoulder and squeeze on my way out. "You never do."

He catches my arm. "Where are you going?"

"Don't worry. I'm not off to instigate a new war unless chess counts."

"You're really just going to play chess?"

"I know, right? I've become too boring for my own good."

He gives me a quizzical glance, but he lets me go. "Remember, Lan. If you fall back into your manipulation and chaos patterns, it won't work."

"Yes, Mum." I do a mock salute and I'm rewarded with Bran's snickering.

On my way out of the mansion, I shoot my cousin Eli a text.

Landon: Remember the exchange of favors we once talked about?

Eli: Ready to go down like a little bitch?

Landon: Only if you turn into a smaller bitch than my highness.

Eli: Your arrogance will get you killed one day.

Landon: Not when your arrogance is alive and thriving. Now, as much as I love talking shit, I need something.

Eli: The question is, do you need it enough to lose your bargaining chip?

Landon: Yes.

Eli: Prepare to lose the race as the best King grandchild.

I ignore him. Eli thinks that I have only one bargaining chip, but he'll learn, after I get what I want, that there's no pushing Landon King to the side, not even by the hands of another King.

After sending him instructions about the possible proof that can make my theory a reality, I drive to the chess club.

Now, I don't expect Mia to show up after she specifically asked me not to pester her, but it doesn't hurt to try.

Yes. Unfortunately, I've become so irrevocably obsessed with the little muse that I'm surviving on the mere hope of being able to see her.

Desperate much? Abso-fucking-lutely.

I park my McLaren opposite the entrance and step out, only to be greeted by the most miserable weather England has to offer. The wind slaps me across the face, and I close my eyes to ward off the assault. When I open them, I see none other than Mia getting out of her car.

My lips pull in a wide smile.

Despite her occasional reluctance, she can't get enough of me either, and her face lights up whenever we meet. Which is why I had a hunch she would be here…

As she approaches me, her black tulle dress swishes, and her ribbons fly in the wind. She comes to a slow halt in front of me, her eyes entirely fucking wrong.

I cross my arms even as I keep my smile in place—only, it's much more fake now. "I thought we weren't supposed to meet since you're apparently scared shitless of everyone in your family finding out about us. Changed your mind?"

"This is my club, too, last I checked," she signs and lifts her chin.

"Which you knew I'd be coming to. Does that mean you miss me?"

"In your dreams."

"I'll take that as you don't mind Nikolai and the others finding out about our very secret, very intimate rendezvous."

Her cheeks heat and rage blares in her eyes that are more wrong than vanilla sex.

"It doesn't matter, because I'm getting bored and could send you packing any second. In fact, I'm doing it right now."

"I'm disappointed." I release a dramatic sigh. "You put all this effort into pretending to be someone else, so the least you can do is be more subtle about it, Maya."

She flinches, but instead of trying to go on with the charade, she clicks her tongue and says, "What gave me away? Not too many ribbons? Not quick enough sign language?"

"Neither. You could've done the outside to perfection, but you still wouldn't have fooled me. Your eyes are entirely wrong and extremely revolting."

"Fuck you, asshole."

"No, thanks. I much prefer your sister."

She hikes a hand on her hip. "Of all the people who could've warranted your deranged attention, why did it have to be her?"

Because she makes me see sides of me I didn't know existed before.

But I don't tell Maya that since I don't owe her shit, and she narrows her eyes. "Just so you know, I don't approve."

"Just so you know, I can't find any fucks to give." I pause. "Besides, shouldn't you all learn how to respect her wishes? Ever thought that this excessive overprotection might be suffocating her?"

"We just want what's best for her."

"And she doesn't?"

"That's not what I said."

"That's what you mean. She's old enough to make her own decisions without your or anyone else's unwanted interference."

She opens her mouth, but she looks behind me and her eyes turn into big pools of panic.

I stare back and catch a shadow of two men before they disappear into a side building.

"Maya?" I call her name and snap my fingers in her face.

She startles and the fear spreads to her shaking limbs. It's similar to Mia's state when she was scared shitless of the dark.

"I... I have to go." She runs back to Mia's car and has to try twice before she can open the door.

I continue staring at where the men disappeared to. Interesting. I shelve that information for later as I text Mia.

Landon: Your sister just pretended to be you so she could break us apart. I figured her out the second I saw her pretentious eyes. Don't I get a reward for that?

No answer.

I tap my finger against the back of the phone for a few beats, then type again.

Landon: In my modest opinion (I'm just playing—there's nothing modest about me), the forbidden love vibes are hitting so hard. But fuck that, am I right?

Again, she reads the text but doesn't reply.

While Mia gets a kick out of playing the role of a medieval princess who's into courting and talking about feelings, she hasn't been ignoring me lately.

Or maybe she was the one who sent Maya over—

No, she's not the type who shies away from confrontation. If she wanted to tell me something, she wouldn't hesitate to invade my space and give me a piece of her mind.

My phone lights up in my hand and I stare at her name. Mia doesn't call, for obvious reasons. She's not a fan of FaceTime calls either, except for when her parents are involved.

Unless—

I answer it. "Is something the matter?"

"Everything is grand, minus your annoying interference. Mia and I are having a good time, so how about you piss off?"

Beep.

Beep.

Beep.

I stare at the screen of my phone as that very familiar—soon very dead—voice rings in my ear.

Fucking Rory seems to have been praying for his funeral.

What am I if not an extremely good sport?

TWENTY-NINE

Mia

TODAY HAS BEEN AN EPIC PROPORTION OF COMPLETELY random events.

First, Maya asked to take my car because hers broke down and she refuses to have her bodyguards drive her in their, and I quote, 'super-old businessman Mercedes.'

Second, I walked in on Nikolai nearly falling off the balcony in his sleep and had to pull him inside with Gareth's help.

He asked me if I'm still seeing Landon, and when I didn't say anything, he walked away without a word.

Niko has always been my and Maya's champion. The brother who walked around school announcing that if a hair on either of our heads was touched, they'd have to start preparing for their lifetime vacation in hell.

He was also the one who hid our troublemaking habits from Mom and Dad, though he did give us an earful about it sometimes. Other times, he joined in.

Mostly, he gave us space to live outside the shackles of our mafia princess lives.

So the fact that he's both mad and disappointed in me makes me feel like shit. Gareth said he'll come around, but he didn't sound like he believed his own words.

To make things even worse, I'm trapped by this asshole as soon as I'm finished with classes and walking down the street.

His name is Rory, if I remember correctly. I know him because I've often seen pictures of him with Landon at their tacky Elite parties. The reason I remember him so well is because he's usually beside Nila, whom I personally researched after I heard her talking in Landon's room.

I was just curious. Nothing more. Okay, maybe I was a little jealous and wanted to see who I was up against.

At any rate, Rory decided that today of all days was the perfect time to make my acquaintance. He's taller than me, a bit too lean, and has curly blond hair that looks too big for his head. The most striking feature about him, however, is the bloodshot eyes that could be cast in a horror movie.

When he first interrupted my walk, he was wearing sunglasses, but now, he doesn't seem to care for his rich English boy image.

Under different circumstances, I would've faked a smile and pushed past him, but he went ahead and pissed me right the fuck off.

As I was reading Lan's message—and cursing Maya for the stunt she pulled—this asshole confiscated my phone, held me at arm's length, and called Lan to tell him blatant lies.

"You're welcome." He dangles the phone in front of me after he hangs up.

I snatch it back, rage building at the base of my belly and a thousand curses tingling at the tips of my fingers.

Rory stares over the length of me with complete apathy and obvious disregard as if I'm a doll in a store window. "I have no clue what he sees in you."

Excuse you?

I'm about to type that, but he continues, "You're nothing more than a cunt that he could get in the hundreds if he as much as wants to. What's so special about yours?"

The audacity of this motherfucker. *You messed with the wrong person today of all days.*

But before I can type a few choice words, he steps into my space, trapping me against the wall of an old closed pub.

"You're distracting him from what's important, and we can't have that. Without Landon plotting mayhem, our club won't survive."

That's a good thing, if you ask me.

But preppy boy Rory doesn't seem to agree, because his eyes narrow on me in their bloodshot glory. "If you're gone from the picture, everything will go back to the way it's supposed to be."

I type with jerky movements, then show him. "You sure you want to hurt me? One, your balls will be in jeopardy because they'll be brutalized by yours truly. Two, Landon won't take kindly to that."

"Who said anything about hurting you?" A knowing smirk lifts his lips, completely unhinged and entirely evil. "Violence is never really the answer when something a lot tamer will make a better impact. See, Lan might dote on you, but you are and will always be just a phase, and I've figured out exactly how to end his irrational fascination. Do you know the one thing Lan doesn't care for? No? Let me enlighten you, then. He completely loses interest in soiled goods."

I'm still processing his words when he leans in, pushes my pigtails to the side, and sucks on my neck like a disgusting hyena.

I shove at him, but he's surprisingly strong for someone who's made of bones.

So I lift my knee and hit him as hard as I can.

His howl rings in the air as he falls back. I immediately slap a hand on where his lips touched my neck. Judging by how much it aches, the bastard got me good.

He comes back, face red and fist raised in the air, but before he can attack me, my bodyguard immobilizes him and throws him on the cobbled street.

Rory falls on his ass but quickly stands up, snarls at me with the animosity of an unruly animal, then runs away.

My bodyguard inspects me. "Are you okay, miss?"

I nod, still clutching my neck. For some reason, I don't want anyone to see what the asshole has done.

"Do you need me to go after him and break his legs?" my bodyguard asks.

I shake my head and sign, "I already brutalized his balls as I previously promised. Just drive me home."

Any desire for a walk has completely disappeared. I just need to hide this stupid mark first.

We ride to my apartment in eternal silence.

I pull up Landon's texts and type a few of my own.

Maya is just being a little shit. Never mind her. Like you and Bran, we've always been overprotective of each other.

You're right. Fuck the forbidden love concept.

Also, what Rory said just now was a lie. You know that, right?

I delete each and every one of them. I sound guilty when I did nothing wrong.

Instead, I type.

About that statue you made for my birthday, I think I'm ready to see it now.

I stare at my phone for the rest of the journey, but there's still no reply.

My shoulders drop as I exit the car and get inside the apartment, still having a glaring competition with my phone.

He hasn't even read it.

Don't tell me he really believed what Rory said. Worse, was Rory right and Landon loses all interest in soiled good, as he so disgustingly put it?

"Where were you?"

I startle at Maya's uncharacteristically monotone voice. She's been waiting by the corner, in darkness, I now realize. All the curtains and blinds are pulled.

After I slide the phone into my pocket, I hit the light switch and sign, "I just got back from class."

She releases a shaky breath and inspects me like Mom would. "Is everything okay?"

"Yeah. You're being weird."

Her brows knit together as she looks at my neck. "Was that Landon?"

I shake my head. "Some other asshole who has a death wish. Speaking of Landon, why did you pretend to be me? We agreed you wouldn't do that again after you tried to vet everyone who had an interest in me during high school."

"Well, they clearly didn't deserve you since they couldn't even tell us apart."

"But Landon did."

She makes a face. "He's so perceptive, it's annoying. Apparently, we don't have the same eyes. He figured me out from the beginning and pretended he didn't, just to see what I was up to."

I smile to myself. That sounds like something Landon would do. He's such a manipulative asshole, it's attractive at times.

Only at times, though.

"Why are you smiling like some proud girlfriend? He's still bad news, Mia."

"Maybe I've always wanted bad news," I sign. "You know I never liked all the nice boys at school and found the bad boys too shallow. Landon is neither and maybe I like that. As long as he doesn't hurt my family, I'm ready to see where this goes."

"You're...serious."

"Yeah. I like him, Maya."

"Ugh. Of all people it had to be him?"

"It's because it's him that I like him. I can tell him things and not feel judged."

"Things like what? You...can't possibly have told him about the kidnapping, right?"

"Well, not all of it." But certainly more than she knows, which I feel bad about.

"You can't possibly trust him, Mia. Besides, Niko will be pissed."

"Niko has no right to control my love life. Landon already announced a truce that he's been keeping despite his destructive instinct. So maybe Niko and the others should do the same."

"You and I know that's not how it works." She rubs my arm. "Just…be careful, okay? You know I'm here for you, right?"

"Always."

She nods, then retreats to her room and closes the door. I hear her talking on the phone, something about wanting to see someone, but I don't linger around to eavesdrop.

I think she has a new relationship going on, and I have a most probable suspect, but I'll let her be until she lets me know herself.

I go to my room and gasp when I see the large hickey on my neck.

Fucking Rory will have more than his balls brutalized the next time I see him.

I apply foundation, but the angry purple is still visible, so I put on a choker, but even that doesn't hide it.

As a last resort, I put on a scarf that's so against my usual fashion choices, but at least it hides the atrocity.

Again, I check my phone, but there's still no reply from Landon.

You know what? I don't need his permission to go and see a statue that's supposed to be my birthday present.

I'm going back to where everything started on my own.

THIRTY

Landon

THERE ARE TIMES WHEN THE BEAST BECOMES SO LOUD, I have no choice but to let him and his demon minions come out to play.

Sometimes, a mere disruption of other people's lives is enough. Other times, that doesn't cut it and there needs to be full-on anarchy. Perhaps arson here, destruction there, and burying seeds of chaos everywhere.

At this moment, however, my beast is not in the mood for small-time felonies. No. It's not about satiating its urges and sending it back into hibernation.

This is about making someone pay.

In blood.

With his fucking life.

He dared to not only look in the direction of what's fucking mine, but to also touch her. Fucking. Touch. Her.

If there's any time I refuse to put my beast on a leash, this is it. In fact, on my way here, I smashed the shackles that kept him in place, so he's out in his full glory.

I've been patiently waiting for the fucking bastard who's living on borrowed time by the corner opposite his flat on the tenth floor of an old building. I don't get agitated, don't pace, and I certainly don't lose my cool. The rage that rushes through my veins doesn't turn me irrational; it turns me deadly calm.

Calculatively murderous.

I've always had impeccable control over my emotions and have never displayed strong ones. In fact, I looked down on the peasants who allowed their distorted feelings to guide their decisions.

Having lived my life preying on other people's sentimental rubbish, I've perfected the art of never allowing them to use mine.

My target appears at the top of the staircase, walking to his flat with nonchalance and looking so happy with himself. Rory has always been a spoiled brat with nothing in his head but drugs and the immense need to seem more grandiose than his rat-like presence.

The reason I've kept him close is because he belongs to my circle and is a useful pawn. But that ended the moment he dared to do the unthinkable.

I wait for him until he's close, my body humming with thoughts about snapping his neck. But that's too little of a punishment. Death is a peace that I won't allow him for the foreseeable future.

The moment he's near the fire escape staircase, I stalk out from my hideout at the corner and slam my body against his from behind. He loses balance and releases a surprised noise, but he turns around, his sunglasses fall and smash to the ground, and I'm met with his hideously bloodshot eyes.

"What the fuck—"

His words end on an *oomph* as I grab him by the collar, push him against the metal railing, and slam my fist into his nose. Pain explodes in my knuckles, but I do it again and again.

Rory's face swings left, then right, then left again under my powerful blows, but he manages to spit out, "Is this about my little visit to your flavor of the week?"

My Mia is everything but the flavor of the week, but I don't tell him that.

"I knew you were daft, but I didn't think you'd be *this* daft, Rory." I kick his shins and he falls on his knees so that he has to look up at me as if I'm his god. At this moment, I might as well be. "You of all people should know by now that I can destroy you and your entire fucking family if you get in my way. Aside from the information I have on you, I can gather more dirt and figure out weaknesses that you have no idea existed, and I would use them one by each one to ruin you until I make you go bloody insane."

I punch him again and blood explodes in his split lip and drips on his T-shirt and the floor. Rory snarls with bloodied teeth like an injured animal. "You should've kept your part of the deal and stopped ignoring us like we were an afterthought."

"News flash, motherfucker. You *are* an afterthought. In fact, you're so fucking useless that I forget you exist sometimes. The Elites is a club I started for my own entertainment and every one of you is a fucking pawn on my chessboard, so when I tell you to jump, you ask how high. When I tell you to throw yourself down a well, you do that with eyes wide open, like you've been doing all along."

"You fucking..." He starts to stand up, but with my merciless grip on him, he only manages to make it halfway. "You said we were partners."

"And you believed it? But then again, you were never that bright, were you, Rory?"

"I was bright enough to make your girl's acquaintance. She was soft and delicate. I can see why you're so obsessed with her."

Blind rage rushes to my head and I lift him up, then wrap my hands around his neck and push him back against the railing so that he's hanging halfway outside. "You don't seem to have any self-preservation neurons in your barren brain, so I'll make your suicidal wishes come true."

His fingers claw at my hands with frantic, desperate movements, but they do nothing to make me loosen my grip. If anything, I tighten my fingers incrementally. First, he gasps and chokes on nonexistent breaths. Then, his face transforms to a deep red, his bloodied lips turning blue.

I can feel the dire gurgles of his last breaths beneath my fingers as his body fights for a chance to live.

Kill him.

Finish his miserable life for daring to touch what's yours.

The voices grow in intensity, clashing and mounting until they're all I can hear.

But I ignore and loosen my hold on Rory's neck. Death is still too good for the twat and I refuse to let him go down in peace.

I keep him on the edge, hanging, close to falling ten stories and losing his miserable life as I say, "You'll leave the island and will never, and I mean *never*, show your fucking face here again or else we'll have problems. And by we, I mean you."

He nods countless times like a broken toy, and I pull him up, then release him.

I kick him one last time, then turn around to leave.

"I left you a souvenir with Mia. Hope you like it."

I stop dead in my tracks and release a long sigh. Seems that he truly is in the mood to fuck with me today. What am I if not a good sport?

Let's hope this rage will be dissipated once I'm done with Rory.

Otherwise, Mia will be in deep fucking trouble.

THIRTY-ONE

Mia

AFTER I REACH THE HAUNTED HOUSE, I REALIZE WITH A BIT
of shame that I don't actually have a key.

Well, screw that.

I'm not going back home now that I'm here.

After a slight maneuver, I park my car near the gate, hop on top of
the hood, then climb the metal bars and jump down on the other side.

My legs take the hit, but I'm good. I stare at my phone one last
time in case Landon has graced me with a reply.

Nope.

Nothing.

My feet come to a slow halt at the front garden. My flowers are
slowly growing. One of them, a lone blue gentian flower, is blooming.

It's not a coincidence.

I can't believe Landon, who proudly confessed that he's the
enemy of everything flora and fauna, has not only been watering the
flowers, but he's also trimmed the grass around it and removed the
parasites.

I crouch in front of them and gently run my fingers along the
seams of a bloom, my heart squeezing for an unknown reason.

Why do I feel so embarrassingly hollow all of a sudden?

After I apologize to the flowers for not visiting sooner, I head to the door and reach into the deep hole in the tree where Landon hides the spare key.

A smile pulls on my lips when I find it, then use it to get inside. My mouth hangs open when I see the interior of the house.

Or more like, renovated interior.

Aside from the new furniture, there's a new wooden floor, windows, and elegant muslin curtains.

The renovated Victorian balcony overlooks a newly mowed back garden. The fallen branches and grotesque trees have disappeared. Instead, the view is much more manicured, elegant, even.

The fact that Landon still made these changes even though I was boycotting this place warms my heart.

I walk into his studio, expecting to find new creations. However, the place is creepily the same as I left it over three weeks ago.

The same half-finished statue of a woman fighting a demon. A man screaming into his own ear. A demon drowning in a pool of his disfigured face.

Landon's art is the same as the man himself. Unpredictable, thought-provoking, and, most importantly, intense.

The only thing different is a statue in the corner, covered by a white sheet.

I remove it with an unsteady hand. Sure enough, I'm staring at myself.

Standing only in panties, I'm glaring down and holding up two middle fingers. My lips part when I realize Lan replicated my look from when he first chased me up to the roof.

I get closer, my heart beating so loud, I hear the rush of blood in my ears. His attention to the details grips me in a merciless chokehold.

He didn't miss a single element from that day. Not my curved lashes, the ribbons tangled in my hair, the lines of my collarbone, the slope of my breasts, the hard nipples, the creases in my panties, and even the chains on my boots.

The closer I study it, the deeper I'm pulled into the lethal beauty that stares back at me. This feeling isn't because I'm looking at myself. No. It's because Landon's hands made this.

I don't even know when he had the time to perfect this…I have no clue what to call it. A masterpiece seems too generic. Too little to encompass the meaning behind what his hands made.

I touch her cheek to make sure it's real and I'm not, in fact, imagining myself as a statue.

I never knew art could bring about these strong emotions.

"What are you doing here?"

I startle and nearly knock the statue over. I catch it at the last second, my heart nearly splattering on the floor.

Slowly, I turn around to find Landon standing at the entrance, a hand shoved in his pocket and his face a map of colossal darkness.

My eyes fly to the splashes of blood on the collar of his white shirt and a dash of panic slithers its way to the base of my stomach.

"What happened?" I sign and point at his shirt.

He doesn't even look at it. "You didn't answer my question, Mia. What are you doing here after you made it perfectly clear that we won't be meeting on my territory anymore?"

It's not only his territory. It's mine, too.

Also, what's with his increasingly somber voice? I wished I was only imagining it earlier, but no. His tone is as dark as the blue pools of his eyes.

It's been a long time since Landon looked at me with such disapproval.

I realize with a heavy heart that he only looked at me like this after I bathed him in pig blood and he was out for revenge.

Only, now, there's no trace of his taunting smirk and godlike confidence that can't even be rivaled by the devil.

"I texted you that I wanted to see the statue. You didn't reply," I sign, holding on to my calm by a thread.

"Oh?" He pushes off the wall and an urgent need to run away slaps me in the face. I don't, though, and choose to stand in the path of the deadly storm.

"So you do know how to text, and here I thought you were ghosting me again."

I track his deliberate stalking, my heartbeat escalating with each step he takes forward. "I wasn't."

"Why not? I thought we weren't supposed to meet today, because we apparently met our quota, no?"

"I changed my mind."

"Hmm."

His voice vibrates close to my face as he stops in front of me. I'm assaulted by the scent of his intoxicating cologne and the ethereal view of his features.

And it's really not a wise idea to think of him as the most beautiful man I've ever seen when he seems to be on the verge of squashing me between his fingers.

"You seem nervous, Mia. Is there a reason for that?"

I shake my head, and for the first time, I'm glad I can't speak or I would've definitely stuttered.

"Let's try again. Is there something I need to know about?"

My lips tremble as the pressure of his gaze strips me naked, leaving me unprotected when facing the overpowering intensity of his eyes.

Maybe I should confess about Rory. After all, he did talk to him over the phone and it's not a good idea to pretend nothing happened. If I tell him that I wouldn't even look in that prick's direction, he'd believe me.

Right?

Still, I sign, "Something like what?"

"Like this." He grabs the edge of my scarf and I yelp as he pulls it free.

I slap a hand on the hickey and I know I've made a terrible mistake when he clicks his tongue.

Shit.

"First, you let someone else touch you, then you do a flimsy job of hiding it with a scarf, and now, you're trying to do it with your hand?" His voice darkens with every word. "Do you honestly believe you can protect the hickey from me?"

I shake my head.

I'm not trying to protect it. And yes, maybe a part of me believes what that asshole Rory said about how Landon stops being interested when someone else touches what's his.

That possibility leaves me inexplicably on the edge. I tried to purge Landon out of my life, but that was a joke.

I seriously don't know how I'd be able to go on without his craziness in my life anymore.

And that's a scary thought that I don't even like to consider.

"Drop your hand," he orders with a tone that could accidentally cut someone—that someone being me.

I shake my head.

Maybe if he doesn't look at it, his anger will dissipate—

In a fraction of a second, Landon grabs my wrist and forces it down.

His lips purse in a disapproving line and his eyes become two black holes that look like they're straight out of hell.

Sweat beads on my spine and temples as I slowly break under the suffocating tension he commands with his eyes alone.

"Seems that you've forgotten who's the only one you belong to and could use a reminder." And with that, he leans down and bites on the hickey.

Hard.

Like a bloodthirsty vampire.

THIRTY-TWO

Mia

PAIN EXPLODES ON THE ASSAULTED SPOT IN MY NECK AND spreads throughout my body like lethal wildfire.

However, I remain stunted in place.

Unable to move.

Unable to concentrate on anything but the feel of his lips on my battered skin and the fiery emotions only Landon can trigger inside me.

I should probably tell him I didn't want Rory to touch me nor did I let him, really, but I can't.

My whole body seems to have lost its functions and I'm seeping into a seamless, weightless reality where I can only exist in the moment.

Landon sucks on the skin with power that nearly empties my soul through my throat. It's punishing, hard, and entirely cruel.

It's also a fucked-up connection I didn't realize we could establish. A liaison through searing pain and insatiable rage.

He finally pushes back, leaving a throbbing, tingling mess where his teeth were.

Blood coats his lips, enforcing the image that he's a vampire who just finished feasting. On my blood.

His eyes plunge into mine, darker and completely hollow in their depths.

Only, Landon is no longer hollow. I don't know when I started seeing him as more than the emptiness that lurks inside him and his need for anarchy, but I unfortunately do.

He tsks and that sound has somehow become part of my wildest nightmares. "It still won't go away."

His words ring in the studio like an ominous promise, and I expect him to bite the skin off, just to make the mark disappear.

"I didn't let him touch me," I sign, reining in the tremors that cause my limbs to spasm.

"He said you asked to meet him."

"And you believed him?"

"No." He points at my neck with a lift in his upper lip. "Until I saw that."

I could offer excuses that Rory was too fast and I didn't see him, but that's all those would be.

Excuses.

I refuse to be dragged into that type of dynamic when I did nothing wrong. So I choose the option to remain silent. Fuck him.

I'm a Sokolov and we don't offer excuses.

Landon wraps his fingers around my throat and I suppress a groan as the pad of his thumb presses against the assaulted skin.

He pushes me and I have no choice but to step back to match his movements.

"You know, I don't react well to someone else touching my things."

"I'm not your thing," I sign, even though I struggle to breathe properly.

"Oh, but you are, Mia. You're my fucking property and that means every inch of your skin belongs to me." He digs his thumb into the injury. "Every part is my fucking property."

My back hits the table, on top of which an assortment of Landon's equipment clatter due to the impact.

I flinch and choke on my irregular breaths. The air around me seems to have plunged into a well of suffocating tension I can't breathe through.

"You don't seem to have grasped the situation, Mia. Just because I give you space and make unneeded truces for your sake doesn't mean you can go to someone else. If you're mine, that's what you'll always be. Fucking. *Mine.*" His other hand reaches to the zipper of my dress and he pulls it down until the cloth pools at my feet.

The night air tightens my bare nipples and naked pussy. My cheeks heat as Landon takes in the entirety of me. Lust mixes with rage in an unholy reunion, hinting at a war that's about to blaze through.

"You've come prepared." His voice drops, mixed with angry arousal. "Or was this view perhaps meant for someone else?"

I shake my head. How can he think that?

Yes. I expected something tonight, which is why I didn't put on any underwear, but that plan is obviously being decimated before my eyes.

"No?" He reaches between my legs, cupping the arousal that's been coating my inner thighs since his lips met my neck.

It's part of the reason why I didn't fight. Why I still refuse to fight. I can finally admit that I'm as crazy as Landon, because every inch of me throbs at the prospect of being manhandled.

He strokes my folds with gentle hands and I get on my tiptoes, chasing the spark of pleasure that spreads between my legs and tightens my belly.

"You're soaking my fingers, Mia. Are you that horny for my fingers and cock?"

I suppress a moan as I stare into his impassive eyes. Anger still rages deep in them, black and encompassing me like a second skin.

But what's troubling me the most is how he keeps calling me by my first name. There's no little muse or any of his affectionate terms that he tailor-made for me.

"Were you also this aroused when that twat touched you? Did you moan and show him your sexy little face that should only belong to me? Did his putrid eyes see this version where you're fighting so hard to hide how much you're yearning to be fucked?"

My stomach dips and I clutch the edge of the table for support. His words leave me hotter and more sensitive so that I only need a little push to come.

"But that won't be possible now, because guess what? Rory will be removing himself from this island effective immediately."

My eyes widen, then zero in on the blood on his collar. So my hunch was right. That definitely was because of Rory.

"I taught him a little lesson that included punching the eyes he looked at what belongs to me with, then I split the lips he put on *my* throat. Then finally, as he begged like a little bitch, I broke the arm he used to touch what's fucking mine. But that's not how his miserable story comes to an end. Far from it. See, I made it my mission to gather information that even he wasn't aware of and I will use it to destroy him inch by each fucking inch. In fact, I'll be there as he inevitably overdoses and my apathetic eyes will be the last he sees. As he spits out his last breaths, he'll know messing with what's mine was the worst mistake of his meaningless life." He slaps my pussy and I yelp as the throbbing pain spreads over my core and clenches my belly.

"Why would you do that?" I sign weakly.

"If it's not clear yet. I'm into you, Mia, and that's a very long-term commitment. I'll protect you, but I'll always keep an eye on you so no one else fancies what's mine. You'll never, *ever*, let anyone get close."

He releases my throat and pussy. An unsatisfied groan spills from my lips, but it ends with a yelp as he pushes all the equipment off the table with a single sweep, sending it crashing to the ground. Then he lifts me up with both hands.

My ass touches the cold table, but that's the last thing on my mind as Landon rips his shirt down the middle, sending buttons flying everywhere.

My mouth waters upon seeing his chiseled abs and a hint of the snake tattoos peeking out from the slope of his muscular shoulder and side.

As I stare at the trail of fine hair leading to beneath his clothes, Landon's fiery eyes remain on me as he unhooks his belt and unzips his pants. He kicks them away and straps the leather around my neck.

My throat throbs, but it's not due to the pain. In fact, there's something reassuring about this position.

The belt remains hanging around my neck as Landon reaches for a bucket beside us, and I watch with utter fascination as he removes the lid and splashes me with the cold liquid.

I'm stunned.

Completely and utterly taken aback by the action. I can only watch as the oily-like liquid soaks my face, clings to my eyelashes, and slithers down the rest of my body before dripping on the floor.

Before I can ask what the hell this is, Lan pulls me by the belt so that I'm on the edge of the table and then swipes his thumb along my lower lip.

His mouth is a breath away from mine as he whispers hot, low words, "You look like my favorite masterpiece."

A shudder leaves me when his lips crush against mine, claiming me in a ferocious kiss that tastes of oily liquid and blinding possessiveness.

I can't help but kiss him back, my body falling for the spell of his intensity, the taste of his unforgivable lips and his unapologetic touch.

A bulge stabs my lower belly and then friction ignites between my overstimulated folds. Lan glides his very large cock over my core in an intimate, highly arousing rhythm, teasing but not getting there.

I roll my hips, trying to lift myself so his cock will slip inside. Lan tightens his grip on the belt and sinks his teeth into my lower lip in warning.

"This is a punishment, Mia," he murmurs against my assaulted lip. "Why do you think you can enjoy it?"

He slides his fingers over the oily liquid on my breasts, then squeezes my nipples to aching pebbles. A jolt of both pleasure and pain shoots to where his cock slides between my folds.

The erotic sounds of the glide echoes in the air and I moan, my heart nearly beating out of my chest.

I grab onto Landon's arm, imploring him with my eyes so he'll end this torment already.

Landon pinches my nipple harder as a reply, then lowers his palm to my belly, then over my hip and down to where his cock meets my core.

"The way you're begging for it while your face flickers between pleasure and shame makes me fucking hard." He slides the crown of his cock into my entrance.

I clench around it as if refusing to let him go, but that only triggers a gorgeous smirk on his face. "You want me to fuck you, Mia? Want me to fill my cunt with so much cum, no one else will touch it?"

I nod, not caring if I look too eager for my own good.

Lan pulls out his cock and I nearly scream from frustration.

"As I previously mentioned, this is a punishment and you don't get to enjoy it. Perhaps I'll leave you starving for some time so you'll be more mindful about who you let mark my fucking skin. Perhaps my cock won't touch you for the foreseeable future until you learn your lesson."

"Oh, please. You can't survive without me," I sign, even though a part of me is starting to think I also can't survive without him.

It's a special kind of hell. It's hard to live with his constant mind-boggling intensity, but it's harder to live without him.

"Doesn't mean I won't teach you a lesson, Mia."

"Muse," I sign slowly. "Don't call me Mia."

"Tell me something I want to hear." He strokes the crown of his cock against my entrance.

I bite my lower lip. For the first time in a long time, I want to say this in my own voice, with my own words.

But since I can't and possibly never will, I sign, "I'm yours, Landon."

I watch with bated breath as the rage slowly dissipates, leaving a place for an avalanche of lust and savage possessiveness.

"Yes, you are. Always were and always fucking will be." He thrusts into me in one powerful go so that the table and whatever remains on top rattles.

My pussy clenches around his cock and this time, Landon tightens the belt around my neck as he drives into me with powerful urgency.

"You're taking my cock so fucking well, Mia. You're my favorite little cum bucket, aren't you?"

I don't say anything. I can't.

Lan pulls me using the belt so that my sticky chest is glued to his and my nipples brush over his hard muscles. My breath is stolen by his grip but also by the absolute unapologetic possessiveness he touches me with.

It's like we belonged together several lives ago and we're just reuniting.

Or maybe we're doomed lovers who finally found our way back to each other again.

His pace grows harder, faster until it's nearly impossible to keep up.

My legs wrap around the backs of his thighs, the heels of my boots digging into his flesh, and my fingers sinking in the slithering slope of the snake tattoo.

I'm holding on to him for dear life, but also because it feels so fucking right to be so tangled together that I have no clue where he ends and where I begin.

"Hold on to me, little muse. Quench this fucking thirsty rage inside me." His words sound sinister in my neck. "You're the only one who knows how."

And then he bites down on the flesh he assaulted not so long ago.

I don't know if it's because of his words or the stimulation or the fact that I missed his crazy touch more than I would like to admit, but I come in a spurt of spasms.

White dots form behind my lids and I'm a mess of tremors, but I don't let him go. It feels vital not to.

Lan fucks me through my orgasm, his thrusts going deeper and faster until the world seems to shake around me.

As I'm still recovering from the orgasm, Lan pushes me back so that my shoulders rest against the wall behind me. He reaches for a piece of his equipment—a metal ball with a handle—licks the ball, and then glides it in the liquid on my inner thighs.

"I need to fill your little arse with my cum, but first..." He pulls out and flips me so that my stomach is on the table, my feet are on the ground, and my ass is in the air.

Landon parts my ass cheeks and I hear it before I feel it. He spits on my back hole as he thrusts his cock into my oversensitive cunt.

"Once I'm done, every inch of you will be mine and mine alone." Then he slides what feels like the ball around my back hole before he slowly drives it inside.

I tense up, not even the pleasure in my pussy making this tolerable. Agonized noises leave my lips and I bite it down.

"Shh. Relax for me." His rhythm slows but deepens, hitting my G-spot over and over again.

Moans slip out of me, and apparently, I relax enough, because he drives the ball all the way inside my ass. I feel the burn, but it's not as bad as I thought it would be.

In fact, pleasure spreads all over my core until it's become all I can think about.

I'm so full and stuffed to the brim, it's both overwhelming and thrilling.

My nails dig into the edges of the table, my breath condensing on the surface as I take in the entirety of the intense emotions.

"That's it. You're taking my cock so well, baby."

The praise coupled with the way he calls me baby is enough to make me come again.

Stronger this time.

Harder.

And I scream, wishing—*no*, I actually try to say his name.

But it only comes out as a long sound. No words.

Just eternal silence.

Landon's pace grows in intensity and he joins me soon after. He pulls out and spreads his cum all over my ass so that my skin is a mess of erotic stickiness.

I can barely breathe, let alone think. My ears ring and my heart seems to be fighting to keep me alive.

However, everything quiets down when Landon leans over, pushes away my hair and ribbons from my face, and whispers, "Fucking mine."

I am.

But then again, so is he.

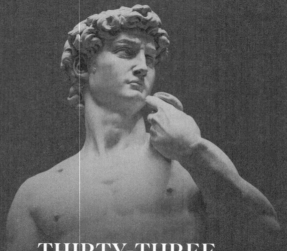

THIRTY-THREE

Landon

MY FINGERS FLOW OVER MY SKETCHBOOK IN A SPORADIC, chaotic rhythm that I have little to no control over.

And I'm the type who thrives on control and having everything under my fucking thumb.

Yet I can't put an end to the figures I've been sketching for hours. Don't ask me how many, because I have no clue what I made during the time I've spent trapped in this endless loop.

It's been so long that I've lost count, and I've also lost the ability to get past this stage.

It's been long enough that my lips have become dry. Since there's nothing to keep them company, it's impossible to tune them out.

What's more frustrating, however, is this rush of creativity that's been possessing my head and limbs but refuses to materialize in real form.

Sketches upon sketches of possible masterpieces fill my pad, and yet none of them makes the cut. My brain is a picky twat with higher standards than the Greek gods.

But then again, if greatness were to come easily, everyone could be a genius.

A soft hand touches mine and I lift my head to meet the eyes of my own Greek goddess. The muse I didn't know I needed until she stood in front of me in the darkness like a perfect imitation of a statue.

My hoodie swallows Mia's tiny frame and reaches the middle of her thighs. Marks of my fingers form a map over the fair skin of her inner legs in a clear show of my absolute ownership.

My gaze slides to the dark blue mark that's spread on her throat. A mark of my own making that bears no resemblance to what I did to that fucker Rory, who's probably fucked off back to his unremarkable hometown in Cambridge as we speak.

After I got that brazen call, I went to the flat he shares with another member of the Elite. I didn't have to wait for long, because he showed up soon after, wearing a smug grin.

That sense of victory was wiped off his ugly face by yours truly after I taught him some basic rules about who calls the shots. Spoiler alert, it's not him.

Just before he passed out, he had the audacity to tell me that he left me a memento with Mia.

That got him the final punch in the face that could or could not send him on the first ambulance to the hospital.

My rage surged the highest after I saw that Mia intentionally hid the hickey he left. As if she was trying to protect the mark or something equally blasphemous.

I've never experienced that type of rage. Not when Bran was made a target. Not when Killian decided my sister was his target.

Not even when I figured out I'd never relate to my parents the way my siblings do.

The moment I saw another man's mark on Mia's skin, I had the urge to destroy Rory so irrevocably, nothing would be left for others to come and pick up.

Then came the need to cut into Mia so deep, my name would be the only one left inside her for any future lives.

But that black rage instantly faded as soon as she said—or, more accurately, signed—the words.

"I'm yours, Landon."

Of course she fucking is.

I didn't need to hear/see the words to know they were true and yet that's exactly what managed to pull me right off a very bleak and dark edge.

She's doing it again right now.

The feel of her soft hand against mine is enough to drag me out of the black hole I got myself trapped in after she fell asleep.

My demons retreat to the shadows, quietly hissing and making their discontent clear.

"Is everything okay?" she signs.

I slam my notebook shut, throw it on the table beside me, and grab her by the waist, then sit her on my lap. She feels small and fucking perfect in my arms—like this is exactly where she was always supposed to be. I bury my nose in her slightly damp hair and I breathe in the magnolia scent.

And yes, I have that shampoo and body wash here.

My lungs expand as I inhale her and I release a long hum. "It is now."

Mia wiggles on my thigh until she's sitting sideways with her back against the desk. Her eyes glitter in a watery blue, like the Mediterranean Sea under the scorching sun.

Was she always so fucking beautiful or am I falling harder onto that bottomless hole?

She studies me closely, which has been the norm since the rooftop date. As if she's trying to get under my skin by using every method at her disposal.

"What were you thinking about just now?" she finally signs.

"Why are you asking?"

"You seemed so lost in thought and I want to know what someone like you thinks about when you're trapped in your own head."

"Nothing good, to be frank." My fingers slide beneath the hoodie and I stroke her hip slowly, sensually.

She shudders but soon recovers. "Tell me."

"It's best to leave some skeletons in the closet."

"But I want to know."

"The skeletons? My, muse. Is this a new kink?"

She teasingly swats my shoulder. "Don't even think about changing the subject."

My smile flattens. "My mind is wired to see the bad before the good. In fact, everything sunshine and rainbows is often an afterthought, never a main idea. My instinct is pro-manipulation, corruption, and anarchy, which means it revolts against the very notion of neurotypical people's socially acceptable behavior. I have a beast that's in constant need of stimulation and if I don't satiate those demands, I'll spiral down a worse path."

As soon as the words are out, I curse myself internally for disclosing that information so easily. In fact, I can't even fathom that I just talked about it to someone other than Uncle Aiden and sometimes Dad.

I've been a proud member of the Antisocial Club to the point where I could be elected as its president. That's why I've always prided myself on being private and secretive. I've never been an open book, not even when I was younger or with therapists. They tried, but as soon as I perfected the game of social emulation and learned emotion, I played them as skillfully as a chess board.

Mia, however, is different. I tried to play her, but I never quite succeeded.

She looks at me with a sense of understanding instead of clinical judgment. Only three people have ever given me that look. Mum, Dad—after he realized it was pointless to put me on a leash—and Uncle Aiden.

And now, her.

Mia.

She watches me for a few beats as if she could skin me alive and insert herself between my ribs. After careful thought, she signs, "Is that why you've been finding it hard to stay still ever since you announced the truce with the Heathens?"

Perceptive little minx.

"Partially."

"What's the other part?"

"You playing an infuriating push-and-pull game."

"Well, I couldn't trust you before."

"Does that mean you do now?"

"I'm starting to." She clears her throat. "Do you feel better?"

I tighten my grip on her waist, my fingers digging into the soft skin. "Now that you're here, yes."

"That's enough?"

"To make the urges dull down, yes."

"Is that why you said I'm the only one who can quench the rage?"

I nod. "You're a good sport."

"But what if I stop being a good sport? Will you dispose of me if I get in your way?"

"You're not a good sport most of the time and you're always in my way. You don't see me pushing you away."

"What if I never change and continue being difficult and too much myself."

"That's what I'm counting on. Don't ever change. You're perfect the way you are."

A shudder rushes through her and she smiles a little. "Did Bran teach you to say that?"

"Fuck no. In fact, I should teach him a few things."

"Because he's an empath?"

"That's a problem as well, but my biggest concern is that he's a bit of a prude and has little to no experience."

"Ever thought that's because girls have used him to get to you?"

I narrow my eyes. "How do you know that?"

"He told me."

"Getting a bit too cozy with Bran, aren't you?"

"He's a very good friend."

"Hmm."

"Stop it." She smiles. "I can't believe you're jealous of your own twin brother."

"I'm not jealous. I'm territorial. Besides, there's a reason I'm more popular than him."

"The fact you're a dick?"

"There's that. He's also extremely emotionally stunted sometimes.

Don't let the image he wears so well fool you. There's another side to him that he keeps under lock and key."

"What is that supposed to mean?"

"Nothing you need to worry about."

She observes me with a slight frown, but, thankfully, she chooses to let it go and points at my pad. "Were you sketching?"

"Yeah. Not much luck, I'm afraid."

"You didn't sleep?"

"Don't have time for it."

"But you never sleep."

"Sleep is overrated." I stop there, not wanting to disclose that I do sleep, just not when she's around.

She's been single-handedly driving my superior creativity lately and I'd rather get the most out of it than sleep.

Mia glares.

I pinch her cheek. "Did I ever tell you that you look adorable when you glare? It gets me hard."

Her cheeks redden as she signs, "Everything gets you hard."

"Not everything. You."

"Not me. The kinks."

"Not the kinks. *You.*" I lift her chin with my thumb and forefinger. "They do offer a sprinkle of spice, and yes, they're undeniably thrilling, but they're not strictly mandatory when I'm with you. I used to go to sex clubs and indulge in all sorts of fuckery because normal stopped working out for me since secondary school. Although I managed to reach physical climax countless times, it was never fully satisfying."

"Even with the kinks?"

"Even with the kinks. You're the only one I've reached a mental climax with."

"In some time?"

"In ever."

Her lips curl in a proud smirk. "Guess that means we're each other's firsts after all."

"Don't get smug Miss Prude Virgin Until Fairly Recently."

"Virgin or not, I managed to offer the great Landon King

something no one else has." She ruffles my hair, seeming so happy with herself.

I grin in return. "You find me great?"

"Get over yourself."

"Impossible."

She shakes her head, but the smile still paints her lips. "What were you working on?"

"Nothing satisfying."

"Ever thought that you're too hard on yourself?"

"Not hard—selective. I don't vibe well with mediocrity."

"Nothing you make is mediocre." She points at her statue. "I love it. Thank you."

"You're welcome, but you can't take it."

"Why not?"

"It's my property, like you, little muse."

She frowns. "I'm not a thing."

"No, you're not. But you're still mine."

"Well, are you mine, then?"

"If you want."

She bites the corner of her lip and releases it, then clears her throat and looks around for another way to change the topic.

That's fine. If she's this rattled by me, it means I'm drawing her deeper into my world. Sooner or later, she'll have no choice but to let her guard down and completely belong to me.

After a few seconds, she signs, "How come you're not smoking and making your lungs as black as your soul?"

"I quit."

"Really?"

"Cigarettes were always an indulgence I could walk away from. I don't get addicted." *Except for when it comes to you.*

It's not only obsession or limerence at this point. And it's definitely a lot more addictive. The fact that my demons immediately calmed down the moment she appeared is both fascinating and alarming.

And yet I wouldn't have it any other way.

"Good. It's not good for your health."

"And your health."

"And the plants!" She smiles. "Thank you for taking care of them. They're alive and pretty."

"I was bored."

"You're never bored enough to take care of plants, so just take the thank-you without being so sarcastic about it." She hops off my lap before I can stop her. "I have to go check on them. It's best to water them this early in the morning."

"Are you seriously exchanging my godly company with some flowers?"

"You can join me," she offers over her shoulder with a flirtatious smile and then she's out the front door.

I'd rather crash and burn in my McLaren as it falls off a cliff.

Twenty minutes later, I'm dressed in sweatpants, a T-shirt, and my wellies as I make my way to the small garden Mia created.

What? I was bored. Besides, I'm not in the mood to be trapped by my own creativity again.

Mia looks up from her crouched position and lifts her gloved hand to shield her eyes from the rising sun. I stand in its path and slide a hand into my pocket. "I'm gracing you with my presence. I accept worship in the form of blowjobs."

She laughs and shakes her head, then signs, "Don't just stand there. Make yourself useful and get me the fertilizer spikes."

The blasphemy. How dare she treat me like a servant for the demon flowers that she's giving more attention than me. I should've squashed them to death when I had the chance and chalked the whole thing up to an unfortunate flower death. Happens every day in many flower shops and wouldn't be frowned upon by any stretch of the imagination.

Since that option is currently out of the question, I go fetch the fertilizer and even put on gloves. Then I, Landon King, the legendary genius of contemporary art, help water the little flower fuckers.

My logic is simple. The sooner she's done with this tedious chore, the faster I can get her to round two. Maybe this time, I'll paint her pretty little body as I fuck her on all fours on the canvas. Or maybe I'll sketch something on her back while I fuck her senseless. I'm nothing less than versatile when it comes to fucking and art. Combine the two together and you get a recipe for guaranteed success.

"You're not supposed to try to stab them, Landon." Mia laughs and catches my hand to show me how.

So I make mistakes on purpose so she can 'correct' my actions further. Now, this I can deal with, unlike entitled flowers that have no business getting between me and my muse.

After I get over my childish, immature feelings about literal plants, I focus more on Mia. I love the carefree, happy expression on her face as she strokes and even signs to the flowers as if they're pets.

"You could make a career out of this," I say when she keeps inspecting the seeds.

"Oh, I will," she signs. "I'm going to be a badass businesswoman who will make the world a better place for plants."

"Pretty sure you're confusing business with activism."

"I can do both. Money talks, so I'll have that and use it to give the plants a better life."

"How about your family's notorious mafia business?"

She lifts a shoulder. "Fortunately or unfortunately, that responsibility falls on Nikolai's shoulders. Mom and Dad promised that Maya and I can marry and do whatever we want. Imagine me having to marry one of the mafia heirs?"

"Not so hard to do, considering your liaisons with Jeremy."

"Jeremy is a responsible leader and a trustworthy friend."

"Hmm. Go on. Tell me a bit more so I can bump him up to the top of my shit list."

"Don't be jealous." She laughs.

"Me? Jealous? I don't process those feelings, love."

"You obviously do. Aside from the Jeremy thing, Bran said you made it clear that I'm yours in order to keep him and Remi away."

"As it should be. Bran is my brother, but even he isn't allowed to mess with what's mine. As for Remi, he's a nuisance."

"No, he's not. He's actually funny and fun."

Funny and fun. Not just funny or fun. It's both funny *and* fun.

I better not see his face in the near future or I'll be tempted to ruin it.

In fact, maybe I should do just that. He's too carefree for his own good and could use a lesson or a few.

I'm still contemplating the best plan to bring Remi down when, all of a sudden, the sky opens up and the rain comes pouring down.

Mia gets to her feet and grabs my hands, then we run toward the gazebo in the middle of the garden.

But it's too late. We soon realize that we're both soaking wet.

We look at each other, pause, and then burst out in laughter.

It's one of the few genuine laughs I've ever had, and it's only because she's by my side.

The rain hammers down on us. Mia's blonde strands stick to her face, but she still looks like a goddess as she laughs, the sound echoing around me like my favorite tune. Droplets of rain stick to her upper lip and then make a path to beneath her hoodie.

Mia stops in the middle of the yard, takes my hand again, then uses it to twirl herself under the rain. Just when I'm about to join in the cheesy dance, she releases me, a sly look penetrating her light irises. "Catch me if you can."

Then she resumes running.

My beast roars to life as if it was never dormant. This is what Mia has that no one else does. She's not prey to my beast, she's its match.

The yin to his yang.

The crazy to his insanity.

I leap right behind her. Mia chances a look back and releases an excited yelp when she sees me within touching distance.

And I realize as I catch up to her inside the gazebo that I wish this moment would last for an eternity and beyond.

But since that's not doable, I will prolong it for as long as possible.

Looks like classes are canceled for both of us today.

Remington: Who the fuck hid my special edition Jordans?

Eli: And you're texting that in the group chat because…? Don't tell me you think someone actually cares.

Remington: You shut up, psycho. Why don't you go torture some miserable soul?

Eli: Why would I do that when I have my own source of entertainment, aka you?

Remington: I'm no clown, twat.

Eli: You're failing to make the case for yourself.

Brandon: I thought you found them the other time?

Remington: They went missing again. Spawn! Help me out.

Remington adds Creighton to the group chat

Creighton: I'd rather be sleeping.

Remington: What the actual fuck? Do you prefer sleeping over helping your lord and savior (who's me by the way)? You're changing, Creigh. Not only are you often with your girlfriend, but you're also not paying my lordship much attention. Remember that if it weren't for me, you wouldn't have had the adequate social skills to even get on Anni's radar.

Eli: And you plan to make him work for that for the rest of his life? Stop bothering my little bro and go find yourself a decent hobby aside from unnecessary arrogance.

Remington: Says the twat who's the definition of the term.

Eli: At least I don't talk about myself in the third person as if that's a perfectly normal thing to do.

Brandon: I'll help you look for them, Remi.

Eli: You don't have to cater to his illogical whims, cousin. Let his 'lordship' solve his own trivial problems.

Remington: You're so unserious, not to mention jealous. Do something better with your life instead of obsessing over me @ Eli King.

Eli: Me? Jealous of you? The bar is so low, might as well step on it.

Remington: You just proved my theory.

Eli: Which is?

Remington: You've always had an inferiority complex because you can never reach my level of blinding charisma. Don't worry, Eli. You can't have everything in life.

Brandon: Come on, let's be rational.

Eli: Something Remi will never know the meaning of, considering his multiple delusions.

All this time, I've been reading the chats while leaning against my car at the corner of REU, waiting for a mosquito to make her presence known.

Since I'm bored anyway, I type.

Landon: He also doesn't know when to shut up, which will soon make him the subject of a ferocious witch hunt.

Eli: Not to mention, give him a dedicated section on some people's shit list. He's too blasé for his own good.

Landon: He doesn't know how to keep his thoughts and tacky jokes to himself. For the record, you're not funny, Remi.

Creighton: I agree. No clue why girls think of him as funny.

Remington: Spawn! How dare you turn on me and take Eli and Lan's side over mine?

Eli: It's the sensible thing to do. My little bro has superior taste, as expected.

Landon: Everyone but Remi does.

Remington: You jealous bitches can go die. The fact remains that I'm besties with all of your girls and always will be. Muahahaha.

I'm going to kill the bastard.

Creighton King has left the chat

Brandon: You shouldn't have fanned the flames, Rems.

Eli: You made a terrible mistake. You better watch your back.

Landon: Should've said goodbye to your beloved Jordans while you had the chance. RIP.

Remington: It's you! I swear to fucking God, Lan, if you don't give them back...

I don't read the rest of the texts. One, because I have no mind for Remi's over-the-top dramatics. Two, because the person I've been stalking better than an MI5 agent walks around the corner, watching her surroundings with eyes as big as a sewer rat.

I slide my phone back into my pocket and move to a hidden spot by a gigantic tree to the side.

Nila stops upon seeing my McLaren, her face pales to a pallid white.

Her heels scratch against the asphalt as she makes a run for her car. I follow behind her, and the moment she opens the door, I slam it shut and say in cold words, "Running from something, Nila?"

She slowly turns around, doing a poor imitation of those horror film airheads. She plasters a smile that's more fake than her lashes and releases an annoying chirpy noise.

"Lan! I didn't see you there."

"Naturally. Since you've been making it your mission to avoid me."

"What...? No, of course I wasn't avoiding you."

"Is that why you haven't been acting like my designated shadow the past couple of days?"

"You said you didn't like that."

"Didn't stop you before." I step closer so that I'm staring down my nose at her. "So let's hear it, Nila. What's the reason that pushed you to be so transparently avoidant of my company?"

"I just have a lot of schoolwork."

"Are you sure that's the only reason? It couldn't perhaps be due to a certain fuckup on your part, now, could it?"

"I don't know what you're talking about—"

Her words are cut off when I grab strands of her hair and pull until tears gather in her eyes. "The time where you can bullshit me does not and will not exist, Nila. Did you possibly think I wouldn't find out that you were the one behind Rory's foolish idea about Mia? He's as thick as a brick, but you're not. You've always been a conniving little bitch who uses your looks and resources to get anywhere you want. But here's the thing, Nila. I taught you half of what you know, which you should've thought about before you went against your fucking maker."

Her face reddens as I pull harder with every word. She tries to claw my hand free, but it's no use. If I choose to, I can squash her faster than a cockroach.

"You're the one who turned your back on the club and us for that bitch!" Her voice grows in volume as she lets her true face show through.

Greed and contempt stare back at me like a disgusting mirror of my old self. I'm no saint and fortunately never will be, but these types of frivolous, shallow emotions Nila represents have long since been washed out of me.

"So you decided to inflame Rory's rage and point him toward Mia. Is that it?"

She purses her lips. "So what?"

"You had the audacity to touch what's mine, Nila, and as I'm sure you found out through Rory's state, I don't react well to anyone threatening what belongs to me."

Her lips lift in a snarl. "What does she have that I don't?"

"Figures. One thing's for certain, you fucked up and this is me telling you, I'll fucking destroy everything you stand for. The friends you think you have? They easily switched to my side after a few words from yours truly. Your beloved papa's company can effortlessly be crushed if my dad somehow pulls his investments. So here's a helpful suggestion. Be afraid, Nila. All your worst fears will come true."

I release her and she crashes against the side of her car, tears streaming down her cheeks.

"She'll eventually see you for who you truly are and abandon you,

Lan!" she shouts at my back. "You can never maintain a relationship, not with her or anyone else!"

I don't listen to her blabbering as I head to where I parked my car and pull out my phone.

Eli was a good sport and sent me some information. Though it's not much and by no means concrete evidence, coupling his findings with what I discovered on my own, I'm getting close to the whole truth.

Another text pops up at the top of my screen.

A smile lifts my lips when I find it's from Mia. She attached a picture of the flowers she's grown in the garden.

Ever since I found her there three days ago, she's been going to the haunted house—that's not so haunted anymore—whenever she has time.

It's for the flowers, she says. But I often catch her trying to sneak and take a look in the art studio like a curious kitten.

When she was asleep, I hid the piece I was working on in a closet and locked it with a key. Other than that, she's free to roam around—which can't be said about anyone else who's not Mum or Bran.

Lately, I often catch her looking at anything that casts a reflection—mirrors, the refrigerator door, the glass top table—opening and closing her mouth as if she's trying to speak. She's probably doing it subconsciously since she usually looks startled whenever she takes note of the situation.

That happens during sex as well. Twice now, she's opened her mouth, struggled, and then only released a guttural scream.

In a way, it feels as if she's battling to remove the mental shackles that stole her voice. I have confidence that after I get rid of the vermin who threatened her life, she'll be able to finally be at peace with her younger self.

I stare at the text she sent with the picture.

Mia: Claudia, Stephan, and Emilia say hi.

Landon: Either you're crazy and actually gave those flowers names or you're also crazy and started talking to the resident ghosts of the house, who are in the process of sending me a stern letter about the recent renovations. No clue which crazy is more serious.

Mia: *laughing out loud emoji* x3 You're effortlessly funny sometimes. And what do you mean that naming the flowers is crazy? Of course they need names now that they're blooming. I'll name the others when they grow as well.

Landon: You do realize they're not pets, right?

Mia: Of course they aren't. They're my friends.

She's so insane, I love it.
My smile turns to a grin as I type.

Landon: You better be done with all that voodoo by the time I get to the house. There'll be nothing friendly about what I'll do to you.

Mia: Promises. Promises.

My dick jumps in my trousers and I have to readjust so I don't sport a major hard-on for the world to see.

Fuck me.

I'm definitely going to break a few road rules on my way there.

The new flirtatious version of Mia is completely doing my head in. In a good way.

I love that she's more upfront about what she likes and doesn't shy away from dropping to her knees when I'm trying to work. It's a major distraction, but I prefer coming down her pretty throat to touching cold statues for sure.

Movement sounds behind me and I start to turn, but someone wraps an arm around my neck, catching me in a chokehold.

I lift my hands to push it away, but someone else yanks them behind my back.

The stronger they strangle the life out of me, the more lightheaded I get. The last thing I see is Nikolai's manic face.

"Payback time, motherfucker."

THIRTY-FOUR

Mia

I'M UNDENIABLY UNDERGOING A DRASTIC CHANGE AND THE worst part is that I can't describe it.

All I know is that I've never been happier in my life.

Free.

Wild.

With no limits but the sky itself.

It's all because of the crucial role Landon plays in my life. Ever since he forced his way past my walls, I've been experiencing a curious sense of novelty, adventure, and happiness.

That's when I realized that before him, I was only living, never truly alive. I was so caught up in my childhood tragedy that I let it shackle and dictate how I should live my life.

But it doesn't matter how confident or determined I've been, I still let the monster control the very foundation of my being and steal my voice forever.

Maybe that realization is why the recent bursts of happiness I've been experiencing seem flawed with a huge black hole in the middle.

Unless I deal with it, I know the hole will keep widening and possibly devour the good. At this point, I'm no different than a kid building a house of sand on the beach and expecting it to remain standing after being hit by a wave.

I still choose to hold on to the vain hope and the sparks of happiness with the desperation of a drowning woman.

I just can't consider any different circumstances where complete happiness and peace is entirely impossible.

In a dream, maybe.

If I wake up, I'll never be able to survive.

My heart rate hasn't gone down since I was texting with Landon.

That was an hour ago.

I finished taking care of my garden, removed my gloves, and freshened up, then waited for him.

And waited.

But there's still no trace of him.

I'm by the tall window overlooking the entrance, but my car is the only one in the driveway.

I check my watch for the thousandth time.

He made it seem as if he would be here in fifteen minutes, but that's clearly not the case. He couldn't have texted me from London or something, right?

This is starting to worry me. Especially since he never replied to the subsequent texts I sent asking about his whereabouts. Lan always replies to my texts.

Always.

My phone vibrates in my hand and I check it so fast, I nearly drop it. My shoulders hunch when I see the name on the lock screen, then guilt gnaws at my insides for feeling disappointed.

I'm such a horrible friend.

Brandon: Hey. Lan is with you, right?

My chest tightens and a burst of uneasiness spreads down my spine.

Bran knows about us and even told me that Lan seems to be genuinely trying not to be his asshole self for the first time. However, he never asks about us or what we do. In fact, he's the type who'd rather be spared the details, unlike Remi, who called for a 'meeting' so he could get the latest gossip.

So the fact that Bran is asking now deviates from a pattern and I don't like that. I type with unsteady fingers.

Mia: Why are you asking?

Brandon: Just tell me if he's with you or not. Please.

Mia: He's not. We were supposed to meet, but it's taking him longer than usual to get here.

He reads the text but there's no reply.

Mia: What's going on? Is there something wrong?

Brandon: I don't know, Mia. Maybe you're the one who needs to tell me what the fuck is going on.

I stare at the text with my jaw nearly hitting the floor. That doesn't sound like Bran, especially since I've never heard him curse.

My screen lights up again.

Brandon: I'm sorry. I shouldn't have lashed out at you, but I think, no, I'm ninety percent certain your brother has something to do with Lan's disappearance. He either kidnapped or assaulted him, then threw him in a ditch somewhere. That is, if he didn't fucking kill him. Bloody hell.

My breathing quickens as I read and reread the words.

Mia: How do you know?

Brandon: It doesn't matter how I know. I just do. We need to do something before it's too late.

Shit. Don't tell me…

Maya texted me earlier, inviting me for coffee. When I said no, she kept pestering me and asking where I was exactly and saying she'd come to meet me. But when I told her that I was at Landon's, she finally gave up.

Now, I know why my overly insistent sister who never gives up did. She was probably instructed by Nikolai to make sure I stay away so he could do whatever he wanted with Lan.

I'm already running for my keys at the entrance as I type.

Mia: Meet me at the Heathens' mansion. Give the guards at the front my name and the code 01483.

Brandon: On my way.

I've never driven so fast in my life. The entire time, my mind is invaded by all sorts of bleak scenarios. None of which has a good ending.

After I arrive at the Heathens' mansion, I go straight to the annex house that they use as some form of a torture chamber.

As expected, two buff guards and Ilya stand in front of the door like watchdogs.

Upon seeing me, Ilya steps forward. His large frame blocks the sun so that I'm staring at his poker face and unexpressive eyes. "You should go back, miss."

"Get the fuck out of my way," I sign, not caring that he doesn't understand a thing.

Ilya places an arm in front of me, and I can see him struggle not to push me down like a criminal. He's definitely under strict orders not to allow me access to the room.

I slip from beneath his hold and steal a gun from one of the other guards. I point it at Ilya and motion to the side.

He lifts his hands in the air. "You don't want to do this, miss. It's not your fight."

It absolutely *is* my fight. All of this is happening in great part because of me.

The other part, of course, is because Landon is an asshole who can't breathe without exhaling venom into the world.

But I've come to terms with that, and I foolishly thought Nikolai had, too.

I keep the gun pointed at Ilya and the others as I grab the handle of the door and slip inside.

My hand with the gun falls to my side as I stand at the entrance of a large white room with a gruesome scene in the middle.

Killian, Jeremy, and Nikolai surround Landon, who's on his knees on the floor, his lip cut, one eye swollen shut, and blood smeared over his white shirt.

Some of it splashed on Killian's and Jeremy's T-shirts and Nikolai's naked chest. At this moment, my brother, who I love more than any words could describe, looks like a stranger in the form of a beast.

A weapon of destruction.

An uncontrollable entity of rage.

Landon looks up at Kill with a bloodied grin, coughs, and speaks in a hoarse voice. "Is that all you got? If you're going to fuck up Glyn's trust, the least you can do is make it worthwhile."

"Shut the fuck up." Nikolai drives his fist into his face. "You really thought we'd take the truce and let you mess around with my sister? My fucking *sister*? I'll kill you before you put your hands on her again."

"Then do it." Landon's provocative grin disappears. "That's the only way you'll keep me away from her."

Despite the terrifying scene, I can't help the imaginary hand that squeezes my heart and tightens my stomach.

"You're a fucking dead man." Jeremy kicks his side.

"Highly doubtful." Landon's eyes slide to mine as if he knew I was there this whole time. "Hey, little muse. I believe you should revoke Jeremy's highly underserved nice card, don't you think?"

Three pairs of eyes turn toward me and it's Nikolai who speaks first.

"What the fuck are you doing here? Get out."

I throw the gun to the floor and sign as I stride toward them, "So you can continue to torture him?"

"That's the idea," Killian says. "Remove yourself from the situation, Mia."

"No."

"I don't know what this motherfucker has been saying to you, but you can't believe any of it," Jeremy says.

"Like the fact that he kept his part of the deal and you didn't? You already agreed to a truce, so why the hell are you doing this?"

"I never agreed to the fucking truce," Nikolai speaks in a voice so tight, the veins in his neck bulge with tension. "He does not, under any circumstances, get to touch you and live."

"But that's not up to you!" I get in his face, my movements

brimming with anger. "This is my life and I have the right to decide whoever gets in it. Neither you nor anyone else has a say in it."

"Mia," he growls in warning.

I glare back at him and sign more calmly now, "Let him go."

"No."

"My apologies for breaking up the touching family moment, but hey you, uncultured swine." He looks up at Jeremy, who's now twisting Landon's right arm at an awkward angle. "I know you're jealous you'll never be as artistically genius as me, but you're causing strain on my priceless hand. Let go, would you?"

"Only if you get to free fall to hell, motherfucker."

"Let him go, Jeremy," I sign, watching the unnatural angle he's holding his arm in. If he twists it to the side, he'll break his wrist and the thought of that leaves me in cold sweat.

Landon can only survive through art. If that ability is taken from him, he won't be able to battle the demonic forces inside him. I've seen how calm he gets when he's creating, how grounded and zen his expression gets.

If that's taken away, I'm not sure where he'll go from here.

Nikolai watches my expression closely, then he smiles, but it's manic at best as he leans down to stare at Landon's face. "Want to keep your arm in one piece?"

"Preferably soon, yes."

"Then leave my sister alone. For good."

I push at Nikolai's shoulder, but he doesn't look at me. My chest tightens. Fuck. He knows that's worse than ignoring me. If he doesn't look at me, I can't talk to him. He's basically silencing me in the most brutal way possible.

And it hurts worse than I'd like to admit. Especially coming from my brother, who's always listened to me, even when I talk gibberish.

I don't recognize this version of Nikolai. Not even a little.

"If you don't." Nikolai's face turns somber. "Jeremy will break the wrist you cherish so much."

"Choose carefully, King," Killian says in a casual tone. "Any breaking of arm bones, especially the wrist, could prove to be fatal in an artist's life. Take it from me. As a med student, I can confirm that bones and ligaments never go back to the way they were and you could find immense difficulty in creating anything ever again. Your bright future will be *poof*. Gone. In a fraction of a second."

"Kill!" I push at his chest. "What the fuck is wrong with you? If you watch as his wrist is broken, Glyn will never forgive you."

"She'll never find out, and even if she does, I have a better track record than her emotionless brother."

My lips part. I always thought Landon was the worse psychopath of the two, but right now, my cousin, whom I always considered like my second brother, looks worse than the monster from my past.

Because I know that even if the word got out and Glyn caught a whiff of this, he'd spin the story to look completely innocent. I've seen the way he looks at her and I'm well aware he can't afford to lose her, but he certainly can afford to hurt her brother irrevocably.

"Go ahead," Landon says tonelessly and without emotion. "You can break the other one as well while you're at it. But I'll always touch her, even with casts on. She's mine and neither of you motherfuckers will decide otherwise."

I meet his cold eyes with my alarmed ones and shake my head frantically. *What are you doing, you idiot?*

He's provoking Nikolai and the others. He must know they're not the type to bluff. Especially not Nikolai.

Sure enough, Jeremy starts to twist and I scream so loud, everything comes to a halt. The world, my hoarse voice, and my surroundings.

Jeremy stops. He and Killian watch me as if I'm a wild animal who's about to bite their heads off, which I probably should do.

Nikolai's attention slides back to me, his expression taken aback.

"You're finally looking at me now after you erased and silenced me?" I sign, feeling the burn in my eyes. "How can I talk to you if you don't look at me?"

Some of the tension in his shoulders disappears as he steps toward me and grabs my arm. "Fuck. I'm so sorry, Mia. I didn't mean to."

I push his hand away. "Let Landon go."

"I can't do that. He's a venom that needs to be extracted by the roots—"

"I'll leave him. I won't associate with him again, so just let him go."

"No, you won't." Landon fights against Jeremy's grip for the first time since I came here. "Go ahead and break my fucking wrist, Jeremy."

"Stay fucking still." Jeremy struggles to keep him down.

"Remember, Cecily loved me first." Landon's voice turns eerily calm. Taunting, even. "She loved me so much that she fantasized about me and called me her prince. She loved me so much that she gave me heart eyes long before you came along. Not to mention, we used to bathe together as children. Fucking naked. You must really hate that you'll always be second choice to me."

"You little fucking—" Jeremy twists his wrist and Landon's face scrunches, but he doesn't release any sounds.

One moment, I'm standing beside Nikolai, the next, I'm kicking Jeremy's arm. He's so taken aback that he loses his grip on Landon's wrist.

I help him up and he stands to his feet. However, his arm remains limp by his side.

"Is it okay?" I sign, gulping the lump in my throat.

Landon doesn't even check if his wrist is okay as he grabs my cheek with his good hand. "You're not going any-fucking-where. You understand me?"

"Leave," I sign.

"I'm going to fucking kill this motherfucker." Nikolai comes close, but I shake my head at him.

"Just go." I push Landon toward the door.

He doesn't even take one step.

"Brandon is outside," I sign. "He could be in danger, too."

His upper lip lifts in a snarl and he tsks. "What the fuck is that busybody doing here?"

"He's worried about you. Please go, Landon. For me. Please."

I have no doubt that if he stays here one more minute, he'll provoke them again and they'll make good on their threat to break his wrist.

"You're never leaving me and we won't be over," he says, ignoring everyone else present as he kisses me in a brief passionate kiss. All I taste is blood as Killian pushes him off me.

And then he's out the door.

I release a long breath, then I glare at the three guys I thought were closest to me.

"What?" Killian says. "You should've known this was coming. That motherfucker did a lot worse to us."

"There's nothing worse than breaking an artist's fucking wrist, Killian! Put yourself in his shoes. How would you have survived your medical career if your own wrist was broken?"

"You need to stop defending the bastard, Mia," Jeremy says.

"Not when all of you are ganging up on him."

"Why is Brandon here?" Nikolai asks out of nowhere.

"What?" I sign.

"Just now, you said Brandon is here. Why is he?"

"He texted me that you could've been hurting Lan, which turned out to be true, so I told him to meet me here. I'm glad I did. At least he can give Lan a ride."

"Mia…" He growls as he barges toward me.

"I'm going home," I announce. "To New York. I obviously don't have any rational support here. Maya lied to me and you shut me up."

He curses under his breath as I push past him toward the door.

Maybe talking to Mom and Dad is my best chance to protect the fragile happiness sand castle I've been building.

THIRTY-FIVE

Mia

HOME HAS ALWAYS BEEN MY SANCTUARY. A PLACE IN WHICH I can unplug and be myself.

Not that I've found trouble being myself everywhere else, but whenever I'm in the presence of Mom and Dad, I feel like a kid again. Maybe childishly so.

The second Maya and I step through the door, we're greeted by Mom's radiant face. She's dressed in an elegant knee-length burgundy dress with a belt that enhances her hourglass shape. An off-white jacket rests on her shoulders, giving her a sophisticated edge.

Her eyes glitter in a dreamy blue as she engulfs me in a bear hug. As soon as I inhale her warmth, the urge to burst into tears hits me out of nowhere.

All of a sudden, I'm that little girl who was trapped in the darkness with no way out. This moment is similar to when she and Dad found me.

I felt the same sense of crippling emotion when he personally came to pick me up at the airport after our private jet landed.

Yes, my parents have a private jet. It was actually Mom's wedding anniversary gift from Dad. He got a lot of shit from Grandpa about it, but Dad told him he's the reason their family has so much money in the first place, so if he decides he'll buy his wife a plane or the moon itself, he has no say in it.

Grandpa Mikhail is more old-fashioned than the English monarchy, but he's been present our entire lives. While he clashes with Dad sometimes, they actually get along pretty well. Mom said they found each other late in life, so that's probably why Grandpa dotes on us more than his other grandkids. He's spoiled us rotten since we were young and has never hidden the fact that we're his favorites.

He learned sign language for me at an old age and often invited us over, despite having countless other grandchildren.

So it's no surprise that he also accompanied Dad to the airport. Grandpa said that he wanted to see 'his girls' first. He received a call about some trouble one of my uncles is causing and we separated at the airport, but not before he told us we need to spend a day or two with him before we go back to the 'tasteless' Brits.

He and Dad definitely agree that we should've stayed on US soil so they could keep an eye on us.

My fingers dig into Mom's back, probably harder than needed. But she doesn't complain and even strokes my hair. "I missed you so much. I can't believe I haven't hugged my babies for months on end."

"My turn." Maya basically pushes me away so she can hug Mom.

Dad wraps an arm around my shoulder and I hug his waist, leaning my head on his chest. Since a young age, Dad has always had a smart, casual style and he rocks suits, like his current black Armani, better than a model. Whenever he and Mom are in public, they attract more attention than celebrities.

It's part of the reason why I prefer not to go out with them much. Maya, however, is all over that crap, considering she needs attention as much as air.

I crave my parents' company in private, though. Being surrounded by them offers me a much-needed escape from my head. So I tighten my hold on my dad. He smells like cedarwood and safety. This scent reminds me of when they first found me in that basement. As Dad carried me in his arms, I hid my face in his chest and remained so still, I don't remember even blinking.

It took me a few minutes to fill my lungs with him and realize it was finally over.

Or was it really?

It wasn't over. Not then.

Not now.

Mom pulls away from Maya to stroke her face. "You girls have grown so much. You look absolutely radiant."

"Of course." Maya flips her hair and then smooches Mom's cheek. "We take after the best."

"Where did you get the sweet talk from, I wonder?" Mom gives Dad a knowing look.

He grins and winks. "Proud of it, princess."

Maya physically swoons. "You guys are goals! Come on, I want a selfie."

"You can't post my face on social media, Maya. You know that's a hard rule," Dad says.

She releases a dejected sigh. "Okay, fine. I'll just keep it to myself. Come on."

Dad starts to push me toward her, but I shake my head. He throws me a look, but then he gets in the shot for a selfie with Maya.

After she takes it, she pouts. "Are you going to stay mad at me for long?"

I cross my arms and look at the elegant, modern interior of our entrance area. This used to be a lake cottage, but Dad renovated it into this extravagant mansion at the edge of the lake.

Elegant pillars lift the three-story house and provide high ceilings and a symmetrical architectural structure. Tall French windows offer a direct view of the lake and illuminate the space with natural sunlight.

The luxurious mansion is crafted from premium rocks and enjoys an elevated, charming position in the middle of nowhere. Large balconies provide a front-row seat to mesmerizing sunrises and sunsets. Before we left for college, it was our family ritual to watch them together.

Nikolai, Maya, and I often played outside by the garden and swam along the shores of the lake, then splashed each other until we were giggling and out of breath. My twin and I usually conspired against Nikolai, but he often won. And whenever he didn't, it was only because he felt sorry for us and let us beat him.

He's often been our knight, but yesterday, he definitely didn't act like one.

I understand his animosity toward Landon, and I get his need for revenge, but the fact that he shut me out so cruelly still hurts.

I texted Landon on my way to the plane.

Mia: I'm going back to New York to visit Mom and Dad. Maybe this is a good opportunity to put some distance between us.

Landon: Nonsense. The word distance doesn't exist in my vocabulary. It's for cowards who don't know what the fuck they want. I know exactly what I want. The question is, do you?

I didn't reply to that text.

I couldn't.

My mind has been a mess since the whole encounter with the Heathens.

"What's going on?" Mom studies me and my sister closely.

"It's nothing." Maya throws her hands in the air. "She's just being unreasonable."

I glare at her and she glares back.

She wasn't supposed to come home with me for this long weekend that coincides with a bank holiday, but she likes to think that we're twins attached at the hip.

"It's not nothing," Dad retaliates. "You weren't speaking on the ride here, which is unusual, to say the least."

"Well, Mia is being unnecessarily dramatic." My sister releases a long breath.

I narrow my eyes on her, but I refuse to reply when she doesn't even want to admit what she did wrong.

"What's this all about, girls?" Mom asks. "You know it's a house rule to talk about our problems so we can resolve them."

Maya sighs and lets her phone with some fashion design case drop to her side. "Well, Mia has a crush on this British guy who's more notorious than Satan himself, but she wouldn't listen to reason when everyone—Niko, Kill, Gaz, and I included—told her that he's bad news. Like the worst of news, Mom. Imagine Kill on steroids. Yeah, it's that dire. So Niko decided to take matters into his own hands and teach the prick a lesson, and rightfully so. Kill and Jeremy joined in because, well, remember the part where he could give Satan a run for his money? He actually caused shit with the two of them as well, including hurting Kill because he just wanted to date this guy's sister. Mia is illogically mad because I didn't tell her about their plan to teach him a lesson he desperately deserves."

"Illogically mad?" I sign, my lips curled in what must look like either a snarl or a growl. "Niko told him either he leaves me or he breaks his wrist, Maya! Landon said no, so if I wasn't there, an artist's wrist would've been broken to pieces. Is that the lesson you wanted to see?"

"Yeah, well, maybe that would've taught him to stay in his own lane."

"Maya!" Mom scolds, her voice rising a little.

"She's being unreasonable, Mom!" Maya shouts back. "She's been choosing this idiot Landon over me and Niko over and over again, not caring how the fuck we feel about it. Maybe it hurts. Maybe it makes us feel like we've been cast aside, but she doesn't seem to care!"

I swallow, my heart beating fast and erratically. This is the first time in over a decade that Maya has been this mad at me.

Ever since the incident, she's often treated me with kid gloves and overwhelmed me with overprotection. The current situation is far from that.

Dad grabs us each by the shoulder in a firm fatherly hold and softens his tone. "I think we need to sit down for this. How about coffee or tea?"

"Yeah. I have your favorite strawberry pudding." Mom proceeds to the massive open-floor kitchen that's every cook's dream.

Dad pulls out my chair like the gentleman he is. Seriously, considering his very British accent, his style, and the way he carries himself, no one would suspect he's actually the most lethal human weapon anyone could cross paths with.

Maya and I sit across from each other and we avoid one another's gaze as Mom pours both of us coffee. Dad brings out the pudding from the fridge and places one serving in front of each of us, then he sits beside me.

Mom settles beside Maya and places her arms on the table. "Okay. Now that we're more settled in, let's talk in more detail. Is there a reason why you didn't tell me you were in a relationship, Mia?"

"Because he's a psycho who actually physically hurt Niko and Kill, that's why," my twin says. "She was ashamed of him, as she should be."

"Maya," Dad says in a warning tone. "The question wasn't directed at you. Don't speak on your sister's behalf when she's fully capable of that."

Would it be too cheesy to jump Dad in a hug? Probably. I just can't help feeling grateful for his important form of validation of my voice, as nonexistent as it is, especially after Niko ignored me not too long ago.

"Is that true, Mia?" Mom asks.

"Partially," I sign. "I didn't mean to start this relationship, and I certainly didn't think it'd last this long. The facts are, Landon did hurt Nikolai and Kill, but they hurt him back, you know. It's not like they sat there and played poor victims. Besides, I did break up with him when I thought he was going too far, but he made a promise not to hurt anyone and to offer a truce. He kept both and I couldn't stay away anymore. He's the only man I've ever felt comfortable and safe with. I know he's different, but I've come to the realization that I'm different, too, and I'm finally fine with that."

I stop before I blurt that I love him.

Then it hits me.

I actually *do* love Landon. The fact has become clear after the time we've spent together lately.

Is it love if I worry about him more than myself and feel a black hole forming in my chest the more I don't see him?

I think it is.

Shit.

When the hell did this feeling start and why am I having the epiphany now?

"But he's bad news!" Maya slams her hand on the table, causing the cups to shake and her coffee to spill over the side. "You can't possibly be thinking about staying with a psycho like him."

"His sister stayed with Kill just fine, so does that mean you think it's okay since he's our cousin but the other way around isn't? What type of double standard is that?"

"She has a point," Dad says as Maya's face scrunches up.

"I still don't like him and won't approve of him," she says.

"You know I love you and I would appreciate it if you'd accept my decision, but even if you don't, that doesn't mean I'll break up with him due to your and Niko's over-the-top protectiveness."

"You'd choose him over us? Again?"

"Enough, Maya," Mom says. "You're being unreasonable and uncharacteristically agitated."

"Oh, so I'm the problem? Okay, then, fine. Let me remove myself from the situation so it's better for everyone." She jerks up and leaves.

"Maya!" Mom calls, but my sister doesn't show any signs of hearing her.

"It's okay." Dad stands up and fetches her plate of pudding. "I'll talk to her."

He kisses the top of my head and offers me a smile. "I'm proud of you and your pragmatic way of solving problems, baby girl." This time, I do hug him and he strokes my hair. "I still won't approve of this Landon guy until I see him for myself."

I gulp as I sit back down. Mom stands and then sits in the chair beside me. A soft glow covers her face as she rubs my shoulder. "Are you okay?"

"I don't know." I feel a weight lift off my chest as I stop the knee-jerk need to lie. Mom and Dad have always offered me a safe space to tell the truth and I often resisted the urge because I had no confidence in what I might blurt out in moments of weakness.

What if I accidentally told them the identity of the monster and they get hurt because of it?

I would never forgive myself.

"Why don't we talk about this Landon? Is he really Kill on steroids as Maya said? Because if that's the case, we need to discuss it."

"Yes and no. I won't paint him as a saint, but that's the thing, Mom. I've never liked saints. I was never attracted to the boys in school and felt so stupidly broken for that. I don't feel broken when I'm with Lan."

Her brows pull together in a soft frown and she takes my hands in hers. "Don't hide anything from me, Mia. Is he taking advantage of you or threatening you in any way?"

"No. I'd cut off his balls before he did that."

She releases a sigh and smiles a little. "That's my girl."

I smile back. "Whose daughter do you think I am?"

"Mine, of course. Now, tell me everything about Landon."

"He learned sign language for me and helped me set up my own garden. He also plays chess with me and cooks my favorite pasta. He also drives me insane by being so socially and mentally different. But I'm taking my time getting to know him better and he's letting me in."

"That's good."

"You don't think I'm being crazy for choosing someone so different?"

"Love is fundamentally crazy, Mia. If it doesn't have that element of insanity, it's not love, in my opinion. You have two solutions. Either you take it as it is or you let go. There's no in-between."

"You and Dad love each other, and it's not crazy."

She laughs, the sound carrying through the room before settling in the space between us. "Oh, we were more than crazy. Like you, I never liked normal either."

"Really?"

"You think I would've ended up with your dad if that weren't the case? We consume each other, but we also balance each other out. It might be unorthodox, but it works. We have the best three children anyone could ask for. So I'm the last person who'd judge your choices, honey."

I wrap my arms around her. If only Maya and Nikolai thought the same. But for now, Mom is enough.

"Now, tell me more," Mom says as we pull apart.

I do, omitting the details that I believe are too much information.

Mom listens carefully, even though I talk for what feels like an hour. I finish the first pudding and get my second serving and I'm still not done. I needed someone to listen to me without judging me since Maya is out of the equation now.

Dad is the one who interrupts our catching-up session. "Your sister wants to talk to you, Mia."

My shoulders hunch, but I still drag myself up.

"You don't have to speak to her now," Mom says. "You can let her cool off for a bit."

"It's okay," I sign and go to find Maya in the sitting room close to the entrance, arms crossed as she studies some of the crowns we made for class as children.

For some reason, Mom chose to display them above the fireplace like some sort of decoration. Maya's were always more sophisticated than mine, but the teacher praised my crazy patterns. They're different, she said. Art is about being different, not neat.

"They look so ugly now," Maya says, still turned away from me. "I don't know why Mom is being sentimental all of a sudden."

I won't step in front of her so she can see me talk. She's the one who asked me here, so she has to face me. If she ignores me like Nikolai...

Maya turns around, her cheeks red and her eyes glittery. She looks out of sorts, which is so unlike her public image.

"I still love the crowns. They remind me of the times we had fun together," she says, then sighs. "I'm sorry. I was being irrational and overprotective. I guess it's hard for me to let you go and I was a bitch about it. I just don't want to lose you."

All the anger washes away as easily as it settled there. I simply can't stay mad at her for long.

"You won't," I sign. "We're twins for life."

"Does that mean you forgive me?"

"Only if you don't interfere in my life so negatively again."

"I won't. I will try to accept the psycho Landon, I guess."

"That's all I need from you, Maya. You're my best friend and it hurts when you don't talk to me."

"I'm sorry." She hugs me so tight, I can barely breathe. "I'm so sorry, Mia."

I pat her shoulder to tell her it's okay. Actually, the thought of never speaking to her again makes me sick, so I'm glad all's well now.

We hear a commotion at the front door and we head there together.

My steps come to a halt when I see the last person I expected on our front porch.

His face is a map of bruises and one of his eyes is purple, but he still smiles at my parents as he says, "It's nice to meet you, Mr. Hunter and Mrs. Sokolov. My name is Landon King and I'm Mia's boyfriend. May I come in?"

THIRTY-SIX

Kyle

HAVING LIVED MY LIFE AMONGST WOLVES, I RECOGNIZE ONE when I see it.

And this Landon, who claims to be my baby girl's boyfriend, is undeniably one. I wouldn't be surprised if he's the leader of the pack.

His face is fucked up with a rainbow of colors, but he's wearing a spotless dress shirt, pressed black trousers, and premium Italian shoes.

Despite the disadvantage of his bruises and the bandage that peeks from the cuff of his shirt and slithers to the back of his hand, he smiles like a respectable gentleman.

Or more like someone who was either taught or learned the specific ways to act like the perfect socially-accepted man.

He stares behind me and my wife and his grin widens as he mouths, "Surprise."

Mia, who's accompanied by a frowning Maya, walks carefully toward him, eyes bemused but cheeks tinted in red.

And this, ladies and gentlemen, is the first time I've ever seen my youngest daughter blush.

"What are you doing here?" she signs.

"I figured since you were going home, I'd join you and introduce myself. I'm a bit late since my grandfather's private jet took longer than expected to arrive at the island. Please accept my sincerest apologies for my sudden appearance at your door, Mr. Hunter and Mrs. Sokolov. I wanted to surprise Mia."

"Not sure if it's a welcome surprise," Maya mutters under her breath, then when Mia elbows her, she groans. "Fine, fine, maybe it's like a tiny bit welcome."

"Thanks, Maya." He smiles with no humor whatsoever. "I'm glad you could welcome me."

Rai ushers him inside. "Don't just stand there. Come in."

"You mentioned a grandfather," I say, trying not to strangle the fucker and throw him to coyotes. "Judging by your last name, could that by any chance be Jonathan King?"

"The one and only." He walks inside my fucking house between Rai and Mia as if he's been here countless times. "I know Grandpa has a reputation that stretches around the globe, but I didn't realize it would reach you as well. Have you dealt with him in business matters?"

"You could say that."

Now, it makes sense why I found his face, brutalized as it is, exceptionally familiar. Of course Jonathan's grandchild shares his absolutely domineering and highly irritating personality.

"What happened there?" I motion at the bruises.

"A little incident caused by your son, but we've put that disagreement behind us. At least, I did. Not sure about Nikolai."

I raised my son right. He was born for destruction and has no limits regarding his sisters.

Note to self: Call him later to announce how severely proud I am of the methods he uses to resolve conflicts.

My wife leads Landon to the living area. "Make yourself comfortable while I go prepare some refreshments. It must've been a long flight."

"Nothing is too long if I can find Mia on the other side."

My daughter's face turns a deep shade of red. Maya rolls her eyes and Rai mutters an 'Aww.'

Me? I'm ready to bury the motherfucker in my father's new construction site. It'll be brutal but discreet, and no one will hear of the name Landon King ever again.

I'm doing humanity a huge favor, if you ask me.

Maya chooses to go help Rai while I sit opposite Mia and Landon. He interlocks his fingers with hers and places them on his thigh.

I narrow my eyes at the gesture, but he completely ignores the attention and smiles at my daughter, who rewards him with one of her rare smiles.

My lips part.

It's no secret that Mia's smiles have been few and far between ever since the day I failed her as a parent and we almost lost her for good.

My wife and I never say this out loud, but we know, deep down, that we actually lost a huge chunk of our daughter after the kidnapping. She was never the same carefree, bright, and remarkable attention-magnet little girl she once was.

Mia lost a part of her soul and the worst part is that she refused to talk about it. Not to us or the million specialists we employed to help her find her voice again. All of them came up with the same infuriating result.

It's psychological.

She's shackling herself.

Unless she takes the initiative, she won't be able to find her voice again.

So to see her act this way around Landon leaves me with a serious feeling of failure. It took us a lot of time and effort to provide Mia with a healthy, safe environment, and yet this little twat has managed to win both her trust and affection in such a small time frame.

"How long have you known my daughter?" I ask.

Still keeping his snake-like grip on her hand, he graces me with his lewd attention. "A few months, give or take."

"And you already think you're at a place to introduce yourself to her parents?"

"I don't see why not."

The audacity of this twat. He's shameless and wears it like a badge of honor.

"Do you know who we are, son?" I say in my serious tone.

Mia catches the change in my demeanor and her face bleaches, chasing away any remnants of the earlier blushing.

Landon, however, seems perfectly content with his ride on the expressway to hell, because he says. "Naturally."

"So you realize we're the Russian mafia and you still aren't scared for your life?"

"Why would I be when I haven't done anything? Besides, you just called me son, so I take that as you welcoming me into the family."

"You wish."

"I don't do wishes, Mr. Hunter. I make things happen."

I narrow my eyes on him and he stares me dead in the face, unblinking, openly challenging me in my own fucking house.

"Dad," my daughter signs, dread written all over her soft face. "Please."

"It's all right, Mia," Landon says. "I was fully prepared for this level of hostility and would've been disappointed if there was anything less, to be honest. But how about we get past this stage? Since you're acquainted with Grandpa, I'm sure we can come to an agreement."

"And if we can't?"

He lifts a shoulder. "I'll keep trying until we do."

"Even if it takes years?"

"Or decades. I can be both persistent and persuasive."

"Neither of those traits works on me."

"I'll find something that will."

"Highly doubtful."

Mia stands up, remains silent for an awkward pause, then signs, "I'm going to see if Mom and Maya need help."

She shares a look with Landon that only the two of them seem to be able to decipher the meaning of before she reluctantly leaves.

Good. Now would be a good time to abduct the bastard and execute my construction site plan.

"Where were we?" Landon asks. "Right, me trying to win you over. I'm confident we can figure something out. At least you're not as animalistically violent as your son."

"Who do you think is his father? And drop the act now that it's the both of us."

"Act?" He searches his surroundings as if looking for a third presence before focusing back on me. "What act?"

"The doting boyfriend act. That doesn't fly with me."

"I'm not acting, since I am, in fact, attempting to be a doting boyfriend."

"How is that working out for you?"

"Judging by your murderous expression, I'd guess not so good."

"You guessed correctly." I lean forward in my chair. "I know your type, Landon, or rather, I've *crushed* your type countless times before."

"My type?"

"Suave, dishonest predators who only care about their narcissistic selves."

"I don't deny the characteristics. In fact, I take pride in them since they'll allow me to identify similar monsters and protect your daughter from their claws. I'm open to earning your trust in any way you deem necessary as long as it doesn't include breaking up with Mia. Nikolai and his edgy cousin Killian tried, but I assure you they didn't and won't succeed. I promise I'm not a threat. At least, not to Mia and the people she loves."

"Your promise holds little to no importance for me."

"How about information, then?"

I narrow my eyes. "What type of information?"

"Further details about what happened to Mia eleven years ago."

I straighten and grow taller in my chair. "How the bloody hell do you know about that?"

"Mia told me herself because, as I mentioned earlier and you refused to believe, I do happen to be a doting boyfriend and worked hard to earn her trust. Which included suppressing my own nature, but I'm sure you're not interested in those details."

"What the fuck do you know about what happened?"

"Enough to formulate a dangerous theory."

One moment I'm sitting there, the next, I grab him by the collar of his shirt and lift him up. "What the fuck do you know?"

"Whoa. Here I was complimenting your coolheadedness compared to Nikolai, but the apple doesn't fall far from the tree. Am I right?"

"I know a hundred and one ways to kill people, so unless you're ready to experience the most brutal one, I suggest you talk."

He grabs onto my arm, but he doesn't push me away. "I will if we have mutual trust. I must say, your reaction doesn't encourage any future collaborations."

The sound of Maya's talking reaches me and I release the little fucker. He falls against the sofa and readjusts his collar as if nothing happened.

By the time my wife and the girls join us, I'm already in my seat and thinking of a thousand ways to kill the bastard in his sleep. Forget about the construction site; that's too mild for him.

But first, I need to figure out what exactly he knows and why the hell Mia trusts the sleazy fucker enough to tell him about that part of her past.

"What were you guys talking about?" Rai asks while placing the tray of tea and biscuits in front of him.

"Mr. Hunter was just telling me you make great tea and I must admit, I'm curious to find out."

I narrow my eyes on him, but he continues to smile at my wife, who tells him that's a major exaggeration on my part.

We sit down for tea again, but despite my deep-rooted Britishness, that's not my focus at all. I keep watching for telltales to expose the twat and reveal his true face.

That mission proves to be increasingly hard when he keeps saying all the right words and gives Rai the perfect answers to all her questions.

He's as skilled at lying as trained spies, but then again, maybe he isn't, in fact, lying but rather good at mixing the truth with the right words, depending on the audience.

But what actually takes me aback is Mia's talkativeness. She signs a lot and tells the epic story of the survivors Claudia, Stephan, and Emilia, the flowers who are living their best lives due to her and Landon's care.

"Wait." She turns to him. "Who's taking care of them if you and I are here?"

"I gave Bran the keys and specifically told him that I might revoke brotherly rights if something happens to your precious flowers."

She hits his shoulder. "You're so mean to him. You better appreciate him more."

"Yes, Mom." He salutes.

Mia tries and fails miserably in hiding her smile.

"Who's Bran?" Mom asks.

"My twin brother." Landon scrolls through his phone and then shows it to my wife. "We're identical, as you can see from the picture. I'm, however, fifteen minutes older and definitely claimed the elder brother position."

"Oh my. You and Mia are both part of identical twins."

"I know, right? I never believed in fate, but this small detail might very well change my mind."

Maya stops herself before she rolls her eyes. Her gaze meets mine and she mouths, "He's so full of shit."

I know, baby girl. I know so well.

After some time of being stuck in the happy-go-lucky conversation and witnessing a different side of Mia that I thought was long dead, I excuse myself.

I retreat to my home office on the other side of the house and close the door behind me.

The lake extends in the distance as I stand by the tall window and scroll through my contacts.

I find the name I'm looking for and tap it.

He picks up after a few rings. "Jonathan King speaking. Who is this?"

"Kyle Hunter. Remember me, Jonathan?"

A pause stretches between us, then he says in the same tone, "Yes. I was wondering when you were going to cash in on your favor."

"Now."

"What do you have in mind? Stock? Discounted investment in my empire? A certain property you have your eyes on?"

"None of the above. I told you at the time you used my services that I have no interest in money whatsoever."

"What do you want, then?"

"Your grandson a few continents away from my daughter."

Another pause. "Which grandson?"

"Which one is the worst headache?"

"It's a tough competition between my two eldest Eli and Landon."

"It's the latter."

"Ah."

"That's all you have to say? Your unruly grandson has his eyes on my daughter and I need you to keep him away."

"I'm afraid I can't do that."

"You're his grandfather. You can force him."

"Unless I'm God, I can't force him to do anything."

"We agreed on a favor, Jonathan."

"And I'm keeping my part of the deal. Asking for the sun is more doable than demanding I keep Lan on a leash. He doesn't react well to any form of authority, so take my advice and let him sort it out with your daughter instead. Any interference on your part will only backfire and make your case a lot worse."

The door of my office opens and I track my wife's movements as she stops by the entrance.

"Thanks for nothing," I tell Jonathan. "I'll be in touch."

"Hopefully not as in-laws," he says and hangs up.

Was that amusement in his tone?

He's as much of a bastard as his grandson.

My wife walks up to me, looking more beautiful every day. It's been over twenty-seven years since I met her, but she still looks as breathtaking as when I first laid eyes on her.

Elegant, majestic, and brutally demanding of my attention.

This woman hasn't only changed my perspective about life from feeling unwanted to accomplished, but she's also been by my side through everything.

The good, the bad, and the disgustingly ugly.

We don't only love each other, we literally complete one another in ways I find hard to describe.

"Am I interrupting?" she asks.

I wrap an arm around the small of her back and pull her flush against me, then kiss the top of her head. "You're never interrupting, princess."

She strokes the lapel of my jacket. "Are you okay? You didn't seem yourself back there."

Of course my woman would pick up on my change of attitude, no matter how successful I am at hiding it.

"I don't trust him and I don't like how close Mia allowed him to get to her."

"I know. I'm wary about him as well, especially since I'm seeing firsthand how similar he is to Kill."

"Why do I feel a but coming on?"

"Mia truly loves him, Kyle. From my initial assessment of the situation, I can see that he genuinely cares about her and is not just putting on a show. Have you seen her around him?"

"I have. That's why I'm disturbed."

"You should be happy for her, not disturbed. Besides, we'll keep an eye on him the next couple of days and if something doesn't seem right, we'll take care of it. What do you say?"

"I say we take care of him now."

"We can't. It's been a long time since I've seen Mia so wildly happy. We can only judge him on his actions."

"Then let's hope one of his actions is to slip and crack his neck open."

She laughs. "You're so bad."

"You know you love it."

"I do." She gets on her tiptoes and brushes her lips against mine. "But I love you more."

"Fuck, princess. You're the only one who knows how to cheer me up."

"Always." She interlinks her fingers with mine and I let her guide me out of the office.

I'll find a way to make fucker Landon disappear.

But I'm more concerned about my beautiful wife's company now.

My one and only.

My forever.

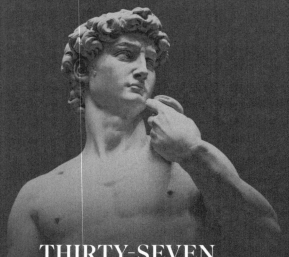

THIRTY-SEVEN

Landon

To say Mia's father doesn't like me would be an epic understatement.

Not only has he been keeping a close eye on me since I showed up at their door yesterday, but he's also been threatening me with bodily harm every chance he gets. Behind the backs of his wife and daughters, of course, so he won't seem like the bad guy.

Too bad for Kyle, Rai tolerates me. Don't get me wrong, she's still suspicious, probably due to a bad marketing campaign Maya has led against me, but I'm nothing short of the best PR representative you'd ever encounter, so I've been changing my image.

Namely, now that I'm meeting Kyle's father and Mia's grandfather.

He invited the family for lunch at his place, and because I refuse to be separated from Mia, especially since I have my suspicions about this trip, I joined.

When I think of grandfathers, mine come to mind. My paternal grandfather Jonathan King from is a ruthless monarch who only shows affection to my nan and Glyn. My maternal grandfather, Lord Henry Clifford, is a posh, sophisticated man who still has the posture of a forty-year-old.

Mia's grandfather, Mikhail, however, has a significant belly and the distinguished look of a mobster in his beady eyes. As I stand in front of him while Mia introduces me, I'm not sure if he'll pull out his gun and shoot me between the eyes or ask the buff men stationed at every corner of his house to do it for him.

He looks at Mia the entire time she talks and only after she finishes does he direct his ruthless attention toward me. His voice carries in the air with a notable Russian accent. "So you're the one my precious granddaughter chose."

"My name is Landon King. It's a pleasure to meet you, Mr. Kozlov. Mia has told me so much about you." I offer him my hand.

He takes it with a slight lift of his brows. "Like what?"

"Like how much you've spoiled her since she was young and how you were one of the first to learn sign language for her. Not to mention that she loves spending time in your house because she feels loved and safe."

Don't get me wrong. Mia never really told me these things and I haven't been able to ask her or get alone time with her when Kyle has been acting like my designated warden. But I witnessed her talking to Maya and Rai earlier this morning and saw how excited she was to visit her grandpa's house again. Since I'm a mastermind at linking patterns, I managed to create the image of everything I said just now.

My effort is greeted with a smile from Mikhail. "I see. I always knew Mia was smart and would know how to choose properly."

"Naturally, Sir. She had a brilliant upbringing, and from what I see, a fantastic family support system as well."

"Don't call me 'Sir.' It's too impersonal for my Mia's boyfriend."

"Of course... Grandpa?"

"Much better."

Mia gives me two thumbs up as her grandfather guides me to the extravagant living room that's decorated with animal heads and gruesome renaissance paintings.

This 'Grandpa' has no qualms about appearing entirely unwelcoming. In fact, I suspect he does it on purpose to blow fear into his enemies' veins. But then again, I wouldn't expect anything less from a man who probably spent his whole life in the Russian mafia and survived to reach an old age.

Maya and Rai walk alongside me and Mikhail, but Kyle wraps his arm around Mia's shoulder and glares at me.

I meet it with a smile.

What? I'm working hard for his approval, and I doubt that would be achievable by being a dick.

And while I have no fucks to give about other people's opinion of me, Kyle matters because he happens to be the man who contributed in the making of my little muse.

I'll dance to his tune until he realizes that he can't get rid of me. His father definitely likes me and he should follow his lead. Not going to lie. It's irritating to be seen as a threat by him when I've been so dutifully stopping myself from planning to break Nikolai's arms and chopping off his legs for his stunt a couple of days ago.

He had the audacity to not only try to keep Mia away from me, but to also try to break my genius hands. But then again, just because I can't and won't hurt him physically—which he should thank his sister for—doesn't mean I won't destroy him emotionally.

Nikolai made the mistake of messing with what's mine, not once but twice, and I don't react well to being threatened, now, do I?

He better sleep with one eye open going forward.

But that's a thought for another day. Right now, I'm more concerned with making a good impression on Mia's aunts and uncles, who are being introduced to me by Mikhail.

I compliment one aunt on her scarf and another on her massive ring that could accidentally blind someone. I also talk American football and hockey with the three uncles, which they respond to with enthusiasm. I had some help from Mia in this regard. I texted her to ask about her family's interests and she sent me a whole list of what each of them enjoys.

Currently, as she watches me capturing their attention like the god I am, her mouth is agape. She must be wondering how I've managed to remember all of this, but I'm a bit wounded. I thought she would know by now about my superior genes, but anyway, Operation Charming Mia's Family is a staggering success. By the time we sit down for lunch, I seem to be the center of attention.

Mikhail even says that Nikolai was being overprotective and could've taken it too far by ruining my handsome features.

Don't worry, Grandpa. He'll pay for it in due time.

After lunch, we go to sit in the garden, and I notice something in their family dynamic. Everyone here—and I mean everyone—looks up to Kyle and Rai. They keep cornering them together and separately for a brief conversation, and I can tell Kyle is so done with his family's shit.

Rai, however, is more diplomatic. She listens carefully and nods along.

That's probably why she's more receptive to me than her closed-minded husband.

I meet his eyes across the room, and he narrows them as he tightens his hold on Mia's shoulder. I smile again.

Just wait, old man. I managed to win over your difficult daughter and it's only a matter of time before it's your turn.

Since Mia is unfortunately out of reach, I slide up next to Maya, who's sitting on a chaise lounge and obsessively checking her phone.

"Waiting for an important text?" I whisper close to her ear from behind the chair.

She startles, and in her surprise, the phone falls to the grass beside her. She grabs it hastily and glues it to her chest. "What the hell do you want?"

"I was asking an innocent question." I cock my head to the side. "But judging by your highly suspicious reaction, I have reason to be curious. What are you hiding, Maya?"

"None of your business."

"I'm afraid it is."

"Don't push your luck just because Mia chose to like you."

"Jealous?"

"Fuck you."

"As I previously mentioned, I'm interested in your sister, not you."

Her lips lift in a snarl as she jerks up and storms away, still holding the phone in a death grip.

As I watch her leave, Rai walks toward me. I straighten and stop glaring at her daughter.

I lift my hands in the air. "I was only asking what she was doing. I swear I had nothing to do with her sour mood, even if it seems like it."

"I believe you." She smiles and shakes her head. "Maya has always been Mia's closest and best friend, so she feels a bit threatened that Mia has someone of her own now. You understand that since you also have a twin, right?"

I nod. The day Bran finds someone, though it's very unlikely, I'm not sure what sort of beast I'll turn into. I'd like to think that I've changed some of my mindset, but my brother has always been a red line that couldn't be crossed by anyone—our parents included.

"Maya has the right to have as much antagonism toward me as she pleases. As long as she doesn't get between me and Mia, I can tolerate her attitude." Mostly because I couldn't care less about her entire existence. Her only merit is being my Mia's sister.

"I appreciate your understanding." She pauses and looks across the garden to where Mia's telling Kyle and Mikhail a story about her plants.

All I can see is her carefree smile and the way her light eyes twinkle under the afternoon sun. I have the urge to go there and devour that smile and feast on her full lips. But since I'm sure that would only result in my balls being cut off by Kyle, I focus back on his wife.

She studies me closely. "I admit I wasn't comfortable with the idea of you after Maya told me you're like my nephew Killian, and I'll probably always be wary of that."

I knew Maya was campaigning to be the president of my anti-fan club.

"However," Rai says. "I can see how much Mia has changed since the last time I saw her, and according to what she told me, it's all because of you that she smiles more now and seems more comfortable expressing herself. So thank you for bringing back my daughter, Landon."

"As much as I would like to take the credit, I can't. Mia is the one who worked on herself and is fighting to find her voice. And I'll be there every step of the way until she manages to do so."

And I mean it.

I don't care who I have to upset for Mia to regain what she lost against her will.

If that means her family will hate me, so be it.

None of them matter.

The only one who does is the girl who keeps stealing looks at me whenever her dad isn't looking.

"Is everything okay?" she signs from the distance.

I nod but stop there before I accidentally say what I'm thinking.

Everything is always okay whenever she's in my sight. Not even my demons could interfere with this sense of peace.

She's managed to tame them by merely existing.

And I'll make sure to bring her demons to their knees before they hurt her, even if it's the last thing I do.

THIRTY-EIGHT

Mia

I F SOMEONE HAD TOLD ME A FEW WEEKS AGO THAT LANDON would be a doting boyfriend, I would've called the psych ward.

But here we are, two days after we got to New York and he's already met—and completely charmed—Aunt Reina, Grandpa Mikhail, and even my uncles and aunts from Dad's side.

His bruised face didn't stop him from conjuring the charming god in him. He openly told them it was Nikolai being slightly overprotective. He even had the audacity to tell Aunt Reina, "I never liked Killian, but now that I see you're his mother, I can try to tolerate him for your sake. And my sister's, of course."

He was invited to dinner with Grandpa—who's more paranoid about strangers and security than a US president—and even played against him in chess.

Mom was a bit wary of him, despite not saying it out loud, but she eventually warmed up to him.

Even Maya has kept her illogical distaste to herself and, as promised, tried to be civil.

The only unchanging variable is my dad. The more others liked Landon, the harder he glared at him and threw jabs in his direction.

He does it less in my presence, especially since Mom and I elbow or try to stop him.

And while Lan's muddied relationship with Dad saddens me a bit, it's not enough to drown out everything else.

For the past two days, we've been on a rollercoaster ride. We eat together. Landon introduced himself to my family as my 'boyfriend' with a hand at the small of my back. If he couldn't do that, he inter-linked our fingers together. At the end of the dinner we had with Grandpa, Lan said, "We'll surely see each other again, Mr. Kozlov."

I never expected Landon to be perfect boyfriend material, but he's proved that he's so much more than that. Maybe it has to do with his superior people-reading skills. Or the fact that he knows exactly what people want to hear.

While a part of me likes this. The other part is confused, to say the least.

"Why do you think he's doing this, Iris?" I ask my favorite flower on my balcony. A whole bed stretches over the entire terrace, sparkling in different colors. This is the only place where the monster couldn't slither into the corner.

In fact, I developed my love for plants and flowers because it was the only sanctuary where I could escape the monster's sharp claws.

Aunt Reina has done a marvelous job at keeping them beautiful and alive. I can tell they missed me, though, because they've become much brighter since I came back.

Or maybe I'm seeing them through the rosy lenses I've been wearing lately.

Sweat trickles down my temples and I wipe it with the back of my arm.

The sun descends in the lake, casting an orange reflection on the clear water. And just like that, our stay here will come to an end.

We'll have to go back to the island tomorrow.

But why do I feel like every ounce of happiness I experienced will vanish as easily as the sun?

I crouch in front of the flowers and stroke Iris's rosy petals. "You don't know either, huh?"

"Please don't tell me you're talking to flowers again."

My spine tingles at the very familiar voice and a sudden frisson erupts at the back of my neck. I tilt my head to the side to find Landon standing in the middle of the terrace, his usually impeccable shirt slightly untucked and his hair ruffled and finger-raked.

I slowly stand up and search behind him. "What are you doing here?"

"I jumped through your sister's balcony." He points a thumb behind him. "I always wanted to try and see what it's like to climb walls and windows for your beloved à la Shakespearean. Not too bad. Four out of five would recommend."

"Why only four?"

"Whether or not I add the fifth star depends on the results of this." His darkened eyes rake over my satin shorts and thin camisole. "So far, it's looking promising."

I suppress a smile. "You should probably leave before Dad notices your absence from his immediate surroundings and comes knocking at my door."

"We better be quick, then, or else I'll fall victim to his relentless cock-blocking."

I bite my lower lip and inspect our surroundings. It's probably better that I push him out, but then again, he's not the only one who's sexually frustrated. With Dad keeping Lan on a leash—as much of a leash as Landon will allow—it's been impossible for us to get time alone. Especially since Lan has made it his mission to meet every single member of my existing family.

"So you want to spend time with me now?" I sign. "I thought you were more interested in Grandpa, Aunt Reina, and the rest of my family."

He searches around the flowers.

"What are you doing?" I sign.

"I'm checking to see if one of these edgy flowers is perhaps poisonous and might cause hallucinations. Otherwise, why in the ever-loving fuck would you think I'd rather spend time with your family than you?"

"Well, didn't you want to meet them all?"

"Yes, but only because I figured it'd make you happy if I get to know the people you love." His brow furrows. "Did I miscalculate something? Is my spending time with your family perhaps not something you want and actually makes you displeased instead?"

My lips part as I study his face.

He looks genuinely confused. He was going against his nature to provide me with a form of happiness, but I shot him down.

I wrap my arms around his waist and bury my face in his chest. Lan engulfs me, his larger hands covering my back in a protective cocoon.

"If you don't speak to me, I won't understand, Mia. Do my actions have the opposite effect of what I intended?"

I shake my head against his chest and then push back. "It does make me happy. I guess I was a bit salty because I missed you these past couple of days."

A wolfish grin lifts the corner of his lip and he strokes my cheek. "Say that again."

"It makes me happy."

"No, the other part."

I smile. "I missed you, Lan."

"You did, huh?"

"Don't get too cocky."

"That's part of my charm, though. Besides, I'm allowed to according to your aunt, who I like very much, by the way, no clue how she's the tasteless Killian's mother, but I digress."

"Aunt Reina said you're allowed to be cocky?"

"No, but she did mention that I'm the only guy you ever introduced to the family. There was apparently this Brian in high school, but he barely met your mom and only due to a coincidence. By the way, what's his full name?"

"Brian Muller. Why?"

"I just want to know the name of the loser so I can disrupt his life."

"Don't be unreasonable. Brian and I went on five dates max and we didn't technically do anything."

"I know, which is why I said I'll *disrupt* his life, not *destroy* it.

Now, define *technically* because the answer to that will certainly decide his fate."

I purse my lips.

"Did he touch what's mine, Mia?" He wraps his fingers around my throat. The grip is loose enough to let me breathe, but it's firm enough to establish who holds the power. "The lack of answer is an answer, muse."

"No, it's not. I just refuse to succumb to your unreasonable demands."

"Tell me, then. Did the loser Brian touch this pretty little throat? Did he feel your pulse point and get hard by the notion that he holds your life in his hands?"

My heart nearly stops beating as Landon slides his free hand beneath my camisole, over my stomach, and to the swell of my breasts. My nipples tighten against the satin cloth and he twists one, then pulls. A shudder flashes through me and an ache blossoms between my legs.

I can't stop the way I respond to him or even tame it.

Maybe I don't want to.

The reason I've been addicted to Lan isn't only due to his intensity but also how utterly unhinged he tends to be.

"Did he play with these, then? Did he tease your nipples like an inexperienced pubescent who's only seen real tits through porn? Did you enjoy his touch?"

A moan slips out of me as he twists the other nipple, but it ends in a gasp when he pinches it to the point it hurts.

It hurts enough that my eyes water.

It hurts enough that my inner thighs feel sticky with wetness.

There's definitely something wrong with me. Otherwise, why the hell am I so attracted to this?

"He did, didn't he?" Landon's voice darkens, lowering to a frightening edge. "He put his hands on what's mine."

"I wasn't yours then," I sign with shaky hands, barely able to keep my wits about me.

"Highly doubtful. You were always mine, Mia. We just hadn't met yet." He slides his open palm down my stomach, then pushes my shorts and panties down enough to grab my aching pussy. "What else did this Brian who'll soon be wiped off the face of the earth do? Did he dry hump my cunt? Did you like the feel of his limp dick?"

I shake my head.

"Is that a no?" His eyes darken on me until I'm completely at the center of his attention.

"I never liked his touch. It was too gentle."

A smirk that could only be described as nefarious curls his lips. "And you don't like gentle, do you, my little muse? You don't like to listen to sweet words whispered in your ear while being fucked missionary style. You prefer the kinks and the unknown. You get off on the rough and the fucked up."

Slap.

I gasp as throbbing pain flares in my pussy. The crazy bastard did it again and I can't even bring myself to pretend I'm offended anymore.

"Bet you didn't get this wet for Brian. Did you?"

I shake my head.

"That's my girl."

He releases my neck and unbuckles his pants, the sound echoing in the air around us. I barely catch a glimpse of his hard cock when he lifts me up.

My shorts and panties slide to the ground and I'm butt naked in his arms. Letting him carry my weight, I sign, "We can't, Lan. Dad will find out."

"I won't fuck you. I just need to feel you."

My protests stop at the back of my throat when he slides his cock against my soaking-wet folds. The feel of his skin on mine offers a reprieve from the throbbing pain of the slap.

It's always been this way with Lan. Pleasure can only come with pain—rough, decadent, and absolutely delicious.

I wrap my arms around his neck. In the descending darkness, he looks savage and absolutely rugged. The fading bruises add a dangerous edge to his already ferocious nature.

And yet I've never felt that I belong like I do in Landon's arms.

My fingers stroke along the mole beneath his right eye. His gaze captures mine as his cock slides up and down my folds and over my clit. Pressure builds in my core and I bite my lower lip so I don't release a loud sound.

"Fuck. You feel so good, baby."

My chest aches and butterflies erupt at the base of my stomach, malevolent but addicting. Destructive but entirely delicious.

I used to think butterflies were a cliché, but it took finding Lan to realize I want to feel them whenever possible.

He dry humps me, though I'm not sure about the dryness when I can hear the evidence of my arousal.

Just when I think I'll come from the constant pressure on my clit, Lan slides the tip of his cock into my opening. My eyes widen.

What is he doing? He said—

"Change of plans. I don't think I'll keep my word." And then he thrusts inside me in one go.

I groan as he fills me entirely, his cock thrusting into me from below. I grab onto him, nails sinking into his neck and the collar of his shirt.

He pushes me so that my back hits the wall, then slams his palm by the side of my head.

My eyes meet his dark ones as he drives into me with the urgency of a madman. "Your cunt is taking me so well. I'm the only one who can fuck you like this. Own you like this. No one else touches what's fucking mine, baby. No. One."

His rhythm turns animalistic and I hold on to him for dear life as the pressure from earlier explodes into one ferocious orgasm.

I'm still riding it as Landon pulls out, puts me down, and turns me around.

"Palms on the wall and arse in the air. Let me see my hole."

My limbs shake and I can barely stand, but I grab onto the wall.

Lan parts my ass cheeks and slides my wetness to the back hole. I squirm every time he touches my core, all my nerves still sensitive from the orgasm.

His fingers dig into my ass cheeks pulling them farther apart and then he spits. I can feel it sliding down my legs, and for some reason, it turns me on.

"Your cunt is mine. Your arse is mine. Everything you have to offer is fucking mine, Mia. It's time I own you entirely."

He lubes his cock with my arousal and slides into my back hole. I get on my tiptoes, teeth sinking into my bottom lip.

"Relax." He slaps my ass and I yelp. "If you get tense, it'll only hurt."

He slaps my ass again and I jerk.

His fingers dig into my hip, keeping me upright. "Unless you want it to hurt?"

I must make a subconscious nod because Landon's deep and absolutely toe-curling laughter echoes in the air. "This is why you're my one and only."

And then he thrusts deep inside me. This is different from the toys he put inside me before. Lan is a huge man and I feel every inch of his cock filling me to the brim.

I pant, my head leaning against the cool wall.

"Mmm, I knew your arse would be custom-made for me, just like your cunt. You're taking me like such a good girl, baby."

I wiggle my ass against his cock and he chuckles. "Impatient, are we?"

He reaches to my pussy and massages my clit as he thrusts into my ass.

"Fuck, you're strangling my cock so well, baby."

His rhythm increases until I'm completely full of him, his intensity, and his raw power. My nostrils fill with his scent until it's my aphrodisiac.

Pleasure floods my core as he expertly teases my clit, touching, twisting, and bumping it against his thumb over and over.

I come with a long scream, and for a moment, I think this time I'll definitely say his name.

I don't.

Still, the orgasm is stronger than anything I've experienced. I feel it at the base of my stomach but more in my aching heart.

Why does it hurt so much?

Lan curses under his breath as he pulls out and comes all over my ass.

I can feel the stickiness sliding down my legs and pooling at the bottom of my slippers.

"Fuck. That felt good."

He releases my hip, and with the only support gone, I nearly fall to the floor. Landon grabs my elbow last second, then lifts me up in his arms and carries me into my room.

As my arms wrap around his neck, a smirk lifts the corner of his lip. "Maybe we should go for a second round on your bed before your dad comes in?"

I keep staring at him, my heart still beating loudly.

I don't like the realization as to why my chest still hurts.

But deep down, I know that I enjoyed the sex so much not because it's only sex, but because it's so much more.

"I'm just kidding." He grins. "Or not, depending on your reply."

"I love you," I sign before I can even think about it.

He stops at the threshold of the room, but it's only for a second before he continues to the bathroom. "Let's get you in a bath."

My lips tremble, but I control the urge to scream and rage.

I knew Lan doesn't subscribe to the notion of love, but still, it hurts to say the words and get nothing in return.

I wiggle out of his hold, so he puts me down and I face him. "Aren't you going to say something? Anything?"

He pauses, seeming lost for words for the first time ever. "Do you want me to say it back?"

"Not if you don't mean it."

He looks at me with that frown again and it hits me then.

Landon is a blank page in the emotions department. He's an emulator and a master adapter. None of the sentimental feelings are his own.

And I just demanded that he feel an emotion he absolutely can't.

"Forget it," I sign. "Those words were said in an emotion high and didn't mean anything.

I go to the bathroom and close the door.

Then I slide to the floor and cover my face with my hands.

I always thought I'd be okay as long as Landon was a decent human being who didn't just get off on violence and anarchy.

But now, I can only watch my heart bleed as I realize I want more. I want the love he'll never be able to give me.

By the time I finish showering, I feel worse than before, but, thankfully, Lan is already gone.

He tried to come in and even attempted to open the door by force, but after I sent him a text to leave me alone, he did, though reluctantly, and only after he promised that he'd be back.

I change into a black dress and boots, then slip out the back door to take a walk by the side of the road. Growing up, I often did this whenever I felt suffocated and needed more space.

The edge of the lake has better aesthetics, but it's not as well lit as the road. And since our house is the only one in the area, no cars venture out this far.

The night chill blows beneath my dress and triggers goosebumps on my arms. I should've brought a jacket, but oh well. Maybe cold will be good on this occasion.

My phone vibrates and I bring it out, then smile when I see the name on the screen.

Brandon: How is everything? Did Lan cause trouble?

Define trouble, because if it means stomping all over my heart, then he did that with flying colors.

Mia: I wouldn't call it trouble. He's been excellent with my extended family.

Brandon: Charming people is what he does best. I'm glad it went better there than the disaster that happened here.

Mia: On that part, it did.

Brandon: Does that mean it didn't on another part?

Mia: Maybe.

Brandon: Oh no. What did he do now?

Mia: Nothing disastrous. Don't worry. At least, not yet. It's just that I'm not sure where we're supposed to go from here if I love him so much and he doesn't know how to love. How do you deal with it, Bran?

Brandon: I just love him. But as I said, I have no choice, he's my identical twin and the one person I know the best. It's in our DNA to love our twins, no matter what they do. Besides, he might not know how to love, but he is learning how to care, and I can assure you that he cares for you more than I've seen him care for anyone else—himself included. The day I picked him up from the Heathens' mansion, he looked both monstrous and shell-shocked. He mentioned you promised to leave him so Nikolai wouldn't break his wrist. He looked me in the eye and said, "You told me to act against my instinct and try to understand what she thinks instead of what my beast dictates. We have a problem, Bran. I think Mia is the one who doesn't understand and could use your boring lessons. If she truly ends things between us to save my art career, I'll cut my own wrist and send the evidence of self-mutilation to her fucking brother via post. Perhaps if I do that, she'll finally understand which one is more important."

I read and reread Bran's text, not believing my eyes.

Mia: He really said that?

Brandon: Yes. I've only ever known Lan as an artist. Sculpting is what puts a leash on his demons, even if temporarily. So the fact that he's willing to give that up for you is colossally important. Maybe it's not that he doesn't know how to love, it's more of a case that he does it differently.

My crushed heart that was burned not too long ago resurrects from the ashes, ready to sacrifice itself at Lan's altar or break against his harsh edges.

Everything Bran said is true.

If I look at the time I've spent with Lan, he's been so adamant about caring for me and making me feel comfortable.

It's not really about words, it's about actions.

How the hell could I forget that he was ready to lose his wrist and his flourishing art career instead of losing me just because he didn't say 'I love you'?

Footsteps sound behind me and I smile to myself. Of course Lan wouldn't leave me alone for long.

My smile freezes when I stare into the eyes of darkness I would recognize anywhere.

Any-fucking-where.

The monster from my past.

The reason why I'm forever broken is staring back at me from behind a gun.

"We meet again, Mia. I heard you've been saying things you shouldn't have."

THIRTY-NINE

Mia

MONSTERS TAKE DIFFERENT FORMS IN PEOPLE'S imaginations.

Some see them as phantom-like figures that could be mistaken for ghosts. Others imagine them as the ghoulish beast hiding under the bed or lurking behind the closet door.

For me, a monster has always taken the form of a stern, square-faced woman with a tight auburn bun and a cruel ruler.

Over the years, she's started to blur into images of the yellow-eyed monster who's been creeping into every corner of my room, waiting to pounce on me.

But now that I see her face again, all memories of the wooden ruler drift back into my consciousness.

Mrs. Pratt.

She's a short woman with a plump figure and now sagging cheeks. She's wearing her usual black skirt and gray cardigan like a timeless figure. She was my and Maya's nanny for years, but she quit when we were around seven years old because she wanted to take care of the family farm with her husband.

But that wasn't the last I saw of her. No.

The person who kidnapped me? It was her. She had a male accomplice, who attacked our car, killed my bodyguard, and took me away. I suppose he was her husband, but I never saw his face in that black, dirty hole.

The only person who terrorized me to within an inch of my life was Mrs. Pratt. During the days I was there, she disciplined me with her ruler to the point I can still feel the painful blows against my flesh. While hitting me, she said she regretted not having the chance to use the ruler to 'correct' my behavior before. And that she knew I was asking Mom to replace her, which is why she quit before she was kicked out.

I did tell Mom that I didn't like Mrs. Pratt, because she was so stern and no fun. I preferred someone who'd let me and Maya play instead of always focusing on our curriculum.

What was an innocent request became the reason for my childhood trauma.

People assumed my kidnapper was a man and I let them believe that, not seeing the need to correct them. All these years, my main priority was to make sure she and her dangerous husband couldn't hurt my family.

That's all I cared about.

That's what I lost my voice for and why I've never gotten it back.

I believed that if she could kidnap me, kill our bodyguard, and nearly take Maya as well, she could do anything. Our tight security means jack shit to this woman.

Deep down, I thought maybe one day I'd get over the crippling anxiety and devastating fear I felt in the darkness of that basement.

Maybe one day I'd be able to use my voice again.

But seeing her now brings everything tumbling down.

My legs tremble and every fiber in me tells me to run.

Now.

"Don't even think about it, child," she says, her voice low and unpleasant.

I never liked Mrs. Pratt. Even before the kidnapping. Call it a self-preservation instinct or pure disdain for stunted people. I just never felt comfortable around her and preferred my Russian teacher at the time. Something Mrs. Pratt didn't react to so well.

She takes a few steps toward me, her hold on the gun steady, and I nearly hyperventilate.

Stop coming closer. Stop coming…

"Now, tell me, Mia. Did you open your mouth, or—more accurately—your hands to tell that boyfriend of yours about the past?"

I gulp, sweat trickling down my back and gluing my dress to my skin. I can't move.

I can barely breathe.

As if paralyzed, all I can do is stare at the monster from my past.

A shudder snakes through me and I can barely breathe, let alone think about escaping.

Is this the end?

Finally?

"You couldn't have, right? It was supposed to be our secret, wasn't it?" She stares up at me with her lifeless eyes.

I often saw Mrs. Pratt as an educated, normal woman, but it wasn't until the kidnapping that I realized monsters aren't only disfigured beings and can take different forms.

Monsters aren't the work of cartoons and comic books. They're not even the big buff men with scarred faces that Mom and Dad deal with on an everyday basis.

They could be something entirely different.

An apparently harmless woman with a strong moral compass could suddenly become a monster herself. Or maybe she was a monster all along, but she excelled at camouflaging that part of her.

"I warned you about what I'd do to anyone who finds out, didn't I? Does that mean you're ready to see your boyfriend's blood splashed all over your pretty little face?"

Panic explodes behind my rib cage and shatters all over the ground around me.

Don't touch him. Not him.

I open my mouth, but none of the words come out. My hands remain limp at my sides as if they refuse to speak anymore.

"You were so good at keeping secrets for over a decade, so what's changed, Mia? Why are you being stupidly stubborn now?"

I want to open my lips and beg her not to hurt anyone I love.

Please. Not Landon or my parents or...

"Mia!"

Maya runs down the street, her clothes disheveled and her hair flying all over the place. Her face is so white, it could be mistaken for a ghost's.

I've never seen her like this, except for when I came back home after the kidnapping.

She was bawling her eyes out. I stood there in complete bewilderment.

If anything, I just wanted her to stop crying.

My sister grabs me by the shoulder and faces Mrs. Pratt, her chin trembling.

I push her away, horror bleeding into my bloodstream as I sign with shaky hands, "Go, Maya. Just go."

"No." She wraps her arms around me tighter and I can feel her shaking worse than a leaf in the aftermath of a storm.

"Maya, Dear. What are you doing here?" Mrs. Pratt asks in the soft voice she used to speak in when she was our nanny. It sounds creepy at best when she's pointing a gun at us now.

"Go away," Maya says—no, she orders. "You said you'd never come back or show yourself in front of Mia, so why are you here?"

"That would've only worked if you'd both kept your part of the deal, but you didn't, now, did you?"

Wait...what?

I stare at Maya, whose lips are trembling and her eyes are filled with unshed tears. This can't be what I think it is. It just...can't.

"Oh, right," Mrs. Pratt says. "Seems you're not up to date with what Maya did, so here it is..."

"Shut up," my sister whispers then yells. "You promised!"

"You also promised to keep her quiet, but you didn't keep your promise, so why should I?" Mrs. Pratt directs her twisted attention toward me. "See, Maya was always jealous of you, Mia. You were the bright, smart twin who attracted everyone's attention. Even your aunts and uncles preferred you over her. Before she transformed into this beautiful swan, she was the introverted twin who would spend time alone and only had you as company. Your teachers preferred you to her, despite you having the same level of intelligence. You were outgoing and kind. Always got flowers for your teachers and called them pretty. Always complimented their looks and smell and hugged them goodbye. Maya didn't or more like she didn't have the capacity to fake her emotions at the time. The more they treated you better than her, the deeper her grudge toward you grew. She didn't show it, though, because she genuinely loves you.

"One day, she muttered under her breath, 'I wish Mia would disappear even for a few days,' so I made it happen, though a year later. See, I was more attuned to Maya's emotions than your mom, who just focused on giving you equal attention and opportunities. I recognized that hidden jealousy in her and nurtured it well. After all, I was always treated as inferior to my more accomplished sister and could recognize it in others. So a year later, when I *accidentally* met Maya outside her school and asked her about the route, she willingly gave up the information. I couldn't ask you, because you were much more suspicious and would've told your parents about it. Maya wouldn't because, deep down, she always wanted you to disappear. For good."

"That's not true!" Maya screams, tears streaming down her cheeks. "I only told you because you said you were going to pay us a surprise visit. I didn't know you were going to kidnap her. I didn't!"

"Not at first, but you did after the attack, no? My husband told me you saw his face and recognized him, but you didn't say anything to your parents, because you were scared they'd hate you forever if they found out what you'd done. You didn't care if Mia was abused within an inch of her life or eventually died. It's okay to admit it, Maya dear."

"That's not true…" Fat, ugly tears stream down Maya's cheeks as she stares at me. "You can't possibly believe her, right, Mia? I was about to tell Mom and Dad, I swear. But they'd already paid the money and gotten you back so…so…"

"So you decided to stay silent?" My movements are robotic at best.

"She threatened me." Her voice shakes. "She showed up at my

piano practice and said if I say a word about what I knew, she'd tell you and the whole world that I helped in your kidnapping. I couldn't... I couldn't risk losing you, Mia. You know how much I love you."

"If you loved me, you wouldn't have hidden something so important from me," I sign. "Do you know how much I struggled to keep the truth to myself while Mom and Dad begged me to let them in and tell them anything about the perpetrator? I'm mute because of it, Maya!"

She flinches, her face appearing more ashen under the orange streetlights. "I'm so sorry, Mia. I *really*, really am. I've been living with guilt for eleven years."

"Fuck your guilt." I push her away.

Maya stumbles, but she glues herself back to me. "I know that you hate me and that's okay, but I can't leave you alone with this woman. Her husband was keeping an eye on you in the UK."

Even though pain and anger mix inside me, I can't help looking at Maya. Bemusement must be written all over my face.

"I only found out about him that day when I disguised myself as you and went to the chess club to test Landon. He's the owner of that club, Mia."

Mr. Whitby...

I stare at Mrs. Pratt, who's been watching the whole exchange with a satisfied expression. "Of course we have to keep an eye on you, child. If you'd opened your mouth, everything we built would've broken to pieces. I can't risk your parents' wrath, now, can I?"

"You risked it enough to kidnap Mia!" Maya screams and gets in Mrs. Pratt's face.

She pushes her back using the gun. "Yes, but I got away with that twenty-five million richer. Money can buy you multiple identities and, most importantly, immunity. You wouldn't know this because you were born with a silver spoon hanging from your mouths. You don't know what it's like to see your life's work fall to pieces in front of your eyes because you don't have enough means to keep it afloat. You don't know what it's like to lose a child because you didn't have the money to save his life. You know nothing!"

"But that's not our fault!" Maya screams. "Mom and Dad treated you so well. Is this how you repay them?"

"I don't see anything wrong with taking some of the endless dirty money they own. Besides, both of you are in one piece, for now." She points the gun between the both of us.

Maya stands in front of me, even though she's shaking uncontrollably.

"Here's how it'll go, girls. You'll both keep your mouths shut or I'll personally kill the mom and dad you care for so much."

"Here's another deal for you. Drop your weapon or I blow your head off." The click of a shotgun follows next and I nearly cry when I see Landon standing behind Mrs. Pratt.

"Oh my. Seems that I have more of an audience than I bargained for," she says. "Did you tell him when I called, Maya?"

"No, she didn't," Landon says. "But I've seen her behaving completely out of sorts and figured something was up. The same happened when she was acting out of character in front of the chess club, so I started gathering information. I suspected both Frank and the college professor Kayden since they were standing there when she nearly lost her marbles. Kayden, though suspicious as hell, had a strong alibi almost eleven years ago. In fact, as I was snooping around him, he asked me how well I knew Frank, because a few things weren't adding up. Such as how he suddenly developed a British accent. That was enough to make me dig further into Maya. I had a friend install spyware on her phone. I saw the text she sent you when she found out about Frank. How she was agitated and threatened that if you didn't keep him from Mia, she'd tell her parents everything. She also told you that if you wanted to take care of anyone, it should be me since I apparently know more than I should. It was also because of her that you figured out they were coming back home. So I made sure to be here when you showed up. I knew you couldn't let such an opportunity pass. But not everything is going according to your plan, Kirsten. I'm happy to tell you that your husband is currently being detained by the local authorities. Now, whether or not he gets transported to prison or dies in a freak accident on the way there, I guess we'll know soon. But first, I suggest you drop the gun. I don't have much training with this thing, so I might unintentionally or intentionally end up blowing your head off."

Mrs. Pratt's face turns a deep shade of red as she turns around all of a sudden.

A scream bubbles in my throat and everything crashes down in matter of seconds.

"Landon, noooo!" I shriek as a shot rings in the air.

And then another.

And then my vision turns blood red.

FORTY

Mia

LIFE CAN FLIP UPSIDE DOWN IN A FRACTION OF A SECOND.

Eleven years ago, everything I knew crashed and burned into a thousand shreds.

That nightmare shaped my life, and now, once again, I find myself in a similar situation that I have no control over.

Once again, it's silence.

But this time, it's different and more potent.

Like remnants of destruction, all I can do is watch as life is pulled from beneath my feet and shoved down my throat.

My temperature rises and tears haven't stopped streaming down my cheeks since I witnessed the bloody scene.

Mrs. Pratt shot Landon.

After eleven years, she actually did what she promised all those times and hurt someone close to me because I failed to keep my mouth shut.

It's all my fault.

Everything.

If I'd just told Mom and Dad, I'm sure they would've found her and eliminated her and her husband.

But when I was younger, I wasn't emotionally or mentally strong enough and allowed her to get into my head. I believed her when she said that if she could get to me, she could get to Mom and Dad and slice their throats in their sleep.

I believed her more when she used her wooden ruler to shut me up when I started to scream. She slapped and threw me against the nearest wall the moment I started to be a nuisance.

So no, there was no reason why I wouldn't believe she was capable of much more with Mom and Dad. She managed to infiltrate our airtight security, so why wouldn't she do more to the two people I loved the most?

And worse, what if she also targeted Maya and Niko as well?

A part of me was ready to remain silent forever if it meant I would protect them. I was prepared to sacrifice my voice for good in order to make sure everything remained as it was.

But it wasn't until I saw her pointing a gun at Landon that all hell broke loose.

I didn't only scream his name, but I was also ready to take the bullet for him if I could.

I couldn't, though, because it was already too late.

Landon was shot. Blood exploded everywhere. I screamed and screamed as he was falling down.

But, in reality, he only hit the ground after he fired his own shot and Mrs. Pratt's head exploded all over me and Maya.

I couldn't care less about the pieces of goo and brain that covered my clothes at the time. All I could do was drop to the asphalt and hold Landon in my arms and cry.

I haven't stopped crying since.

"Say my name again." He grinned as he wiped my tears away.

That's the last thing he muttered before he lost consciousness.

Due to the sound of the shots, Mom, Dad, and an army of their guards found us then.

Now, everyone is in the waiting room at the hospital. The nurse assured us it was just a shoulder graze and should be okay, but if that was the case, why did he lose consciousness?

"It's going to be okay, baby girl." Dad places a hand on my shoulder to stop me from pacing the length of the sterile waiting area.

A few guards are scattered in front of the two entryways, led by Mom's senior guards, Katya and Ruslan. They often played with us and made us feel safe growing up. But right now, nothing seems safe.

The walls are closing in on me and bile gathers at the back of my throat, threatening to make me vomit the contents of my stomach.

"How do you know, Dad?"

He stands in front of me, his face creasing with awe and searing happiness.

"What?" I ask.

"You called me Dad after such a long time. I..." An unnatural shine glints in his eyes. "I thought I would never hear you say that or talk again."

"I guess I just needed another shock." More tears stream down my face. "I'll never forgive myself if anything happens to him."

"Don't say that, Mia."

"He put himself in that position because of me. What if...what if..."

My father wraps me in a hug and I cry in his chest, my fingers digging in his jacket, but even his scent and warmth don't offer me the usual calm.

I *can't* stay calm.

Not when the life of the man I love is in danger because of me.

When we break apart, I'm greeted by Mom's frowning face.

She looks anxious, stressed, and far from being the badass woman who's not rattled by anything. In fact, her face is similar to the day they found me in that basement and she hugged me and cried.

I didn't.

A teary-eyed Maya trudges close behind her, fingers interlinked and expression lost, as if she's back to being a child.

"What are you doing here?" I scream at her. "I told you I don't want to see her face, Mom!"

"Honey," she speaks in a soft voice and strokes my arm. "She told me everything and I understand why you're mad at her. I'm disappointed in her, too, but it's best we talk about it."

"I have nothing to say to a backstabbing, lying bitch. She ruined our family, Mom!"

"I didn't mean to." Maya takes my hands in hers. "Please, Mia. Please don't stop talking to me. I'm ready to do anything…"

"Give me back my voice for the last eleven years of my life."

She pales, her words coming out shaking. "You…know I can't do that."

"There you have it, then." I slap her hands away.

Maya sinks her nails into my skin. "Mia, please. We're not only twins, but we're best friends. I can wait for you to forgive me as long as it takes, but please don't throw me aside."

"Best friends don't do this to each other." I unscrew her fingers. "I trusted you most in the world, Maya. I was stupid enough to think you were protecting me, but all this time, you've been stabbing me in the back."

"Mia…" She tries to hold on to me again, but Mom pulls her back.

"That's enough, Maya. You both need time off. You're on a high of emotions and this clearly can't be resolved right now."

"But…" Maya protests. "I can't lose Mia."

I look the other way, refusing to give her the time of the day. I still can't properly process what she did. All those years she offered me comfort and made sure I was never alone in the darkness wasn't because she loved me. It was because she felt guilty.

The reason she stopped her jealousy fits after the kidnapping wasn't because of a screwed-up sense of sisterhood, it was because of guilt.

The way she insisted I tell her first if I remembered anything wasn't because she wanted to be there for me. It was because she needed to warn Mrs. Pratt or shut me up if I ever decided to come forward.

The reason she was so jealous and disapproving of Landon wasn't because she wanted to protect me like Nikolai does, it was because she was worried I was slipping between her fingers and confiding in someone else other than her.

Everything was lie after damn lie.

I don't even think I know her anymore.

But I can't focus on that when someone a lot more important is fighting for his life on the other side of the wall.

I always thought Maya was the closest to me, but she didn't care for me unconditionally, Landon did.

He's the one who told me for the first time in my life that I should kill the monster in my life instead of dying trying. He's the one who encouraged me to talk again, even unknowingly.

Maya starts crying and calling for me, but Dad physically removes her and says he'll take her home.

I don't care. I just need her out of my sight for the foreseeable future.

Hell. Maybe it would be a good idea to never see her again.

Mom rubs my arm. Her face is ashen, her eyes a bit molten, as if she finds it as hard to process the situation as I do. Good. That way she understands how disoriented I feel about the entire thing and won't force me to 'talk it out' with Maya.

"I'm so sorry, honey."

"Forget it, Mom. I don't want you apologizing on her behalf." I'm talking and signing at the same time, I realize. I did the same earlier as well. Subconsciously. Until Maya grabbed my hands.

"I'm not apologizing for Maya. I'm apologizing for disappointing you as a mother. I should've seen the signs of Mrs. Pratt's authoritarian nanny style. I should've paid more attention to Maya's small bursts of jealousy and her overindulgence in asking for attention. I chalked it up to coming-of-age symptoms and I'm so, *so* sorry, Mia."

It's my turn to rub her arm. "It's not your fault, Mom. You… couldn't have guessed it was Mrs. Pratt when she quit a whole year beforehand. As for Maya…that's all on her. I'll be seriously mad if you offer excuses for her."

"I won't. I believe we all need time to process this before we take any further steps." She strokes my hair and cheek as if trying to remove some of the blood stains.

I washed up and changed into Katya's spare bodyguard suit as soon as we got here, but I must still have some of Mrs. Pratt's remains on me.

Mom's eyes fill with tears. "I don't know what would've happened if she'd gotten you this time."

"I'm here, Mom. It's okay."

"Oh, honey." She pulls me in for a hug and I can feel her sniffling in my neck. "I'm *so* happy to finally hear your voice again."

"Me, too, Mom. Me, too."

"Excuse me?"

I disengage from my mom to look at the doctor, who just entered the waiting area. My steps are awkward and uncoordinated as I run toward him.

My heartbeat roars in my ears as I ask, "How's Landon? Is he okay?"

"Perfectly fine, miss. Luckily, the bullet only hit some fat and tissue, and we were able to remove it successfully. The patient has been moved to his room and has regained consciousness if you wish to see him."

A long breath heaves out of me. "Thank you! Thank you!"

Mom squeezes my shoulder. "I'll be right here, honey."

I nod and head to the recovery room. I pause for a second before I slip inside.

My heart beats in a frightening rhythm when I see him sitting in bed, half naked. Some blood forms a transparent sheen on his chest and a thick bandage is wrapped around his shoulder, hiding some of the snake tattoos underneath.

The longer I see him, the stronger the need to cry hits me.

He's fiddling with the IV tube as if he wants to remove it. I jog to his side and place a hand on his. "What are you doing?"

He looks up at me, his face a bit drowsy and his eyes unfocused. "Mia, is that you?"

"Yeah. What are you trying to do?"

"Coming to see you."

"But you've been shot!"

"Why should that stop me?" He strokes my hair behind my

ear. "Fuck. I knew I'd love your voice since the first time I heard you whisper."

I frown. "But I never spoke to you before."

"You did while you were dreaming."

"I did?"

"Yeah. I've loved it since and did everything in my power to make sure I'd hear it again."

My gaze falls to his shoulder and pain explodes behind my rib cage. It hurts to see him in this state. Probably worse than if I were the one who'd been shot.

"But you got hurt because of me."

"Worth it. Would do it again in a heartbeat."

"Including killing Mrs. Pratt?"

"Especially that. She signed her death certificate when she hurt you."

I cover his hand with mine. "Thank you."

"For what?"

"For being there for me. I wouldn't have been able to do this without you."

"I will always be here."

The butterflies from earlier tonight explode again and I taste their sweetness on my tongue. I grip his hand tighter and my voice shakes as I whisper, "Why?"

"Why what?"

"Why would you do that for me?"

"In case it's not clear yet, I care about you, and when it's someone I care about, which is decidedly few and far between, I protect them."

"I still don't understand. Are we in a relationship or are you just having your fun with me? Why would you care about me if…if you're unable to feel love toward me?"

"Who says I'm unable to love you?"

"You couldn't say it earlier."

"Because I don't like to label what I feel for you as love. This"— he points between us—"is much more potent and twisted than mere love. If loving someone means letting them go and wishing them

happiness with someone else, then I don't subscribe to that definition. But if love means protecting and wanting to take care of you till
my dying day, then I love you more than anyone has ever loved another human being."

My lips tremble. "You...do?"

"Depending on your definition of the word." He takes my hands
in his bigger ones, leans his forehead against mine, and closes his eyes.

I study his sharp jawline and the fluttering of his lashes over his
skin. I've never seen someone so brutally beautiful as he is. And yet,
at this moment, he feels like a different man.

No, not different. *Changed.*

I used to only see a monster in him, but I've found out he's so
much more than that.

No, he'll probably never be normal, but I'm irrevocably in love
with him, faults and all. He was born different and always will be, so
why should he comply with social standards?

"Listen to me carefully, Mia. My whole life, I've been a desolate,
empty entity of anarchy and violence. My black soul couldn't survive
without inflicting some form of chaos or producing a decadent burst
of creativity, but even that has dwindled and started to drift from the
center of my being. Without art, I'm nothing but a serial killer in the
making. Ever since you came along, not only have you pushed my
creativity to heights I never imagined would be possible, but you also
filled up the emptiness with your stubborn submissiveness and stupid
flowers with names. While I can't possibly be your Prince Charming—
and rightly so, since he's an overrated idiot—and I can never be neurotypical, whether genetically or mentally, I promise you this, Mia.
I'll always see your perspective before mine, not because I have to,
but because I want to. I'm in for the long haul."

I stroke his cheek, careful not to press where his fading bruises
are. "What if you get tired of me down the road?"

"Complete and utter nonsense. I'd get tired of myself before I'd
ever get tired of you, and we both know that I believe myself to be
God's gift to humans."

I chuckle and he opens his eyes, a sly grin lifting the corner of his lips. "Say it again."

"What?"

"That you love me. I want to hear you say it."

I release a sigh. I have no qualms about how different and absolutely thrilling being in a relationship with Landon is. I know if maybe down the line, I find someone else or end things between us, he'll revert to his toxic ways faster than I can blink.

But that's the thing.

I'm definitely as crazy as Landon is, because I do believe that we are the forever type of couple. For us, breaking up is impossible.

If he doesn't make sure of it, I will.

There's no way I'd let another woman have him. Not in this lifetime.

I grab his face with both hands and whisper against his mouth, "I love you, Lan."

He inches closer until his lips nearly brush against mine. "And I love you, Mia. Forever."

His lips meet mine and he seals the confession with a searing kiss.

EPILOGUE 1

Mia

Three months later

LIFE HAS NEVER MADE AS MUCH SENSE AS IT DOES LATELY.
Or maybe it started to make sense after Landon slid into my life and wreaked havoc on the very foundation of my being.

In return, he offered me himself—unfiltered, unapologetic, and absolutely unhinged.

Today, he's offering something more in the form of a peek into his past.

He brought me to London so I could meet his parents over the summer vacation.

He's tried to bring me here countless times, but I've always told him I wasn't ready, more out of cowardice than anything else; however, he's always respected my decision and hasn't pushed me to make the trip.

His parents should've come to New York after he got shot, but Landon asked my father, who's now a big fan of his—since he saved both me and Maya—to bury the incident so that his parents wouldn't find out.

He disguised the injury as something minor he suffered while working out and said it was pointless to worry his parents.

"The time some prick stabbed me, they didn't leave my side for days and Mum wouldn't stop crying. I prefer not to repeat that," he said.

Naturally, no police were involved in the incident due to my parents' influence. Mr. and Mrs. Pratt were dumped somewhere no one but my father knows and their names were casually added to the MIA list. Landon's name was never mentioned in regards to her death and he faced no legal inquiry whatsoever.

At any rate, I couldn't push back the date to meet his parents anymore. Besides, I've always been curious about the two people who made Landon, Brandon, and Glyndon. Three siblings with entirely different personalities.

As we step to the front door, I pull on my blue dress, even though it reaches my knees. "Are you sure you told them I was coming?"

"On my face? Why would I tell Mum and Dad that?"

"Landon!" I hit his arm. "Can you not talk about sex when your parents are on the other side of the door?"

"Why not? They have sex, too. All the time, if I might add. We're sex-positive in this household. If any of us were to bring home an alien, they'd welcome it with open arms."

"Are you saying I'm an alien?"

"The sexiest alien."

I'm about to hit his arm again, but the door opens and my spine jerks into a straight line.

"I told you to wait until they come inside," a tall, well-built man with strikingly blond hair says. I recognize the resemblance between him and his sons right away. Lan and Bran have his jaw and the same mythical blue shade of eyes.

He has his arm on the small of a shorter woman's back. Her green eyes, which she definitely passed down to Glyn, twinkle with mischief and I can't stop staring at her shiny long brown hair that falls in waves. "I'm just a bit impatient to meet Lan's special guest."

Landon wraps an arm around my waist, mirroring his father,

and says, "Mum, Dad. Meet my girl and your future daughter-in-law, Mia Sokolov."

I stare at him.

Future daughter-in-law?

I don't have time to focus on that as Landon's mom, Astrid, offers me a big, welcoming smile. "It's so nice to meet you, Mia. I've been dreaming about the day Lan would introduce us to his special someone. He's never brought anyone over, you know."

"None of them were worth it," he replies simply, without batting an eye.

"I heard from Glyn and Bran that you single-handedly put a leash on Lan's crazy," his dad says. "I like you already."

"We're officially impressed," Astrid says. "This one right here has always been a wild horse."

"And always will be. I just happen to have a partner in crime now." He pulls me closer to his side. "Let us in. I'm starving."

Astrid grabs my arm and leads me inside, leaving Lan in his father's company.

"Any news about your brother?" I hear Levi ask.

"Working on it. Don't worry, Dad. I'll make sure everything falls into place."

"What about what we discussed the other day...?"

Their voices become distant and unintelligible as they stay behind while Astrid gives me a mini house tour. Their mansion is a lot bigger than I imagined, with rustic, high Victorian ceilings and wide, tall windows that overlook a manicured garden.

They have three built-in studios. One for Astrid, the second for Lan and Bran, and the third for Glyn. All of them were carefully constructed by Levi as gifts to his wife and children.

Astrid takes me to Landon's room and shows me all his awards from multiple activities. Football. Art shows. Spelling contests. Language competitions. The overachiever has done it all.

Astrid seems absolutely proud of his wins, as if they were her own. She sits on the edge of his bed as I study the keepsakes from the endless activities he's taken part in. He definitely wasn't lying when he said he's a genius and a fast learner.

"Lan did everything while growing up—the good, the bad, and the entirely screwed up," she says with a sad smile. "He thinks we didn't realize this, but his father and I always knew that he took part in countless events and activities to fill the emptiness that kept growing inside him. The bigger the hole got, the more intense his hobbies turned. Levi and I let him do whatever he pleased and gave him room to enroll in violent sports, not because we encouraged it, but because we were at a loss for what could benefit him. Therapy didn't help. Restraining him had the opposite effect, and monitoring him made him vindictive. I guess what I'm trying to say is, thank you, Mia."

I face her, hugging an art award to my chest. "I…didn't do anything."

"You gave him the balance he spent his entire life searching for, and that's everything. You gave him what we couldn't."

"That's not true. He knows you tried your best. That's all that counts."

She smiles, her expression soft and reminiscent. Now I get why Lan really cares for his mom and dad and didn't want to worry them about his injury. They let him be himself when he needed it the most. They did it in the hopes that he'd get back on the right path one day, and I think he realizes how hard it was for them. More importantly, he knows the many troubles he caused them over the years.

"He's also been showing me his most recent pieces and saying he found his muse," she says. "I'm guessing that's you."

"I suppose. I wanted to ask you since you're an artist yourself. Is there anything else I can do to help him?"

"Not really. Just be yourself. He's finally finding his distinctive style and it's euphoric to watch."

"He hadn't before?"

"No. I don't deny that Lan was born a genius. He has the perfect technique and a unique imagination. I've always told him that he surpassed me in his teens, but he often showed me his work and I felt happy that he still sought my validation. But ever since he started being a professional, I could see his creative and technical superiority, but there was no soul. Lately, that's fundamentally changed. Now, I'm sure he'll soar to the sky with his talent. With your help, of course."

"I don't really do anything. I just sit there." And sometimes suck him off just to mess with him.

"Don't underestimate the role of a muse. Some say it's inseparable from our souls."

Why do I like the thought of being part of Lan's soul? Probably because I'm as possessive as he is and want to engrave myself inside him as deep as he's inside me.

Astrid stands. "Come on, let's go down for dinner. Maybe I can dig out his baby albums afterward."

I grin. "I would love that."

When we get downstairs, we're greeted by two new people, or more like, one new face.

I recognize the first one as Eli. I met him fleetingly in the Elites' mansion and Landon always made it a point to separate me from him. For some reason, that made Eli more insistent about interacting with me, which, in turn, provoked Lan's toxic, over-the-top possessive traits.

The man accompanying him is Aiden, who's an older copy of Eli. Tall, imposing, and intimidating without even trying.

I don't see him in that light, though. According to Lan, his Uncle Aiden has always been his number one fan, the enabler of his anarchy-driven mind, and the one who understands his antisocial behavior the best.

His dad does, too, now, but it took him some time to come to terms with the fact that Lan is and always will be different—mostly because he used to treat his siblings in an antisocial manner.

"And what are you doing here?" Lan glares at Eli.

"What's with the cold welcome, dear cousin? I was terribly wounded in my nonexistent heart when you invited Dad for dinner and didn't consider including me." Eli wraps an arm around his father's shoulder. "We come as a set."

"Did he force his way to come with you, Uncle?"

"Pretty much," Aiden says with a poker face. "He said, and I quote,

'Of course my presence is welcome. Who wouldn't enjoy my godly company and stimulating conversationalist eloquence?'"

"Me, for one." Lan grins. "I can think of someone else who wouldn't either. Maybe I should text that someone so they can judge your *stimulating conversationalist eloquence.*"

"Dad…" Eli says, all humor absent. "Remember when I said I want Lan gone?"

"Yes, constantly."

"I still want him gone."

"Too bad I'm here to stay." Lan makes a face. "And stop asking your dad for help like a little bitch. How old are you? Six?"

"You're playing with fire, twat."

"Burn, dear cousin. Burn."

"Boys," Levi says, pinching the bridge of his nose. "When are you going to grow out of this meaningless rivalry?"

"Let them be." Aiden smiles. "It's amusing."

Lan's expression goes from playful to burning hot when he spots me with his mother.

He comes to escort me, his hand landing on the small of my back as he guides me to the center of the living area.

Eli offers me his charming smile. "We meet again, Mia."

"Hi."

"Isn't it about time you decide this one right here isn't worth your time?"

"Ignore the waste of space." Lan doesn't even pay him attention. "Uncle, meet Mia. The future queen to my kingdom."

My cheeks heat and I hope it's not as obvious as I think it is. What's with him and all the labels today?

I offer my hand. "It's nice to meet you, Mr. King."

"Please. Call me Aiden." He returns the shake with a firm but brief one. "I must say, you're one brave young lady for putting up with someone like Lan."

"I've been saying that for months," Eli agrees.

"Hey." Lan seems offended. "You're supposed to be on my side, Uncle."

"It takes courage to put up with you, so of course I have to give credit where credit is due." He leans over. "Give me a call if this one gives you trouble."

"Me, too," Levi says.

"Dad!" Lan scoffs.

"Leave my boy alone." Astrid wraps her arms around his waist in a hug and he smirks, then pretends to be wounded.

"See, Mum? No one understands my worth."

"I'll add my number to the Landon Hotline," Eli says, almost too excitedly.

"Can't be busier than the Eli Hotline," Lan shoots back. "I know because I've been taking care of the fallout for years."

Eli glares at him and Lan merely waggles his brows.

Aiden and Levi share a look, then shake their heads, almost exasperatingly.

I only just met this family and I already love them.

They're different from mine. While I always thought we were so close-knit, what Maya did ruined everything.

We've been taking it slow, but I'm learning to forgive her. She hit rock bottom after that incident. Apparently, as I suspected, she had a major crush on Ilya, Jeremy's senior bodyguard, and probably even started a secret relationship with him.

But evidently, she did something so unforgivable, he broke up with her. Then the thing with Mrs. Pratt happened and I cut ties with her.

She had a mental breakdown.

I was there for her. Unlike what I would've thought, I couldn't just watch her disintegrate. She's still my twin, and like Bran said, it's in our DNA to love our twins, no matter what they do.

Our family has been healing, but I'm not sure how long this process will take. I guess, as the family counselor said, it can take as long necessary.

The positive thing is that Nikolai apologized again for ignoring me that day and promised not to interfere in my relationship with

Landon from now on. There's no love lost between them, but I'll take any peace offerings I can get.

"What are you thinking about?" Lan whispers in my ear as we fall behind while everyone else goes to the dining room.

"How much I like your family."

"Everyone except for *the nuisance Eli, you mean*!" he shouts the last part.

"The only nuisance is you, prick!" Eli shouts back without hesitation.

"Hey, Lan." I stop in front of him and wrap my arms around his waist.

More than his gorgeous statues, he's the brutal beauty that always, without doubt, steals my attention.

"Yeah?"

"Thank you for letting me into your world."

"Thank you for being my world."

"Thank you for helping me get my voice back."

"Thank you for letting me hear it."

"Seriously, you've been taking Bran's lessons so well."

"No lessons are needed. Besides, Bran is the one who's in dire need of lessons, not me."

The bell rings and he frowns. "Mum, are we expecting someone else?"

"I invited someone over." Eli comes rushing through.

As he opens the door, Glyn jumps Lan in a hug. "Surprise!"

The surprise is, of course, that she brought Kill along.

I wince. This is such a terrible idea.

It doesn't matter how many truces exist between the Heathens and the Elites. Lan and Kill can't stomach each other to save their lives.

"Your presence isn't enough, so you added another obnoxious presence?" Lan asks Eli.

"Of course. The more the merrier, am I right, Kill?"

"Right." My cousin grins as I greet him with a hug. When I back away, his face reverts to the usual coldness. "Landon."

"Killian," he says with the same destructive energy. "For the record, I still don't like you."

"I don't like you either."

"The solution is simple. Leave my sister."

"Only if you leave my cousin."

"No."

"We'll agree on that, then."

I meet Glyn's gaze, which looks so done with their shit, and we both roll our eyes.

"My favorite psychos." Eli grabs each of them by the shoulder, but they disengage. Lan grabs my hand and Killian does the same with Glyn.

"Rude," Eli mutters under his breath.

"Let's get the fuck out of here," Lan whispers in my ear.

"No. I'm not bailing on your parents. Besides, this is fun."

"As long as it amuses you." He seems unhappy, but he's definitely faking it.

I get on my tiptoes and kiss his cheek, then murmur, "I love you, Lan."

"Fuck." He smiles a genuine heart-stopping smile. "You sure know how to calm the beast inside me, little muse."

And I always will.

It doesn't matter how the world sees Landon.

He might be crazy, but he's my crazy.

EPILOGUE 2

Landon

Two years later

REMEMBER THAT THING I WAS WORKING ON FOR SOME TIME? Well, I might have gotten a bit sidetracked and the task took me longer than I planned.

Two years longer, to be specific.

But what's a win without a few struggles along the way, am I right?

Actually, I'm not right. I know it's rare, but it's true at times. This meaningless fucking hurdle has been bothering me for a while.

But here I am. Finally. In the middle of my own exhibition.

Now, to be perfectly clear, I've had multiple offers from renowned domestic and international art galleries to host my first solo art show ever since I was at uni.

I refused each and every one of them because, as I mentioned during my earlier moaning about timing, I was simply not ready.

And while that might sound like a flimsy excuse, it actually is true.

The Landon from two years ago needed a bit of a shake and a kick in the arse so he'd get his shit together and finally produce the masterpiece he was put on this earth for.

While I didn't agree to solo exhibitions, I did take part in multi-artist and charity-funded exhibitions. I grew my name and left the art community brimming with excitement for when I'd finally show them what I've been secretly working on.

Safe to say, my masterpieces don't compare to the decent but not-so-special statues I made before.

Things that were called 'marvelously stunning,' 'achingly beautiful,' and 'brutally captivating' pale in comparison to my new creations.

So, I might have gone a bit overboard and instead of producing one masterpiece, I have a few.

Or more like thirty of them.

The subject and the exhibition's name? *The Mystery of a Muse.*

Statues of Mia fill out the gallery. For the first time, the subject of my obsession and addiction is revealed to the general public or anyone who's not a staff member.

I stand in the corner, watching everyone falling head over heels for my genius and the reason behind my genius.

The muse whose existence I didn't believe in until I was trapped by her forever.

The muse who filled up the emptiness so thoroughly, it's become impossible to picture a world whose center she doesn't occupy.

Mum was the first one who told me that my art finally has a soul, and I can see exactly why. Before Mia, I didn't have a soul, and while some might argue that I still don't, the truth is, I could only find my drive after Mia came into my life.

I needed a way to translate those feelings and unleash them onto the world so they could see how much she means to me. It might also have to do with the fact that I wanted to announce irrevocable ownership so everyone sees that she's fucking mine and no one gets any funny ideas.

The statues filling the gallery are of Mia in different situations. The day I first met her after I brutalized her cousin's car. The day I cornered her in the bathroom and she bathed me with blood. The day she kicked me in the nuts because of her adorable jealousy. With a flower in hand. In front of a field of her named arseholes that she sometimes gives more time than me. On the day of her graduation. The day she screamed my name for the first time—secretly my favorite moment.

However, my favorite statue is the one I chose as the main theme of this event. The piece I spent two years perfecting.

The piece everyone gawks at like it's their custom-made god.

A giant statue of Mia stands in the middle of the gallery. She's wearing her gothic dress and boots. Ribbons interlace her hair and her eyes stare at nothing. Her lips are sewed shut with stitches. The stone dips under each one, looking painful and deep and impossible to undo.

Two large wings blossom from her back, leaving gashes in the stone. One of them stands proud, but the other is crooked, broken, and half fallen. Red is splashed on the edges—her virginal blood that I got on a canvas two years back.

She holds out both her middle fingers. Like she did that day she let me chase her and showed me the side of her that spoke my language fluently.

The world is caught in a chokehold by my favorite—and possibly my only—masterpiece.

But not more than me.

I found myself in complete awe of my creation after I finished it. And, in a way, I experienced a strong sense of emptiness at the thought that I was done. My only solace is that I can make more masterpieces as long as I have Mia.

The woman in question appears by my side, her eyes blindfolded, guided by Bran and Glyn.

And she's wearing a blue dress.

A color she reserves only for super precious occasions.

My art exhibitions belong on that list.

She's snatched Mum's position and has easily become my number one cheerleader. She just graduated and is ready to start working on her businesswoman dream, but she still models for me and pouts so adorably when I say she can't see what I'm working on.

"Where are we going? Glyn? Bran?"

My siblings grin and give me the thumbs-up before they join Mum, who's fighting tears as she gives a few interviews. Dad is by her side, looking proud and content. Let's just say my decision to stop bugging my siblings for sport has improved things dramatically within the family.

Turns out, I was the problem and the drama king. Shocker, I know.

But anyway, this is the moment I've been waiting for.

"Bran?"

"It's me, muse." I brush my lips against her cheek.

It flames in a bright red color. "Lan?"

"Yes." I take her hand. "Follow my lead."

"When can I see the statues? I've waited long enough."

"Patience."

"I've been patient for two whole years. I don't understand why you're being so secretive when I'm your so-called muse."

"It's for a good reason, believe me."

The crowd parts like the Red Sea for Moses.

I get past all our family and friends, including but not exclusive to Rai and Kyle—yes, we're on a first-name basis now, as I'm obviously their favorite future son-in-law and anyone who tells you otherwise is lying—Maya, who's been apologizing to her sister for the past two years, Nikolai, Uncle Aiden and Aunt Elsa, Grandpa and Nana, and our extended group of friends.

"Are we there yet?" she asks again.

I stop her in front of the statue and remove her blindfold. She blinks against the sudden light, but as she refocuses, her lips part.

The ethereal color of her eyes widens the more she takes in the details. Her gaze turns to the rest of the statues and she cups her mouth with her hands.

I can't help watching her, falling for every spark in her wildflower eyes all over again. I thought the world was an utterly pointless loop of nothingness but then realized I was empty. I thought I came to peace with that part of myself, but that was until Mia showed up in my life and unlocked a side of myself I didn't know existed.

She finally faces me, her face flushed and her lips still parted.

"These are so…so…beautiful. No, that's an understatement. I can't believe you've been making these the entire time."

"You're the reason this masterpiece exists." I lower myself to one knee and pull out the ring that I had custom-made from a rare jewel that matches her eye color. "You're not only my muse, but also the sole reason I create anymore. You don't complete me, you fill me up with your hope, determination, and constant nagging. But I digress. Only slightly, though." I let my charming smile show through. "I used to believe I didn't have a soul, but it turns out, I just needed you to fill it up. Now that I found you, I can't and won't live without you. Mia Sokolov, would you marry me?"

Tears shine in her eyes as she gets on her knees in front of me and nods frantically, then signs, "I love you."

"Is that a yes?" I sign back.

"Yes. A million times yes, Lan."

I slide the ring on her finger and then kiss her in the middle of cheers, hoots, and camera flashes from everywhere.

As we break apart, I whisper, "I love you, too."

I know how much she needs to hear that, and while I don't believe in love as an emotion, I believe in her.

My woman.

My muse.

My forever.

THE END

You can check out the books of the couples that appeared in this book.

Kyle Hunter & Rai Sokolov: *Throne Duet*
Levi & Astrid King: *Cruel King*
Killian Carson & Glyndon King: *God of Malice*
Jeremy Volkov & Cecily Knight: *God of Wrath*

WHAT'S NEXT?

Thank you so much for reading *God of Ruin*!
If you liked it, please leave a review.
Your support means the world to me.

If you're thirsty for more discussions with other readers of the series, you can join the Facebook group, *Rina Kent's Spoilers Room*.

Next up is the story of Nikolai Sokolov and Brandon King in the standalone MM book, *God of Fury*.

ALSO BY RINA KENT

For more books by the author and a reading order, please visit:
www.rinakent.com/books

ABOUT THE AUTHOR

Rina Kent is a *USA Today*, international, and #1 Amazon bestselling author of everything enemies to lovers romance.

She's known to write unapologetic anti-heroes and villains because she often fell in love with men no one roots for. Her books are sprinkled with a touch of darkness, a pinch of angst, and an unhealthy dose of intensity.

She spends her private days in London laughing like an evil mastermind about adding mayhem to her expanding universe. When she's not writing, Rina travels, hikes, and spoils cats in a pure Cat Lady fashion.

Find Rina Below:

Website: www.rinakent.com

Newsletter: www.subscribepage.com/rinakent

BookBub: www.bookbub.com/profile/rina-kent

Amazon: www.amazon.com/Rina-Kent/e/B07MM54G22

Goodreads: www.goodreads.com/author/show/18697906.Rina_Kent

Instagram: www.instagram.com/author_rina

Facebook: www.facebook.com/rinaakent

Reader Group: www.facebook.com/groups/rinakent.club

Pinterest: www.pinterest.co.uk/AuthorRina/boards

Tiktok: www.tiktok.com/@author.rinakentt

Twitter: twitter.com/AuthorRina